FULFILMENT

To Jared.
With love + Best wishes,
Grandpa
x x x
25th October 2008

Also by the author

FULL CIRCLE

FULFILMENT

H. R. Henley

A CIP catalogue record for this title is available from the British Library

ISBN 978-0-9556228-3-0

First published in 2008
Two Plus George Ltd, 25 Warren Way, Barnham, PO22 0JX
Printed and bound in Great Britain by Cpod, Trowbridge, Wiltshire

Acknowledgement

*My grateful thanks to my family
and many friends who gave most willing support
during the preparation of this book*

PART ONE

1919-1928

FROM WAR TO PEACE

Chapter 1

Autumn 1919 was well advanced when Francis and Margot returned from their honeymoon in France. Coming ashore at Plymouth they were glad to set foot on land as the ferry crossing had been rough, with passengers restricted to the lounges below decks. Formalities completed and the luggage stowed aboard the train, they took their seats in a first class compartment to begin the journey for Bristol, where they planned to spend a few days with Francis's mother Fanny before continuing to the Manor House at Farndene, Hampshire.

As the train sped towards Exeter, Margot, a true Scottish lass from St Andrews, was a little homesick as she gazed at the Devonshire countryside but nevertheless felt comforted to be back in England. The freshly ploughed fields had a pleasant pinkish tint that contrasted with the browns of the almost leafless trees and hedgerows, while the black skeletal trunks and branches were stark against the sky, where a hazy sun endeavoured to pierce the stubborn blanket of mist. Francis put his newspaper to one side and asked with a smile, 'A penny for your thoughts darling?'

Margot, a little startled, smiled in return and then looked more serious as she replied.

'I was thinking about our visit to your mother.' She paused and looked out of the window for some moments before continuing, 'I have to admit I'm apprehensive,' she looked searchingly at Francis, 'Darling, I hardly know her!'

Francis put his arm round her and, looking into her eyes, spoke with feeling, 'Let me put your mind at rest, my sweet. Mother is the most generous of persons and I'm positive she's delighted to welcome you into our family. She's blessed with great qualities of affection and common sense, so please don't worry your pretty head about her anymore.'

'That's all right for you! You happen to be her son while I'm a daughter-in-law, and as such I'll have to watch my Ps and Qs!'

He leaned across to give Margot a lingering kiss just as the compartment door opened and the guard, clearly covered with confusion, entered.

'Beg pardon, sir, sorry to interrupt, but may I see your tickets?'

Moments later, after a search, Francis handed the tickets to the guard who checked and clipped them.

He spoke as he passed them back, 'I see you're going to Bristol, sir. This is the London train so you must change at Exeter. I'll check the connection when I get back to my cabin and let you know in good time.'

As soon as the guard had closed the door Margot collapsed with the giggles, 'Caught in the act! So, Francis, no more kissing until after the little man returns with the timetable!'

They both enjoyed the joke and chatted as the train followed the river course all the way to Exeter.

Like all railway stations, Exeter was filled with bustling crowds of travellers; some single, others family groups with countless children of all ages and with pet dogs. Soldiers, sailors and airmen, with their military paraphernalia of kitbags, bedrolls and rifles stood in groups, chatting and smoking. Porters with trolleys piled high with luggage pushed against the mass of humanity like an icebreaker nosing through pack ice. In addition, groups of friends gathered to say farewell to their loved ones while others welcomed new arrivals with the usual flurry of excited chatter and hugs and kisses. All this activity was against the noise of engines entering and leaving the station in clouds of smoke and steam, and the ever present menace of flocks of pigeons which roosted above on the girders when not scavenging for food dropped by the travellers.

The London train pulled slowly into the station and Margot and Francis looked on with some trepidation at the intense activity before them. Once a porter had been engaged to deal with their luggage, Francis suggested they go to the first class waiting room until the Bristol train arrived in about three-quarters of an hour. Margot was not so keen and said she would like to stretch her legs, 'Let's have a little walk round, preferably outside the station, and get away from the deafening noise inside; what do you say?'

Francis agreed and arm in arm they strolled along the platform and out of the main entrance.

They stopped for a moment to take in the scene on the cobbled forecourt where, by a hansom cab rank the drivers talked and smoked as they waited for fares. The road sweeper stood with a shovel and broom, always ready to clear the 'inevitable' from the cab horses. Along the pavement a group of porters stood chatting and smoking, with barrows available to help incoming passengers. At the station entrance a newspaper vendor, with a bundle of papers under his arm, shouted the current headlines, 'read all about it!' But the next words were, as usual, inaudible. A wounded ex-service man, with a leg missing, sold matches and boot- and shoelaces from a tray. Francis bought two boxes of matches and received grateful thanks for a two-shilling piece.

As they moved away Francis remarked, 'so much for the land fit for heroes our government made such a song about! Seeing a man like that without a proper job is a scandal.' To one side of the forecourt, a horse-drawn coffee stall stood with a tall chimney belching black smoke, while in the shafts a withered specimen of a nag stood motionless with its head stuck in a nosebag.

To one side a muffled figure stood on the cobblestones turning the handle of a barrel organ and as pins plucked the strings, the strains of 'Pack up your Troubles in your Old Kit Bag' echoed around the area. The organ grinder held a tin mug in his free hand and acknowledged any contributions with a nod and an inaudible movement of his lips. The local policeman stood nearby, enjoying the musical interlude and tapping his foot to the rhythm.

At that moment their attention was drawn to a disturbance at the coffee stall where four urchins, probably eight-year-olds, had stolen buns from the stall counter and pelted away as fast as their legs would carry them. The stall owner, a heavily built man, gave chase with shouts of, 'Stop fieves, stop 'em,' at the top of his voice.

One boy made straight for the station entrance and as he passed near Francis and Margot, tripped and fell headlong on the ground. Before the boy could get up, the stall owner grabbed him and commenced to slap and punch the terrified child who squealed for mercy. The stall man unhitched his leather belt and with an oath, was about to beat the small boy – 'you li'l bugger, arl teach yer ter nick fings!'

Without further comment he brought the belt down heavily on the boy who screamed with pain.

Francis moved quickly to grab the man's arm, 'that's enough! There's no need to brutalise the child.'

The stall owner was taken aback by Francis's intervention, 'Push orf and mind yer own bisniss.'

Unimpressed, Francis increased his grip on the man's arm as he spoke forcibly, 'Do as I say or I'll report you to the policeman. There are plenty of witnesses to your brutality.' He nodded towards a little crowd of bystanders who were in agreement.

The man realised he was in a difficult situation and released the boy, but retorted with anger in his voice, 'it's orl right fer you! You're a toff and ain't lorst nuffink. 'E nicked 'em buns wivart payin'.'

Francis felt he had to make a gesture: 'Well how much did they cost? I'll give you half a crown, and that should more than cover your loss.'

Having received the money the man, muttering, departed to his stall.

Meanwhile, Margot attended to the boy who had cut his hand and with two handkerchiefs covered the wound. He was pitifully thin and shivering, as his clothing consisted of a threadbare jacket and knee breeches, a cloth cap and a pair of boots several sizes too large for him, but no socks.

Margot bent over the small weeping figure to comfort him, 'What's your name laddie?'

The tear-stained face looked up at her, 'Rupert, miss,' and with a fearful expression, 'Don't let the police take me. And please don't tell my Mum!'

Margot put her arm round his shoulder and assured the boy that wouldn't happen.

'What's your other name and where do you live?'

It was a moment before he replied, 'Tupper, miss, and I live at eight, Penny Lane with Mum and my brother and sister. My dad was killed in the War and Mum hasn't got much money.'

Francis leant over the lad and asked gently, 'Why did you take the buns from the stall?'

'I was hungry! I hadn't had nothing to eat since yesterday when Mum got a loaf and we all had bread and dripping.'

Francis promptly walked over to the coffee stall and returned moments later with a hot meat pie, which the boy ate ravenously.

He then took a pound from his notecase and gave it to the lad, 'Rupert, I want you to put that in your pocket and take it straight home to your mother. Tell her I'll write to her shortly as I may be able to help your family. Now run along home as quickly as you can.'

With a flicker of a smile Rupert thanked them both and scampered away.

Francis looked at his watch and, taking Margot's arm, hurried back into the station, 'We've about five minutes to catch our train so we must look sharp Mrs Vining!'

Margot stopped short and turned to Francis, 'I love to hear you say that darling, it gives me a wonderful feeling being Mrs Vining,' and putting her arm round his neck, gave her husband a large kiss.

'Hey! Steady on young woman, you mustn't flirt with me in public!' at which they were both helpless with laughter.

Boarding the Bristol train in good time they settled in the first class compartment, and took stock of all that had happened in the last half hour.

Margot spoke first, 'Rupert's mother, as a war widow, is in an appalling situation! I think it's a national disgrace so little is being done for them. I imagine that family is typical of thousands of others who exist without any quality of life and little hope for the future.'

Francis nodded his agreement: 'My thoughts exactly darling and they are being let down by our country. I intend to do something as soon as we get back to Farndene; in fact I'll write to Mr Lloyd George, our Prime Minister about it. I'll also try to find out with which regiment her husband served, as they may be able to help his widow.

The time passed as the train sped on for Bristol and the 'Rupert Tupper' episode dominated their conversation for much of the journey. In her forthright legal manner, Margot declared, 'The Tupper family, like many others have every right to expect happiness now and in the years ahead and to have the means to feed, clothe, and educate their children as they grow up. Our government has a duty to look after the fatherless and to do it adequately!'

'Bravo! Well done, Margot! I heartily applaud all you've said and together we'll do all we can to help! In fact I'm sure mother will also help us.' Francis felt strongly about the war widow issue and he and Margot intended to do something about it.

As the train neared Bristol, Margot became quiet again, thinking about the very close relationship Francis had always had with his mother. How much those ties would continue troubled her. Very soon she would be meeting her mother-in-law and she was now more apprehensive than ever.

Chapter 2

Fanny Dewar, meeting her son Francis with his new wife Margot, arrived in good time at Temple Meads Station, Bristol, and, having spent a short while looking at the latest novels on the Smith's book stall, decided to sit down and take in the splendour of the *Brunel* masterpiece.

Moments later she was a little taken aback as a tall naval commander came up to the seat and addressed her. 'Please excuse me, but are you Mrs Vining?'

Fanny, a little disconcerted, replied quickly, 'Well, yes and no! Why do you ask?'

Smiling, the officer sat down and continued, 'I knew it! You haven't changed a bit in all these years! Please forgive me; I haven't introduced myself. I'm Hilary Marchant and I was a pall-bearer for Norman Vining, way back in 1904. Of course I was a mere lieutenant in those days, but we had a great friendship and he helped me considerably when I first joined his ship.

Fanny thought she recognised the man who sat next to her and, touching his arm, spoke with great feeling, 'How very kind of you to remember and speak to me. Although I lost Norman fifteen years ago, at times it seems just like yesterday. However, I'd better explain my first comments. I married Angus Dewar in 1908 and we had ten wonderful years together; sadly he died in 1918. But please tell me about yourself?'

'There's not a lot to tell; as you can see I survived the war but my younger brother Michael didn't. He was lost at the battle of Jutland serving with Admiral Beatty's squadron. I was married in 1912 but my wife left me for another serving officer and I've since been divorced.' He smiled wistfully, adding, 'but that's the way of the world at present, one has to get on with life by making a fresh start. In other words, look forward to the future and not back to mistakes that cannot be undone.'

Fanny felt sympathy for him and was touched that he had taken the trouble to speak to her, 'I'm so sorry to hear about your marriage ending so soon but I appreciate your making my acquaintance, it really is a pleasure to meet you,' Fanny paused thoughtfully for a moment, 'do you know anything about the other pall-bearers?'

Hilary shook his head, 'Sorry, I've lost touch but I'll find out if you wish.'

'Yes, please, I would like that.' She looked up to see a train approaching. 'My son and his wife are on this train, so if you have a short while to spare I'd like you to meet them. They are returning from their honeymoon to stay with me.'

As they stood up Hilary took her hand, assuring her, 'Of course I'll stay! Thank you for being so understanding.'

Amid the noise and bustle of the train arriving, Francis, and Margot, were greeted by Fanny with excited hugs and kisses. They were also introduced to Hilary who shook Francis's hand warmly, remarking, 'You're so like your father and it's a great pleasure to know you.'

Fanny suddenly realised she had no idea where Hilary lived so asked him for his address.

'Oh! I'm staying with a cousin in Bath so I'll give you her address.' He proceeded to write the details on the back of his own visiting card, which he handed to Fanny.

'Thank you Hilary, and here's my card. If you are free, perhaps you would like to join us for dinner tomorrow evening?'

Hilary jumped at the invitation and details were exchanged before he departed to catch the Bath train.

As they emerged from the station, Fred Gutteridge, their chauffeur, gave Margot and Francis a beaming welcome and soon ushered them into the waiting car.

Once home, Fanny suggested they take some light refreshment but it was soon evident Margot and Francis were suffering the effects of their journey. 'You've had a long and arduous trip and I'm sure you are both tired! So why not go to your bedroom and relax until dinnertime this evening? I'll see you get a call in good time to get ready.'

Margot replied quickly, 'Thank you, Lady Dewar, it's most kind of you; to be honest I'm ready for forty winks!'

Fanny sensed Margot had difficulty in what to call her mother-in-law so made a suggestion, 'Margot, you are part of our family now so there's no need to be formal; would you like to call me Mama?'

Clearly relieved, Margot agreed with Fanny. 'That sounds just right.'

Shortly after, Fanny entered the kitchen to discuss the menu with the cook, Mrs Sheila Monroe, and found arrangements were well in hand for the dinner party that evening, particularly a special cake to welcome home the newlyweds. The cake stood on a silver tray and looked wonderful. Fanny was obviously impressed and congratulated Sheila, 'It's a masterpiece, quite beautiful and I like their two names piped across the top, I'm sure they will be delighted. Sheila, I would like you to bring the cake into the dining room and present it to Francis and Margot!'

Sheila coloured up as she replied, 'Oh! You are very kind madam. Do you really want me to?'

Fanny nodded her agreement, 'Well that's settled, now we must check the rest of the arrangements as tonight's dinner is very special.' With that remark they got down to business.

Having previously warned Francis the dinner party was in fact a family gathering, he and Margot were able to put on their 'glad rags'. As they came into the drawing room everyone greeted them and, to piano accompaniment, joined in singing 'Here comes the Bride' to Margot, followed by 'Poor Old Joe' for Francis! A wonderful start to what was to be a splendid occasion.

The surprise of the evening was the presence of Sir Roger Vining, Francis's grandfather, who put his arms round Francis and Margot, giving them a huge hug and explaining, 'Fanny suggested I should come down to stay for a spell and I thought it a very good idea. I'll stay here until you two young ones are settled in at the Manor House, so it'll be easier for you with me out of the way for a week or two.'

Francis and Margot moved round the room to talk to their family and friends and, as a matter of courtesy, started with Aunt Lotte who stood with her daughters, Jessica and Mildred. Lotte explained how much she was enjoying her 'grandchildren to be' as she put it. She called across to her son, 'Alex, bring Angelina over and tell them your news.'

They were joined by Alex who soon explained what his mother meant: 'The fact is Angelina and I hope to be married very shortly but it all depends on you Francis!'

Francis caught on straight away, 'Alex, I know! You would like me to be your best man. Well there's no problem as far as I'm concerned, just tell me where and when.'

And so the party got underway and with so much to talk about, the time went quickly before dinner was announced.

The seating at the dinner table was carefully arranged for Francis and Margot to sit next to Fanny's parents David and Ruth, and the grandfather and grandson were soon reminding each other of Francis's younger days, which Margot found highly amusing.

Fanny watched the family gathering with pride and was thankful they all seemed to get on so well. However, once or twice she felt a sudden loneliness as she realised Francis had 'flown the nest' and would be living in Hampshire from now on. She missed Angus so much on these occasions and realised at her age of forty-five she would probably be on her own for the rest of her days.

At nine o'clock Fanny asked everyone to stand as Sheila, the cook, brought the celebration cake into the dining room to a round of applause. Comments of approval and congratulation greeted the splendid confection Sheila had made.

Once again the family started singing as the newlyweds cut the cake and this time it was the famous wartime song 'If you were the only girl in the world and I were the only boy'. To the delight of everyone, Francis took Margot in his arms and they were locked in a long embrace. He stood, beaming, with his arm round his wife to thank them all for a most wonderful welcome home.

'Words can't adequately express the sheer joy this party has given us and our thanks go to each one of you but in particular to my dearest Mother for organising such a memorable evening. I have no doubt we will always cherish this gathering and I speak from the heart when I tell you I believe our family has, over the years, always been able to unite in times of happiness or sadness and tonight's gathering of the clan in celebration is no exception. The words the Reverend Digby Fletcher spoke at our wedding come to mind and they are truly appropriate to us all, 'Love and support each other within the "Full Circle" of your family! Margot and I are so thankful we belong to such a loving family.'

Francis went straight over to Fanny, who had tears in her eyes, to hug and kiss his mother amid applause from all sides.

Over coffee in the drawing room groups of family and friends chatted, exchanging the latest news, and it was then that Margot told them about the heart-rending incident at Exeter Station that morning, 'We were distressed by the sight of wounded ex-servicemen, reduced almost to begging by selling matches and bootlaces.' There were murmurs of agreement as she continued, 'A coffee stall stood in the station forecourt and suddenly we were witness to several urchins stealing buns from it. They scattered in all directions, chased by the stallholder. One boy ran towards the station entrance and as he reached us, tripped and fell headlong, cutting his hand in the process. The stallholder grabbed the boy and slapped and thumped him before beating him with a leather belt.' Her listeners responded with cries of 'Oh! No, surely not.'

Margot waited and then continued, 'Yes, the man was a bully but Francis intervened and stopped him and to calm the situation, paid the fellow for the stolen food. I have to tell you the lad was a pitiful sight and he pleaded with us not to hand him over to the police or tell his mother what he'd done. He was quite terrorised by the ill treatment he'd received, clearly undernourished for his years and wearing threadbare clothes. We were able to calm the boy, who told us his name was Rupert Tupper and he lived with his widowed mother and a brother and sister. He also said he was starving hungry, not having eaten that day and the family had only bread and dripping for their meal the previous day.'

The general reaction was of sympathy and several were of the opinion that something should be done, particularly as they learned the husband, a sergeant in the Royal Artillery, had been killed in the war.

Margot assured them she and Francis intended to look into the tragic case and would do so when they reached the Manor House in Hampshire.

Ruth, Fanny and Lotte told Margot they were willing to help and suggested it may be preferable for someone to visit the unfortunate widow. Fanny suggested, 'I'm happy to go if you wish but only as company for you.' Both Ruth and Lotte pledged their support for any action.

While the ladies were discussing the Tupper affair, Francis was in deep conversation with his grandfather, Sir Roger, who was most interested to hear his grandson's thoughts concerning the possible development of the Manor House and estate at Farndene, comprising some three thousand acres of farm and woodland.

The conversations went on well into the night and it was quite late when the party broke up. Fanny invited her parents and Aunt Lotte's family to dinner the following evening to meet Commander Hilary Marchant but unfortunately Jessica and her fiancé were unable to come.

A little later, in the privacy of their bedroom, Margot and Francis were glad to lie in bed, chatting over all that had happened during the day. 'You know, darling, I really enjoyed the party and I'm sure I'll get on with your mother. I must say she is quite a person and young in heart!'

Half dozing, Francis replied, 'That's great, bearing in mind you were apprehensive this morning.' Then there was a long pause as he was almost asleep.

'Darling, you're not going to sleep are you? We're still on our honeymoon! Or have you forgotten?'

Francis sat up quickly and, taking her in his arms, responded, 'Did I hear the word honeymoon? Well I don't need second bidding my sweet!' And with that they were soon making love, once again sealing the bond between them.

Chapter 3

The following day dawned a beautiful autumn morning and as soon as Margot and Francis had breakfasted, they decided to take a walk through Castle Park to the river. The air was clear and warm in the late sunshine and as they strolled arm in arm the conversation covered many aspects of their life. A seat by the river was a convenient resting place and here Francis put his arm round Margot and kissed her several times. Her response, with a little giggle, 'careful lover, we are in public and there may be a "peeping Tom" watching us with a spy glass.'

His response was a further kiss and, 'If there is an observer we might as well give him something to look at!' At that moment she suddenly exclaimed in a lowered voice, 'Seriously Francis, I can see eyes watching us!'

He turned to look in the direction Margot indicated only to see some ducks and drakes coming out of the water onto the river bank as the seat was clearly a favourite feeding place for them. They had a good laugh after which Margot talked about the family, saying she now felt a part of it. She was thoughtful for a moment before turning to Francis, with a part statement and part question, 'I know we are both fond of children, but what sort of family do you want?'

He replied with a cheeky grin, 'Oh, just boys and girls I suppose.'

'You're not being serious darling but I want to know exactly how many of each?'

Francis gazed across the river before he spoke and then, looking into her eyes and holding her hands, told Margot what he hoped would be their good fortune, 'Dearest, I would love to have two daughters and two sons, particularly if the girls were as good looking as you!'

She couldn't resist, 'That suits me down to the ground but I insist the boys are as handsome as their father!' And more laughter followed after she had the last word, 'Well that's that, so we had better get on with it … but not here!'

Still giggling, they stood up to resume their walk just as a smartly dressed elderly gentleman passed with his dog. He stopped and, with a twinkle in his eye, addressed Francis earnestly, 'the young lady is very good looking and I know from experience! So if you take my advice, marry her before someone else beats you to it.'

Francis, in a waggish mood, responded, 'Thank you sir but I'm unable to do as you suggest as I'm already married!'

The gentleman was flabbergasted and was about to accuse Francis of acting like an unspeakable cad when Francis stopped him saying anything further, 'Sir, so there's no misunderstanding may I introduce you to my wife, Mrs Vining.'

The gentleman was most apologetic and after a pause suddenly reacted to what Francis had said: 'Did you say Vining?' Francis nodded, 'Yes, but why?'

'I served on General Sir Roger Vining's headquarters Staff in France. Is he related?'

'Well, indeed, yes, he's my grandfather.'

'How remiss of me, I haven't introduced myself.' The gentleman proffered his hand as he spoke, 'I'm Colonel Robert Oulton, Royal Engineers.'

They shook hands and chatted for some minutes before Robert noticed his black labrador, Milly, was missing, having disappeared into thick bushes along the riverbank. After three short blasts on a small whistle, the excited animal came bounding out of the thicket to be reunited with her master, 'Good girl, now stay!' he commanded and the dog sat at his feet.

'What a beautiful animal and such a pretty name,' Margot suddenly felt homesick as she remembered her dog. 'I've a black labrador back in St Andrews; his name is Jock and, like Milly, he has a lovely nature.'

Milly enjoyed the attention she got from Margot and Francis and it was then Robert made a suggestion, 'Look here, would you care to walk back with me? I live on the other side of the park and I'd very much like you to meet my wife, Edith.'

They both agreed without hesitation and some ten minutes later reached his house, a large Victorian residence overlooking the park.

Letting himself in, Robert called to his wife, 'Edith, I've brought home some very interesting people to meet you.'

Robert's wife, a petite figure with white hair and a strikingly attractive face, came into the hall. Over her dress of pale green velvet she wore a single string of pearls completing her well groomed appearance. She greeted Margot and Francis with a smile, 'My dears, how very kind of you to come to see me.' She took them by their hands, 'Now do come in and I'll arrange for some coffee. I'm sure you could do with something after your walk.'

They followed Edith into a charming drawing room with large armchairs covered with beige moquette and long curtains at each window to match. Shortly a maid brought a tray of coffee and biscuits. Margot smiled as she saw a dog biscuit on a separate dish and watched Milly sit up and beg before getting the prize.

Sipping his hot drink, Robert eagerly told them about their early days.

'We were both born and brought up in Rochdale, Lancashire. My father was a railway engineer, dealing mainly with the construction of bridges and I became interested in my father's profession and, when I was old enough, went with him to a number of construction sights. When I left school I passed the Army examination and was accepted to train with the Royal Engineers at the Shop in Woolwich and later at the Academy at Chatham. But that was the easy bit.' Turning to his wife he said, 'Edith, tell them about the stroke of good fortune we had when we first met.'

His wife smiled, 'Yes, my dearest, good fortune is the right word,' and, addressing Margot and Francis, 'You see I was lucky enough to be trained as a schoolteacher and, as my mother had been a headmistress, it was a natural course for me. Our home in

Rochdale was in the northern belt of the cotton industry where the weaving took place and, as you are probably aware, the working conditions for women employed in the mills was nothing short of drudgery. The families providing the mill labour lived in very basic houses, with no adequate heating, cramped living accommodation for parents and large numbers of children, and a privy in the back yard. There was much poverty and the women were obliged to work for a few shillings a week to help feed and clothe their children as the men were also on low rates of pay and often out of work.

'In my school I saw the effect of many undernourished boys and girls; the poorer ones often had threadbare clothes and suffered dreadfully in the cold weather. But for the help of charities, who provided some outer clothing for the most needy, many wouldn't have survived the winters.

'I'm telling you all this as my mother and I became involved in the women's suffrage movement to give all women the vote and thereby give them a voice in Parliament. We joined the National Union of Women's Suffrage Societies [NUWSS]. Mother and I were organisers for our local area and we held regular meetings for the women and some male supporters.

'It was at such a meeting in the Co-operative hall in Rochdale, where I was interrupted during my talk by a man who shouted abuse: "You're nothing more than a rabble-rouser stirring up strife in the minds of all these bloody women who should be at home looking after their husbands and families," he said. His ramblings, laced with expletives, went on for some minutes while I stood listening but not interrupting. When the man had exhausted his rhetoric, I calmly told him to sit and listen and then asked if after the meeting he would be going to the local pub, to which he nodded. I proceeded to point out that while he enjoyed his pint and a chat, his wife would be washing, ironing, mending clothes, cleaning the house, baking bread for the week, preparing meals each day and going to the mill for a shift to earn extra money to help with the housekeeping. "She can't go to the local for a pint and a chat! The women in this hall are all living in conditions similar to your wife and as nobody seems ready to champion their cause we have decided to do it ourselves."

'The applause was deafening and went on for a little while, during which the abusive man slunk to the rear of the hall where Robert confronted him.'

She turned to her husband, 'My dear, you tell them what happened.'

Robert took up the story, 'I went to the Rochdale NUWSS meeting with my parents who were firm supporters and I must say I was very impressed by the way Edith dealt with the obnoxious man who heckled her. As he was about to leave the hall I stopped the fellow and told him his conduct was disgusting and he should be thoroughly ashamed. He left with his tail between his legs.

'After the meeting I was invited with my parents to Edith's house for refreshments and it was there I congratulated her on the masterful way she dealt with the heckler.

'It was during that evening I realised I was drawn to a most attractive young woman who had a compelling but sympathetic way of speaking. But I'd better explain by taking you back to the beginning.'

Robert was thoughtful for a moment or two before going on.

'I have to admit I found Edith attractive and her presence disturbing in a most pleasant way!'

Edith's eyes sparkled as she recalled the occasion, 'He was not the only one with a disturbing experience! For my part I'm glad to admit I thought Robert very handsome and it was no time at all before we realised we had fallen, head over ears, in love. We had a short engagement of six months and were married in November 1903, exactly sixteen years ago. Looking back it has been the most wonderful part of my life and I couldn't have wished for a better husband.' Sitting next to her, Robert leaned over and smiled as he squeezed her hand and nodded agreement.

Francis and Margot were completely fascinated and found themselves wanting to hear more and glad when Edith continued.

'After our marriage, mother and I went on with our work for

the NUWSS and it was then a terrible thing happened which could have cost me the sight of an eye or possibly my life.

'A very large meeting was arranged in the Co-operative hall in Nelson, and it was packed, with many standing at the rear. Mother opened the evening and, from the start, it was clear there were several groups of men determined to interrupt proceedings. I started my talk and immediately there was shouting of abuse from various parts of the hall. My reaction was to tell the men to listen and they would benefit as much as their wives.

'At a signal from the most vocal man they all started to pelt the speakers on the platform with eggs, rotten tomatoes, apples, small raw turnips and beetroots, and believe it or not, live mice by the handful, at the same time telling us to go home and look after our husbands. Just at that moment I was hit above the right eye by, what turned out to be, an old cricket ball. I was knocked unconscious and fell to the floor with a large gash in my forehead from which blood gushed over my face and clothes. The result of my injury turned the meeting into a near riot as the women set about the hecklers. As they vastly outnumbered the men, they soon had the rowdies cornered. The police were called and several men and some women were arrested.'

Robert intervened, 'My poor girl had a frightful wound and will carry the scar for the rest of her life. Luckily the sight was not affected but, had the ball hit the eye, the result would have been much worse. However, I was determined to find the culprit if possible and decided to visit the local cricket club with the offending ball. The secretary was saddened to hear about the attack on Edith and assured me he would look into it with the members.'

Edith took over the story again. 'I had a charming letter form the club secretary in which he told me he had not been able to trace my attacker but, on behalf of his members, enclosed a £5 note for the NUWSS as they all felt the conduct of ball thrower was "just not cricket". It was a charming gesture and a splendid help with our funds.'

Margot was thrilled with what she had heard and asked, 'Have you continued with the NUWSS work since?'

'Of course my dear, now more than ever and as you know we obtained the vote for women over thirty in 1918 so we have to campaign with renewed effort to obtain the vote for all women; will you please support us?'

Both Margot and Francis agreed to help if they could, promising to start as soon as they returned to Hampshire in a few days' time.

Robert finished his coffee and enquired where they were staying, 'Are you visiting relatives?'

'We're visiting my mother, Lady Dewar, as well as Aunt Lotte Henshaw and my cousins. Do you know them by chance?'

'Know them? Of course we do, particularly Fanny who we see frequently,' continuing, as he turned to his wife, 'We do, don't we dear? She's wonderful company and a great bridge player!' Momentarily he was thoughtful, 'We also know Lotte Henshaw and remember her late husband Albert with affection. He was a lovely man whose knowledge of wines was enormous.'

Edith, clearly delighted at meeting Margot and Francis, suggested to her husband, 'Why don't we ask these young people to come to dinner with Fanny and Lotte and the cousins if they are available? It would be just wonderful to meet them all again!'

'A capital idea Edith,' and to Francis he said, 'May we presume upon your good nature to speak to your family and let us know when it will be convenient?'

Francis assured them he would do just that and they sat chatting until Margot told her hosts the story about Rupert Tupper on the forecourt of Exeter station, 'The wee fellow was just skin and bone and starving hungry into the bargain. His mother is a war widow with three children to feed and clothe on a pittance of a pension.'

She explained she and Francis intended to take some firm action when they reached Farndene, later in the week.

Edith's eyes shone as she gave her view of the Tupper situation. 'Now you can understand why there is the utmost necessity for women to have the vote and thereby a voice in parliament. What is going on in this country with regard to women and their children is a public disgrace and our male government members either don't appreciate the situation or they're not interested. Well, we intend to change that as soon as we are able. Robert and I will give you any assistance you require so you've only to ask.'

Margot and Francis were delighted and most profuse in their thanks.

They left shortly after, walking across the park to Fanny's house.

Chapter 4

There was certainly a buzz of conversation over luncheon that day, during which Fanny accepted the suggestion to go to dinner with the Oultons. It was decided two days later would be convenient and she undertook to contact all concerned and let Edith and Robert know in good time. Sir Roger said he looked forward to the occasion with much pleasure and told them, 'Robert Oulton was an outstanding sapper officer with a natural aptitude coupled with a wealth of experience. He was one of the strongest members of my Headquarters Team. It'll be a great pleasure to meet him again.'

Francis picked up the conversation, 'It's good to hear what you say Grandpa, as I'd already formed the opinion he is a thoroughly dependable and likable person, which brings me to the point. As you know we have already discussed possible developments of the Farndene Estate, part of which is the construction of an airfield on the higher ground to the north of the house and in this context Robert may be interested advising in a feasibility study. I like the man and would value his advice.'

During the ensuing conversation neither Francis nor his grandfather ate much, which prompted Fanny into action, 'Now you two gasbags, you know the family saying at meals, "if you don't eat your first course, you won't get any pudding!" So what about it?'

The result was miraculous with clean plates amid much leg pulling, particularly from Margot who had a very keen sense of humour. She put her oar in with the observation, 'I hear all you say but that may conflict with my own idea to raise a large beef herd of shaggy highland cattle,' and with a cheeky smile, 'Angus steers don't need specially levelled fields and they certainly don't make anything like as much noise as aeroplanes!' For the rest of the luncheon the lively banter continued and all the while Margot felt more and more at ease.

The time slipped by for Margot and Francis with visits to the various members of the family in Bristol, but it was the dinner party with Robert and Edith Oulton that claimed pride of place in their minds. After the meal, Francis outlined his development ideas to Robert who was clearly attracted to the scheme and agreed wholeheartedly to take part in the feasibility study, 'Good Lord, it'll be great fun, just like old times. I can't wait to get into the action again,' he paused and, glancing at Sir Roger, continued, 'and into the bargain I'll be on your patch so perhaps we can reminisce from time to time.'

Sir Roger smiled and nodded his head, 'that will be capital and something to look forward to, so let's get on with the action!'

While the men were deep in their conversation, Margot discussed the burning issue of Rupert Tupper and his family with Edith, Aunt Lotte, Fanny and her mother, as well as the other ladies present, and they all decided to do something definite as soon as possible. Edith promised to write to Mrs Tupper and suggest one or two of them should go down to Exeter to meet her and see what help could be arranged. Margot was impressed with Edith's drive and felt sure the Tupper family was in good hands. She also realised the experience Edith had had as a member of the Suffrage Movement made her an ideal person to deal with the problem.

So, after many happy hours spent with the family and friends, Francis and Margot said their fond farewells and departed in the Bentley touring car, left to Francis by his late father-in-law Angus, and headed for Farndene, their future home. Aunt Lotte made them promise to come back for Christmas saying it would probably be the last time she could do the entertaining, 'I'm getting on a bit and anyway the younger members of the family are keen to take on the responsibility of the annual gatherings of the clan.'

During the journey Margot shared the driving with Francis and they talked endlessly about their future together. She returned to the subject of the coming Christmas and told Francis she looked forward to joining the family in Bristol but wished to go north to St Andrews to be with her family and friends to celebrate Hogmanay. 'You may not know Darling, the last day of the year is very special to all Scots, a time to give and receive gifts and it is, if anything, more important than Christmas north of the border.'

Francis smiled and assured his wife he was aware of the festival. 'I know all about New Year's Eve and the giving of gifts; usually in the form of lots of wee drams, with the effect half Scotland never sees the New Year's Day as they are overcome by the effects of scotch! But never fear, my sweet. we will certainly go to join your family for Hogmanay, I promise you.'

By this time Margot had the giggles and told her husband he was incorrigible but also adorable and with that, put her arm round his neck and kissed him several times. His response was immediate, 'Hey! Stop that! Don't touch the driver like that as it may cause him to overheat!'

They stopped at Salisbury for luncheon at the White Hart Hotel and enjoyed the rest and warmth, as the weather had turned decidedly cooler which, of course, was seasonal for the first day of December. The remaining journey was uneventful and as they neared Farndene village, Francis told her he had written to the butler telling him not to have the staff outside the house to welcome them but the formal greeting should take place in the drawing room.

'Francis, that is what I like about you, you're so thoughtful about others and in particular the house staff. I have a feeling we are going to get on well with them all. Please tell me what you can about them?'

Francis was quiet for a moment or two. 'To be honest darling I only know the name of our butler, Phelps Bertram, known as Bertie to all. He came to grandpa from the late Sir Teddy Makepeace and I believe brought Annie Bloom the cook with him. By all accounts he is an excellent butler so we may expect a well run house.'

They were soon at Farndene and as the car turned into the Manor House drive, Margot gripped Francis's arm tightly and with tears in her eyes told Francis her thoughts: 'My dearest I feel so very, very happy now at last we're home. This is really the beginning of our married life together and I promise I'll do everything in my power to make this the loveliest place to live for both of us.'

Francis stopped the car and taking her in his arms, kissed his wife. 'Margot, you are a wonderful woman and I know you mean every word you have said and I'm sure this house will give us great happiness in the years to come. Thank you, my darling, for telling me what a splendid future we can expect.'

As the car drew up at the front of the Manor House, the door opened and Phelps Bertram walked over to greet them. 'Madam, sir, it is with great pleasure I welcome you home and I trust you have had a good journey.'

After the preliminary handshakes, he continued, 'If you care to come into the house with me I will introduce you to the staff after which I will arrange for your luggage to be brought in.'

They followed the butler into the drawing room where the other staff members were waiting.

Francis greeted them collectively: 'My wife and I are touched by your generous welcome and look forward to getting to know you individually in the coming days. I expect Mrs Vining will have a few words with you Annie about menus but meanwhile our thanks again.'

The staff moved out of the room leaving the butler, who stopped at the door to tell them, 'Dinner will be at seven thirty and please let me know if you require anything in the meantime.'

Francis nodded, 'That'll be fine Bertie and thank you for arranging such a charming welcome.'

Alone together, Francis and Margot sat quietly on a large sofa in front of the fire, neither saying a word for some minutes. Margot broke the silence, 'Darling, it's lovely to be home and this place will be just perfect to bring our four children up in. So after dinner I think an early night will be appropriate, don't you?'

Grinning, Francis agreed and added, 'Yes, we've had a long day and I expect you are feeling pretty tired, my sweet.'

'Not a bit of it,' she replied with a twinkle in her eyes, 'Don't forget we have four children to raise so we must get on with it and, as far as I'm concerned, tonight's the night so you can forget all about being tired!'

Francis burst out laughing and grabbing her in a tight embrace, 'That's what I like about you, sweetheart, you're so practical about life and I look forward to a continuous honeymoon for the foreseeable future. In my view love transcends all else in our relationship both now and in the years ahead and although you may tire of some aspects of our marriage, please never tire of me!'

Margot said nothing in reply but put her arms round his neck to kiss him in a long, passionate embrace.

'Gosh! You're really hot stuff!' he gasped.

'Not at all darling, that was just a starter; just wait till I'm really in the mood!'

With arms tightly round each other they got up and left the room to prepare for dinner.

Chapter 5

At breakfast a week later Bertie chatted as he served Francis, 'I hope you won't mind my saying Sir, but the whole house has come to life since you and your wife came. I speak for the staff when I say it's a delight to have younger people to serve. Not that we didn't like serving Sir Roger who was always a kind man to work for but, just to give you an example, Annie the cook told me how much she appreciates Mrs Vining taking an interest in the menus and the welfare of the staff. Sir Roger always left it to Annie regarding the meals and rarely suggested anything different. I hope you understand what I mean sir?'

'Of course I understand what you mean, Bertie. There are changes ahead for all of us but I assure you they'll be beneficial and will bring fuller life with plenty of interest,' adding with a smile, 'and now I'll have the kippers you so thoroughly recommended.'

Bertie positively beamed as he made for the sideboard to arrange a fine pair of Craster kippers on a plate, returning to place them in front of Francis, 'there you are, sir, and may I ask, is Mrs Vining breakfasting today?'

'Yes, she will be in shortly but is not a kipper lady. Perhaps a rasher or two with some toast but I'm sure you will have alternatives to suggest.'

Moments later Margot entered the dining room and sat opposite Francis.

'Good morning, madam.'

Margot smiled, 'Good morning Bertie and what have you to offer today?'

'Well, madam, I understand you are not a lover of kippers so I'll proceed with alternatives. We have some excellent back rashers from Denmark with the freshest lamb's kidneys from our local butcher and mushrooms that excel in flavour to accompany them. Cook has made a fresh cheese soufflé of the utmost lightness while there is an abundance of fresh fruit of all kinds from our local fruiterer.'

'Two rashers, with some toast and some coffee please, Bertie.'

Again Bertie beamed in satisfaction as he placed the food in front of Margot, 'I do hope you enjoy your breakfast, madam, you have made a wise choice.'

As Bertie moved away she could not help noticing Francis was having difficulty stifling his giggles.

During the meal Francis outlined his day, starting with a meeting at which Harry Bradshaw and his two assistant game-keepers were to report.

'It'll take about an hour and as soon as we finish I'll let you know darling, so they can meet you and you will know who they are and what they do.'

Francis felt the need to explain the rearing of pheasants but was quickly put in his place by Margot, 'My dear husband, I probably know as much about the rearing of game as you do. In Scotland we have some of the finest grouse moors in the British Isles and large herds of red deer. I often accompanied my father on shoots and, I may add, I'm a pretty good shot, rarely missing a bird. However I look forward to meeting the gamekeepers, I assure you.'

Francis said nothing for a moment and then, in a rather condescending way, said, 'My sweet, you are full of surprises.' He smirked as he continued, 'But tell me, is there anything you aren't expert at?'

His remarks touched a raw nerve in Margot and she bridled at the tone of his reply. 'Your comments are completely uncalled for and I resent what you have just said. If you can't conduct a civilised conversation I suggest you keep your mouth shut!' And pushing her chair away from the table, she stood glaring at Francis as she gave him a final verbal broadside, 'You'll have to learn I will not be patronised!' With those words stinging his ears, she swept from the room leaving Francis thoroughly bemused.

He sat quietly for a moment before remarking to Bertie, 'I reckon I've put my foot in it, good and proper.'

Bertie made no reply but came to the table, 'Shall I clear away now, sir?'

Francis nodded, 'Yes, please. I've finished in any case.'

To the clink of china and cutlery as the table was cleared, Francis left the dining room with a heavy heart, wondering how on earth he could retrieve the situation.

About ten minutes later, Margot walked out of the Manor House front door into the bright December sunlight and made her way down the drive, turning at the main gates towards the village. Although well wrapped up in a winter overcoat with a thick fur collar, a woolly hat and sheepskin gloves, she felt chilled as a result of the spat over breakfast.

She walked briskly at the same time going over the incident methodically in her law-trained mind, trying to fathom why Francis had been so sarcastic. She walked along the lanes, bordered by fields, still white with the overnight rime, with groups of trees silhouetted starkly against the vivid blue sky. The scene looked wonderful and Margot felt a calming comfort radiating from the countryside around her. She passed nobody and saw only cattle, standing in groups, gazing at her through a light haze as their breath drifted out in the frosty air.

In a little over fifteen minutes she reached the twelfth-century village church of St Paul and stopped to admire the flint-walled building and tower, complete with a gilded clock face, the hands at two minutes to ten.

Margot felt drawn to the church and entered through the south porch, in which various notices were pinned to a board, along with details of the services and the name of the rector. Just as the clock struck ten with its resonating bell, she noted his unusual name, the Reverend Shadwell Legion, and wondered what he looked like.

The door creaked as she stepped into the nave; looking up she beheld massive oak timbers lining the inside of the roof, illuminated by the sunlight filtering through upper windows. Along the walls were various brass and marble plaques, erected in memory of notable parishioners who had departed this life; one caught her attention as she walked towards the west end of the church.

There was a simple white marble rectangle on which she read the inscription, 'In loving memory of Lieutenant Commander Norman Vining, RN, who died on 5th October 1904 in the service of his country. "Greater love hath no man than this; that a man lay down his life for his friends."'

Margot realised she was looking at the memorial to Francis's father; it had an immediate effect on her. She sat in the nearest pew and quietly took stock of her situation, questioning why she had responded so forcefully to the comments Francis had made.

She concluded her adjustment to married life needed more time and decided to make a determined effort to overcome what possibly was a slight lack of confidence.

Looking down she noted the various boys names carved on the pew shelf, probably executed during lengthy sermons, reading Bobby, Daniel, Fred, Andrew, Walter, Josh and others that were damaged beyond legibility. Were they still alive and how many had perished in the Great War? They had carved their names with pride but, like those mentioned on the wall plaques, would they be remembered in the years ahead?

Margot moved down the nave towards the altar, admiring the delicate tracery of the rood screen spanning the chancel entrance. It was at this point she became aware of two elderly ladies polishing the choir stalls and chatting in low tones

'Good morning, I hope I'm not intruding?' Margot smiled a she approached them.

They both stood up and looked a little flustered, 'Oh! We had no idea there was anyone else in the church. You made us jump!' The taller of the two appeared to be the spokesman.

'I'm sorry if I startled you but I was just looking round this beautiful church for a few minutes. It is in such good condition and no doubt due to your care.'

The cleaners were pleased with the compliment Margot paid them and enquired, 'Are you visiting Farndene?'

'No, I moved into the Manor House with my husband a week ago and today is the first opportunity I've had to come to the church; perhaps I ought to introduce myself: I'm Mrs Vining and my husband is Francis Vining.'

Both ladies straightened their aprons and the taller again spoke up, 'Oh, madam, it's a great pleasure to meet you, as we heard you was coming from Sir Roger when he looked in one morning. I'm Charmaine Brench and this,' she said, pointing to her friend, 'is Rose Green. We cleans the church regular, if you know what I mean. The rector calls us his Holy Polishers.'

They stood chatting for a while before Margot said goodbye and, as she walked out through the south porch, the clock struck eleven.

A quarter of an hour later she arrived at the front door of the Manor House and, having no key, rang the bell. Bertie opened the door with a smile, 'I trust you have enjoyed your walk Madam? Mr Francis was enquiring for you about ten minutes ago when he ordered coffee for his meeting. Shall I include coffee for you madam?'

'Yes please, Bertie, I'm ready for a hot drink.' Margot left her outdoor clothes in the hall and, as she entered the study, Francis and the three gamekeepers stood up to welcome her.

'Thank you for joining us, darling; I would like you to meet our gamekeepers.' Francis introduced them individually, after which they sat talking and enjoying the coffee. Harry Bradshaw was most interested to hear about the red deer and suggested some consideration might be given to starting a herd on the estate. He also told Margot how well Alec Briggs had picked up the rudiments of pheasant rearing and hoped he would take over as head gamekeeper when Harry retired at the end of the year.

She was keen to learn more and enquired if there were any problems at present.

Harry gave a few details and told her the major difficulty, 'Poaching is always something we have to deal with, but it reaches alarming proportions each December and this year has been no exception. There's a ready market for the birds at Christmas time and organised gangs take not one or two but dozens in a single night.'

Francis came into the discussion at this point, 'We are planning patrols using as many of the estate workers as we can for the next two weeks and hopefully we'll catch some of the poachers. We think they come out from Southampton with a motor van and take the birds back there to a prearranged market.'

As soon as the meeting broke up and they were alone, Francis started to say how sorry he was for the situation at breakfast, 'Darling, I regret very much what I said this morning and want you to forgive me for being such an ass!'

At this point, Margot put her arms round his neck and gently kissed him, 'Dearest, I was as much to blame for our little spat and wish to be forgiven!'

The forgiveness was obvious as they were locked in an embrace for some minutes after which Francis pleaded, 'Don't let's quarrel anymore sweetheart, it hurts so much!'

Margot squeezed him and promised. She went on to tell him about her walk to the village church and all she saw there, particularly the memorial to his father. 'You know, darling, going into the church made me think about our marriage and I'm convinced a change took place in my whole attitude as a result of that visit. I came away with a feeling of confidence and determined to live up to our expectations by being the good supportive wife you are entitled to expect. I love you very dearly and am longing to make this house our home by putting our seal on it.'

Still holding her in his arms, Francis told her, 'You are a remarkable person, Margot, and I too love you with all my heart and will support you in our homemaking.'

They were enjoying a further lingering kiss when there was a tap at the door.

'Come in,' they both called and Bertie entered to announce that lunch would be ready in five minutes.

Taking his arm, Margot marched Francis towards the door with the exultation, 'Come on, laddie, let's go and eat. I'm starving!'

Chapter 6

As promised, Edith Oulton wrote to Mrs Janine Tupper in Exeter, suggesting a visit in the next week. A few days later Mrs Tupper replied, saying she was looking forward to their meeting. Consequently Fanny, Aunt Lotte and Edith departed early for Exeter on 8th December driven by Fred Gutteridge, enjoying the journey in bright winter sunshine and arriving by midday. After a quick lunch at the Royal Hotel, Fred drove them towards their destination.

Fanny suggested they walk the last part of the way and, on reaching Penny Lane, the dilapidated nature of the area became apparent.

The shabby appearance of the terraced houses, many with cracked window panes in frames lacking paint, was set off by scattered rubbish along the road. Here and there groups of children played hopscotch on frames drawn with chalk on the road, or bowled iron hoops. Girls were skipping, while boys kicking a ball against the front of one house brought an angry woman to the door, shouting expletives with threats. Her threat had little lasting effect and often provoked cheek from the boys who continued ball kicking against the house as soon as she closed her door.

As the ladies walked along the road the children stopped what they were doing to stand and stare, obviously curious that three well-dressed ladies should come down their street

Reaching number eight, Fanny noticed a chimney sweep's barrow, bearing a name board 'John Foston, The Clean Sweep', parked at the kerb next door.

The door opened quickly in answer to their knock and Mrs Tupper smilingly invited them in. The house was a typical 'two up, two down' with a small scullery at the back, in which they could see a single cold water tap above a shallow earthenware sink. Through the rear window was a small backyard with an outside privy against the adjoining wall. The stairs to the upper bedrooms rose, parallel with the road, between the two ground floor rooms.

Janine Tupper, a petite figure, speaking with an attractive French accent, invited the visitors into the rear living room and, after introductions, they sat on café-style bent wood chairs round the well-scrubbed kitchen table. In the chimney breast a small black-leaded cooking range shone and a large black tea kettle simmered on a trivet against the fire. The place was clean in spite of the obvious shortage of money and the light brown lino covering the floor was well polished.

The three children stood along the wall as Janine introduced them each by name, 'Mollie, my eldest who is ten is my little helper.' The quite pretty girl with dark hair smiled and Lotte noticed her dress was a faded blue woollen cloth. 'Next is Rupert who is eight,' Janine smiled wistfully as she added, 'he's usually a good boy but sometimes gets into the wrong company with other boys and up to mischief.' Rupert had similar dark hair to his sister and was good looking with a cheeky smile. He was tall for his age but clearly underweight. Again his clothes were thin and his jacket elbows patched.

'And my baby Tom is six and has fair hair like my dear Charlie.' Tears welled in her eyes as she mentioned her late husband.

Fanny spoke to all three about school and how far they had to walk and the children were soon in relaxed conversation with their visitors. Edith Oulton made a popular move when she asked if there was a sweetshop near and received a loud chorus in reply, 'Yes!'

Janine explained the corner shop along the road sold practically everything and was run by Pat and Maureen Bessant, 'They are good Irish Roman Catholics and have been very supportive, allowing me to buy food "on the slate"; I don't know what I would have done without them.'

Edith produced three pennies from her purse and, amid thanks, the three children departed without delay for the sweetshop. 'I thought it right the children should not be present while we discuss your personal situation,' she said with a smile, 'so we have three pennies worth of time and must make the most of it.' She turned to Janine, 'Now tell us all about yourself and your present difficulties and we will see how we may be able to help you.'

Janine started by explaining her origin, 'I am a Breton woman, born and raised in a small town called Plonéour Lanvern, south of Quimper. My family bred horses for all purposes except racing and my father Andre Cabellou, with my brothers Alain and René ran a successful business. Most of the feed and straw bedding was grown on our farm for the hundred or so horses we kept.

'My late husband Charlie also came from a horse breeding family just outside Exeter and he and his father often came to Plonéour Lanvern to buy fresh brood mares. After we had met several times over two or three years we realise we had fallen in love. As I was then twenty-one we decided to be married but my father, on hearing Charlie was a Methodist, forbade it and said I had to marry a Roman Catholic.' She stopped momentarily to wipe away a tear. 'The consequence was we eloped and I was married in the local Methodist Chapel in 1908. The Tupper family were very kind but sadly my mother-in-law died with consumption the next year and never knew her grandchildren. The Tupper business did well but my father, out of spite, would not sell them horses so they had to buy elsewhere.'

Fanny interrupted to enquire, 'Haven't the Tupper family helped you since you husband was killed?'

'Well no. But perhaps if I continue you will understand. When the war broke out my Charlie and his younger brother Gregory decided to join up, choosing the Royal Artillery rather than being drafted into the infantry. They were expert with horses and both were soon promoted, Charlie as sergeant and his brother as bombardier. Sadly Gregory was killed at the battle of the Somme in 1916. Charlie survived until August 1918 and was lost during the final campaign in Belgium. The loss of his two sons devastated my father-in-law and he was a broken man.

'In January 1919 he sold his farm and horse business to a circus company who intended to use the stabling as winter quarters for their animals. He has since disappeared and I've no idea where he has gone. I wrote to my sister-in-law Megan but got no reply. I never did get on with her and I think she resented my marrying Charlie, her favourite brother.'

'Couldn't your own family help you by sending a little money from time to time?' Lotte just couldn't understand Janine's father and mother leaving a widowed daughter without their support.

'I also wrote to my parents to tell them my position but some weeks elapsed before I got a reply, which came from my dear mother, Stella. She told me my father wanted nothing to do with me and forbade her writing to me.' With tears running down her cheeks, Janine had difficulty continuing, 'Mother sent five hundred francs but asked me not to write again. My financial situation got steadily worse and I had to pawn the few trinkets Charlie gave me and last week my engagement ring went to provide enough money for food.'

At this point she broke down weeping and Lotte put her arm round the unhappy young woman for comfort. Fortunately the large black kettle began to boil and, pulling herself together, Janine suggested a cup of tea for her guests and they agreed.

All declared the brew was just what was wanted and the discussion continued until Janine spoke about Rupert again, 'He's a lovely boy but too much for me to handle and he needs a man's influence now and for a few years to come. I just don't feel I can cope with him.'

Fanny said she understood, explaining briefly how she was widowed with a small boy to bring up, 'As it happened I remarried and my second husband was a great influence on my son. Please don't misunderstand me, I'm not suggesting you remarry but perhaps consider fostering for the lad.'

Janine was not familiar with the term and asked what it meant.

'Let me explain,' Fanny continued, 'a family home is found for Rupert where he can be brought up with other children under the care, influence and love of a mother and father. He would spend term time with them but come home to you on all school holidays. The arrangement is entirely voluntary and you would be able to bring Rupert back at any time if you were unsatisfied.'

Janine sat quietly for some moments, absorbing all Fanny had said and then she asked, 'Which family are you talking about and where do they live?'

Fanny responded without hesitation, 'I have one of the workers on the Farndene Estate in Hampshire in mind, who is married with a good wife and three children.

'He is employed as a gamekeeper and has an excellent character reference from the Royal Navy, where he served during the Great War. I have to tell you he married a Methodist and the family go to the local chapel each Sunday.'

'Would it be possible for me to meet the family you have in mind?' Janine was attracted by the fostering idea but needed to be sure her son was going to the right people.

'I'm sure that can be arranged and I'll speak to my daughter-in-law who lives in Farndene and make arrangements for you and the children to go there.' Fanny made a special note in her diary.

Edith then talked about money and discovered there was an outstanding bill of three pounds at the Bessant shop. Janine was given twenty-five pounds to clear her debt and to help in the coming weeks, and an additional sum to retrieve her things from the pawn shop.

She told Edith, 'A disabled officer from the Royal Artillery visited but he had to undergo surgery on the stump of his leg and had not been back for some time. He spoke of a Regimental Trust set up to help the families and widows of former members.'

They had been talking for nearly one hour when the children returned to show their purchases from the sweet shop. Each had a twist of paper containing a mixture of aniseed balls, humbugs, sherbet cushions and toffees. Tom said he chose dolly-mixture sweets as there were lots more to eat. Mollie and Rupert also had a stick of liquorice. The ladies politely declined the offered sweets from the children and shortly after said goodbye to the Tupper family. Fred Gutteridge met them with the car a short distance from Penny Lane.

At afternoon tea back at the Royal Hotel they all agreed the visit had been heart-rending but most interesting and unanimously declared they must do all they could to help. Fanny said, 'I'll contact Francis and remind him to write to David Lloyd-George about the plight of thousands of war widows.'

'Good for you Fanny!' Edith's response was wholehearted, 'and I'll back that up by going to see the PM in person to up the pressure on him. He will remember me from our encounters over women's suffrage. He'd better look out as we're on the war path!'

Chapter 7

Sir Roger Vining returned to Farndene at the end of the second week in December and Francis welcomed his grandfather back by inviting him to dinner. There were just the three of them as Francis and Margot wanted to discuss personal matters relating to the estate. They all enjoyed the occasion and Sir Roger was sincere in his appreciation of the menu, 'I haven't enjoyed a meal like that for many a moon and I do congratulate you Margot. I can see why my grandson married you. You're not only very good looking and intelligent but into the bargain you know how to charm we men with food fit for the gods!'

They all had a good laugh and Margot's face flushed with appreciation and, turning to Sir Roger, she made him a promise, 'Grandpa, next year I'll cook you the finest handmade haggis with tatties and bashed neeps on Burns Night, so please come and join us.' He accepted without hesitation, putting a note in his pocket diary.

They adjourned to the drawing room and over coffee Francis outlined his ideas for the development of the Estate: 'I've been looking at about three hundred acres on the ground to the west of the house and, if you agree, will carry out a feasibility study as to its suitability for the construction of an airfield.'

Sir Roger nodded but wanted to know who would make the study, 'It's important we get a good man to look at it for us.'

'As you know I've spoken briefly to Colonel Robert Oulton and he is very interested. As a retired sapper he has vast experience from his days in India where he was responsible for railway construction and maintenance and, during the early part of the Great War, airfield preparation in France for the Royal Flying Corps and the Royal Naval Air Service.'

His grandfather was impressed and suggested a new limited company should be formed to finance the whole project. 'You and Margot must be the shareholders but I'm willing to put up some capital by way of a loan to get the thing started.

'May I say how astute you are being in sighting the field well away from most dwellings in this area. The noise created by aircraft taking off during the light hours will be offset by other daytime activities and it is hardly likely the airfield will ever operate at night.'

Francis was thoughtful before replying, 'In life I've learnt never, to say never. None of us know what the future holds, but at present the intention would be to have daytime flying only.'

At this point Margot put forward her idea for stocking the grazing areas with highland cattle to produce beef and Sir Roger was attracted to the suggestion. She continued, 'I've another idea which may or may not appeal to you. In Scotland we have large herds of red deer and there is a ready market for venison, which fetches a high price. Additionally deer stalking is a very profitable operation and clients come from Canada, the USA, France, and many other European countries to shoot. Several parts of the Estate are heavily wooded, quite suitable for rearing deer and I suggest we try a small herd for a couple of years.'

Smiling, Francis glanced at his grandfather who was looking wide-eyed at Margot. Nodded his head, he replied, 'by Jove Margot, there is a lot more to you than I'd realised; I think both your suggestions are well worth examining and I'm particularly attracted to the idea of a deer herd. By all means exploit the asset and what you have both put on the table will enhance our income but not, in any way, detract from the natural surrounding beauty of this place.'

They talked for a couple of hours, covering all aspects of the business side of the Estate and by half past eleven Sir Roger said he had to stop drinking any more coffee, otherwise he wouldn't sleep, 'I have to tell you two it gives me great pleasure to know you are my near neighbours and I've a feeling in the coming years you will rejuvenate this whole place, including the village. Now please excuse a tired old man who must go home.' With that he kissed and hugged Margot and shook Francis's hand warmly.

'I'll get Bertie Bertram to run you to your house; he's a good driver and never drinks when he's on duty.' His grandfather accepted Francis's offer with thanks.

After Sir Roger had left, Margot and Francis sat in front of the fire talking until past midnight and she again told her husband how the visit to the local church last week had been a revelation, 'I told you how I felt at that time and the feeling is even more intense now. I'm so very happy and I'm proud to be part of the Vining tradition.'

Francis took her in his arms and held a long embrace to the point they were both gasping for breath.

'Gosh, Francis, you're certainly a goer! So now you're in the mood I suggest we go to bed. Don't forget we want four children so let's get on with it.'

During the next week Margot had little time to spare as there were so many things concerning the house to arrange whilst she and Francis were away in Bristol for the Christmas holidays. Bertie the butler would be staying in the Manor House with Mrs Gertrude Reynolds, the housekeeper and Mrs Annie Bloom, the cook as well as two of the maids and the stable man, Larry Forbes; the rest of the house staff were given leave and some would not be returning from seeing their families until the New Year. As the remainder of the outside estate staff lived in the village they would spend the holiday with their loved ones.

She also had a long telephone call from Fanny during which her mother-in-law explained the problems Janine Tupper faced, particularly with Rupert. Before she and Francis left for Bristol, Margot promised to discuss the proposed fostering with Alec Briggs, the assistant gamekeeper and his wife Beatty.

At the last moment on the morning of their departure on 20th December, just as they were preparing to drive to Bristol, Larry Forbes reported one of the hunters had developed a cough.

Francis telephoned the vet, Luke Yardley, who was already out on a call. His wife, Rose, promised Francis she would tell her husband as soon as he returned. Consequently they were delayed and Francis called his mother so she would not worry. It was almost half past two when Luke Yardley arrived, apologising but explaining he had been to an outlying farm to deliver a calf. He and Francis entered the stable where they met Larry Forbes in a very distressed state.

'She's in a bad condition, sir, and has got worse in the last couple of hours.' Larry stood to one side to let the vet look at the mare. After a thorough examination, he turned to Francis, 'I'm afraid it's bad news, she has serious lung infection, a kind of equine influenza and it's in an advanced state. She has a massive temperature and is coughing blood. There is nothing I can do for her now. She is a fine beast but I'm very sorry, it's best to put her down as she is in great pain.'

Francis was upset and shaking his head, 'What a tragedy. She was always a wonderful horse to ride and I'll miss her.' He was quiet for some moments before making up his mind, 'She must not suffer! Please go ahead, Luke, and will you please arrange for the carcass to be removed.'

As he walked back to the house he heard a single shot and realised it was all over.

Margot was distressed and wept when she heard the news. She recovered somewhat when her next thoughts were for Larry Forbes, 'Francis, he'll be very sad. Perhaps we should ask him in for a drink and we can talk to him for a little while before we leave.'

Minutes passed and Luke came into the kitchen, where he removed his boots and asked if he could wash his hands. As he scrubbed under the running tap he talked to Francis, 'I've told your man not to let anyone touch the carcass and, if I may, I'd like to telephone to arrange for a special carter to collect the remains. You see, I believe the infection is serious and must be reported to the authorities to carry out a post-mortem. It may be a viral infection imported from France when hundreds of our horses were repatriated to England at the end of the war and disbursed mainly in the south. Will you please arrange for the stable to be fumigated thoroughly and all straw litter to be burnt?'

Margot suggested tea and Luke jumped at the idea, 'Thanks. I could do with a hot drink to get my circulation going again.

They went through to the drawing room and, once seated, Francis asked where Luke had spent his war years.

In between sips of tea, Luke replied, 'I was commissioned into the RAMC at the outbreak in 1914. I spent some time in this country before going to various parts of France and Belgium until 1916, when I was put in charge of a large unit near Amiens, dealing with wounded horses.'

At the mention of Amiens, Francis's interest sharpened, 'My final base was at Amiens where my squadron saw the German air force off for the last time.'

'I remember seeing your planes taking off over our place; the horses were usually excited by the noise and careered around the large pens. We managed to patch up most of the wounded and the recoveries were due, to a large extent, to my two Canadian assistant vets who came from Edmonton and Calgary respectively. Sadly both died in the influenza pandemic, when hundreds died at the Canadian Army base at Grayshott Heath, south of Hindhead. It seems tragic having survived the war only to die in such a way.'

Margot agreed, adding, 'I understand a memorial is being provided in the shape of avenues of Canadian Maple trees on Grayshott Heath and some of the money will come from local subscription. The Canadians were very popular with the nearby villages.'

As soon as Luke departed, Margot called Larry into the house and gave him hot tea, which Francis laced with scotch.

It was four o'clock when Larry finally left, having consumed three more large whiskies. 'It helped to deaden the sadness of losing the mare,' he said with a smile, 'I've always thought scotch is a wonderful healer and I'm just about healed thank you.'

Looking across the room at Francis who was sitting gazing into the log fire, Margot realised he had suffered quite a shock. 'Francis, darling, I think we should stay the night here and make our way to Bristol in the morning. You're upset and tired and in no state to drive all that way in the dark. What do you say?'

Francis smiled as he crossed the room to take Margot in his arms and kiss her. 'Sweetheart, you are always so considerate and I do appreciate it. Yes, let's do just that and I'll telephone mother straight away.'

'And I'll cook you a lovely meal which we can eat at our leisure.'

Francis perked up at that news and promised, 'We'll have a nice bottle of wine to round off the evening.'

'After which we can have an early night in our own bed and, you know, if you're not too tired ...' Margot added with a wink.

Francis enjoyed the light-hearted way Margot was dealing with the situation and, kissing her again, responded, 'You're good for me my sweet. Cheering me up, promising to cook supper and you obviously love me as you've invited me to help with the family plan!'

'Francis, you're cheeky, but I do love you!' Margot and Francis were both laughing as he went through to the study and she to the kitchen.

Chapter 8

On 16th December, with Christmas looming fast, Fanny, Edith and Lotte tried their best to sort out the Tupper family difficulties. The most pressing problem was, in fact, the most simple to resolve, it being the provision of food and presents for Janine and her three children.

Fanny suggested, 'my parents' Food Store can arrange for a hamper to be dispatched in good time for Christmas and we can enclose cash to provide new clothes for them all. At this stage we might as well give the money ourselves and decide later how extra funds can be obtained.'

The contents of the hamper had to be sensible foodstuffs for a family, enough to last for about a month, by which time more permanent arrangements would be in place.

Turning to the question of a foster family, Fanny told them she had spoken with her daughter-in-law, Margot, on the telephone. Margot discussed the matter with Alec Briggs, the assistant gamekeeper, and his wife Beatty; they were more than willing to take Rupert Tupper for six months on a trial basis.

She went on, 'they have three lovely children, Jenny just eight years old, Connie six, and Raymond, four and the two older children are bright little buttons, according to their school teacher.'

'We need to provide some subsistence allowance for Mr and Mrs Briggs and I think I know where I can tap some money.' Edith, as always, was most thorough in her assessment of a situation, 'I'll talk to Robert this evening to see what can be done.'

Fanny returned to the most difficult problem: 'If you remember, Janine Tupper quite rightly wanted to meet Alec and Beatty Briggs and we agreed to make this possible. Well, the visit could take place after Christmas during the school holidays. Margot suggests Janine and her children travel to Farndene by train and are put up at the Albion Inn in the village for a day or two. It'll give all parties a chance to get to know each other and any difficulties can be ironed out. Margot said she and Francis can keep a watching brief on the proceedings and give any help required.'

And so the necessary arrangements were put in place and Fanny said she would let Janine have all the details.

On the morning of 18th December Francis and Margot felt able to leave the Manor House for their Christmas holiday in Bristol. At a last minute meeting with Harry Bradshaw, the head gamekeeper told Francis he had received a 'tip off' that a large scale poaching operation was to take place that night. To meet the threat he had organised fifteen of the estate workers, split into three groups to lay ambushes in the most likely spots, adding, 'I hope we catch the blighters and put a stop to this sort of thing once and for all.'

'How are you arming yourselves?' Francis felt he needed to know his men were adequately protected.

'We will be carrying our usual sticks and some clubs in addition, but no firearms. I've stressed on no account should anyone take a gun.'

Francis was satisfied and congratulated his gamekeeper, 'Well done Harry! I wish you every success tonight.'

After a good journey Francis and Margot arrived at Fanny's house by mid-afternoon and were soon relaxing for tea in front of the drawing room fire.

There was plenty to talk about, discussing the forthcoming visit of Janine Tupper and her children to Farndene and subsequently the various arrangements for the Christmas holiday.

Fanny went on, 'Edith and Robert Oulton are coming to dinner tonight and I've also asked Commander Hilary Marchant, the officer who was a pall-bearer at your father's funeral.'

Francis's pulled a face and was clearly not impressed with the news; in a pouting tone of voice he challenged Fanny, 'Mother, I remember the fellow when you met us at Temple Meads station and I thought him a pompous individual! I hope we're not having him any more over Christmas.'

Fanny bristled slightly, 'Now, Francis, you're not being very charitable! He is on his own in Bristol and I just think we should offer friendship, particularly at this time of the year. He's dined here once or twice and I find him pleasant company.'

Margot was also a little put out by the attitude Francis had struck and remonstrated with him, 'Darling, you have only met this man once before and it was a very brief occasion if I remember correctly, so wouldn't it be better to see how you get on with him tonight? And in any case your mother has every right to ask whom she pleases to dine at her house.'

Francis realised he was under siege on two fronts and held up his hands in capitulation, 'All right. I've got the message from both of you. I promise I'll behave myself at dinner tonight.'

The dinner party that evening was a pleasant affair but Francis found Hilary Marchant's company somewhat overbearing. As he had promised his mother and Margot, he made an effort to be sociable.

When the ladies withdrew to the drawing room, Francis, Robert Oulton and Hilary Marchant enjoyed port and cigars while discussing the airfield to be built at Farndene. At about a quarter past nine Oliver Perkins, the butler, came into the dining room to inform Francis there was an urgent telephone call for him.

Francis went to the study and picked up the receiver. He was surprised to hear his grandfather's voice, 'Francis, I'm glad I've got hold of you without delay. I'm sorry to tell you there has been a terrible accident here tonight!'

Francis closed the study door and sat down to receive the news in a long conversation with his grandfather.

About twenty minutes later he went to the dining room and told Robert and Hilary they had better come with him to join the ladies as he had just received some dreadful news.

Once in the drawing room Francis explained that there had been an accident on the estate that night. 'Grandpa told me a large organised gang of poachers had been ambushed by Harry Bradshaw and his men but, during an ensuing fight, one of the poachers shot Harry. Subsequently the man with the gun had been shot dead during a struggle with our chaps. Several of the poachers had been detained and handed over to the police who had answered the emergency call very quickly. The police are questioning Alec Briggs and Larry Forbes, our two fellows who grappled with the man who died, to ascertain exactly what went on.'

There was a shocked silence as they all took in the terrible news. 'How is Harry?' Margot was clearly upset as she recalled meeting the gamekeeper so recently, 'Is he seriously wounded?'

Francis put his arm round Margot as he went on, 'At present I don't know; he was taken to Southampton Hospital but Grandpa didn't think the injuries were life threatening. The hospital surgeon is operating tonight and promised to keep Grandpa informed.'

'Francis, this is awful!' Margot was anxious to know more,. 'Do they know who the dead man is? And are any of the other estate workers injured?'

'At present the identity of the deceased isn't known but the police are questioning the captured poachers and hope to find out very soon. There was no news of the estate staff but I told Grandpa I thought I should return to Farndene in the morning. He wouldn't hear of it and we said we should stay in Bristol for Christmas as planned. He will telephone again in the morning to let us know the up to date situation.'

Fanny had listened to all her son had said and spoke from experience, 'Francis, you forget your grandfather is a retired General and from my experience he is more than capable of dealing with the situation. He'll be in his element and will see that the police get on with the job of rounding up the poachers who escaped. It's sad that Harry Bradshaw was injured but even sadder someone died.

'Now, I think we could all do with something to buck us up so I'll get Perkins to bring fresh coffee, and perhaps some brandy wouldn't come amiss!'

There was general agreement and once it arrived the buzz of conversation went on until late hours.

After the guests departed, Fanny, Margot and Francis sat talking for another half hour before they said goodnight to Perkins as he cleared away.

Fanny was clearly delighted to have Margot and Francis staying and told them so as she kissed them both on the way to bed.

It was almost lunchtime the following day when Sir Roger telephoned to report the current situation at Farndene; Fanny took the call.

He explained, 'I'm pleased to tell you a lot has happened and the police have really got on with the job of rounding up the poachers who escaped last night. From information given by one of the captured men, they raided several houses in Southampton and arrested five more criminals, together with the van used in the raid, which still contained a large number of stolen pheasants as well as some dead sheep and deer.'

'That's excellent! But what is the news of Harry Bradshaw?' Fanny was most concerned to learn how he was progressing.

'I was just coming to that, Fanny. Harry will be all right in a week or so; he's had a bullet removed from his left thigh. A second bullet passed between his left arm and his body, grazing his chest. Last night our estate staff acted superbly and apart from some scratches and bruises, feel very pleased with themselves.

'I've arranged for extra pay for them all and each has been given a bottle of brandy. One cheeky fellow said he is willing to turn out each night for such a reward!

'Now I've left the choice bit of news till last: the dead man has been formally identified and, you'll never believe it, his name is Ranolph Mandrake, grandson of Admiral Sir Monty Mandrake our near neighbour. The poor man is devastated particularly as Ranolph, a lieutenant in my regiment, deserted in France in January 1917 and until last night had not been seen or heard of since that time.'

Fanny could hardly believe her ears, 'Oh, how terrible, and I'm sure his grandfather must be awfully sad.'

'Jack Snapper, the superintendent in charge of the case, is coming to see me later this afternoon to discuss a number of problems so I'll telephone again if there is any fresh news.'

Fanny thanked Sir Roger and made careful notes of all he had said to tell the family when they returned.

It was just a family gathering for dinner that evening and Fanny's parents, David and Ruth, Aunt Lotte and Jessica, Alex and his fiancée Angelina. Mildred and her fiancé Bert Fingall didn't come as they had volunteered to look after Angelina's two children.

The guests had not seen Francis and Margot since the wedding so there was much to talk about. However the main topic centred on the terrible news from Farndene and Fanny gave a good account of her conversation with Sir Roger at lunchtime.

'He told me there appeared to have been a pitched battle between the estate men and the poachers, among whom were several army deserters living on organised crime. They were led by Ranolph Mandrake, himself a deserter from Sir Roger's Regiment. He was the grandson of Admiral Sir Monty Mandrake a near neighbour of my father-in-law.' She explained how Harry Bradshaw had been wounded and continued, 'Ranolph Mandrake fired at Harry but was himself killed in a struggle with two of our men. The police have rounded up most of the gang who are now in custody.'

Fanny turned to Francis, 'I told you Grandpa would be in his element dealing with the police and that is exactly what happened. He said "I got behind the coppers and they understood I wanted action! The result is the superintendent will call to report to me today." So you must not worry and we'll hear more in the morning.'

Francis took in all his mother has said but felt concerned he was away from Farndene at a very difficult time for everyone there.

After dinner they talked at length about family matters and

the time passed very quickly with the result it was past midnight before the quests left and they all said goodnight.

Once in their bedroom Margot put her arms round Francis and kissed him at the same time realising he was worried. 'My darling, please don't be too concerned about Grandpa. He's a robust character and will cope with the situation I feel sure!'

Francis smiled in response, 'Thank you, my darling, but we need to go back to Farndene as soon as possible after Christmas. How would you feel about returning the day after Boxing Day? That would give us time there before we go to Scotland on, say, 29th December.'

'I'm quite happy with your suggestion and will help with any arrangements we need to make at home before going to my parents for Hogmanay.' With her arms still round his waist she was aware he had other matters on his mind, 'Darling, what else is worrying you?'

'To be honest, sweetheart, it's my mother and this confounded Hilary Marchant.'

Margot was taken aback and wanted to hear more, 'What on earth has he to do with your mother? The man's good looking but his manner is on the condescending side; I also thought him a bit effeminate.'

'My thoughts exactly, but in addition I've a feeling he is cultivating mother in a very obvious way.' Francis paused for a moment, 'I watched him at dinner the other night as he acted the courtier to her, turning on the charm each time he spoke.'

'And what was Mama's reaction Francis?'

'She didn't dislike it but I feel the situation dangerous, particularly as mother is a wealthy and titled person, but still a woman. She's a widow and the prospect of spending the rest of her life alone will have crossed her mind.'

Margot was thoughtful as she summed up all he had said, 'Francis darling, aren't you exaggerating the situation a little? While I agree a wealthy widow is a catch for a lonely man, do we know Hilary is embarking on a fishing expedition for a comfortable future, free of money worries?'

Francis was nodding, 'You see my point dearest. Neither of us knows exactly what Hilary Marchant intends but the seeds of doubt have been sown in our minds, don't you agree?'

'Yes darling, you are right and I think we need to know a lot more about the Commander. What action do you suggest?'

'Well, Margot, as soon as we return from Scotland discreet enquiries must be made and a private detective employed if necessary. For mother's sake we must make absolutely sure the man is of good character. I'll also have a quiet word with Aunt Lotte to get her view on the subject.'

It was now well after midnight and both were quite exhausted from the day's happenings, so bed was the only course open to them.

Chapter 9

Francis and Margot travelled back to Farndene from Bristol on 27th December, very relieved to find their grandfather very much in command, things having calmed down following the shooting. He was pleased to join them for dinner, thus giving him an opportunity to relate all that had taken place, and wasted no time giving a full account in detail.

Sitting back in his chair, he outlined events on the night of 19th. 'It must have been shortly after eleven o'clock when a policeman called to ask me to go to the Manor House as there had been a serious accident. Bertie Bertram arrived moments later with a car so I was at the house without delay. Here I found a state of, what I can only call, near chaos with people coming and going, coupled with a large police presence. On the humorous side, I was stopped at the front door by a zealous young constable enquiring who I was! Luckily Tony Hemp, our local police sergeant, arrived at that moment so the young bobby was "informed", and muttered apologies.

'I found a number of our men in the hall, all very cold and shivering, while some were suffering from severe cuts and bruises, so I instructed Bertie to take them to the kitchen and arrange for Cook to prepare hot cocoa to be provided suitably laced with rum.

'Sergeant Hemp told me the body had been examined by Dr Maurice Strickland for the police and had confirmed death. The deceased, unknown at that time, was taken to the police mortuary pending further enquiries to be conducted by Superintendent Jack Snapper, who was in charge of the case. An ambulance arrived to take Harry Bradshaw, who had been shot, to hospital together with four of our more seriously wounded chaps.' Momentarily he paused, giving Margot an opportunity to enquire more about Harry Bradshaw.

'Grandpa, tell me, how is Harry following his operation and are any of our men still in hospital?'

'Harry is quite comfortable and expects to come home in about a week's time. As far as the others are concerned all were discharged the same night after treatment but, naturally, will be a bit sore for a while. Each was given a bottle of brandy, which I felt was the least I could do in the circumstances and I understand they enjoyed the Christmas holiday.'

Francis had been listening intently but needed to know more. 'Grandpa, exactly where did our men intercept the poachers?'

'It was in Farley's Croft which, as you know, is roughly half a mile from the Manor House. The beggars came in a large van along Farley's Lane and drove the vehicle a short way into the woods. They had killed a number of birds before Harry Bradshaw's men caught up with them and from that moment a pitched battle took place. Some of the poachers had already taken the pheasants to their van and on hearing the "set to", drove off at high speed. Our chaps put up a tremendous fight and completely overwhelmed the poachers who gave in when their leader was shot dead.'

'Grandpa, what happened when Superintendent Snapper came to see you?' Margot's legal mind was working, 'and what happened to the pheasants the police recovered?'

'Jack Snapper called and gave me details of the investigation, and I must say he impressed me immediately. Apparently he mustered the whole of his force in Southampton, raiding several houses on the information given by one of the poachers. They succeeded in rounding up the gang plus several other criminals engaged in various rackets.

'As you know, Ranolph Mandrake was killed and at this stage it appears he and others were involved in a number of illegal enterprises, including handling stolen goods, including jewellery, and antique furniture, and smuggling from France and Holland. The rustling and poaching were seasonal sidelines and involved deer, sheep and pheasants. He indicated the net was closing on other people and declined to tell me names at this juncture.'

'What a story and no doubt the best is still to come,' Margot was wide eyed and her legal training focused on the coming action. 'It looks as though this will be a big case when it reaches court in the New Year.'

'You're absolutely right, Margot, and I hope the scoundrels are sent down for a long spell. But you asked about the stolen pheasants – well I've arranged for the birds to be sold and the proceeds passed to my regimental charity which helps widows and orphans of soldiers killed on active service. In addition to the pheasants, two dead sheep were found in the van but at present nobody has claimed them.'

After dinner, over coffee, the conversation moved to the plans for the estate and to the airfield in particular and here Francis outlined his thinking: 'As you know, Grandpa, we go to Scotland on the 29th for Hogmanay with Margot's family but as soon as we return in the New Year I intend to start the project in earnest.'

Margot, still concerned about Harry Bradshaw, declared, 'I think I should go into Southampton tomorrow to visit Harry in hospital. I feel it would be a little thoughtless if we just took off for Scotland without making any contact with him; what do you say, Francis?'

'I agree, darling, and I'll come with you. We can ask cook to bake a cake for him. As she has a soft spot for Harry I'm sure she'll be delighted.'

They talked at length and as Sir Roger left he again remarked, 'you two have no idea how much good your coming here has done for me; bless you! The Manor House has come to life again!'

The next day Margot and Francis went to Southampton Hospital as planned and, on entering the men's ward, were impressed by the spick and span appearance of everything. Beds were lined up in military precision with large vases of flowers on the three tables in the centre of the ward and the all-pervading, hospital smell of disinfectant. The nurses looked polished in their pale blue uniforms with starched collars and cuffs, black stockings and shoes, and stiff white headdresses.

Met by the ward sister, they were escorted down to Harry's bed. He was quite overwhelmed by their visit but delighted to receive a large box containing cakes and biscuits, freshly made that morning by Annie Bloom, and with a smile, 'Oh, from my favourite cook.' As he opened the box his reaction was typical, 'there are too many for me so I'll share them round the ward with the other chaps.'

Francis told him not to think about coming back to work until he was thoroughly fit and asked if there was anything he needed at present.

Harry shook his head, 'Nothing, thank you, but there is something that worries me in this ward. You see the dark fellow in the last bed on the opposite side, well he has a broken leg and I've found out he was one of the poachers! I feel sorry for him, as he hasn't had any visitors since he came in. Now I have a crutch and can move about a bit, I went over to talk to him yesterday.'

Margot was very interested and wanted to know more, 'What did you learn Harry?'

'Only that he is resigned to his fate and convinced he will be sent to prison as soon as he's fit again. He said he's worried about reprisals as he gave the police the address of the gang in Southampton. The poor chap was severely wounded at the Battle of the Somme in 1916, serving with the South Hampshire Fusiliers and subsequently invalided out. When he returned home he found his wife had left him for someone else and had disappeared. He is a trained carpenter but found it difficult finding work after the war and his only income, a small disability pension, was insufficient to live on.'

Margot persisted as the case intrigued her, 'But how did he get involved with crime?'

'That was quite simple! He did some repair work for Ranolph Mandrake who offered further lucrative opportunities, which involved moving packing cases to a warehouse in Southampton. Unfortunately, he found out later the cases contained smuggled goods and Ranolph Mandrake then blackmailed him to continue.'

Having taken in all Harry had said, Francis added, 'I think I'll speak to the fellow before we leave as we may be able to help him, particularly as he served with my grandfather's regiment.'

After leaving Harry they crossed the ward to the poacher, who told Francis his name was Wally Clarkson. After a discussion, Francis promised he would talk to Superintendent Snapper about any charges and also to Sir Roger concerning the regimental connection, 'I'll do what I can to help you but promise nothing at this stage.'

Wally was overcome with gratitude and thanked Francis, 'You're very kind to me Sir and if you give me a chance I'll not let you down.'

Back at the Manor House Francis wrote a note to his grandfather and also a letter to Superintendent Snapper giving details of Wally Clarkson's situation.

Dawn broke on 29th December heralding a new day of sunshine but a cold easterly wind so that people went about their business wrapped in big overcoats and scarves, rarely stopping for casual conversation.

Francis and Margot left Farndene by the mid-morning train, arriving in London by noon where they met the Reverend Digby Fletcher, now retired and living at Brown's Hotel in Dover Street. They had a leisurely meal and their host was eager to hear all the news from Farndene. Margot and Francis gave a full account of the events involving the poachers.

'Gracious me! What a carry on!' Digby was clearly taken aback at the news. 'What a tragic situation for poor Monty Mandrake having a scoundrel of a grandson. I knew the boy in his teens and there was something about him I disliked, although I couldn't put a finger on it. I'll write to Monty and perhaps go down to see him a little later on.'

Francis was eager to learn how Digby was getting on in London and smiled at the reply he got.

'My boy, the situation couldn't be better as I have so many churches to visit I could go to a different one each Sunday for a year. And as you know I love the theatre and this city is probably the finest in the world for stage productions; I'm a great "First

Nighter". Finally there are countless good restaurants so I need to watch my figure! When you are settled, come up to town and give Margot a treat for a long weekend; you can put up here at Brown's quite easily.'

They sat talking for some time and, after tea, left to go to Kings Cross station to catch the night train to St Andrews. As Margot and Francis said goodbye, Digby promised to visit them in the spring, adding with a smile, 'When birds do sing, "Hey ding-a-ding ding", I'll be there! Now God bless you both and I wish you a safe journey.'

Chapter 10

In spite of the comfort of a first class sleeper, Margot and Francis arrived in St Andrews early on the morning of 30th December, decidedly weary after their journey. All tiredness evaporated, however, as they were met by her father, David, with a car and many were the hugs, kisses and handshakes before leaving the station.

The chauffeur was most attentive and insisted, 'Mr Norton, you get into the car with your daughter and son-in-law and I'll attend to the luggage, sir.'

As soon as they entered the house, Lorna, Margot's mother clung to her daughter with tears of joy running onto her cheeks.

'Margot my dearest, it has been a long two months and we've missed you so much but now, thank God, you're safely here.'

David and Francis stood smiling until Lorna, recovering, invited them into the dining room, 'Now come along all of you and while we breakfast you can tell your father and me all your news.'

In turn, Margot and Francis related the highlights of their honeymoon and the journey back, giving a graphic description of their encounter with little Rupert Tupper at Exeter. Margot painted a vivid picture, 'there was this poor wee bairn, no more than eight years old in threadbare clothes, from a very poor family living on the pittance of a widow's pension. He stole from a coffee stall to eat but fell almost at our feet as he ran away. To sum up, Francis and I are going to help the family if we can.'

Her parents were shocked and Lorna made her views known: 'It's a disgrace our war widows are not receiving the help due to them and it shames our Government!'

Francis went on to tell them the poaching saga and his in-laws were amazed as the story unfolded.

'What a wild lot you have to contend with in the "deep" south!'

David had a twinkle in his eye as he turned to his wife, 'Lorna, we must take care when we visit Margot and Francis or we could be held up by outlaws!'

After breakfast, while Margot went off with her mother, Francis explained his plans for an airfield at Farndene to David. He went on to elaborate the potential, 'my idea is to establish a flying school to train pilots and navigators as well as ground staff to service the planes. Additionally, a flying club will be formed and members encouraged to buy their own machines, although there will be club planes available for those who can't afford their own.'

David was most impressed and reacted to what he'd heard, 'I've got to hand it to you, Francis, the whole concept sounds good and I'm sure it'll be a money spinner; but when do you start?'

'Immediately we get back in the New Year I'll get down to business and hope to have the airfield up and running by next September. The first student has already enrolled to train as a pilot.'

At that moment Margot and her mother came into the room and Lorna's comment was to the point, 'You talk about us women gassing but you men can beat us hollow!'

David smiled, 'Aye, we can talk a lot but our subject calls for intelligence. Francis tells me his new flying school has already enrolled the first student to train as a pilot.'

Lorna congratulated her son-in-law, 'My, you're a good businessman, Francis, but tell me, who is the lucky man?'

Francis smiled at his wife across the table, 'Your very own daughter and she can't get airborne quick enough.'

Both Lorna and David looked astonished at the news, shaking their heads in disbelief. David's only comment was, 'She's a bonnie lass with a first class brain and she'll not disgrace you.'

I'm sure she won't, but I'll tell you something else' – Francis was enjoying 'setting out his stall' – 'all being well, the next time we come north it could be by air! With a suitably adapted plane, Margot and I could share the flying, stopping en route only to refuel. I've worked out a course and it is definitely feasible.'

At this point Margot chipped in, 'The beauty of flying will be the tremendous time saving but, best of all, not having to make the beastly train journey.'

While discussing this exciting prospect Lorna suddenly remembered she hadn't told them her news.

'Oh! I've just remembered Madeline and her new husband Grant Sheldon are coming from Whitby tomorrow and our two darling grandchildren Sam and Marion.'

Margot's face lit up as she hugged her mother, 'Whoopee! What a super prospect for Hogmanay with the whole clan together; it's seems so long since I saw Madeline and the two children.'

With so much to catch up on they sat talking for another hour during which the subject of a visit to Farndene came up and Margot wanted to know when her parents were coming south.

'Why not come down in the spring when the better weather should be here? Easter Sunday is 4th April, so you could travel down before Maundy Thursday and stay as long as you wish.'

Lorna's smile reflected her enthusiasm, 'Margot that would be wonderful,' and, looking at David, 'We have an invitation from Fanny in Bristol, so why don't we go on to see her after our holiday with Margot and Francis?'

'That's good thinking, Lorna, and as a true Scotsman I cannae help thinking two holidays for the price of one train ticket is good book-keeping!'

They continued to enjoy each other's company until Lorna suddenly realised the time had flown.

'Good gracious me! It's nearly eleven and there are countless things to be done for the lunch tomorrow when Madeline and her family come; we'll just have to bustle.'

David decided he wished to discuss business with his son-in-law, 'Francis, perhaps we can go along to the study and look at your airfield project further?'

Francis nodded and they left the room as the ladies chatted endlessly, apparently oblivious to the men's departure.

New Year's Eve dawned with a grey sky and a stillness in the air which resulted in hovering patches of mist and fog lingering along the shoreline and on the slate green sea until late morning.

After breakfast David and Francis spent the morning going over the plans for the Farndene airfield and it was clear David was completely attracted to the scheme.

'Francis, what you have shown so far convinces me the operation is sound and well conceived, so if you need some extra capital, I'm willing to come in with you. I don't wish to be involved in the equity but perhaps on an interest bearing Loan Stock. Naturally you and Margot must keep the Equity Capital of the company; think over my suggestion and let me know in due course.'

Francis was flattered by his father-in-law's remarks: 'Your offer is generous and I'm heartened you have confidence in my scheme. At this stage we're talking in broad terms but I foresee we may need substantial funding as the business expands. I have made a diary note of your kind offer for future reference.'

The following day lunch was delayed until Madeline, Grant, Sam and Marion arrived from Whitby and it was half past one before the excitement of the families meeting settled and the meal got under way. With so much to talk about, a constant buzz of conversation ensued, frequently punctuated by bursts of merriment, making the occasion a happy and delightful experience.

Over an hour later they adjourned to the drawing room when, for the first time Margot and Francis were able to talk to the children. Sam, who had overheard conversation about the airfield, wanted to know more.

'Uncle Francis, please tell us what sort of aerodrome you're going to build?'

With the children's eager faces watching, Francis was delighted to talk about his pet subject.

'Well, Sam, first of all it will not be an aerodrome but an airfield, which is really a flat clear area of grassland over which planes take off and land. There have to be support buildings including hangars for the maintenance of the aircraft and these will be on the edge of the field. There will also be a watchtower having an overall view so that planes taking off and landing can be checked for safety reasons.'

Sam and his sister listened wide eyed and they wanted to know if their uncle would take them up in a plane when they came to Farndene.

'Of course I will and I promise I'll take both of you for a flight over Southampton.'

Marion said a heartfelt thank you, 'It's ever so kind of you uncle. I'd love to go up to see everything from above like a bird. We'll ask Mummy when we can come and stay with you and Auntie Margot.'

Margot, listening, suggested perhaps the autumn half term holiday as the airfield would probably be working by then, 'I'll talk to Mummy and see what we can arrange.'

Mild and sunny weather ushered in 1920, the start of a new decade with the population of Britain slowly recovering from the tragedy of the Great War. Unemployment was high, especially in the industrial areas of Scotland, and Francis had long talks with David, telling his father-in-law of his concern about the unrest at the Dewar factory and foundry being 'fanned' by the Trade Union.

As the weather held, the whole family, including the dog Jock, went down to their holiday cottage, 'Morton's Reach' at Kingsbarns, enjoying a beautiful day there walking along the coast and on the beach at Cambo Sands. It was a nostalgic time for Margot and Francis and as they lingered on the seashore she held his hand tightly, whispering, 'Dearest, this will always be my very special, heavenly place where we made love on the first night of our honeymoon,' and with a smile, ' I think we did quite well for beginners, don't you?'

Francis was on the point of making a cheeky reply but was prevented as the two children came running up to them.

All too soon the holiday drew to a close and some tearful goodbyes saw Madeline, Grant, Sam and Marion leave for Whitby. Late the following evening Margot and Francis were driven to St Andrews station to catch the night sleeper for London. After many handshakes and kisses, David and Lorna waved them off as the long express drew slowly out into the night.

On board as the train rattled along Francis gave Margot a goodnight kiss with the comment, 'That's all you get tonight as it's totally unsafe to make love in this contraption!'

Margot smiled, 'Fair enough, darling, and if we fly next time it will be just as difficult, so let's wait till we get home and make up for lost time!'

Chapter 11

With their stay in St Andrews a happy memory, Margot and Francis were back in Farndene by 5th January and were greeted by, among other things, a pile of correspondence including a letter from Fanny. Opening the envelope Francis took out two sheets of closely written script and started to read,

43, Lower Castle Street,
Castle Park,
Bristol
1st January 1920

My dear Margot and Francis,

My first letter of the New Year is to send you my love and fondest wishes for the coming year in the hope it will be a healthy and successful one for you both. I expect by the time you read this you'll be back in Farndene and I trust the visit to Margot's parents was a great success.

We had a quiet New Year's Eve celebration and, naturally, missed you, Francis, to do the first footing for us. Aunt Lotte wasn't well after Boxing Day and took to her bed on the following day. As no improvement was evident by Tuesday 30th December, I called the doctor and he diagnosed a chest infection. He gave a prescription and told Lotte she should stay in bed, promising to call again in a few days. Unfortunately your aunt decided to get up so she could see the New Year in! I did my best to dissuade her but you know Lotte is strong minded and insisted on taking part in the celebrations. She's now back in bed and the doctor ticked her off when he called today.

The other news concerns Janine Tupper who is travelling to Farndene with her three children on Wednesday 7th January. She will stay for two days in order to meet Alec Briggs and his wife, the couple who are willing to foster Rupert Tupper. If it helps, I will

come over to Farndene with Edith Oulton, to meet Mrs Tupper and act as an intermediary, as she may be more relaxed with someone she has already met. I hope you see my point but it will be lovely to see you both in any case. Give me a call on the telephone when you've thought it over. Will you book accommodation for them at the Albion Inn in the village as you suggested?

I've seen a lot of Alex and Angelina and know they hope to get married sometime in February, so keep it in mind when you are making arrangements for that month. They are settling in well and the children are very happy to be in England. No doubt Alex will be in touch with you shortly to suggest a final date.

Hilary Marchant has visited me several times and was pleased to join us for the New Year's Eve celebrations. I enjoy his company and find him a pleasant and considerate person in many ways.

That's all the news for now so I'll close.

My fondest love to you both,
  Mother

Francis sat for some minutes, taking in what his mother had said; the last piece of news about Hilary Marchant worried him considerably.

He passed the letter to Margot to read with the rider, 'Tell me what you think of mother's news particularly the last paragraph.'

Having read it, Margot put down the letter and looked keenly at her husband before saying, 'Darling, I know you're worried that Hilary Marchant may not be all we desire but let's be honest, it's your mother's affair and from what I know about her, she's quite capable of forming her own judgement of someone paying court to her. All the same, perhaps some discreet enquiries wouldn't come amiss as you suggested before Christmas.'

'That's exactly what I intend to do and will contact our solicitor tomorrow to get the wheels turning. However, we have urgent things to put in hand to make arrangements for the Tupper family who arrive in two days' time. Incidentally, I think mother's offer to come over with Edith Oulton a good one; what do you think, dearest?'

'Yes, I agree she will be very helpful in settling the family in and guiding Janine Tupper over the fostering of Rupert. Your mother's vast experience in dealing with people will be beneficial for all parties in this case. Now I really must get on as I have a number of letters to answer and I must write to St Andrews to thank my parents for the wonderful time they gave us. I'll also drop a line to Madeline to suggest she, Grant and the children come down to stay in the early summer.'

Margot gathered up a pile of correspondence and walked round the desk to give Francis a big kiss as she left the room.

'Hey, what was that for sweetheart?'

'That was just for being a good boy and a very good husband.' Margot giggled as she paused at the door, 'and to try to stop you worrying about your more than capable mother!'

Before Francis had time to reply she was away and he could only marvel at his good fortune in having such a wonderful wife. He picked up the telephone and asked for the Bristol number to speak to his mother.

The next two days passed quickly and Fanny and Edith Oulton arrived late Wednesday morning driven over from Bristol by Edith's husband Robert, as Fred Gutteridge, the chauffeur, was ill with a feverish cold. After luncheon, promptly at two thirty, they gathered on the platform of Farndene station to await the arrival of the Tupper family.

As the train steamed along the platform, they searched eagerly for a sight of Janine Tupper and her children. In the commotion of people getting on and off the train, with doors banging and porters shouting instructions, Fanny suddenly spotted a petite figure alighting and, pushing her way through the throng, put her arms round Janine in greeting, 'Welcome to Farndene my dear.'

The next few minutes were spent in introductions, after which the Tupper family were installed in the Albion Inn. Later that afternoon Janine and the children met Alec and Beatty Briggs in a private room at the inn. With Fanny and Edith present, the meeting was successful and later on they all went to the Briggs cottage to be introduced to Alec's children.

In the evening, after the children had gone to bed, Fanny and Edith had dinner with Janine at the Albion Inn during which the fostering of Rupert was discussed. Janine said she was more than happy with Alec and Beatty Briggs.

'I was impressed with the relationship and loving nature towards their children. I'm happy to leave my Rupert in their care for a trial period as you suggest, but I would like him to come home to Exeter on school holidays.'

Fanny was not surprised at Janine's decision and assured her concerning the holidays, 'It's very important he should be with his family regularly and we'll see that takes place, have no doubt. Now the only other urgent matter is the school. The children go back next Monday 12th January and Rupert needs to be there at the start of the term.'

Janine responded quickly, 'I'd thought of that, so I packed some extra clothes on the offchance. But I'd like to meet the headmistress while I'm here if that's possible.'

'I'm sure that can be arranged so I'll call on Miss Gertrude Turner, who lives in the village, and make arrangements for tomorrow.' Fanny smiled as she went on, 'Miss Turner is a wonderful teacher but a strict disciplinarian and the children just respect her for that. She has a young assistant teacher, Miss Bunty Fenwick, who joined the school last autumn and she is very popular with everyone. Her parents lived in Newcastle but she decided to come south after qualifying, to be near her older brother, Brian, a practicing solicitor in Southampton and well known to the Vining family.'

They sat talking for some time until Edith noticed Janine's eyes were drooping and promptly suggested they call it a day: 'You've had a long day and I'm sure you must be very tired so we'll say goodnight.'

With tears in her eyes, Janine thanked them again for their kindness, 'You have no idea how much your support has helped me, and I'm deeply grateful for all you are doing for my family and for me.'

As they closed the door of the Albion Inn to drive back to the Manor House both Edith and Fanny felt a profound sense of satisfaction and fulfilment which warmed them on a cold night.

True to her word, Fanny contacted the headmistress of the local school and as a result she, in the company of Edith with Janine and Rupert, made their way up the garden path of the school house for a meeting at two o'clock the following afternoon.

The house, an attractive late Victorian building was constructed from locally made red bricks on the ground floor and the hung tiles on the first floor took the eye to the roof. Here tall chimneys with bright red pots, sitting like sentinels, overlooked the whole scene. Windows with leaded lights in teak frames completed the very pleasing picture.

They were welcomed by a smiling Miss Gertrude Turner, a tall, well-proportioned lady in her mid-fifties. Wearing a high-necked dress with a small cameo brooch at her throat and her slightly greying hair neatly drawn back and secured with a large comb, she was indeed an imposing figure, well known and respected for her discipline, but loved by many for her excellent teaching.

After the usual introductions, they sat in the front parlour, in the window of which reposed a large aspidistra plant, set on a low mahogany table.

Miss Turner told Rupert to stand by her chair and asked him a number of questions, including, 'What do you most like doing at school Rupert?'

He stood thinking for a moment or so and then out it came, 'I like doing sums and drawing and music, miss.' Followed by a long pause.

'I see,' Miss Turner produced a sheet of paper and a pencil. 'Now, Rupert, can you write something for me about your brother and sister?'

He took the pencil but wrote nothing for some minutes and turning to the headmistress, 'I don't know what to say, miss. But I can draw you a horse if you like.'

'Thank you, Rupert, I'd like that and will you also put the

names of any horses you have known under the drawing?'

They all watched as the boy drew a fine picture of the horse adding names as he had been asked.

Miss Turner looked at the result and was obviously impressed. 'Thank you for a nice picture and I see you have put eleven names on the sheet, three of which are in French. How did you know these?'

At this point Janine intervened to explain, 'I have to tell you I'm a Breton woman, and my late husband dealt in horses all his life, running a stud near Exeter with his family. He told Rupert a great deal about horses and taught him to ride from the age of four. As far as language is concerned, all my children are bilingual and can write in both English and French.'

After further discussion, Miss Turner told Janine she would like to have Rupert in her school. 'Can you see he comes along next Monday when we start the Easter term? He will also meet my assistant teacher, Miss Fenwick, who joined the school last autumn.'

Janine assured her Rupert would be there and would come in the company of the Briggs family.

Chapter 12

January 1920 saw a great deal happening in Farndene and especially at the Manor House where Francis and Margot had happily settled in. Margot set about redecoration of all the rooms, to be phased over the coming months, the priority being the kitchen area.

She was appalled at the antiquated layout and equipment and explained to Francis what she intended, 'I think we should strip out everything and start from scratch, calling in a good builder who can work to our specifications.

'We need to install electricity, do away with the old and dirty coal fired ranges. I have checked and there are some new electric cisterns producing hot water and boilers for cooking. The stone floor needs looking at, to be replaced with something more modern and hygienic. With new cupboards, fresh marble working surfaces can be brought in. It'll take a couple of months, so I suggest we set up a temporary kitchen in the large breakfast room at the back of the house.'

Francis looked quite bewildered but responded, 'Darling, what you have said is perfectly true and the kitchen is well overdue for replacement. My only thought is, have you discussed the plan with our cook, Annie?'

'Of course I have, sweetheart. She and the other kitchen staff are thrilled with the prospect and Annie's only reservation was "I'll need some help learning all about this electric thing", so we have their one hundred per cent support.'

'Good! Let's get started by finding a good builder and getting a quotation for the overall cost. Margot, I have to say I think your approach to the running of our house absolutely first class.' And with that he took her in his arms to give her a long embrace.

With a cheeky smile Margot responded, 'Please make a note I'll expect a similar kiss as each room is redecorated throughout the house and I won't want any excuses!'

The morning of 12th January was cold but, thankfully, dry as the children reassembled for the start of the school term. The scene in front of the red brick building was one of constant activity and noise as the boys and girls gathered in the playground. Some mothers had seen the younger ones to the gate in the surrounding iron railings and stood chatting among themselves.

Promptly, at five minutes to nine, Miss Turner emerged from the double entrance doors with Miss Fenwick at her side. The assistant teacher rang a large brass bell vigorously and the children collected in their class groups forming little queues.

Miss Fenwick then gave instructions, 'No talking, children,' and to the youngest pupils, 'Now lead on to the hall,' and to the older children, 'Follow on in class order.'

All went well under the eagle eye of the headmistress, who greeted the whole school in the main hall, 'Good morning children and welcome back to our school. I hope you all had an enjoyable Christmas holiday.' The children responded with a lusty, 'Yes, thank you, Miss Turner'.

Prayers and a hymn followed, after which the older children dispersed to a nearby classroom while the little ones stayed in the hall to be taught by Miss Fenwick.

Rupert, guided by Jenny Briggs, stood in the classroom with the older ones until Miss Turner told them to sit. She introduced Rupert and another new boy and the lessons started.

At break time the playground was a mass of children engaged in very many forms of play and activity. Rupert kept himself much to himself, just talking to one or two children until a large ginger-haired boy, accompanied by two or three of his friends, came up to him.

'I'm Bartle Fellows and if you want to get on in the playground you'll have to do what I tell you,' and with that he gave Rupert a violent push against the school wall, much to the amusement of the other boys with him. 'See what I mean!' Bartle was very pleased with himself, 'Well what do you say?'

Rupert took stock of the situation and realising he was smaller than Bartle, chose his words carefully, 'I hear what you say, Bartle, but why are you threatening me? I've done you no harm.'

Bartle was affronted and immediately grabbed Rupert, ruffling his hair and punching him in the chest, 'Don't cheek me Rupert or I'll give what for.'

At that moment Jenny, who was skipping with some girls near-by, saw what was happening and came straight across to Bartle, 'Lay off him you big bully and pick on someone your own size.'

Bartle sneeringly replied, 'Mind your own business Jenny, you're only a girl.'

Jenny, a well-built girl for her age stepped up to Bartle and slapped his face hard and, as he put his hands up to defend his head, she hit him twice in the solar plexus with her elbow, completely winding him. Her parting shot was, 'Don't meddle with me again Bartle and leave Rupert alone.'

Fortunately for all concerned, the bell for the end of break sounded at that moment.

From that day on Rupert and Jenny became firm friends and Bartle gave both a wide berth in the playground.

And from the day he joined Alec and Beatty, Rupert settled and became part of the family. Beatty, a very loving mother watched the boy and comforted him at the times he was homesick. She also made sure he wrote a short letter to his mother each week telling her all his news.

Early in January seven poachers were brought before the Magistrates Court in Southampton. Wally Clarkson was bound over following evidence from Superintendent Snapper who told the court Clarkson's help had enabled the police to apprehend all the poachers from addresses in Southampton. Of the remaining seven, two proved to be deserters and were handed over to the Army Authorities to face Court Martial. The remaining three were remanded in custody to appear at the Southampton Assize Court at the beginning of February.

Francis and Margot, who had attended the hearing, spoke to Superintendent Jack Snapper as they left; Margot's question brought a prompt reply.

'I reckon the three on remand are the better off as each will probably only get two or three years inside.'

Margot pressed again, 'And what about the other two deserters?'

Jack Snapper shrugged his shoulders, 'Oh, they'll probably be shot but in my opinion they will both deserve what they get.'

As they stood talking, Francis noticed Wally Clarkson was waiting to speak to him. The poor man was quite overcome by the court finding and thanked Francis profusely, 'Mr Vining, how can I repay your kindness? But for your help I would be with the others waiting trial next month.'

Francis responded, 'I'm pleased justice has been done and you are free. As soon as your leg has healed come and see me at the Manor House in Farndene and I'll try to find permanent work for you.' After receiving further thanks he watched as Clarkson limped away from the court on his crutches.

When Fanny, with Robert and Edith Oulton, had visited Farndene early in the month, Francis took the opportunity to discuss his airfield project with Robert, who examined the proposed site and took measurements. By the third week of January Robert sent draft plans and rough estimates of cost for Francis's consideration and said he would come over to Farndene to discuss them and add more detail. Francis was delighted and a further meeting was arranged near the end of the month.

The only problem was the weather, which turned very cold with frequent snow showers and hard frosts at night; their 'get together' had to be postponed until the first week in February.

Robert arrived on 3rd February and he and Francis spent two days refining the original plans, with the result they were able to assess the cost more accurately. It was decided to employ a secretary and a draughtsman to produce sets of the final plans and make a separate office in a ground floor room at the Manor House for the whole operation.

On the second day of Robert's visit, he and Francis were alone in the study when Fanny's name was mentioned in conversation.

Francis decided to broach the subject of her association with Hilary Marchant and was startled at the reply he got.

'I have to tell you both Edith and I are extremely worried about your mother's attraction to this fellow.' Robert paused as though searching for words to continue. 'Please don't think we're considering interfering in your mother's life but there's something I think you should know about. One evening last month, Edith and I were guests with others at Fanny's place and after dinner a lady visitor kindly played the piano in the drawing room. At the end of the recital Fanny and Marchant left the room together and, as I had consumed several drinks during the evening, I decided to visit the toilet. As I passed the study, the door of which was ajar, I distinctly heard Marchant say, "I only need three thousand until the end of the month when I'll repay everything."

'I felt embarrassed at what I had overheard and quickly went on my way.'

Francis sat, for moments unable to believe what he had just heard. When he regained his senses he said, 'Robert, I'm most grateful for what you have told me and, to be perfectly truthful, I've had suspicions about Hilary Marchant from the first time I met him. I consider he is an unscrupulous scoundrel and Margot and I need to do something about it. I know you will respect my confidence when I tell you I have already instructed my solicitor to make discreet enquiries and we await news any day now.'

Before leaving the Manor House, Robert promised to keep the whole matter in mind and let Francis know of any new developments, 'I think the world of your mother and feel very sad she is being taken in by this fellow. Rest assured, I'll do everything possible to help.'

At the middle of February it was necessary for Francis to have a meeting with his mother to discuss a report on the Business Group left to them by the late Angus Dewar. He stayed with his mother for two days and made good progress with the business arrangements.

At dinner the second evening Hilary Marchant's name cropped

up and Fanny was very quiet and. obviously embarrassed. Francis took the opportunity to enquire, 'Are you all right, mother? Is something worrying you?'

Fanny turned to him with tears in her eyes and slowly told him all, 'Francis, darling, I don't know what you will think of me when I tell you about that man.

'I feel he's played on my good nature and affection and now seems to have disappeared. Since just before New Year's Eve I have lent him several sums of money and on each occasion he has told a very plausible story why he needed more cash. On the last occasion – about the second week in January – he wanted more and, reluctantly, I gave him a further two thousand pounds and he promised to repay all I had lent him at the end of that month. Form that day to this I haven't seen or heard from him and a letter I sent to his cousin's address in Bath has been returned with the answer "not known at this address". I'm at my wits' end to know what to now.'

Francis then asked what the total loans came to and was astonished by his mother's reply: 'Francis what I did was in good faith and I genuinely felt he reciprocated my feelings. I can now see that was not the case. Darling you will think me mad when I tell you he has had fifteen thousand pounds.' With that she broke down weeping.

Francis drew a chair up and put his arms round his mother to comfort her with reassuring words, 'Mother, please don't reproach yourself as you have been taken in by a man who is a clever, scheming scoundrel. It grieves and angers me that you have been hurt in such a way and I'll do everything I can to bring Hilary Marchant to book. Margot and I have been suspicious for a while as the man danced his attention on you.'

Fanny confessed she had been attracted to Hilary and he seemed to understand she was lonely, following Francis getting married and leaving home, 'He was always very attentive and courteous and told me a convincing tale about his financial transactions which were slightly delayed in coming to fruition. That was the basis of his need for temporary help and, on the last occasion I lent him money, he told me emphatically all would be repaid by the end of January. It now seems his promise is like "Bunter's Postal Order", it's always in the post!'

As his mother was telling him the sordid details, Francis suddenly had a brainwave, 'Mother, were all the sums lent given by way of cheques?

'Why, yes. But what difference does that make?' Fanny looked puzzled.

'It makes all the difference in the world; we can trace where he keeps his account. Now I want you to go to your bank tomorrow and ask for the paid cheques you issued to him. From those we can start to trace where he banks.'

Fanny smiled hopefully and promised to do as she had been asked.

They talked for some time before saying goodnight and as Fanny kissed her son, she put her arms round him with the comment, 'Thank God you understand Francis! I feel so much better now I've told you everything. After all what is money? I still have Margot and you with the rest of my family, which is worth all the gold in the world.'

After his mother had gone to bed, Francis went to the study and had a long telephone conversation with Margot, telling her everything about Hilary Marchant.

No sooner had breakfast been finished on the following morning than Fanny and Francis welcomed cousin Alex and Angelina who dropped in for a chat. Alex was very interested in the plans for an airfield at Farndene and asked Francis to 'keep him in the picture'. After chatting about the family, Alex came to the point, 'What I really came to see you about is our wedding. We hope to tie the knot at the beginning of March. Will you be my best man, please?'

Francis shook his cousin's hand firmly and told Alex he would be delighted. 'As so much time had elapsed since Angelina arrived from Germany, I thought you'd never ask me! As soon as you fix a final date let me know and I'll be there, have no doubt.'

Chapter 13

February was well under way as building work in the Manor House progressed, undertaken by Richard Hull, a local man, who expanded his workforce to cope with the contract. Among the additional men employed was the former poacher Wally Clarkson, a skilled carpenter, who proved to be a very versatile tradesman often assisting the plumber as well as painting if needed. Mr Hull found him digs in the village with a widow and it did her a good turn as she was finding difficulty living on her meagre Army pension.

Margot supervised on a daily basis and would not pass work if she considered it below standard, always putting the question to Mr Hull in a nice way, 'Now we can't expect everything to be perfect but I know you will be unhappy if the finished job is mediocre, as it will bear your name!'

He took the hint on each occasion and saw that the offending workmanship was put right.

At breakfast on 16th February, Francis told Margot he hoped to begin constructing the airfield just as soon as the contract was signed at the end of the month.

'I'm using a Southampton firm, vetted by Robert Oulton and given a clean bill of health. He was impressed with them and the managing director, Roy Hersey, is a retired sapper so we expect the work to proceed rapidly as spring approaches. I understand Hersey has several ex-army barrack huts which will be erected on the site here to accommodate the workers, consisting mainly of Irish navvies who will do all the labouring work. So you see darling I've not been idle while I know you've had so much to do with the house. Is everything going smoothly?'

Margot smiled and reassured her husband on that point but then told him there would be extra expense on top of the original costing.'

'Extra, darling? I thought we had gone over the figures very carefully.'

Margot looked down at the table and then broke the news, 'Dearest, we need to spend quite a lot on one of the bedrooms to make it into a nursery.'

It took a moment for the import of Margot's comment to sink in. Suddenly Francis realised what she had said, 'My darling, is it true? Are you expecting?'

He straightaway got up and, pulling a chair beside Margot, put his arms round her to hold her tightly.

'Yes it's true. I'm pregnant as I've missed for the past two months and I saw our doctor yesterday and he has confirmed by the sample I left with him.'

She turned to face him and after they were locked in a long embrace he just gazed at her with loving eyes, 'Sweetheart, that's the most wonderful news you could possibly have given me. So when will the baby be born?

'All being well our son or daughter will arrive sometime around the end of September. Darling, isn't it wonderful? We now know at last our family has started!'

In this happy state they sat talking over all the things to be done to prepare for the happy event in the autumn. 'We must tell your mother and my parents darling,' Margot was thinking of others, 'and Madeline and Grandpa; can you think of anyone else?'

Francis was literally scratching his head as he shook it, 'No, dearest, those are the most important people; others will find out by various means. Of course mother will tell Aunt Lotte and her family.'

Following the announcement that Margot was expecting, it was decided to speed up the work on the house. At a meeting with Richard Hull, he promised to increase his workforce with extra painters and Francis and Margot agreed to meet the additional wage cost. However, the main stumbling block was the kitchen where most of the construction had been completed but the new electrical equipment, some of which was American, had not arrived. Mr Hull explained the problem stemmed from the fact so many people were changing to electricity that the equipment manufacturers couldn't cope with the demand. Francis appreciated the point Richard Hull had made but suddenly realised his own business, the Dewar Group, were supplying many of the electrical engineering companies with steel frames.

'Leave the matter with me, Mr Hull, and I'll see what I can do to speed up deliveries.'

And so within a couple of weeks, with a little coaxing from Francis, most of the new electrical equipment was in place and the kitchen nearing completion.

By the end of February the refurbishment of the house was completed but Margot and Francis decided to postpone a house warming party until 5th April, Easter Monday, when her parents and Fanny would be staying for a short holiday. If all went well, Fanny would to take Margot's parents back to Bristol with her to meet the family there.

On 1st April Roy Hersey came to the Manor House where Francis and Margot had gathered with Robert Oulton and Joshua Hicks the solicitor, for the signing of the contract for the airfield construction. The contract was completed by late morning followed by luncheon and providing ample time for some detailed discussion about the airfield.

Hersey emphasised the absolute need for drainage, 'I've looked at the site and extensive land drainage must be installed and, as a brook flows through part of the field, it will be necessary to divert this watercourse at an early stage. The other important work will be the felling and removal of several large trees for which I have some splendid equipment.'

Robert raised a number of points and the discussion covered these and many more.

'Tell us about the style of permanent buildings you intend to put up?' Margot wanted to know there would be no eyesores, and Francis reassured her.

'All the main buildings are to have brick façades and will harmonise with their surroundings. Away from these, the workshops and stores will be Nissen huts but painted green and suitably screened by fresh tree planting. The only other large building is the hangar which should big enough to hold ten planes comfortably.'

The guests departed leaving Robert with Margot and Francis to enjoy the rest of the day, during which she happily gave them a conducted tour of the newly decorated house. As they reached the kitchen Robert let out a long whistle as he gazed at the transformation, 'Great Scott! What a superb result you have achieved Margot. I can tell you Edith will be green with envy when she sees this wonderful place.'

Margot felt quite thrilled at the compliment and her face coloured as she thanked him.

Quite thoughtfully, Margot had invited Grandpa to join them for dinner and he and Robert enjoyed reliving some of the times they had spent together during the Great War.

Grandpa continued his military theme by taking a very profound view about the present peacetime.

'We're all liable to be lulled into a false peaceful state of mind; from the experience of history such a situation never lasts long before aggression rears its ugly head. The importance for the safety of our country lies in our ability to be strong and on our guard so that we're able to stand up for ourselves. And one final point if, and God forbid, another war occurs we must be ready and have an adequate air force; the air is where the battles will be fought!'

The three men continued to discuss the theory propounded by Grandpa but as they did so, Margot allowed her mind to wander. She thought of all the future hopes she and Francis had for their children to be and recalled the happiness she and her husband had discovered at Farndene, especially the times they had joined Grandpa, walking the estate with him and his two cocker spaniels, Lulu and Pickles. These and many others were simple things that, in total, represented a vital quality of life in peacetime that had been denied during the last war.

Quite suddenly, Grandpa noticed her distraction and, putting his hand on her arm, asked if all was well, 'Margot, have I upset you? I know my comments were much to the point but that is how I see the picture. Please be assured I'm not attempting to forecast what will happen.'

'Grandpa, it was kind of you to ask, but I'm really all right. I was just dreaming about the wonderful quality of our life here in what is now peacetime and realising how much we had to forego during the Great War. You're perfectly correct in your assertion we must be strong and on our guard to protect our liberty, but the danger may rest with those who don't see the situation the way we do and want to disarm.'

Grandpa was enjoying one of his favourite topics as he replied, 'That's true and while such people are sincere in their beliefs they are often naïve, believing the rest of the world will ultimately see the sense of ridding the universe of all weapons of destruction. Now this reminds me of a story on this very subject that took place long ago in darkest Africa.

'A warlike tribe had for generations made knives and spears with which they frequently fought and killed other neighbouring tribes. One day the Head Man, who was a great disarmer, persuaded them to get rid of their weapons and they all agreed.

'A large fire was made and all the knives and spearheads melted down in it. The result was a ball of metal, the size of a very large football, which the head man told them to get rid of. So a large catapult was constructed and loaded with the metal ball. With a great ceremony the retraining strings were cut and the ball hurled into the distance.

'It travelled a considerable way, landing in the midst of a neighbouring warlike tribe and killing their witch doctor. Their head man examined the metal ball and, perceiving it was made of many knives and spearheads, took it to be an act of war. The result was his tribe attacked the ball-making tribe who had nothing to defend themselves with and were consequently all slain. So you see Margot we should always "Be Prepared" as Lord Baden Powell recommended and be able to meet any eventuality.'

She was smiling, having enjoyed Grandpa's yarn. 'Of course such a situation could only have happened in darkest Africa. But as all the "Do Gooders'" tribe was killed who told the rest of the world all about it?'

There was general laughter for some minutes until Francis suggested they all adjourn to the drawing room for coffee. Once seated, Grandpa added his praise for the redecorations, 'You've done a splendid job, Margot, and the result is certainly professional. Perhaps you will come over to my place and give me a few tips as the house needs a face lift?'

Margot promised that the very next time they went for a walk she would look in and make some recommendations.

Progress on the preliminary work for the airfield was slow, as the February weather produced a mixture of rain, sleet and snow, but during the last week it was dry enough to make up for lost time and construction went ahead. A new road was soon put in place linking the whole site to the main street about half a mile away and vast quantities of building materials began to be brought in by lorry. Francis visited the site daily, if he could, and on one occasion met his herdsman who was worried about the effect of aeroplanes on his cows. He assured him the cows would soon get used to the sound of aero engines.

Thankfully March came in like a lamb, enabling the foundation work for the buildings to proceed apace. The drainage schemes amounted to dozens of cross trenches into which clay pipes were laid to take water away from the airfield. The course of a brook that intersected the main field had to be changed by constructing a parallel tunnel into which the water was diverted. The original brook was then filled and levelled with the rest of the field.

Two large pits to hold massive tanks for oil and petrol were to be dug but as work commenced on the second one, the workmen came across a large number of human bones. Work stopped while an archaeologist examined them. He concluded they related to a mass grave during the civil war, the period being identified by some artefacts and pistol remains found with the bodies. All were removed and a week later the Southampton Coroner completed an inquest on them. A number of the Irish labourers refused to work in the pit, saying they were not gravediggers; in truth some were superstitious but would not admit it!

In the village school the children had settled into a rhythm and Rupert enjoyed his lessons, making good progress in all things except his reading. Although Miss Turner appeared awesome to most of the pupils, Rupert felt confident enough to push his luck at times by being cheeky, once paying the penalty by getting the cane. However, the headmistress secretly admired his pluck and liked the wholehearted way he joined in the class activity.

Talking to Miss Fenwick after school one day she commented on a few of the brighter boys and girls, 'I've made a list of several children I consider are scholarship material and they must be given extra help. We must take this group separately twice a week to coach them; I'll take the group on Tuesdays and I'd like you to teach them each Thursday. I've included Rupert Tupper in the group as he's a bright boy but needs to work up his reading. See what you can do for him Miss Fenwick.'

At home Rupert thrived with the Briggs family and as the lighter evenings came along he was often out on the estate with Alec and Jenny, learning all about the countryside and the wild flowers and animals. Punctually each Thursday after tea, Beatty supervised Rupert's letter home to his mother telling her all his news and he always added a little sentence in French. 'Why do you do that Rupert?' She asked one evening.

'It's because if the postman opened it he wouldn't understand what I've said.'

Beatty was no French scholar so she asked him to translate.

'It says I love my mother, Mollie and Tom and miss them. I tell her you are like a mother to me so I'm very happy here.' He looked up at her with a cheeky grin, 'well you are aren't you?'

Beatty gave him a motherly hug and watched him seal the envelope, printing 'SWALK' on the back.

'What's all that about Rupert?' to which he replied with the same grin, 'Sealed with a loving kiss!'

Chapter 14

Beware the Ides of March! The village people didn't need reminding about the ancient Romans as the children at the local school were affected by the first cases of rubella – German measles – on the 15th of the month. Within the week almost fifty per cent of the pupils were suffering. The Briggs family were included in the casualties as Jenny and Rupert brought it home, giving it in turn to Raymond the youngest. Beatty said she hoped Connie would get it as well, 'It's better for a girl to have German measles as a child, because contracting it later in life when having a family can be dangerous for the unborn baby.' As she spoke to Alec, he became very quiet and was obviously concerned.

'Is something the matter, love?' Beatty realised her husband was worried and wanted to get to the root of the matter, 'It's about an unborn baby, isn't it?

'You're right, Beatty, dear, so I'd better explain. I know Mrs Vining is expecting, and the reason I know is because Bertie, their butler, told me in confidence. I don't know if he should have done so and that's the trouble. With all this German measles in our family it is possible I may be a carrier and possibly pass it to Mrs Vining. So, do you think I should tell them?

Beatty nodded her head, 'Most certainly you should and the sooner the better.'

Alec arrived at the Manor House later that afternoon and went straight to see Francis. He explained the situation about his family having German measles and said he believed Mrs Vining was expecting, 'Bertie Bertram told me in confidence but I'm worried I might be a carrier and pass it on to your wife.'

'It's very thoughtful of you, Alec, and as you say it is important we know the situation in your family. I very much appreciate you letting me know. Tell me, how are your youngsters progressing? I hope they will soon be well and about again.'

'Thank you, sir, they're all a bit spotty still but over the high temperatures. They must be on the mend as appetites have returned and my wife says she's sure the children are eating more than ever, which I suppose is a good sign.'

Francis remembered Alec and his wife were looking after Rupert and thoughtfully took a pound from his notecase, 'Take this, Alec, and get some fruit, particularly oranges, for the children.'

Alec took the money and thanked Francis as he left.

After the meeting, Francis went straight to Margot and asked one simple question, 'Darling, have you ever had German measles?'

Margot looked up from her book a little startled, 'Well, yes, as far as I can remember. I think I had it twice; once on my own, and the second time when Madeline caught it. But why do you want to know?'

Francis sat next to her and explained all that had taken place minutes earlier and the concern Alec had. 'Apparently Bertie had told him you are expecting but it puzzles me how Bertie got to know about it.'

Margot smiled as she kissed his cheek, 'I have to admit I may have said something during a meal time and, knowing Bertie, can well appreciate nothing gets past his ears. But, all's well that ends well, as I should be immune having had Rubella twice. All the same I'll keep away from the children in the village as far as possible until the infection passes.'

They sat talking and inevitably the airfield came into the conversation. 'Francis, darling, you really are quite thrilled with the whole project, aren't you?'

'Of course I am and, forgive my complete enthusiasm, but I see enormous possibilities in the future years. Who knows what lies ahead? The objective I have in mind is an expanding flying school and one day travel by air for the ordinary people of this world.'

Margot put her book down and, linking her arm through his, cuddled close to her husband, 'That's what I adore in you, darling, you're a complete visionary and see the goal ahead through the clutter of present day business. I'm sure what you say will one day be a reality and for my part the sooner the better! I can't wait to start flying lessons, so if you can speed up the completion of the airfield it'll suit me fine.'

Francis's smiling face began to change as he looked at Margot, 'Dearest, do you think it wise to begin flying now that you're pregnant?'

She looked astonished at his remark and responded in a forthright way, 'My dearest boy, I intend to lead as near normal a life during the coming months as I can and that includes flying lessons. Later on, when the burden of our little one increases I may have to take things easy but until then I don't see why I should coddle myself!'

Putting his arm round Margot's shoulder Francis hugged and kissed her. 'You've always been an independent person, thank God. Your mother told me you were strong-minded from an early age, insisting always with the phrase, "I'll do it my own self" and apparently you invariably did it your own self! You're very precious to me so please understand I just want you to be careful for all our sakes. Another thing, I've never been an expectant father before and find it rather thrilling.'

Further discussion went on as Francis explained the various phases of the airfield construction with completion hopefully by the end of August. 'We must have a grand opening occasion to which we can invite the family and as many friends as we can. I may be able to contact some of the Royal Flying Corps and Royal Air Force pilots so we can have a flying display.'

At that moment Bertie entered and asked if they would like tea served and Margot laughingly replied, 'Yes please, just as soon as my husband comes down from the clouds!'

When everything seemed to be going well, an objection came from an unexpected quarter. During the last week in March, Francis received a letter from Messrs Fenwick and Bushel, Solicitors of Broad Lane, Southampton, acting for Sir Lancelot

Stratham-Boyne, who owned a large estate to the west of the Manor House.

Francis read and re-read the communication with increased dismay.

> *Messrs Fenwick & Bushel,*
> *Solicitors & Commissioners for Oaths,*
> *5, Broad Lane,*
> *Southampton*
> *22nd March 1920*

Dear Major Vining,

I am requested by my client Sir Lancelot Stratham-Boyne to bring to your notice certain activities taking place on your land that are causing him annoyance and must cease. For some weeks construction work has been taking place on your estate the result of which has created vast amounts of extra traffic on the Southampton Road bordering his land. On several occasions construction material has fallen from trucks and ended up blocking drainage ditches on his property.

A large number of Irish workmen appear to be quartered on your land and frequently they trespass on Sir Lancelot's estate, poaching pheasants, hares and rabbits. On one occasion a fruit store was broken into and apples taken. My client insists you take action to remedy the foregoing without delay and ensure that no further trespass by Irish labourers occurs. To put it mildly, Sir Lancelot feels the construction work you are engaged in on your property can only be detrimental to the surrounding countryside and possibly lower the intrinsic value of adjoining estates.

Your early reply will be appreciated,
> *Yours sincerely,*
> *B. Fenwick*
> *Solicitor*

Francis passed the letter across the breakfast table to Margot, 'What do you think of that, darling?'

She studied the missive with raised eyebrows and clearly

found it extremely unpleasant. 'Who is this Sir Lancelot fellow? It strikes me he is a hyphenated man with a hyphenated mind! I need to look at the various points raised in more detail but from the first impression I get, he appears to be trying to tell you what you can do or not do on your own property. Leave it with me, dearest, and I'll frame a suitable reply.'

Francis was obviously relieved, 'Thank you darling, I thought you'd enjoy dealing with that. However, in the meantime I'll speak with Roy Hersey to make sure the Irish contingent don't stray onto Sir Lancelot's hyphenated land!' They both had a good laugh as Francis added, 'He's not going to like aircraft flying from our field but I've checked and there's nothing he can do about it.'

March swept on its course and true to form, having arrived like a lamb departed like a lion with gale force winds and rain and sleet making life particularly unpleasant for all concerned. For several days the children, unable to go out at playtime, were naughty and some received the cane. Rupert disliked being kept inside and was whacked by Miss Turner for playing up. He received a double dose having cheeked the headmistress in French forgetting she understood exactly what he'd said.

After school that day she talked to Miss Fenwick about it, 'Rupert Tupper is a very bright boy but must learn to behave a bit more. Maybe it would help if he were given some tasks to complete at home; what do you think Miss Fenwick?'

Bunty Fenwick was flattered to be asked: 'I think you're right Miss Turner, he needs stretching mentally and something like that would be good for him. At the same time perhaps we should also give tasks to Jenny Biggs so as not to give Rupert a false idea of his own importance.'

'An excellent suggestion; we'll start tomorrow. Now I have another personal matter I wish to talk to you about.' Bunty Fenwick wondered what it could be that concerned her personally but she didn't have to wait long to find out.

'I believe you have a brother who is a practicing solicitor in Southampton?'

Bunty nodded, 'yes, that is so. Brian is my older brother and his practice is in Broad Walk in Southampton. But why do you ask?'

'I need to discuss my will with a competent legal man but as I teach each day I cannot travel to see a solicitor during the week and they don't work on Saturdays. Do you think it possible your brother could come to see me here one day after school finishes? I'd be most grateful if you could ask him on my behalf.'

'Of course, I'll be happy to do that for you Miss Turner. I'm seeing him this weekend and will let you know next Monday if and when he can come.'

'That's most kind of you! As I retire in three years' time I want to put my affairs in good order beforehand. I'm the last of my family as my younger sister died a few years ago, so it's important I get on with the business.

'There is one other matter I ought to mention as it will affect the school: the Parish Council started building ten new houses for ex-servicemen and their families this week, so we may expect a large influx of new children next autumn.'

'I've drafted a reply to your neighbour, dealing with the various points his solicitor raised,' Margot was clearly enjoying herself as she came into the study waving a sheet of paper at Francis. 'Mind if I sit down, darling?'

'Help yourself and thank you for taking the trouble to answer that missive.' Francis spread the sheet on the desk and started to read,

Dear Mr Fenwick,

I have received your letter of 22nd March setting out various problems your client, Sir Lancelot Stratham-Boyne, has suffered but I am surprised he should feel they concern me.

If I may, I'll deal with the points in the order of your letter. Starting with the building material he states has fallen from trucks travelling along the highway. Has he actually witnessed such happenings? The haulage company is, of course, responsible and

will be liable for any pollution of roadside ditches on your client's land. As far as poaching on his estate is concerned, may I say I have great sympathy and I'm sure he'll be aware I too suffered at the end of last year when an organised gang was intercepted by my gamekeepers and estate workers with excellent results; I suggest he enlists the help of the police as I did! He states Irish labourers trespassed on his land to poach but has he any proof? It is easy to condemn working class men and I'm aware they are simple folk but nevertheless honest, God-fearing individuals.

Finally, I take exception to your client attempting to dictate to me in peremptory tones what I may or may not do with my own property. If I need his advice or opinion I'll ask for it!

With a broad grin on his face, Francis turned to Margot, 'Splendid darling! Thanks very much and I bet you enjoyed every minute writing that to Sir Hyphenated Busybody. I'll get that off today without fail. Reading your effort has made me think: Are you, with your Scottish qualifications, permitted to practise as a solicitor in England?'

Margot shook her head, 'No, I would have to qualify through the Law Society in London. I may consider doing that in due course, it wouldn't be difficult.'

'That might be a better idea than you realise dearest. You see, you could then do the legal business for all our companies,' said Francis adding, with a cheeky grin, 'and I might get it at half price!'

Margot looked hard at her husband and with a faint smile, 'You forget, darling, I'm a Scot through and through and we have a reputation for being a wee bit canny.'

Francis took the remark in good part but pursued his line of reasoning, 'Joking aside, darling, I think you would enjoy getting back into the legal world. Do give it further thought.'

'You're right. I do miss the activity of the courts and, yes, I'll consider applying to the Law Society. It could be convenient to do the necessary reading to qualify, during the coming months. Who knows, it may result in our little one growing up to be a legal genius! Now you must get on with the letter and be sure you use your best handwriting.'

Margot patted him on the head as she left the study.

'You're a delightful slave driver, dearest, but I love you very much,' Francis blew a kiss as she disappeared from the room.

Chapter 15

The Easter weather proved to be warm and sunny, making life more pleasant for everybody and the holiday at the Manor House which brought the family together was a complete success. Margot's parents enjoyed their stay and went on to Bristol with Fanny as planned. The airfield construction, now well advanced, interested Margot's father, David, who spent some time on the site with Francis, He emphasised again his willingness to provide a loan if it were required and Francis told him it would probably be needed after the flying school had started in the autumn.

Janine Tupper, like most mothers, was delighted to have Rupert home at Exeter for the Easter holidays and detected a distinct change in her son. He had obviously grown and soon would, no doubt, be as tall as she was.

'Rupert, you're going to be a big man like your father was and if you work hard at school you will get on well when you leave. Do you like your school?'

Rupert thought for a moment or two, 'Yes I do' and after a slight pause, 'Yes, I do very much. You see, mother, we have two teachers, Miss Turner the headmistress who is very strict and gives a whack with her cane if you don't do things properly and Miss Fenwick who is very nice and helps if you don't understand anything. She doesn't whack with a cane but can smack hard if someone is naughty.'

'And has Miss Turner caned you?'

Rupert had no problem recalling the occasions he'd had three strokes on his hand, 'Well yes, once was for cheeking her in French. She understands French, so I'll not do it again. I'm good at arithmetic and Miss Turner told me as we left for Easter I'm the top of the class for it.'

Janine put her arms round her son and hugged him. 'Rupert, I'm so pleased for you and although I miss you a lot I don't mind if you are getting on well at school. I know you are happy with Mr and Mrs Briggs, and their children, as they wrote a letter to me telling me just that.'

'That's right Mother, they're so kind and particularly Mrs Briggs who always kisses me goodnight after we've said our prayers. But there are some times when I miss you and Mollie and Tom.' He had a little weep and Janine just hugged him harder and gave him several kisses.

'My darling, you are a very brave boy and I'm so proud of you. Now I plan to come to see you next term and will bring your brother and sister with me.'

They talked for some time during which Janine told her son she had found a job working for a dressmaker. 'I go each day after I've seen Mollie and Tom to school. The shop is in the High Street and is called "Madame Baume" and is really run by Mrs Nellie Ranft with her husband Abraham helping her with the books; lots of well-to-do ladies go there for their clothes. I do special work as I'm experienced and do lots of embroidery. From my wages I can now send money to Mr and Mrs Briggs for your expenses.'

Rupert was pleased to hear all his mother had said, 'I think you are the best mother in the whole world and when I grow up and get work I'll look after you!' He gave her a big kiss and squeezed her arm, 'and now I'm hungry after all that. When are we going to have tea?'

Janine laughed, 'Oh! You haven't changed a bit thank goodness. I'll put the kettle on and see what I can get for tea. Tell Mollie and Tom it will be ready in about ten minutes time.'

While they ate their tea, Janine told the children she would be going to the dressmaker only each morning during the two weeks' school holiday: 'Mrs Ranft kindly said I could finish at midday so I'll be able to come home to get your dinner. In the afternoons we can all go out to do something special; one day we can go down the river on the motor launch and see the big ships in the docks. Another time perhaps have a charabanc ride to the country and take a picnic.'

The children thought their mother's ideas exciting and Rupert asked if it would be possible for all of them to go on a train excursion to the seaside, 'You know, mother, it's quite cheap if you go on a special day; I saw a poster while we were waiting on the platform at Farndene station.'

Janine said she liked the idea, 'I'll make some enquiries tomorrow and see what we can do. Now eat up your tea and then I'll read you a story.' They all murmured approval, 'the story will be in French, to make sure you are keeping up with the language!'

There was a general chorus of disapproval, 'Oh, do we have to? Can't we have an English story?'

Janine relented, 'Well, a short French one first and then a long English tale to follow.'

They all helped to clear the table and wash up before trooping into the front room to listen to their mother. When they had all settled and Janine was about to read, she looked up and saw Rupert was playing with the fire irons, 'Rupert, stop fiddling and put the poker back on the stand.' Glancing up from the book she added, 'Now pay attention children and I'll begin: the story of the little donkey lost on the mountain. Once upon a time a small donkey left his mother and wandered onto a large mountain ...' the children listened intently as their mother read two pages of exciting episodes the little animal became involved in, before finishing, ' ... he ran down the hillside where his mother was waiting for him.'

Janine looked at her little brood and smiled as she recognised the relief on their faces as they realised the tiny donkey had come home to his mother safely, 'Did you enjoy that?'

They all nodded, although there seemed to be a slight uncertainty in the way Tom, the youngest, replied. There followed the second tale entitled 'The Enchanted Forest', a great favourite with all three children. Mollie and Rupert then played card games and dominoes with their mother and Tom drew pictures and coloured them with wax crayons, his pet pastime. All too soon for the children it was time for bed and after cocoa and biscuits and prayers, Janine tucked them up with a goodnight kiss.

To the gentle hiss of the gaslight, she worked for the next two hours checking the children's clothes, replacing a button or two and darning holes in socks and stockings as well as making small repairs to their things. Placing the mending in a neat pile she sat back taking stock of her present life and recalling the happy times she had had with her dear late husband Charlie. She remembered how caring he'd always been and how much he loved her and the children; she missed him very much indeed. With a sigh she lit a candle, turned out the gaslight and went upstairs to bed.

The rest of the week was very busy but, as promised, Janine had found out about excursions and on Saturday morning the family, consumed with excitement, made their way to the railway station. The platform was already packed with dozens of children with their parents all happily waiting for the special train due at ten o'clock. Their high-pitched chatter and laughter was hushed as the massive locomotive steamed into the station with several sharp blasts on the whistle. The scores of people and children were soon swallowed up by the long line of carriages and after the porters had slammed numerous doors, the guard waving his green flag and blowing his whistle, started the train, which lurched forward several times before settling down to a steady rhythm.

Occupying one side of a compartment, Janine and the children began their journey out of Exeter as the train wound its way steadily along the river Exe estuary where several sailing boats and ships were plying. Soon after, they passed Dawlish Warren, Dawlish and then Holcombe, with wonderful views of the sea sparkling in the morning sunlight, eventually arriving at their destination, Teignmouth, sitting at the mouth of the river Teign.

Hurrying along with the children skipping beside her, Janine soon reached the beach with its beautiful sands and selected a spot to sit. It was a wonderful sunny spring day with a slight sea breeze and soon the children were occupied building sand castles with the two wooden spades and a bucket their mother had bought en route. Janine sat taking in the scene and appreciating every moment as she watched crowds of children playing on the beach accompanied by the soft hush of the calm sea as it lapped across the sands.

Further along, she saw a yellow van next to a group of donkeys where a tall man rang a large brass bell calling the children for rides along the beach, while above masses of mewing gulls wheeled and dived watching for any titbits the day trippers threw for them.

She agreed the children could take off their shoes and socks and paddle, joining the scores already dabbling at the edge of the sea: 'Now roll your things up and make sure you don't go in too far and Mollie, look after Tom.'

They scampered off and Janine kept a weather eye on them as she took out her knitting. Shortly after, the donkeys came past in a long line, like a caravan of camels crossing a desert and she counted nine of them, each with a smiling child on its back, the whole procession led by the tall man who had rung the bell. She was fascinated by the quiet plodding animals but thought it a hard way to earn their keep, day after day on the beach in all weathers.

Her gaze returned to the seashore but she was unable to see the children at all, which was worrying, as she had told them to keep in sight. Janine stood up to get a better view and at that moment Mollie, looking distressed, came running up to her.

'Whatever is the matter, Mollie?'

The child was panting and with tears in her eyes blurted out her reply, 'Mummy, Tom's gone. Rupert's looking for him.'

Janine put her arms round the frightened girl to comfort her, 'All right, darling, now tell me quickly, which way did Tom go?'

Still panting, 'He didn't like the sea so he went a little way back to play with children who had some bouncy balls. I did watch him a lot but suddenly he wasn't there and I couldn't see him anywhere.'

'All right, now go and find Rupert and bring him back here while I go over to the yellow van to ask the man with the donkeys if he's seen Tom.'

Mollie sped off and her mother hurried over to the group of

donkeys as fast as she could.

Arriving at the van she saw a lad of about fourteen helping the next lot of children to mount. Seeing her agitation, the man in charge asked if he could help. Janine explained she had lost her youngest boy and gave him a description.

To her surprise the man smiled and invited her to step to the back of his van: 'Just look in there, madam, and I think you will recognise your lost property!'

Janine did as she was bidden and to her surprise and joy found Tom sitting on a long seat looking at a book of photographs of all the donkeys, 'Tom! We've all been looking for you! Why did you come here?'

'Oh, I can answer that for him,' the man chuckled as he spoke, 'He came to ask me if the baby donkey we have tethered by the van was the one that was lost on the mountain and he told me a lovely story about a little donkey you had read to him.'

Janine felt very relieved, 'I can't tell you how grateful I am, Mr ...,' she hesitated and he pointed to the side of his van where his name and address appeared in black lettering, 'It's Ellery Hales, madam.'

Janice took his offered hand, 'I'm Janine Tupper,' and she introduced Mollie and Rupert who had just arrived.

Ellery Hales stood looking intently at Janine before speaking. 'Tell me, are you any relation of Charlie Tupper, a horse dealer?'

She was startled: 'Why, yes, Charlie was my dear husband, but how did you know him?'

'It's a long story really going back to the time when Edward the seventh was on the throne. Your Charlie gave me tremendous help when I started up with horses and donkeys and advised me over many years on what to buy and what not to buy. Without him I would never have succeeded and now, not only do I have the donkeys here but also a riding stables my wife Beryl runs with her cousin. It was a great tragedy poor Charlie was lost and you have my sympathy, Mrs Tupper.'

Janine thanked him and, turning to the children, asked, 'Would you like a donkey ride?'

A chorus of 'yes, please' and they were each assisted onto a donkey by the youth who Ellery said was his eldest boy, Andrew. When Janine offered to pay for the three youngsters, Ellery wouldn't hear of it, 'No money, please. It's a pleasure to give Charlie's family a helping hand.'

Later, the family sat on the warm sands where Janine spread a cloth, pinned down at each corner with large stones, on which she spread their picnic. The children were wide eyed as she put out ham and potted chicken paste sandwiches, followed by jam tarts, lemon and fruit cake and a banana for each of them. They sat enjoying a veritable feast after which Mollie and Rupert fetched a tea tray, containing a pot of tea, milk, sugar cubes and cups and saucers, from a nearby beach café. Needless to say all the sugar cubes were eaten!

After the picnic they all had a final paddle before packing up their belongings including a long piece of seaweed, a bucket full of shells, a star fish and a crab, both thankfully dead, as well as their coats and bags. As they made their way to the station to catch the special excursion train at six o'clock they lingered on the promenade for a last look at the sea and beach. It was then Janine realised that day had been wonderful for all of them and she promised to have another trip to the seaside during the summer holidays.

The Easter holidays passed quickly and previous routines were re-established. Margot had overseen the completion of redecoration of the Manor House and, with the new kitchen equipment installed, the result was delightful. Francis congratulated his wife, 'Darling, you've rejuvenated our home and I think you're a marvel! It looks wonderful and, even better, the whole job is only a fraction over budget.' He put his arm around her waist and gave her a long kiss, 'Now you must take things easier from now on.'

Margot smiled and squeezed his hand, 'Of course I'll take care of myself, sweetheart. I'll do nothing untoward!' She giggled as she sang, 'I'll sit on a cushion and sew a fine seam and feed upon strawberries, sugar and cream.'

Laughing helplessly, Francis collapsed with Margot onto a divan and they were locked in a tight embrace as Bertie entered the room. With a slight cough, he announced, 'Luncheon will be ready in about ten minutes, madam, sir,' and exited quickly, leaving the door open.

As they went to the dining room, Francis promised to tell his wife how the airfield building was progressing.

Month succeeded month during the summer of 1920 and by August the airfield buildings and flight area were almost complete. After drainage, the levelling had proved more difficult than anticipated but, with the help of Robert Oulton, with his vast knowledge and experience as a sapper during the Great War, the problems were eventually overcome and the flight field was finished by the middle of the month.

Francis, meanwhile, had purchased several redundant aircraft from the Royal Air Force and these arrived, dismantled and crated, by the third week of August.

One airframe and two aero engine fitters were recruited, having previously served with Francis's Royal Flying Corps squadron in France and since demobilised. Their first task was to assemble a Sopwith Camel fighter plane Francis intended flying to test the suitability of the airfield.

The completed plane was wheeled out on 31st August and having run the engine up for fifteen minutes, Francis climbed in. Watched by Margot, Robert and all the airfield ground crew, he taxied out to the take-off point marked clearly in white on the grass.

He glanced at the yellow windsock billowing in the wind and moments later, as the engine came to life, the plane roared down the field. It was quickly airborne, ascending rapidly and turned to circle the airfield. Soon it was out of sight, although the distant hum of the engine was still audible, and the waiting onlookers chatted about the success of the first flight. Five minutes later their peace was shattered as the plane came roaring overhead at tree height, almost touching the grass before climbing fast to loop the loop and perform several aerobatics, all well received by the spectators.

Having landed, Francis taxied to a parking point and cut the engine. As he clambered down, Margot, now very much an expectant mother, ran forward and gave him a huge kiss to the applause of all those present. Immediately surrounded by a congratulatory crowd, Francis declared the airfield in good condition and turning to Bertie, 'Get the bubbly and glasses Bertie, and we'll all drink to the future of this enterprise.'

The butler hurried to the car and, with assistance, produced champagne for all. Robert stepped onto a small crate and proposed the toast, 'Will you all please join me in saluting this wonderful airfield, the brainchild of Francis who has overcome so much to achieve the success we see before us,' and, raising his glass, 'Congratulations, Francis, for all you've done, particularly the splendid air display moments ago!'

In thanking Robert, Francis told them the whole project would never have succeeded without the expertise and dedication of this outstanding sapper. 'So raise your glasses again to Robert, the unflappable, who overcame countless problems many of us would have blanched at and declared insuperable, but to his agile mind were solvable.'

And so the airfield was born and all minds turned towards the official opening of the base to be held during September.

Chapter 16

Warm autumn weather welcomed the official opening of the airfield and all the plans so carefully prepared came to fruition on 28th September 1920. Francis and Margot held a family luncheon inviting everyone from Bristol, including his mother and Aunt Lotte's family, together with Edith and Robert Oulton. Also included were Margot's parents from St Andrews and Madeline, Grant, Sam and Marion from Whitby together with Francis's grandparents, David and Ruth Edwards and Sir Roger Vining. The occasion, a great reunion, gave them a wonderful opportunity to hear all the latest news from each branch of the family.

Shortly after two o'clock they made their way to the special enclosure where seats were arranged for all the special visitors and the pageant atmosphere greeted them on all sides. Flags, banners and bunting adorned the whole arena and the gathered crowds, including all the children and teachers from the local school, were entertained by the regimental band of Sir Roger's regiment, the South Hampshire Fusiliers. In front of the main building the maintenance staff assembled with several aircraft on display.

Francis, accompanying the Prime Minister, David Lloyd George, arrived just before two thirty, to the cheers of the assembled crowd. At half past two exactly, the Prime Minister made a short speech declaring the airfield 'open'. This was followed by a blessing performed by the Rev. Shadwell Legion, the new rector of St Paul's, Farndene. Four massive rockets then streaked skyward to burst with deafening explosions to the gasps of the crowd.

The drone of approaching aircraft could be heard a short while before a squadron of Royal Air Force fighter planes passed in formation over the airfield. Within minutes they had landed and the pilots joined a special visitors' reception held in the main building. There were many congratulations from all sides and Francis felt the opening ceremony had been most successful. To complete the occasion, the RAF pilots took off and gave a wonderful flying display before returning to their base. The Farndene Flying School was now indeed on the map.

At home with the Briggs family that evening, Rupert wrote his weekly letter to his mother and told her all about the wonderful afternoon he and the other schoolchildren had had, 'we all went to the airfield with the Headmistress and Miss Fenwick and saw all the aeroplanes. Some landed and then went up again to do loop the loops and flying together and things. After that we all went into a big hall where there were other aeroplanes and we had currant buns, ginger pop and an orange each. Mr Vining said we must come again when there were other planes flying. I think I'm going to be a pilot when I grow up. Miss Fenwick blushed when some of the pilots talked to her and Miss Turner laughed. I wish I could just give you a big hug Mother but I can't in my letter so I'll put kisses for you and Mollie and Tom instead.' He then wrote, 'lots and lots of love, Rupert,' and added nine kisses. Asked by Rupert, Beatty Briggs read the letter to tell him if he'd made any spelling mistakes and she smiled at the comment about Miss Fenwick: 'It's all right, Rupert, but are you sure you saw Miss Fenwick blush?' Rupert nodded, 'Oh yes! She always blushes when she talks to young men 'cos I've seen her.' The letter was put in an envelope and sealed with the usual SWALK written on the back.

Beatty made sure Jenny and Rupert did their homework before they were allowed to play games.

In Exeter, Janine was completely settled in the dressmaking business and had managed to have time with the children during their summer holidays due to the generosity of Ellery Hales, who had invited her and the children to stay with his family in Teignmouth. They got on very well indeed, so much so that the children stayed on for extra weeks, during which they helped in the stables, grooming the horses and donkeys and cleaning up generally, in return for which they all had riding lessons each day.

While the children enjoyed the freedom on holiday, Janine was able to return to Exeter to work full time at her job, subsequently returning to collect the children in time for the return to school for the autumn term.

On an early October morning she hurried to the shop and before starting work, enjoyed chatting over a hot cup of tea with the girls of the sewing room. Several were discussing Mr Ranft in quite derogatory tones, one saying, 'Yes, he's a randy old man all right, and he tries it on any time he gets a chance!' While another elaborated, 'He's a groper! Yesterday he grabbed me and when I broke away he told me to "get used to it" if I valued my job. I told him he was a dirty old man.'

Janine was taken aback by what she had just heard, putting the question, 'Why don't you tell Mrs Ranft? I'm sure she would do something.' The immediate unanimous reply was shocked: 'She wouldn't believe us and you can be sure Mr Ranft would deny anything, so we'd likely get the push.' Just at that minute Mrs Nellie Ranft came in greeting them, 'Good morning. I hope you're all well and ready for work. We have a very busy day ahead of us with a complete outfit to make for Lady Grassmere. She is going to America with her husband, the new ambassador, and they sail next week so we must look sharp.' The girls went to their various tables to start as Mrs Ranft called Janine into her office. 'Janine, I find myself in a very tight spot as Cecily Dendy, my head seamstress and cutter, is suffering with a severely poisoned hand and will be away for some while. Will you be willing to take on the cutting while I supervise the girls in the sewing room?'

The import of what her employer had said took a minute or two to sink in but Janine was convinced she could do the work, so replied with confidence, 'Yes, Mrs Ranft, I'll do the cutting if it will help you. All I'll need will be the patterns and the sequence in which the various garments are to be cut.'

Mrs Ranft said she would be available to guide and advise. With that, Janine went to the cutting room and started, laying out the materials and patterns in the correct order set out in the notes her employer had prepared.

It was quiet in the room and, working alone, Janine enjoyed the pleasant atmosphere as she cut round the patterns with a large pair of scissors, stopping from time to time to clear the trimmings into a large sack. With her back to the door she didn't hear it open and close quietly and was shocked when a voice asked how she was progressing.

'You seem to be managing very well and I congratulate you Janine.' Looking round, she found Mr Ranft had entered and had sat on a small chair near the door.

'Mr Ranft, you made me jump! Is there something you want?'

He smiled as he shook his head, 'No my dear, I looked in to see how you were getting along.' Janine felt slightly uneasy, sensing from his manner he was not telling the truth but decided to get on with her work.

'You may not be aware of it Janine, but you are a most attractive person,' he continued in a flattering voice. But she decided to put a stop to his comments and, turning to face him, replied with force, 'Mr Ranft, if you decide to stay will you please not talk as this is particularly difficult work.' With that, she continued cutting.

'Oh, I'm so sorry. In that case I'll go.' He got up but stopped suddenly as he went to the door, placing a handkerchief to his right eye, 'Confound it! Something has gone in my eye; would you be kind enough to have a look for me?'

Janine stopped cutting and turned to give assistance as he stood in front of her. Taking the handkerchief she looked into his eye but could see nothing, 'I'm not aware of anything in the eye, Mr Ranft, you must be mistaken.'

Before she could do or say anything else he grabbed her round the waist and attempted to kiss her mouth at the same time groping her breasts with his free hand. Janine screamed and fought with both hands, scratching one side of his face but he was a big man and he pushed her backwards onto the cutting table with the words 'calm down and you won't get hurt'. With his arm across her neck he tore at her skirt, pulling it up to expose her underwear then tearing it apart with the obvious intention of having intercourse as his flies were open revealing an erection.

Unable to move because of his weight, Janine struggled and as she freed her right arm, the elbow touched the cutting scissors. She grasped them and with all her force, lunged at his body piercing his buttocks in a dagger like motion, the blades sank into his flesh and struck the pelvic bone.

The result was electric as he leapt up with a mighty howl, then collapsed and writhed in agony on the floor.

At that moment the door opened as one of the girls entered with some tea for Janine. The cup and saucer crashed to the floor scattering in all directions while her screams brought Mrs Ranft and other girls rushing to the room. The poor woman was horrified seeing her husband moaning and semi-conscious on the floor with blood pouring from his wound. She quickly pulled the scissors out, staunching the spurting blood with a towel and telling a girl to call an ambulance. A few minutes later she went to the assistance of Janine who had passed out, falling to the floor. Other girls helped to lift her onto a chair where she recovered enough to tell Mrs Ranft what had happened.

An hour later, after Mr Ranft had been taken to hospital, Janine sat in Mrs Ranft's office while she discussed the whole episode. 'I've had my suspicions for a while now and in view of what has happened I've decided my husband has to go. I cannot put up with his behaviour any longer and will divorce the man as soon as possible. Your situation is somewhat different though Janine, because he attempted to rape you and that is a criminal offence, so you have every right to inform the police who will charge him.'

Janine was fully aware of the legal position and had already thought about the consequences of a rape trial for her and Mrs Ranft. She therefore put the case very succinctly to her employer.

'Mrs Ranft, you intend divorcing your husband and I feel you have every right to do that, but what if he won't agree unless there is a financial settlement?'

Mrs Ranft looked puzzled, 'I suppose that's a possibility, in which case I'd have to pay him something.'

Janine responded with a neat suggestion, 'You have no need to pay him anything. This is how I see the situation: if he agrees to the divorce without strings all well and good. But if he proves difficult I'll then bring a charge of rape against him. He can make his choice.'

'That is very generous, Janine, and I appreciate what you are doing for me,' Mrs Ranft took her hand as she spoke with feeling, 'I'll not forget this, you will see.'

The fifth day of October proved to be one of utmost importance also for the Vining family, and one of the happiest for Margot and Francis. Her labour started in the early hours and the nurse in attendance summoned Dr Strickland who arrived at nine a.m. with a midwife. During the ensuing hours, Francis tried to concentrate on business papers in his study without success and he regularly went up to the door of the bedroom to enquire if there was any news. Just after midday the nurse hurried down to tell him Margot had been delivered of a daughter but it was a case of twins and the second child had yet to be born! Francis felt elated but still worried for Margot and hoped all would be well shortly. To his great relief the nurse returned at twenty-five to one to say he was the father of a daughter and a son and it was all clear for him to see his wife.

As he entered the bedroom a lump came into his throat as he looked at Margot, sitting up in bed radiant with two tiny babies, one on each arm. Francis, sitting on the bed, put his arm round her shoulder and told her what a wonderful wife she was, 'Darling you will never know how happy you have made me and I'm so very proud of you!'

Dr Strickland congratulated both of them, 'You have two lovely healthy children and provided Margot can cope with feeding them, they should make good progress. I'll look in again in a couple of days and check all three. I have to tell you Francis, your wife handled the birth splendidly.'

Margot said she had made a list of all the people who had to be telephoned about the twins with Fanny, her parents and Sir Roger,

'I know he will be thrilled to be a great grandpa you'll see!' And after a pause, she added with a wry smile, 'We've started our family in a wonderful way, now I've only two more to produce and we'll be there!'

Francis looked thoughtful, saying, 'But what if you have twins each time? Why – we could end up with six children and I'd have to buy a charabanc to take you all out!' They laughed and kissed and talked for some time about the future for their children, including the arrangements for christening in about six weeks' time at their local church. Francis made the point, 'I'd really like Canon Digby Fletcher to baptise them, so we'll have to approach the Rev. Shadwell Legion, tactfully, to ask his permission.'

Margot nodded at his suggestion and was thoughtful for a moment or so, 'I agree darling. You see I have met Shadwell Legion and, to be perfectly honest, I didn't take to him. He appears very pious but I feel that's only a veneer and there is something about his manner I frankly dislike.'

'How interesting; I had the same impression when I asked him to the opening of the airfield to give a blessing, but if he won't agree to Digby taking the service, what do we do?'

Francis had a look of despair as he contemplated the problem. Margot's response was immediate, 'There are plenty of other churches in Hampshire and I have no doubt Digby will have somewhere he can recommend so we'll ask him if need be.'

Francis's face lit up as he applauded her suggestion, 'What a brilliant idea, darling. We'll do just that if Shadwell Legion proves difficult. Now that's settled I'll go down and tell the staff all about our two wonderful children,' adding, with a smile, 'produced by my wonderful wife!' As he reached the bedroom door Margot blew him a kiss, 'Well you did help a little yourself, didn't you, sweetheart.' With a grin and a nod he closed the door.

Chapter 17

The days of October passed quickly and for the Vining household the two new arrivals soon made their presence felt without ever realising they were having such an effect on the family.

The question of names and the most convenient date for the baptism exercised the minds of both parents. So at the beginning of November Margot decided to make a decision once and for all. On 6th November, as soon as breakfast was over she went into the study with Francis and sat down, refusing to budge until the big issue had been addressed. 'Francis darling, we really must decide on names now.' He smiled and slowly opened the desk draw from which he produced a long list of boys' and girls' names which he pushed across to Margot, 'Take your pick, dearest. I'll be happy with any of them but I don't want more than two names for each.' Margot picked up the list and browsed, shaking her head slightly here and there, then put the sheet down and looked straight at her husband, 'Darling you are very clever to have given so much thought to our problem but have you any real preference?' Francis replied without hesitation, 'Yes, I have. One of our son's names should be Norman, after my father; what do you think?' Margot nodded, 'Yes, I agree that would be a wonderful way to keep his name alive in the coming generation. Do you remember anything about him?'

Francis was thoughtful and obviously trying to recall his early days, 'Yes, I do, although I was only seven at the time of his death, I saw him when he was on leave from the navy. A tall man with a lovely smile, who always seemed to have time to spend with me. When he was home he would see me to bed and tell wonderful bedtime stories. He was a most affectionate father.'

Margot smiled sweetly as she looked at her husband, 'Darling, you've obviously inherited his characteristics and I think you're going to be a super daddy to our two. But we still have only one name between two children, so do you think David would be all right for Norman's second name?' 'That's splendid darling, I'm sure both your father and my grandfather will be thrilled. What about our little girl?'

Margot had also been busy and from a file she produced her preferred list of female names. She put it on the desk for Francis to read, at the same time stating her first choice, 'I like Juliet as much as any unless you have other ideas?'

'Oh, that's a lovely name! Have you any others?'

'Well, yes, I have as it happens.' Smiling, she continued, 'My mother's name Lorna has always sounded beautiful to me and I'd love to use it with Juliet; it sounds just right don't you think?'

Francis stood up and sat on the edge of the desk and with a broad grin handed back the list Margot had given him, 'I've no need to read this list as I consider your choice excellent. So the name game is settled and we can get on with our lives.The difficulty now facing us is simply whether or not we can have the christening in our local church. I'd better go along to see the Rev. Shadwell Legion as soon as possible to find out if he will allow Digby Fletcher to take the service. In fact I'll telephone the rectory and see him at once if he's in.'

Margot left the study and went to her own desk to write to her mother and to Fanny telling them the names they had chosen for the two little ones.

Moments later Francis came into the room, beaming and looking very pleased with himself. 'Darling, you'll never believe what I'm going to tell you; the Rev. Legion has agreed to our request for Digby to take the baptism in St Paul's church and suggested Sunday 14th November at three o'clock. I thanked him and said I'd confirm the date as soon as possible. He said he would like to be part of the service by taking a short intercession. Again I felt that to be reasonable because, after all, it is his church.'

Margot's response was natural, 'I agree. It looks as though the rector has leaned in our direction and the date will suit us admirably though I'm still not attracted to the man. However, Digby will christen our two and that's all that matters.'

They sat talking for best part of an hour during which they decided the godparents were to be Alex, Madeline, and Robert Oulton for Norman, and Lorna, Jessica and Grant for Juliet.

The Sunday chosen for the christening would see the gathering of all branches of the family and, as many would be travelling long distances, accommodation was needed. Margot, excited at the prospect, enjoyed making the plans, 'We shall just have to squeeze everybody in and the young ones will have to make do with whatever we can provide.' Francis saw the funny side of it all, 'Well, that's all right by me; so some might be bedding down in the stables or maybe sleeping in tents on the lawns!'

The family gathered on Saturday 13th November, the day before the christening, arriving throughout that afternoon. Dinner that night saw twenty-four family and friends sit down for the meal.

The Rev. Digby Fletcher said a simple Grace: 'God bless the food we eat, God bless the friends we meet, God is our guiding light, Protect us through this night, And keep us in thy sight. Amen.' Then, looking round at the huge gathering, remarked, 'That's the signal for you all to tuck in!' The buzz of conversation and the bursts of laughter indicated the gathered company was enjoying the occasion and it set the scene for the rest of the evening.

After dinner, little groups of family sat talking over coffee and it was after eleven before the guests retired, some going to stay with Sir Roger, who had kindly offered to accommodate eight, providing they got their own breakfast.

A beautiful dawn greeted the following day and by the afternoon, when the christening party reached the church, the autumn sun shone bravely. They gathered in the pews round the ancient font at the west end of the church and the Reverend Digby Fletcher beamed as he conducted the service.

Francis whispered to Margot, 'Just think, both my father and I were named at this font and probably many Vinings before us.' Her confidential reply caused her husband to smile, 'and there'll be a lot more little Vinings coming here in the future if I have anything to do with it!'

While they waited, Margot sat looking at the pew shelf on which many boys' names were carved. She recalled the day last December she had looked at those same names and wondered who and where those boys, now men, were. It troubled her and she made a mental note to ask the rector if he could trace any of them.

They stood up as the godparents formed a semicircle around the font; Lorna held Juliet and Madeline held Norman. After the opening prayers, the Rev. Digby took Juliet and, addressing Lorna, asked her, 'Name this child.' Without hesitation she replied, 'Juliet. Lorna. Fanny.' A slight gasp was audible from the bystanders but it was too late and Juliet was baptised with three names.

No other surprises greeted the christening of Norman David, who was given the two names his parents intended.

At this point the Rev. Shadwell Legion started the intercession which went on and on, as he prayed for one thing after another for some ten minutes and it was only the intervention of baby Norman who howled, setting off his sister, that the rector gave up.

As everybody left the church, a small, excited crowd of villagers and estate workers waited outside to greet them, all eager to see the two babies and for the women, particularly, to admire the ladies clothes!

Back at the Manor House all enjoyed the reception laid on by Francis and Margot, during which a champagne toast was drunk to the twins. Most of the guests departed during the late afternoon, leaving just the family who were staying one more night.

During dinner that evening, the christening service was a prime topic and Margot, pointedly, asked her mother why she had added Fanny's name to Juliet's, 'You knew very well, Mother, Francis and I wanted both babies to have only two names, didn't you?'

Lorna replied, with a smile, 'I take my duty as a godparent very seriously and I realised that wee bairn would be better off with both grandmothers' names. I'm sure Juliet will be so pleased when she grows up; I also felt Fanny wouldn't mind.'

A hush descended as Margot took in what her mother had just said but slowly her face registered approval as she spoke, 'You're right mother. It was a bit of a surprise but thank you for being such a good godmother.' Margot recalled from earlier years how steadfast her mother was and had no doubt Lorna would carry out her duties as godparent with great sincerity.

The next few weeks up to Christmas were busy for the Vining household, particularly for Margot as she coped with feeding the twins and applying her mind to preparations for the coming holiday. She and Francis had decided they would stay at home for Christmas and the New Year, as travelling with two small babies was out of the question. However, they gave an open invitation to the family to come to Farndene to stay as long as they liked, the result being acceptance by Fanny, Aunt Lotte and Mildred, Alex and Angelina and the two children. Margot's parents decided to go to Whitby to be with Madeline, Grant and the children for Christmas and the Hogmanay celebrations.

The holiday weather was particularly mild and the whole family walked to St Paul's church for the morning service on Christmas Day.

As they proceeded with the twins in a perambulator, pushed alternately by the nurse and Angelina, Aunt Lotte remarked to Fanny, 'This reminds me so much of my own children when they were young. Dear Albert always insisted they all went to church on Christmas Day and, once there, he looked after the youngest in the church by whispering little stories to them about the birth of Christ. He was a lovely father and I still miss him, especially at times like today.'

Fanny squeezed her aunt's hand to comfort her, 'Uncle Albert will always be my favourite and we are right to remember him today. He would have been so proud of you and the children for all you have achieved, so we will drink a toast to his memory after dinner today.'

The service included all the favourite carols and the rector's address was quite short – some said because he had been invited to an early Christmas dinner – so they all got back to the Manor House in good time where the staff, traditionally, were served their meal by Margot and Francis, helped by Fanny and Aunt Lotte, before the family sat down at about two o'clock.

Later they foregathered in the drawing room where an enormous tree stood in darkness in one corner, much to Aunt Lotte's disappointment. 'Why no candles Francis?' she asked.

He told them all to sit down before going behind the tree, 'Now all please shut your eyes and open them when I say so.' All conversation was hushed for a moment and then he shouted, 'Open them now!'

They beheld the Christmas tree, completely illuminated by dozens of small electric bulbs, flooding the room with light and causing many hanging glass baubles to flash. A great 'Ooh!' went up. Francis emerged from the back of tree looking very pleased and, turning to Lotte, said, 'Well Aunt, what about that? This is the very first time a Christmas tree has been lit by electricity in this house and, who knows, maybe in the country!'

Lotte went across the room and, putting her arms round her nephew, congratulated him with a big kiss. 'You're a very clever boy and I think the tree is just so beautiful. But where did you get the electricity from?' The whole room was hushed again, eager to hear Francis's reply.

'It all started back in September when the airfield hangar was completed and we needed electric current for the new tools we had bought for aircraft maintenance. So I installed a generator and it produced plenty of power for our needs. I then reasoned, if our airfield buildings can be electrified why not a Christmas tree? In addition to the small generator I installed earlier to power the kitchen equipment, I now intend putting a second one in the stables next month to electrify the whole of this house.'

His audience was astonished, realising the import of what he was saying. Lotte thought it wonderful and asked the family to join her in a round of applause. They all stood and, with her, clapped their host.

The Christmas party was a huge success and the following days were a bonding time for them all.

On New Year's Eve, Francis undertook the duty of the man of the house and 'first footed' for Margot, a task he would be repeating for many years to come. As the family greeted each other at the beginning of 1921, many recalled past years but all looked forward to a new year unsullied at that moment and for most, full of promise.

Chapter 18

By 1926 there had been great changes in the village of Farndene. Its increasing industry attracted an influx of people, and the village had expanded into the surrounding countryside.

Many of the new arrivals were technicians drawn to the flying school and to a number of small supporting industries that had developed over four or five years. During that period, time flowed silently and uninterrupted like an ever coursing river going down the years into the future. The village, now almost a young town, had witnessed an increase in the number of new houses, an extension to the school to accommodate the many fresh children, and a new police station as, sadly, there was more crime. Additional train services were provided for the increased number of people travelling daily to Southampton to work, and, of course, a bigger garage was built to cope with the increased motor traffic.

Farndene was thriving, due in no small measure to the opening of the airfield on the Manor House Estate. Another great event occurred when the village was connected to the National Grid and even the gas street lamps were electrified.

The increases were not confined to the village, as Margot had given birth to a son, Bruce Duncan, on 5th March 1922. Later, she had a second pair of twins, Clara Frances (born twenty minutes before her sister) and Constance Ruth, on 8th June 1924. All three children were delivered in the Manor House, maintaining the family tradition. The Vining family was now well and truly established and, barring mishaps, Margot did not intend having more children. With good nursery assistance and a full time nanny, Margot was able to put her mind to other things and qualified through the Law Society to practice in England. She also took flying lessons and obtained her pilot's licence in the autumn of 1925.

In Bristol, Alex and Angelina had been married in July 1921 with Canon Digby Fletcher presiding over a truly splendid family wedding. Sadly, Aunt Lotte's health deteriorated during the late summer of 1924 and she died in October that year. Fanny described her passing as the closing of a chapter of their family life.

Over the recent years changes had also affected Janine Tupper and her family. Janine had met and fallen in love with a Major Philip Kirkwood, a retired Royal Artillery officer. Although twelve years her senior, he was still an active man in spite of a war injury to his leg. From his first meeting with the family he had taken a keen interest in Janine's three children and they all got on well with him. He worked for the Regimental Trust helping war widows and had obtained additional funds for Janine when she was desperately short of money.

Philip Kirkwood, a single man, had himself suffered sadness some years earlier when his fiancée died in an influenza epidemic. Janine married him in May 1923 and they moved to a new house in Exeter, nearer to the Madame Baume business, where she continued to work.

In December 1925, fourteen-year-old Rupert left school, starting a five-year engineering apprenticeship with part of the Dewar Group, arranged by Francis Vining, and with an emphasis on aero engine construction. Rupert now stood a little over six feet tall and was the image of his late father Charlie, good looking with dark brown hair and a wonderful sense of humour. Janine was, quite naturally, immensely proud of him.

Industrial unrest again reared its ugly head in 1926, as a massive General Strike was called by the Trade Unions in support of the miners. Although Farndene was not directly affected, people living there found some articles and foodstuffs, requiring transport, unobtainable.

However it was a different story in some of the larger provincial towns and in London where extraordinary scenes were witnessed. Manufacturing industries suffered greatly and in many cases became idle as shortages of fuel and raw materials occurred, due to stoppage of basic transport.

The national press also suffered as strikers shut down Fleet Street. Mr Winston Churchill, the Chancellor of the Exchequer, took over the offices and machinery of the *Morning Post* and organised the production of an emergency newspaper entitled the *British Gazette* which was produced daily on a single sheet while the strike lasted.

The response to the Government's call for help was overwhelming and the public came forward in large numbers with volunteers driving buses and trains. They also drove lorries delivering food, convoyed under armed escort by soldiers for fear of attack by militant strikers. These measures eventually broke the strike on 12th May and the country slowly returned to normality although there was still much bitterness among working class people.

Francis and Margot were delighted with the news of Alan Cobham's epic flight – he arrived in Melbourne on 15th July 1926 – and both went to London to join the tremendous welcome for his homecoming at the beginning of October. Cobham graciously accepted an invitation to visit the Farndene Flying School the following month.

And so early November saw great preparation at the Manor House, in anticipation of the arrival of the special guest. Margot took care to see Alan Cobham would be comfortable. At the Flying School, Francis and his staff did everything possible to ensure a high state of efficiency. An invitation to the Royal Air Force to join in, was also readily accepted.

Blessed with good weather, a large crowd turned out from the village as well as a number of specially invited guests – in all, some three hundred people thronged the airfield to welcome Alan Cobham as he flew in on the appointed day. The local school children cheered enthusiastically after he landed, so much so, he broke away from the formal welcoming group and, walking across to the children, signed autographs for some minutes for all who had pencil and paper handy.

A Royal Air Force squadron arrived shortly after, flying over the field in tight formation in salute. The reception in the main airfield building lasted about an hour after which the RAF pilots took off, completing a formation loop the loop before flying away to the west, the signal for the crowds to go home.

Comfortably installed at the Manor House, Alan Cobham enjoyed his overnight stay, particularly meeting the Vining children and was impressed by what Juliet and Norman knew about aircraft. Norman explained, 'Daddy is making a new plane which will have room for six passengers in a cabin and fly for hours and hours.'

Alan picked up the information with interest, 'My, that sounds like a very big plane, Norman. I think I'll ask your father all about it.' And, turning to his host who was smiling broadly, 'Francis, what's this I hear?'

'What Norman has told you, Alan, is only part of the story. Actually, I'm building a passenger plane with some help from my friend, Geoffrey de Havilland, but the problem is finding a powerful enough engine to cope with the increased weight.'

Alan nodded, 'I understand your predicament but have you considered a twin-engine aircraft?'

'Yes, we have and by doing so I believe we can increase the pay load to eight passengers which makes a great deal of sense from a commercial angle.' They talked for some time on the subject of new aircraft and their use for passengers and concluded a new era of transport was dawning.

Alan also expanded his own ideas on flying, 'I know there's a lot of interest among the public who want to get airborne but can't afford the cost of belonging to a flying club. It's in my mind to form a flying group to tour the country, staying here and there for about a week at a time and offering cheap flights to all the visitors. There are plenty of good pilots who would welcome the chance to join in and earn a living.'

Francis warmed to the suggestions and offered the use of the Farndene airfield, 'What an excellent idea! Please keep me in the picture and I'll be happy to arrange accommodation etc., when you come here.' As they shook hands, Alan replied with a grin, 'Good! That's just what I want to hear!'

The weeks moved on relentlessly into December and, as in previous years, Francis and Margot kept Christmas and the New Year celebrations in their own home. As Francis remarked, 'Taking the Vining Tribe away is a major operation.' He and Margot reserved such occasions for the summer holidays when they saw as much of the family as possible, particularly visiting the grandparents. However the family came together for Christmas at the Manor House and stayed on to welcome 1927.

Over the past few years, Francis had completely reorganised the various parts of the Dewar Group of companies, a move necessary as, since the war, Government orders had thinned out. This meant he had to spend long periods away from home, particularly when visiting the Dumbarton Aero engine factory and foundry. The vein was disarmament and Great Britain seemed to lead the field during the latter part of the twenties. Unemployment rose and the mood among the working population deteriorated as more firms went into liquidation. Bright spots were the remarkable solo flight of the Atlantic by the American aviator Charles Lindberg in his plane 'The Spirit of St Louis' on 27th May, followed by Great Britain winning the Schneider Trophy race in Venice, at speeds over 281 miles per hour on September 26th. There was, naturally, great interest among the staff of the Farndene Flying School. The year ended spectacularly with bitterly cold weather, severe ice and snow which, sadly, added to the misery of the many unemployed whose families were suffering privations.

With improved and much warmer weather in the early part of 1928, hope was kindled in the minds of those still out of work but the Government was slow with initiatives to create jobs and the Unions took a belligerent attitude towards employers. At the Manor House, Margot struggled with the running of their home with fewer girls wanting to go 'into service'; bus and train transport was easy into Southampton where shop assistants were wanted. Although these jobs paid low wages the young women were free when they returned home each evening, whereas in service their duties were a full week with only one day off.

Things came to a head one morning when Bertie the butler

reported a problem in the kitchen. He explained to Margot, 'The truth is, madam, Cook boxed the ears of Rose, the kitchen maid, for not doing her job properly, who, to cap it all was then rude to Mrs Bloom, calling her a silly old bitch.'

Margot interviewed the girl who was very sullen, telling her employer, 'I'm a member of me Trade Union and the seketary told me I'm bein' exploited here fer next ter nuffink wages.'

She stood looking defiantly at Margot who quietly invited the girl to sit down before speaking to her. 'Rose, I hear all you have to say but I didn't ask you to come here to work in the first place, did I? From my memory you were happy working in the kitchen, receiving cooking instruction from Mrs Bloom and to my knowledge you have made good progress – so much so Cook felt you were due to be promoted with an increase in your wages; why this sudden change of attitude?'

Rose looked down at the floor before replying, 'Wot you said, madam, is true but me boyfriend took me to the Union meetin' and made me join and then the seketary said all that stuff about bein' exploited. I didn't want ter join an' it costs a tanner for the sub every two weeks.' Here she started crying, 'I don't know what ter do Missis Vining, really I don't!'

Margot passed the girl a handkerchief and gave some advice, 'Rose, I can't stop you joining a Union but you mustn't let other people interfere with your work here. If you want to leave I won't stand in your way and will give you a good reference. You must make your choice but it won't help your family if you are out of work. Now go back to your duties and think over what I've said; meanwhile I'll speak to Mrs Bloom.'

The subsequent result was a reasonably happy ending as Rose resigned from the Union and settled down in her job; on the downside she fell out with her boyfriend!

The children's education began to concern Margot and Francis as until then they had employed a tutor, Miss Gladys Fitzroy, who came daily to the house. She was an attractive woman in her early forties, who dressed well and had almost black hair always neatly held in place with a large comb. Although she kept strict discipline, the children liked her and she got good results.

Francis was happy to continue the arrangement for the time being but Margot had other thoughts, 'Darling, the problem is the children are not mixing with other youngsters of their age. I remember Madeline and I got our "corners" rounded off by mixing with our peers. The school playground is a wonderful character-forming place and it sharpens up the mind.'

Francis looked somewhat puzzled, 'So what do you suggest? They can't go to the local school for many reasons and they're too young to travel away on a daily basis; so what are the alternatives?'

Margot admitted she didn't know but was convinced they had to give the matter more thought. Then she had a brainwave: 'Darling, I should have thought of it before! Why don't we talk to Miss Fitzroy? She may be able to help.' So they agreed to consult the tutor the following day.

As soon as lessons finished the next day, Miss Fitzroy joined them for some tea, over which they discussed the children's progress. At first the tutor was naturally a little apprehensive, but soon relaxed when she realised the purpose of the meeting was not so much the current achievement of the youngsters, as the future arrangements for their education. Replying to a question by Francis, Miss Fitzroy then made a startling announcement.

'Mr Vining, I have to tell you I was about to give you notice as I will be leaving your employment in one month's time. Actually I am joining a new preparatory school opening in Farndene after Easter, on 16th April. The school has been set up by a Miss Fenwick who was assistant at the local village school a year or two back but left after Miss Turner, the old headmistress, retired.'

Margot and Francis were at first taken aback but quickly realised as one door had shut another had opened.

'Miss Fitzroy, I have to admit your news is certainly a surprise but the information about the new school is most interesting.' Margot went on, 'Exactly where will the school be situated and what age groups will be covered?'

'Miss Fenwick has obtained a long lease on a large house in

West Street and various alterations are at present being made to enable the property to be used as a school,' Miss Fitzroy looked a little uncertain at that point but endeavoured to answer Margot's second question, 'As far as the age range is concerned, I have to admit we haven't discussed that point in detail but I'd imagine children would start at six and continue until they reached thirteen.'

'That sounds about right from our angle as Juliet, Norman and Bruce would all be eligible. My husband and I will look into the possibility of the three children coming along to the new school after Easter. By the way, what is the name of the school?'

'It will be known as the Farndene Preparatory School.'

'Miss Fitzroy, you have been very helpful and we thank you for giving us this useful information; it's quite likely we'll send our three eldest to the new school, so I'll let you know our decision in a day or two.'

After the tutor left, Margot and Francis had a long discussion and decided the new school would suit them admirably. Margot's only further comment was, 'Well, thank goodness we don't have to worry about schooling again until Juliet and Norman reach their thirteenth birthday in October 1933.' They both gave a sigh of relief.

March entered with a roar and squally rain showers accompanied by fierce winds curtailed activity at the Flying School and there was great relief as the weather calmed in the latter part of the month. Margot looked forward to seeing Fanny who was coming for a couple of weeks over the Easter holiday.

Francis was extremely busy and found running the Dewar Group of Companies, as well as the flying school, exacting. He was away from home frequently and Margot noticed he seemed very tired at times, but he brushed it aside when she mentioned he needed to take things easier.

He was away attending meetings in Southampton when his mother arrived the week before Easter but was expected home the next day. Fanny was delighted to spend time with her grandchildren who all adored her as she spent time playing with them and reading them stories, particularly at bedtimes.

The following morning the family had a late breakfast at half past nine and, as it was a beautiful day, a walk to the airfield was planned as soon as they finished the meal. Francis arrived home and joined them at a quarter to ten and it turned out to be a joyful and happy occasion. Shortly after, the butler entered the dining room to tell Francis he was wanted on the telephone and about ten minutes later he returned looking very upset, 'I have to go back to Southampton straight away as there has been an accident and the police think I may have been involved.'

Margot was alarmed and wanted to know more, 'What sort of accident are the police talking about and in any case why can't they come here to talk to you?'

At this point Francis got very agitated and almost shouted his reply, 'How the hell can I tell you any more at this stage? I'll go to Southampton now and find out what it's all about.'

With that explosive comment he stalked out of the room and minutes they heard his car draw away.

At this point the children sat wide eyed at their father's outburst but Margot, quickly recovering herself, called Nanny to take the children to their playroom.

Once alone, she talked the incident over with Fanny, 'I don't know what's going on but I've never seen Francis so upset before.'

Fanny nodded in agreement and then gave her view: 'Margot, I know my son very well and he has always coped admirably with problems in the past. However, I suspect there is a great deal more to this situation than we know at present. We'll have to wait until he returns to get to the root of the problem!'

Chapter 19

The Southampton police headquarters was contained in a spacious building, housing not only the current force on duty controlling the traffic, patrolling the city to protect the public and of course enforcing the law, but also the many specialist departments that made up the constabulary. Among the latter was the Criminal Investigation Department (CID) overseen by Superintendent Jack Snapper.

In his office the furnishings were comfortable but practical and reflected the character of the man in question; a large chair with a leather seat behind an oak knee-hole desk on which stood a brass inkstand with two steel-nibbed pens and cut-glass pots containing red and black ink. Nearby a large three-tier trolley served as the repository for countless files, all bound with pink tape. The walls were bare except for a large, framed aerial photograph of Southampton City and Docks taken from a Royal Air Force airship, and a circular mahogany 'everlasting calendar', which was adjusted each day by a selection of knobs at one side, and displayed the date clearly: Monday, 1 April.

Jack Snapper sat examining current files when, at precisely a quarter to eleven, an officer knocked and opened the door to announce the arrival of Mr Francis Vining. The Superintendent rose immediately to welcome Francis and, after the formal greeting, got down to business.

'Mr Vining, I cannot emphasise too strongly the importance of this meeting and it's appropriate it takes place in this office. I would like to ask you a few questions and I hope your answers will help our investigation. What can you tell me about your friendship with a woman called Miss Yvonne Makepeace?'

Francis had expected some reference to the lady, as her name had been mentioned during the earlier telephone call to the Manor House and realised he had to give an answer.

'I met Yvonne Makepeace and her twin sister in 1917, during the last war and I knew her parents very well indeed. In fact I was engaged informally to her sister Christine and we would have been married at that time, but as she was underage her father objected. Christine went to visit her mother's family in Regina, Canada and tragically died there in 1919.'

Jack Snapper had made notes while his question was answered and, putting his pen down, asked directly, 'when did you see Yvonne Makepeace last?'

At this stage Francis was put on alert and promptly challenged the superintendent, 'I cannot see what you're driving at and I object to this line of questioning. Unless you can tell me the reason for this interrogation, I regret I will have to leave.'

The superintendent sat back in his chair and surveyed Francis for a moment or so. 'Very well, I'll tell you why I am asking these questions. Miss Makepeace was found dead in her house this morning and it is my business to ascertain exactly how she died.'

The magnitude of this news stunned Francis and for the next few moments he sat in a shocked state, quite unable to grasp fully the terrible import of the message. Before he made any further comment his interrogator spoke in a quiet and compassionate way, 'I'm so sorry, Mr Vining, I can see you are most upset by what I've told you. Perhaps in a moment or two you may feel able to answer my question.'

Francis nodded but his mind was working quickly and he realised there was a hidden meaning in the superintendent's manner. He came to a rapid decision and answered with a firm voice, 'Superintendent, I would like my solicitor to be present before I make any further response to your questions. May I use your telephone to make a call to him?'

'By all means. I have no objection to the solicitor being present.'

While they waited, a constable brought coffee for them both and Francis was glad of the interval to collect his thoughts. The solicitor, Mr Brian Fenwick, arrived shortly and after Jack Snapper had given him a resumé of the business so far, the superintendent returned to the vital question.

Receiving a nod from Brian Fenwick, Francis answered, 'At half past seven this morning, I saw Yvonne at her mother's home, St Augustine House, Forest Side, Southampton.'

'Had you spent the night at her house, Mr Vining?'

'Yes I had.'

The superintendent again looked keenly at Francis as he framed the next question, 'Have you been seeing the lady regularly? By regularly would I be right in assuming you were having an affair with her?'

Francis asked his solicitor if he should answer fully and was told to be perfectly open with the police. 'Yes I was. I hadn't seen Yvonne for about six years until, quite by chance, she met me in Southampton three months ago. We had a meal together and she told me she was lonely as her mother was visiting her family in Canada. We met fairly regularly during the following months but I realised what I was doing was clandestine and I was being totally unfair to my family and, above all, deceiving my wife. Consequently I told her today, it was to be our last meeting.'

'And what was her reaction to that news?'

'She was very upset and cried a lot, but after we had talked for a while she appeared to accept the situation. As I left I remember her final words, "I do understand there can be no future in our seeing each other; you have been a wonderful friend and I'll miss you so much", and with tears in her eyes she went into the house and closed the door.'

The superintendent looked up as he finished his notes, 'Mr Vining, you have been most helpful and I have no further questions to ask you at this time. However I have a request to make, will you let us have your fingerprints? Oh, and I will require your passport for the time being.'

Francis bridled at this and retorted promptly, 'Certainly not! For the life of me I cannot understand why you would want them in any case.'

Jack Snapper smiled as he responded, 'Please yourself, but it may help eliminate you from our enquiries.'

'Oh, I misunderstood, but now you explain I'll be agreeable. By the way you haven't told us how Yvonne died?'

'I cannot tell you at present, but hope to know shortly when the pathologist's report is received.' They shook hands and Francis and his solicitor left.

As they walked towards Brian Fenwick's office, Francis appeared to be in a very distressed condition and, turning to his solicitor, asked what on earth he should do.

'You must not see the police again without me on any account as I suspect there is something quite ulterior about their enquiries. It is imperative you tell your wife everything about this affair as you may need her support. I suggest you go home now and do just that.'

Alone once again, Jack Snapper rang for the duty constable who entered quickly. 'Take that cup and saucer carefully wrapped in a teacloth to the forensic fingerprint department,' said the superintendent, pointing to the coffee cup Francis had used, 'and tell them I want a full set of everything they find on them.' The officer promptly did as he was told and closed the door as he left.

The superintendent took the new file neatly labelled 'Miss Yvonne Makepeace', untied the tapes and started to read the enclosed reports.

The first was by Len Corby, the gardener and handyman at St Augustine House for the past six years who had served with the Royal Marines during the Great War. A tall, muscular and good looking man who was living apart from his wife; he had, he said, been cohabitating with a local woman for some years.

'At seven o'clock this morning I cycled past St Augustine House, Miss Makepeace's home. A green Bentley car stood on the driveway. I spent about an hour on my allotment, returning to St Augustine House at around eight o'clock by which time the Bentley car had gone. I entered the back garden by the side gate and put my cycle in the potting shed, which also serves as my workshop. Miss Makepeace usually leaves any special instructions on the work bench and this morning there was a letter addressed to her mother in Canada, with a note asking me to take it to the post office to catch the first post. There were two half crowns with the letter and her instructions for it to be sent express to Liverpool to catch the next sailing for Canada. I posted the letter as she had asked me and returned to St Augustine House by about ten past nine; it took longer than I wanted as there was a queue in the post office. Mrs Hetty Monks, the cook, was waiting with Meg, the daily help and was concerned as the kitchen door was locked and she couldn't get in. I tried the door but it wouldn't open and it was hard to see into the kitchen as it was a dull day. I got my flashlight from the shed and shined it into the kitchen. I could see someone lying on the floor on the far side. I broke a pane in the door and as I opened it there was a strong smell of gas and I could hear the soft hiss of the gas jets on the cooker. I told Mrs Monks to go to Colonel Shawbury, who lives in the next house, and ask him to call a doctor quickly. With a damp cloth over my face, I went into the kitchen and turned the gas off. I went in a second time and opened all the windows wide. When the doctor came about ten minutes later a lot of the gas had cleared and he examined Miss Makepeace who was lying on the floor; he told me she was dead.'

Jack Snapper sat with both hands behind his head, his customary position when turning over evidence in his mind, and he focused on the gas cooker. Unfortunately Corby had turned the gas taps off thereby erasing any previous fingerprints. But, he thought, 'possibly the original prints were Corby's, what did that suggest?' The superintendent needed more evidence so he closed the file and. taking his hat and coat. left the police building for another look at the Makepeace house and outbuildings.

Arriving back at the Manor House at one o' clock, Francis went straight to his study and rang for the butler who came within minutes.

'Bertie, see if you can find my wife and ask her to come here as soon as possible.'

Minutes later as Margot entered he went to her and took her in his arms; tears were running down his face as he kissed her. Margot sensed he was in some sort of trouble and asked, 'Francis, whatever is the matter? You must tell me otherwise how can I help you?'

He sat down with his hands in his lap and, facing his wife, told her everything that had taken place at the police headquarters. 'Margot, I have deceived you and my family. I have had an adulterous relationship with Yvonne Makepeace, who is now dead, and I believe the police superintendent thinks I murdered her, which is not true.' At this point he put his head in his hands and wept.

Margot felt intensely cold with the impact of her husband's revelation and sat looking at him in disbelief, trying desperately to collect her thoughts. One question immediately came to her mind and she asked Francis, 'Would you have told me about this woman if the police hadn't forced the issue following her death?'

He looked straight at her and answered without hesitation, 'This morning I told Yvonne we would not meet again and explained I had realised I had cheated my family and deceived you. She was very upset at first but later agreed it was the best course for me to take. But to answer your question clearly, yes, I intended to tell you everything after breakfast when we were alone. So you wouldn't have any doubt that I had seen Yvonne for the last time today, I wrote a short letter to you this morning and left it for the gardener to post; it will arrive with tomorrow's delivery.'

Francis, a pitiful figure, then became more and more distressed and Margot, realising she had to take some action, went round the desk and put her arms round him, trying to comfort him. The totally unexpected revelation had shocked her and she was trying desperately to focus her mind. Setting aside her feeling of revulsion at his infidelity, her legal training made her examine the possible charge of murder he may be facing.

'Francis, if I'm to help, you must tell me the time you left

Miss Makepeace this morning and exactly what happened and whether you wrote to her during the past three months.'

He gave her all the information she wanted and confirmed he hadn't ever written letters or left her notes.

'Your mother said she would take the children for a walk to the airfield this afternoon but I want you to take them instead, Francis. It will be good for you at this moment and the children will be delighted. Meanwhile, I want to talk to Mama as she has to know what has happened and I'm sure she will give us good advice.'

Jack Snapper left his car a short distance from St Augustine House, taking in the atmosphere of the quiet upper class residential area as he walked to the house. The road was lined with tall Plane trees and well-kept grass borders separated the pavements from the carriageway. Detached residencies, the homes of the well heeled, were screened from the road by tall neatly trimmed holly hedges, and it was only possible to see the houses through their drive entrances. With regular lamp posts at intervals, the gas lights would keep the whole area well illuminated at night.

Reaching his destination, he was saluted by the policeman on duty at the front door, who accompanied the superintendent to the rear of the house.

'Have you anything to report constable?'

'Well, no, sir. I only came on duty after I'd had me dinner at one o'clock when I took over from constable Blagdon and it's been as quiet as a miser's wedding ever since.'

They went to the rear and entered the kitchen door, aware the slight aroma of gas lingered in the room although the windows were still open. The corpse had been removed to the police mortuary and there was a chalk outline of the exact position of the body on the floor.

'It's a sad business sir. Can't understand what makes people end up like this.'

Jack Snapper nodded but his eye had noticed something that had not been there when he first examined the room that morning.

Earlier he had found the communicating door from the kitchen to the rest of the house locked but with no key in the lock. Now the key was in place on the kitchen side; clearly someone had replaced it.

On the kitchen dresser ledge were a number of articles including a round ebony ruler about eighteen inches in length, the type used by bank ledger keepers when ruling accounts off. Again he was sure that item had not previously been there. Taking a teacloth, he carefully wrapped the ruler, tying the ends with some string he found in a drawer.

Turning to the duty constable he gave explicit instructions, 'The windows must be closed and the back door locked and you are to patrol round the house regularly until a second officer joins you, when he will watch the rear of the property. I want this place guarded twenty-four hours a day.'

The constable saluted as he replied, 'Very good Sir.'

En route to the police headquarters Jack stopped at the local post office and asked the post mistress about the queue earlier that morning.

Her reply was emphatic: 'I don't remember a queue, in fact it was a quiet time up till about ten thirty. I do recall Mr Corby coming in at a quarter past eight with a letter to Canada and a local letter. He was only in here for about five minutes and said he had an urgent call to make.'

Jack Snapper returned to his office where the pathologist's report awaited him and he immediately picked it up and scanned the contents. He read the cause of death was gas poisoning and there were bruises to the body and head possibly caused by a fall. The pathologist stated Miss Makepeace was about four months' pregnant at the time of death.

'Well, well!' Jack thought, 'Who's been sleeping in her bed besides Mr Vining?'

Shortly afterwards, the forensic officer arrived, with some interesting news: 'I got an excellent set of prints from the cup and saucer, which matched those on the round ruler, but there are other prints on the ruler.'

Jack Snapper thanked his assistant and knew he needed to pull in and question Mr Len Corby. Detective Inspector Freddy Gaskin, assistant to the Superintendent, looked in to report and told his boss, 'We have not been able to notify Mrs Makepeace of her daughter's death so far. A cable was sent to the Royal Canadian Mounted Police in Regina and they replied saying Mrs Makepeace was away in the north of Saskatchewan on a boating and fishing holiday and would not be back for another week. They promised to keep us informed.'

'That's a bit unfortunate, Freddy, but there is nothing more we can do at present. Now, I want you to pull in Mr Corby and ask him if he returned the key to the lock of the door leading from the kitchen to the rest of the house. I'd also like a set of his prints; tell him we need them as a routine so we can eliminate him from our enquiries. Take the Makepeace file for reference and also ask him what he knows about this ebony ruler.' He handed over the file and a cellophane bag containing the ruler and the inspector left.

Jack Snapper felt, deep down, that Yvonne Makepeace's death was suspicious and although suicide could not be ruled out, there was a number of points that suggested foul play. His two suspects, Francis Vining and Len Corby, could both have motives and the Superintendent intended to delve until he resolved the case.

At a quarter past five Jack Snapper had almost finished checking through several other outstanding cases, when Freddy Gaskin returned looking very pleased. He produced sheet of paper which had clearly been crumpled up and passed it across the desk to his boss.

'Just look at that, Jack, and tell me what effect it might have had on the recipient?'

Jack smoothed the sheet and read,

"Dear Len, Please take the letter to the post office to catch the early post and ask them to send it express to Liverpool to catch the next ship for Canada. The five shillings should more than cover the postage so you can keep the change. As I shall be leaving here for good I will not require your services after today. Enclosed in the attached envelope is a full month's money. If you have any other expense I have overlooked please see my mother when she returns from Canada. You have been great for me and have looked after me while my mother was away and I don't know what I could have done without you. Yvonne.'

Jack sat for a moment contemplating the neat writing before looking up at his assistant, 'Well Freddy, our Mr Corby has been economical with his information and this note certainly puts a new complexion on the case. By the way, where did you find this?'

'It was under the bench in the potting shed. Now you will also be interested to know his prints were found on the ebony ruler and the gas taps on the cooker. He also told me he replaced the key in the kitchen door that leads into the house; he said Miss Makepeace asked him to straighten it as it had become bent. And I found this hanging on a nail in a small out of the way recess in the shed; it fits the back door perfectly!' He placed the key on the desk.

'Freddy, that's absolutely first class. I think we must bring Corby in for questioning without delay. It looks as though we have our man!'

Chapter 20

As soon as Francis left to walk to the airfield with the children, Margot and Fanny went into the drawing room and Fanny, aware her daughter-in-law was suffering considerable stress, sat prepared to listen. As Margot unburdened herself, relating all that had happened that day, she became more and more distressed until at last she broke down completely and wept in her mother-in-law's arms. For a short while nothing was said until Fanny broke the silence.

'Margot my dear, this is indeed terrible news and it will require a great deal of thought and patience to find a satisfactory solution.'

They sat talking for more than an hour, during which Margot again broke down. After a time she became less distressed and then, more at ease, she made a suggestion, 'I am fully aware I have ample grounds for divorce but I can't take that road for the sake of the children; what do you think Mama?'

'You're a sensible woman, Margot, and that decision took a lot of making. I remember when Norman died, Francis was left without a father during his younger years, but that was a situation over which I had no control. Your decision is common sense and if you can make a suitable arrangement with Francis, the children will be brought up by both of you.' Fanny paused, 'Now I feel we should try to examine why Francis became involved with Yvonne Makepeace. May I ask you a very personal question? Have you and Francis enjoyed a normal healthy married life? In other words have you been sharing the same bed?'

Margot sat, looking at her hands for a moment or so before replying. 'Well, to be truthful we haven't had what you'd call a normal sex life since the birth of Clara and Constance. We didn't want to increase our family and Francis decided it would be best if we had separate bedrooms; with hindsight, perhaps, that course was foolish.'

Fanny's response was practical, 'I ought to tell you, in no way do I condone what my son has done but in 1916, I recall Yvonne was very fond of Francis and, I suspect, was in love with him. However, Francis fell for her sister, Christine, who was a possessive little thing and completely captivated my son. So Yvonne would have been delighted when she met him again and possibly one thing led to another ending with the present calamity. But I have to tell you, Francis would never harm anyone so you can discount the question of murder!'

'Mama, I too know in my heart of hearts that Francis is not capable of wilfully killing someone, so we must discount such a notion. But it still leaves the ghastly problem unsolved.'

For a moment they sat quietly until Fanny spoke, 'At home we always had an aid in situations like this. Why don't we have a nice cup of tea?'

For the first time that afternoon Margot smiled: 'I'll ring for Bertie right away.'

Tea arrived shortly as they chatted about the children and as soon as the butler had departed, Fanny returned to the subject of Francis, 'Margot, I have turned the situation over and over and my reasoning brings me back each time to the nub of the business. It is of course the question of forgiveness and I mention this as I feel sure you have the capacity to ride above the personal feeling of humiliation and the anguish you have suffered; what do you say?'

'You're quite right. My initial feelings of anger and frustration are waning, thank God. I know I still love Francis and I'm aware he has been utterly foolish, a weakness he will probably never again submit to. Equally, I have always tried to live up to the Christian principles I have been taught. Deep down in my mind I understand I must forgive and I appreciate in so doing both our minds can be healed.' Fanny was about to interrupt but Margot stopped her, 'Please let me finish. Mama, I want you to know how grateful I am for the guidance you've given me and I have to tell you I'd have found great difficulty talking to my own mother about this awful business. Thank you again for being so supportive.'

'Margot, I have great admiration for what you are going to do and I also know you have been a tower of strength as Francis's wife.' She put her arms round Margot and kissed her, and with a smile remarked, 'It is surprising what a cup of tea will do! So why don't we have another one?'

Returning from their walk, Francis and the children were quite tired but perked up when it was decided to have tea together with Margot and Fanny. The children were overjoyed when they learned Grandma would read them a story at bedtime and Fanny suggested Francis and Margot have a little drive to enjoy the late afternoon sun.

Shortly after, he brought the Bentley to the front of the house and Margot, suitably wrapped up, got in. A very subdued Francis asked, 'Darling, where do you want to go?'

'Oh, let's go somewhere quiet. What about Butser Hill on the Downs?'

He nodded as they took off and little was said until they reached their destination, where he parked the car, looking at the wonderful view south across the Downs.

'I thought this would be a good place to come to; it's a quiet place for us to talk in an effort to sort out our problems.'

Margot spoke for around twenty minutes, outlining all that had been discussed with Fanny that afternoon, finishing on what Fanny had called the nub of the business: 'Your mother put a finger on the question of forgiveness and I agree with her. My dearest Francis, I know you have been extremely foolish but aren't we all at some time in our lives? For our children's sake and for us to heal our minds, I am ready to forgive and forget. Let us make a fresh start now and put all that has happened behind us.'

Francis sat quietly, but now turned to face her, with tears in his eyes and speaking with great emotion, 'Margot, my darling, you are the most wonderful woman any man would wish for and I have to say, listening to you I can hardly believe my ears. I bitterly regret all that has happened and I know what a fool I've been but your generosity is overwhelming and has given me new hope. I gladly accept every word you have spoken.' He took her in his arms and they kissed for some minutes until Margot suddenly became aware the evening light was fading. Looking up she saw Venus, the first bright star shining in the east, 'Look darling, our guiding star. It must surely be a good omen.'

With Easter almost upon them, Janine, now firmly established as Mrs Kirkwood, looked forward to having all her family around for the holiday. Mollie, now nineteen, a young lady with striking looks, had joined her mother at the Madame Baume dressmaking business when she left school and had made excellent progress. Tom, fifteen, was training as a draughtsman in the offices at the Farndene Flying School, helped by Francis Vining, who had arranged accommodation for him with Alec and Beatty Briggs in the village. Rupert, seventeen, was in the third year of his apprenticeship and with an outstanding record had been given a week's leave.

Their stepfather, Philip Kirkwood was in his element getting to know them all and greatly enjoyed their company. On Easter Monday the whole family walked to the airfield, joining the huge crowd to watch a flying display put on by the instructors and some of their star pupils. Other entertainments included a merry-go-round with galloping horses, various side shows and a coconut shy.

Another great attraction was a hog roast on a giant spit where two chefs dispensed large, mouth-watering sandwiches of freshly roast pork.

Back home in the evening Philip told the family all about the trip he and Janine were planning to take after Easter: 'We go to Ostend by ferry and then by train through Belgium to a village called Ruillemont, not a great distance from the German border, where during the Great War your father was in action. At the entrance to the British War Cemetery my regiment has commissioned a memorial to commemorate all those who lost their lives; your father's name will be on one of the plaques. Your mother and I are attending the dedication ceremony at the end of next week at the invitation of the regiment.'

During the family supper they talked a lot about their late father, Charlie Tupper, and Janine remarked, rather wistfully, 'I'm sure your father would have been very proud of you all, he was a great man and I'm desperately sorry he is not with us today.' She stopped to wipe away a tear or two and Rupert sitting next to her, put his arm round her shoulders to comfort her, 'I understand mother. Now we must all look to the future but also keep his memory bright in our minds; he was a good man and we must never forget that.'

The conversation then moved to other subjects and Philip wanted to know what ambitions the two boys had.

Rupert was the first to answer, 'I hope to qualify as an engineer to design and develop aero engines as I feel the aviation industry will develop rapidly during the next decade.'

Philip nodded and put the same question to Tom who replied eagerly, 'Although I have had only one year's training, I'm really enjoying the jobs I've been allocated. I suppose my ultimate target is to become a design draughtsman for aircraft and as Rupert has just said the changes that will come about in the next year or two will be revolutionary.' Philip told them he was impressed and hoped they would both reach their goal adding, with a smile, 'You two could very well link up in the future as plane makers with a difference!'

He then talked to Mollie to ask what her hopes for the future were and was surprised when she replied, 'I have so many ambitions I hardly know where to start. First of all I love my work and the personal nature of the contact I have with our customers,' and here she had a little giggle. 'Some extra large ladies always ask if their clothes can be made so they will look slimmer, while other very, very slim women need just the opposite, wanting to appear more "robust"! Second I would like to travel to Europe, particularly to see parts of our family in Brittany. And third, to go to America and Canada one day as they seem exciting places with so much to see and do.'

Philip was impressed with her response but put a further question: 'Have you any inclination to settle down? By that I mean get married and have a family.'

Mollie was a matter of fact young woman and had no illusions about married life, having seen her mother struggle to bring up a family with little money for many years and her retort was clear and unequivocal, 'I have decided to remain single for the foreseeable future to achieve some of the things I've mentioned but perhaps later on I'll wed if the right man comes along; I'm absolutely in no hurry whatever!'

After the excitement of having the family home for Easter, Janine and Philip Kirkwood left Exeter in the last week of April to start their travels to Belgium. After a tedious train journey to Dover they embarked on the ferry to enjoy a late luncheon during a calm crossing, arriving at Ostend at half past five, where Philip had booked a local hotel for the night.

The next morning, en route for Ruillemont, they joined the train that passed through the wide open spaces of Flanders, with views across what had been the battlefields of the last war.

Philip was quite moved and remarked to his wife, 'It all seems so peaceful now with the same masses of blood red poppies; these were the killing fields alright, where I lost so many good friends but now there is not a trace visible and only memories to haunt us.'

Janine took his hand and caressed it as she spoke, 'I understand, Philip. I think we're both in the same boat with the shadows of loved ones in our mind but now, thank God, we have each other.'

He smiled as he kissed her and confirmed all she had said, 'Janine, you have brought me great happiness and I love you very much. But it's either that or the travelling making me hungry,' and with a little laugh, 'Jove, I could do with my luncheon now!' Luckily the first class dining car attendant arrived as they were enjoying the joke.

Their accommodation at the King Albert hotel in Ruillemont was comfortable if not elaborate and the morning of 5th May dawned fine and clear. Several of Philip's regimental colleagues with their wives were staying at the hotel and Janine enjoyed meeting them.

The dedication ceremony was scheduled for eleven o'clock and all invited guests were seated in a special enclosure facing the memorial. A large crowd had been assembling during the morning and by the appointed hour numbered several hundred. Janine sat taking in all around her, the masses of flags flanking the whole arena, the soldiers in their dress uniform standing guard each side of the dais from which the unveiling would take place, and the regimental band playing a series of patriotic tunes, many of which had been favourites during the war. As the time moved towards eleven o'clock the special visitors arrived, among them British ministers including Baldwin and Churchill, Belgium government officials, senior military officers from France, Belgium and England as well as dignitaries from the Church of England and the Roman Catholics.

As eleven struck at the local church, field guns situated a distance away fired a salute and the ceremony started. A short service followed, during which Mr Baldwin, the Prime Minister, unveiled the memorial and the British Army Chaplain said prayers of dedication. The formal part of the proceedings was now over and the guests filed past the white marble edifice.

Janine and Philip reached the panel where those who had died but had no known grave were recorded. Here she saw her late husband's name inscribed in gun metal lettering, SGT. C.W. TUPPER and the whole affair was suddenly like a dream as her mind coursed back to the happy days she and Charlie had had together. The effect of seeing his name made her head reel and, but for Philip's timely support, she would have fallen. With the help of colleagues Janine was soon seated and an observant soldier brought a glass of water. After resting, Janine was well enough to join the other invited guests for a reception in an enormous marquee.

Philip and Janine planned to stay in Ruillemont for two or three days to make one or two excursions to places of interest in the area but on the following morning decided to revisit the memorial in quieter conditions. They joined a few officers with their wives taking photographs of various panels and were soon in conversation with them.

Looking away towards the cemetery Janine suddenly gripped Philip's arm and gasped as she tried to speak and with difficulty uttered, 'It's Charlie! I'm sure it's Charlie!' Philip observed two men tidying the gardens and neatening the grass round the headstones. One was a short man about thirty with a swarthy complexion and dark hair, while the other was tall and heavily built with grey hair and a large beard and moustache. By now Janine recovered a little and insisted they should go across and speak to them.

Both men stood up and smiled as Janine and Philip reached them. Janine stood gazing at the tall man for moments before speaking, 'Charlie, don't you know me? I'm you're wife. I'm Janine from Exeter!'

There was not the slightest spark of recognition on the part of the listener, who shrugged his shoulders and muttered something to his colleague. Philip then suggested his wife speak in French, which Janine did without avail. The younger of the two intervened in very broken English, 'Casper, him speak Flemish, him not speak Enklish.'

Philip took his wife gently by the arm and led her away a short distance before speaking.

'My dearest Janine, I'm so sorry but the likeness to your late husband is coincidental. Let us go back to the hotel and have a rest and a little refreshment.' She was clearly upset and glad to accept his advice. As they walked away, the two gardeners stood watching for some moments until the tall man turned to his colleague and shrugged his shoulders.

Settled back in the hotel, Janine felt more relaxed and apologised to her husband, 'Philip, I so sorry to have given you all this worry, but the likeness of that gardener to Charlie was uncanny. He had similar features, dark brown eyes and a slightly abrupt way of speaking with his head on one side. But there it ends I suppose as that man is Flemish, his name is Casper and he hadn't a clue who I was.'

Philip agreed,'My dear Janine, what you've said is true but I believe when you read Charlie's name on the memorial, memories of your time together must have come flooding back and you saw the gardener with your mind conditioned and imagined he was your late husband.'

Janine smiled, 'That's exactly the case, my sweet, and you have put it very succinctly. Now it's nearly lunch time so why don't we have an early meal and go sightseeing this afternoon?'

'Splendid.' Philip then continued enthusiastically, 'I was reading an advertisement on the hall noticeboard before breakfast this morning and it was for an outing by charabanc to a small Flemish town of Geraarsbergen, where an International Hooghuysfestival for all kinds of street organs is being held. It is very popular and the notice said more than 50 organs will be in position along the main street. It will be interesting to see them all but what the noise is like is anyone's guess! So, my love, what do you say?'

Janine nodded, 'It sounds fun, darling! Yes, let's go after lunch.' Philip stood up and offered his arm, 'You have the brightest of notions darling and I do believe this morning's activity has made me feel hungry again.' Chatting happily, they wandered through to the dining room.

Chapter 21

At the Manor House the weeks following Easter passed quickly and the children were soon back in the school routine. Margot heaved a sigh of relief, as the family pressures had been immense. Near the end of April Jack Snapper called and talked for about an hour, indicating the police had suspicions about the gardener and consequently he didn't think it would be necessary to interview Francis again. Although a little easier with that news, Francis still felt apprehensive, reasoning that if the gardener were charged with murder, likely or not, he would have to give evidence, during which some unpalatable facts would become public knowledge. As soon as the Superintendent had left, Francis told Margot the gist of the police interview and was pleased when his wife gave her opinion, 'Darling, from all you have told me, I imagine the police have got nowhere with their enquiries and it's highly likely Yvonne took her own life. Her reasons may never be known and it's best left like that. So stop worrying. We need to get on with our life with the whole episode behind us.'

Francis felt reassured, 'I'll take your advice, my dearest, which brings me to a pressing problem. I have to go to Dumbarton to discuss the reorganisation of the foundry and our new aircraft factory and it will take best part of a week. Will you come with me? You know a number of the senior staff and it will give you a break away from here.'

Margot was pleased he'd asked her and replied immediately, 'It was kind and thoughtful of you to ask me, and my reply is yes. I'll have to arrange cover for the children but that is no problem providing you let me have a few days warning.'

Francis smiled and then told her the special news, 'I've kept the best bit till last! We're flying up to Scotland in the new plane with an enclosed cabin, so the days of freezing open cockpits are over!'

She was clearly delighted and put her arms round Francis to give him a long kiss. 'That's the best news I've heard for a long time and I insist on sharing the flying with you; what a wonderful thought, no more tedious train journeys thank goodness!'

The preparations for the Scottish trip soon got under way and Francis had the plane fitted with extra fuel tanks to increase the range as he had calculated some 'legs' of the journey were too much for the smaller tanks.

The trip was planned for the end of May and Francis contacted a number of private flying clubs en route to check for emergency landing and fuel supplies if the need arose. His flight plan initially was to Bobbington, a small airfield to the west of Birmingham, leaving Farndene at eight thirty on the morning of 29th May and arriving there at about ten thirty. After a rest he intended taking off again at midday, flying to Kendal and reckoning to be there between two thirty and three o'clock.

That airfield was just outside the town where an hotel was booked for overnight accommodation. On 30th May the last leg of the journey was to Dumbarton, where a car would meet them at the small local airfield.

The plans looked pretty good, although the weather was very misty on the first day, delaying their departure for nearly two hours. Margot enjoyed the flying and Francis was surprised at how well she handled the plane. As they approached Kinver Ridge, Francis took over controls in preparation for the landing at Bobbington airfield, now only minutes away to the south of Wolverhampton.

As the field had a number of dips in it the landing was bumpy but, with his experience, Francis made a three point touchdown and shortly after he taxied to the flying control building – an ex-army barrack hut – where a welcoming group awaited their arrival.

As the flying club manager and his assistants greeted them, a large green car arrived and, with a flourish, the driver hailed Francis: 'It's great to see you again, Francis, you old bounder.' He turned to Margot: 'Captain Prendergast at you service Mrs

Vining.' He took Margot's hand and with an exaggerated bow, kissed it twice. They all enjoyed the fun as Francis explained that he and the Hon. Lancelot Prendergast had served in the same Royal Flying Corps squadron in France.

All the carefully prepared plans Francis had put together were suddenly blown apart by Lancelot Prendergast.

'Francis, I insist your good wife and you stay over tonight with us here,' and, turning to Margot, 'You'll enjoy meeting Wendy, my better half – she's great fun! So into the Bentley with you and we'll get going.' Francis realised it was no good arguing so they were soon driving along the lanes to the family seat.

Passing through two enormous brick pillars, each surmounted by a statue of a stag, they got their first glimpse of Weighton Hall, a beautifully proportioned sixteenth-century residence. As the car stopped at the main entrance, Lancelot sounded several blasts on the car's klaxon, which brought the butler and two assistants hurrying from the house.

Inside, they were taken into a large drawing room to meet Wendy, an attractive and charming young woman who imme-diately made her visitors feel at home, 'You both must feel tired and hungry so I suggest we settle you into your room and meanwhile I'll arrange something light to eat to keep you going until dinner tonight.'

The bedroom with light oak panelling looked onto the rear gardens and the distant wooded hills. The ceiling had square floral painted panels in delicate pastel shades, giving the room a light and airy appearance.

Margot flopped onto the four poster bed laughing, 'Well, here's a turn up for the book! Something we certainly never contemplated this morning. But it's great fun all the same and I think we'll enjoy it.' Francis agreed, adding, 'To be honest, darling, I'm starving so we'd better not be too long.'

After a quick freshening up, they rejoined Wendy and Lancelot.

Later that evening dinner was served at seven o'clock and the other guests were Wendy's younger sister Alice Wesmacott, who had been engaged to a pilot on Lancelot's squadron, tragically killed in 1918, and her cousin, Crispin Broyle, who had served as a submarine commander in the Royal Navy. With lively conversation the meal passed quickly, during which Margot became aware Lancelot was observing her on several occasions when she glanced in his direction.

She gained the impression from his conversation he might be a womaniser, particularly as he referred airily to the many conquests in his younger days; she also noted he imbibed freely during the meal.

The ladies left the men to smoke, going to the drawing room where they were joined about half an hour later by Francis, Crispin and Lancelot for coffee. At this point their host suggested they may like a tour of the house, mentioning its antiquity and history.

Passing through several corridors they arrived at a long gallery room on the first floor where Lancelot announced, 'This is known as the King's Room, as it was here Charles I was imprisoned in 1645.'

The room was large, heavily oak panelled throughout with a beamed ceiling. One end was dominated by a large stone fireplace, above which the family coat of arms was conspicuous. Heavy oak doors were situated each end of the room while two bay windows looked down to the terrace running along the front of the house.

Lancelot continued, 'My forebear, Dominic, was a staunch Royalist and, but for the support of his staff who swore he supported the Parliamentary cause, would have ended in prison. From our family records we know this house and the local area were taken over by Colonel Edmund Hatfield, one of Cromwell's associates, commanding a detachment of Parliamentary cavalry in preparation for a large battle, possibly at Naseby. Charles, in disguise, was captured with two of his aides, presumably making his way to Oxford where he had set up temporary headquarters. Hatfield and his lieutenants interrogated the King who gave little information. Charles I was held in this room and after a meal he and his two officers were given the comfort of a straw palliasse for the night. Both doors were locked and sentries posted outside, so the King would be under constant guard. But in the early hours, at around two o'clock, all three prisoners escaped completely and I'll show you how it was accomplished.'

Lancelot walked to the fireplace and touching a spring in the oak panelling to one side, caused a large door to swing open revealing an opening. With hand torches they entered the cavity and descended a spiral stone stairway, passing a 'Priest Hole' on the way. The stairs wound round the massive chimney, all the way to the ground floor. Here another spring released a door into a store room with an outer door next to the kitchens.

'All these arrangements were made by Dominic Prendergast who supplied the King and his aides with cloaks, Parliamentary steel helmets and three horses tethered a little distance away. And so the escape was complete and I'm jolly proud to think my family gave such support! The sad part of the whole business occurred the next morning when the escape was discovered. The sentries were tried summarily, found guilty of neglect of duty and taken out and shot!'

They made their way back up to the King's Room where Lancelot unlocked an ancient desk to show the personal letter written by Charles I to Dominic Prendergast, thanking him for his loyal help in the escape. Wendy said she always felt humbled to read the letter, realising how much danger Dominic had put himself in for his King. Lancelot then told them that wasn't all he had to show them and, stooping, he unlocked the lower part of the desk, withdrawing from the cupboard a highly decorated chamber pot which he held aloft exclaiming with a grin on his face, 'This is the genuine "Po" used by the King! But perhaps you'd like to look inside?' They crowded round and looking into the chamber pot saw the bold lettering written on the bottom,

'Some want to go before their bed at night.
Relief much needed ere they say their prayers.
This vessel small though often out of sight
Gives comfort to those taken unawares.'

156

Roars of laughter followed and after locking the 'po' away, Lancelot invited them all to have a nightcap in the drawing room. Here he continued the theme of the Civil War, explaining, 'In the morning I'll take you to St Botolph's, our local church, where you will see how Hatfield's soldiers ill-treated the place. They stabled horses in the Lady Chapel where the mounts bit chunks out of the surrounding oak screen; their farrier operated in the building and the scorch marks from his fire on the stone flags are still visible to this day. They destroyed all statues and smashed the altar table. The priest went into hiding but was reinstated after the war was over. All the silver communion plate from St Botolph's was hidden in the priest hole on our secret stairway during the Civil War.'

Margot asked why the secret stairway had been built in the first place and her host explained the need arose during a period of religious persecution and had concealed many a priest in danger of his life. I believe our priest hole was the work of Nicholas Owen, a carpenter and builder who built many such hides around the country. He supported the Catholics during the years of persecution and did a splendid job in our house. If you didn't notice, the priest hole on our stairway is a small room with no windows so oil lamps or candles would not show outside at night but it is well ventilated.'

Lancelot promised them a good day on the morrow and insisted on kissing and hugging the ladies when saying goodnight.

Once in their bedroom Margot told Francis she had no intention of staying another day at Weighton Hall with Lancelot and said they must leave first thing in the morning.

'Why so much hurry, Margot? We've had a capital time today.' Francis was obviously puzzled until his wife spoke.

'My darling, you may not have noticed but your friend Lancelot is a lecher! When we went down the secret staircase he insisted on putting his right arm round me, explaining there wasn't a handrail. All the way down he was squeezing and fondling my right breast, murmuring how attractive I must look in bed! As we returned to the King's Room up the stairs he repeated the groping.

During dinner he ogled me with a dirty smirk on his face. So now you know why I intend to leave tomorrow morning.'

Francis was thoughtful, 'My dearest, I'm so sorry and agree Lancelot's conduct was pretty disgusting. I'll telephone through to Dumbarton in the morning and say it's imperative we leave early as there are complications there.' Margot thanked him adding, 'The sooner we are in bed the quicker tomorrow will be here. Unless you are too wide awake to think about sleep?'

Francis grinned, 'Well, well. I've never made love in a four poster before but I'm quite prepared to try.'

Unfortunately the very old bed frame creaked unmercifully at every move.

The following morning Francis telephoned Dumbarton as promised and as soon as an early breakfast had been taken, he and Margot took leave of their hostess.

Wendy apologised when Lancelot failed to appear to see his guests off, explaining he wasn't feeling too well and decided to stay in bed. Margot was quite relieved and well aware the 'illness' was a simple hangover as the result of too much drink the night before.

She and her husband were airborne within the hour and chatted as they flew north. Margot told her husband about the previous evening when the ladies retired to the drawing room after dinner. 'Wendy spoke quite frankly to her sister Alice and me about the way Lancelot behaves, saying from time to time he goes away, ostensibly on business but she knows he sees a former secretary regularly. Naturally the poor girl is very unhappy.'

Francis said he wasn't the least surprised as Lancelot was always 'womanising' when they were in France and had the nick name 'Squadron Ram' among his fellow officers, 'It's unlikely we'll be going back to stay at his place again and there are other places we can refuel in the Birmingham area on our return journey.'

Chapter 22

The flight north went well and after two refuelling stops, Francis touched down at the Dumbarton airfield early that evening to be met by his uncle's car. A short drive away they reached Uncle Hamish Dewar's house at Balloch and were welcomed by the old man, still erect in his clan kilt, although in his late eighties.

He particularly liked Margot and told Francis, 'You couldn't have done better than marry a Scots lassie. It's really great to see you and to have a few days to talk about so many things.' He enquired kindly after Fanny and hoped she would favour him with a visit ere long, 'I don't go so far nowadays particularly on those dreadful trains!'

The next few days were to prove exacting in more ways than one, as it was clear the foundry had been working at reduced capacity due to the falling away of government orders as the disarmament lobby became more strident. However, the aero engine factory had a good order book and, apart from designing their own engines, had contracts to produce for several other companies. Uncle Hamish explained another aspect which needed careful handling: 'At the foundry the Unions are pushing the men to join and I estimate they will cause trouble in due course. They are putting rumours around that about half the staff will get the push shortly and threaten if there are any redundancies they'll call the whole working force out on strike. Two of the foremen keep me quietly informed, and forewarned is forearmed in any business!'

Margot's suggestion was as simple as it was practical: 'It is clear the foundry is over-staffed at present and will run at a loss unless drastic action is taken. Why not expand the aero engine production, offering any redundant foundry men employment and training in the aircraft factory? Such a move will keep the union activity to a minimum and stop them accusing you of just sacking the men without hope of re-employment.'

They agreed Margot's plan was worth examining in detail so set about the task over the next two days, producing all the facts and figures necessary.

Finally, it was decided to call a mass meeting of all the staff at the foundry and the next afternoon Francis and Margot faced some 150 men on the shop floor. Francis did his best to explain the possible outcome of the lack of orders and quoted figures but it was clear the union had already poisoned the minds of a lot of their members and there were angry shouts of abuse from various parts of the gathering.

At this point Margot suggested she might speak to the men. As soon as she stepped up on the dais there were hoots and wolf whistles amid laughter from many.

With complete confidence she raised her hands for quiet and a hush fell on the gathering.

In her broadest Scottish she spoke clearly with a smile on her face, 'I see you recognise a Scottish lassie when you see one and no doubt many of you are married or courting one of us; am I right?' There were shouts of 'aye' from many. 'Well what I have to say to you is this. Why not give the plans a chance? It will mean employment for you all and a better life for your families and your loved ones. Go home and talk about it with your womenfolk and we'll meet again tomorrow afternoon to hear your verdict. We must keep the foundry going as alternatively there could be considerable unemployment and suffering for many. Thank you for listening so patiently.'

The meeting broke up and after a short discussion with the foundry manager, Bertram McBride, Margot and Francis made their way to their car at the rear of the foundry. Suddenly they were accosted by a man running after them.

'Excuse me, Major, but I just had to speak to you and your wife before you left! Do you remember me?'

Francis recognised the face but couldn't put a name to it. Luckily Margot's memory was excellent as she recalled the court action way back in 1919 in St Andrews, 'You're Bob Crantock and my husband arranged for you and your family to come to Dumbarton all those years ago. How are you getting along?'

They all shook hands and Bob explained how well he and his family had settled down, adding, 'Thanks to you, Major. But could I ask a favour for a transfer to the aero engine factory? I haven't forgotten my old Flying Corps skills.' Francis assured him a transfer could be arranged and promised to speak to Mr McBride, the foundry manager.

At dinner that night Uncle Hamish wanted to know how the mass meeting had progressed and was interested in Margot's involvement, 'You're a shrewd lassie Margot and it was a clever move to refer the workers to their womenfolk. The wives will not be swayed by a lot of blather from the union officials and will point out it's the husbands' duty to feed and clothe their families. I'll be very surprised if the men don't accept the offer on the table.'

The old man was proved right when the next day the men accepted the offer with a huge majority. One change Francis introduced was to invite those interested in a transfer to the aero engine works to submit their names to the foundry manager as it was felt many would welcome a change.

By the end of the following week all plans had been finalised and the transition of staff between foundry and aero engine factory started, so it was time for Francis and Margot to return to Farndene.

Fond farewells were said to Uncle Hamish and, on a bright clear morning, the plane roared across the Dumbarton airfield and was soon airborne.

Turning due south on the homeward flight, Francis said he felt more frequent refuelling stops would be a precaution in case they ran into poor weather. 'What we need is a national system of weather forecasts which will help all shipping and aircraft. I'll write to the Prime Minister as soon as we get home.'

With a night stop at a small hotel outside Kendal, the flight home was completed as they touched down at Farndene late afternoon on 10th June, where they were received with a rapturous welcome by the children, delighted to have their mother and father home again and, of course, with the presents sent by Uncle Hamish. As they gathered in the drawing room Margot suggested they all had early supper together so she and Francis could hear the children's news.

In Bristol, life for Fanny had been very active since Easter with her many business commitments and social activities. At the beginning of June she received an invitation to a charitable ball, to be held at the prestigious Bristol Imperial Hotel, in aid of the dependants of those killed in the First World War and organised by the Royal Engineers Association of which many of the local retired sappers were members. Colonel Robert Oulton was an active promoter of the event and he and his wife Edith arranged a party, including Fanny and friends.

The evening was spectacular indeed with some three hundred guests, ladies attired and bejewelled in a variety of wonderful gowns and dresses, offset by their escorts in full evening dress and Naval, Army and Air Force officers in formal mess uniform with a large proportion of Orders and medals adding to the profusion of colour.

After a splendid dinner the dancing recommenced at about half past ten and shortly after Fanny was approached by a tall Royal Naval Officer who asked if his name might be added to her dance list. 'Why of course! The dance after next is a slow waltz; may I have your name please?'

'Matthew Drummond, but please call me Matt as most people do. I'll look forward to our dance, Lady Dewar,' and he strode away and was lost from view in the crowd.

Fanny was puzzled and, turning to Robert Oulton, told him what had happened, 'You see, Robert, I can't understand how this officer knew my name.' Robert smiled, 'Oh, that's easy to answer. I've known Matthew's family for donkey's years, as his father Forbes was a sapper in my time.

'Matt asked me your name as he said he felt sure he had met you at some time in the past. The Navy thinks well of him and with an excellent war record, he was promoted to Rear Admiral a couple of years back. His great sadness is the loss of his charming wife in 1915 aboard the P&O steamer *Persia* in the Mediterranean, torpedoed by a German submarine.'

Matt arrived promptly to escort Fanny to the dance floor where she discovered straight away he was an excellent dancer. The initial conversation covered simple subjects including family. 'Have you any children?' he asked.

'Yes, one son, Francis, who is married with five children,' Fanny enthused, 'My grandchildren are all darlings!'

At this point Matt stopped dancing and, looking hard at Fanny, exclaimed, 'I knew I'd seen you before! You must be Norman Vining's widow. Am I right?'

Fanny was taken aback. 'Yes! But why do you ask?'

'I was one of the six pall-bearers for Norman and, while it was a tragedy for us fellow officers to lose him in a terrible accident, it was nothing to the loss you suffered, left a widow with a very young son. I regretted not keeping in touch with you at the time, but the crippled battleship was decommissioned immediately for major repair work and I joined the fleet in the Far East where I remained until the year before the Great War broke out. I married my darling wife in June 1914 but we were parted when she was killed by a German U-boat in 1915.'

Fanny felt quite overcome by all he had said and suggested they sat at a table on the terrace for a while. Once seated, he started to apologise but Fanny stopped him, 'Matt, I'm so very sorry to hear the tragedy you suffered and can understand your loneliness over these past years. But I must tell you how much our meeting has done for me, coming face to face with someone who knew Norman so well.'

He paused, as if making up his mind, 'Lady Dewar, may I call you Fanny? Because that's how I remember you back in 1904.' She nodded, as he continued, 'Fanny, you may like to hear about the other five who carried your husband into the church?'

'Please, I would very much like to know how and where they are.'

'Josh Bennett, Willie Babcock and Jake Rusper were sadly killed during the war. Besides me, there is Luke Brand now living in retirement in Yorkshire and Hilary Marchant who I believe is somewhere in America.'

At the last name Fanny's face became flushed and she gripped Matt's arm as she spoke, 'The mention of that odious man's name is very distressing to me!'

Sensing her upset, Matt decided to tell her of his own experience: 'Do I gather you have met Hilary Marchant and found him unsavoury as a person?'

Fanny murmured yes, as Matt continued, 'I have to tell you he was known throughout the service as an unmitigated bounder, a cad and a seducer and, but for the outbreak of the war, would most probably have been kicked out of the Navy. Sadly he got away with conduct unfitting for an officer and a gentleman.'

Fanny went on to tell him her experience and the money she had lost, 'But the money in the long run doesn't matter, it was the plausible manner in which he cheated me that hurt so much and made me very wary of my dealings with men from then on.'

'Fanny, I'm shocked to hear your story and can well understand how you feel towards us men.' Then, taking her hand, 'Nevertheless, I hope we may remain friends as I've so enjoyed meeting you and feel we have known each other for all these past years.'

She liked his reply and, smiling, thanked him for being a good listener, 'But we ought to be getting back to the dance floor or perhaps they will think we've eloped!'

With a cheeky grin he stood up, offering his arm and responding quickly, 'What a splendid idea! That is where we could get to know each other more.' Arm in arm they returned to the ballroom.

Robert Oulton stood as they joined the party and promptly asked Fanny for the next dance. Once on the dancefloor he steered the conversation to Matt and asked her what she thought of him.

'Oh, he's a very charming man and we had a long conversation as he had been a pall-bearer at my first husband's funeral.' Robert nodded and said he was pleased to hear she liked him.

The ball ended in the early hours and, not surprisingly, Matt Drummond offered to escort Fanny home. As they said goodnight he asked if he might take her to dinner one evening but added it would be towards the end of July as he had to go to the Mediterranean for about three weeks. Fanny assured him she would look forward to meeting him again.

After her bath she sat at her dressing table brushing her hair and looking at her mirrored image, 'What an interesting evening it turned out to be,' she thought, 'Of all the people to have met, how curious Matt should be there. The last time they had seen each other was on that fateful day in 1904. She saw him only as a young naval officer bearing the coffin but he had seen her as a bereaved young widow and not forgotten her over all the years. She liked his manner and although he wasn't handsome he was certainly good looking and had such smiling eyes. 'Well fate decreed we should meet tonight so we'll see if fate will step in again!' Picking up a dictionary from the book shelf, she looked up the name Matthew to read, 'Hebrew origin, meaning the gift of Jehovah.' 'Well, well. So that's why he has such smiling eyes!' she giggled as she said it aloud.

At the beginning of July, Francis was opening his morning mail when he picked up an envelope, the writing on which was vaguely familiar. Taking out the letter he started to read,

St Augustine House,
Forest Side,
Southampton,
Hampshire
30th June 1928

Dear Francis,
I have been away for some time in Canada and the United States of America and have only just returned to England following the terrible tragedy involving my darling daughter Yvonne. Just before her death she wrote to me in Regina, Canada, but it was

some time before the letter caught up with me. Yvonne told me in her letter she intended to end her life, saying she had never got over losing her dearest sister Christine and felt utterly alone in the world. She spoke very highly of her friendship with you and hoped you will forgive her if that friendship put pressure on your marriage in any way whatever. It was her wish to be buried with Christine in Regina so I'll take her back to Canada with me when I return next week. I would like to meet your wife and family if convenient but please don't worry if that is not possible. Yvonne died intestate so all her estate will come to me but if there is a keepsake that belonged either to Christine or to Yvonne you would like I will be happy to let you have it.

I look forward to hearing from you,
Affectionately,
   Gloria

Francis felt suddenly cold realising he had been involved in a tragic drama in which he had played a major part. Now both the girls he had known during the last war had taken their own life. He sat with the letter in his hand as Margot came into the room, 'Francis, dearest, you look so upset. Whatever is the matter?'

He handed her the letter and she read it carefully. 'My poor darling, you must feel quite awful getting this news.' She put her arms round his shoulders and said nothing for some moments as he slowly recovered.

'It's all over now Margot and I suppose there is nothing else I can do to help the situation!'

Margot nodded. 'Lady Gloria Makepeace would like to come to see us, so why not ask her to come over before she returns to Canada?' she suggested. 'She must feel shattered, poor woman, and it may help her.'

'You're right, Margot. Here am I feeling sorry for myself when in fact she has suffered a tremendous personal blow and needs all the help we can give her. Yes, let's ask her as soon as we can.'

Chapter 23

A warm, early July Saturday afternoon was the right condition for the favourite English game – cricket. An idyllic scene at the Farndene ground revealed well-mown green turf of the outfield petering out at the boundary, where it gave way to some rougher patches, flanked by various trees, an erect row of poplars standing like sentinels being the most prominent.

A batting 'square' cut and rolled to a smooth perfection looked like green velvet from a distance. The white pavilion with a shaded terrace stood out against the backing of bushes and trees.

Many enjoyed the coolness of the terrace, particularly some of the veteran members of the club, where from his elevated position, each could scrutinise and discuss every aspect of the game.

A dozen or so deck chairs, in groups of twos and threes, fronted the pavilion in a slightly disorderly fashion, the occupants either chatting, watching the match or dozing comfortably. Among the spectators, well-known local figures including General Sir Roger Vining and the rector, the Rev. Shadwell Legion added to the scene with a profusion of panama hats and straw boaters.

Under a blue sky, with occasional fluffy white clouds, the teams fought to get the upper hand, either to bowl the best or to knock up as many runs as possible. The local league competition brought Farndene and Middlehurst together and they were evenly matched. Francis had played for his home team for many years and while he was no great run getter, he bowled accurately and could be depended upon to take the difficult wickets. Today's encounter was a 'needle' match with the winner going forward to the semi-final of the competition.

Margot and the children had come along to support Daddy, who had completed a spell of bowling without success, but the youngsters were enjoying various games of their own under the watchful eye of Nanny Chandler. Fanny had arrived from Bristol that morning and was glad of the opportunity of a long talk with her daughter-in-law.

'We had a visit from Lady Gloria Makepeace last week and I think it did both her and Francis a lot of good,' Margot paused as a shout of 'howzat' came from the field as another wicket fell. 'You know, her daughters took their own lives and as Francis knew both he felt responsible in some way. However, they had a long talk and Gloria made it perfectly clear to Francis he shouldn't have a guilt complex. She is a wonderful woman and has seen a lot of tragedy in her family but still looks at her problems objectively. She had gone back to her birth town Regina to be with her family. She also told me confidentially she has a close friendship with a distant cousin and might one day consider remarrying.'

Fanny listened, nodding occasionally, until her daughter-in-law finished before telling Margot her own experience at the ball she attended in June, 'I met a quite charming Rear Admiral who had been one of the pall-bearers at my first husband's funeral. He is Matthew Drummond and his family are great friends of Robert and Edith Oulton.'

'And are you attracted to him?' Margot smiled as she put the question.

Fanny flushed slightly, 'Well, yes I suppose I am, but after the terrible experience I had with Hilary Marchant I'm a little apprehensive about closer relationships. Can you blame me?'

'I understand your reluctance, Mama, but he's from a good family by all accounts, so the risks are minimal. By the way, is he or has he been married?'

'He was married in 1915 but sadly lost his wife when a U-boat torpedoed her ship. I hope to meet him again when he returns from the Mediterranean.' Fanny was thoughtful for a moment or so before putting her next point: ' Margot, do you think I could bring him down to meet you and Francis, perhaps for a weekend?'

'Why, of course. I think it will be a splendid way to meet him without any fuss. We'll fix something up before you go back next week.' At that moment the last Middlehurst wicket fell and they were all out for 156 runs.

'Good,' Margot said as she called the children, 'Now we can have our picnic.' The hamper was opened and as the players filed past into the pavilion for their tea, Clara and Constance ran out to Francis to hold hands as he came off the field. He stopped momentarily to have a few words with his mother and Margot. 'We've done fairly well but we need to be careful not to lose our openers cheaply and with a bit of luck we'll pull it off. I'll see you after tea before I go in to bat.' With that he disappeared into the pavilion.

Margot and Nanny gathered the children and with a large travelling rug spread on the ground, the picnic hamper was unpacked and plates and cups were passed round. Silence reigned as sandwiches, sausage rolls, buns and cakes were soon disappearing, all helped down with ginger pop and lemonade while Grandma Fanny was in her element helping the little ones with jam tarts and sticky buns. Margot enjoyed these relaxed occasions and was glad to chat to her mother-in-law about the Bristol end of the family.

With their tea over, the Middlehurst team took to the field and the two Farndene batsmen made a cracking start, soon putting 30 runs on the board.

Meanwhile the picnic finished and Margot and Nanny took the children into the pavilion to the toilets and to deal with sticky hands and faces.

With 95 runs scored without loss, Farndene suddenly lost four of their best batsmen as their opponents brought on the 'ace' bowler. Francis told his team, 'We'll have to watch this fellow or he'll win the match for them,' and to the next man in, gave advice, 'Play him carefully and don't try any heroics, just wear him down.'

Francis went in when the score stood at 120 and had made five runs when his batting colleague was clean bowled. Rupert Tupper, was last man in. A tall, well-built seventeen year old, he was in fact a substitute for one of the assistant gamekeepers who had broken a toe in an accident.

Rupert strolled on to the field, taking a leisurely glance round as he took up his crease. The 'ace' bowler smirked as he ran up to deliver a short ball but was more than surprised as Rupert stepped forward quickly, hitting the ball with force to the boundary. He went on to make sixteen runs from the next four balls.

In between overs Rupert told Francis, 'Just stone wall until I can take on the bowler again.' Francis did exactly that and later Rupert hit four more boundaries, making the Farndene total 155.

Francis now faced the bowling again and an in-swinger took the off stump clean out of the ground. But lady luck was on hand as the umpire called a 'no ball'. Francis left the next two alone but as he hit the fourth ball with all his strength high into the air, a passing motorcycle suddenly backfired with tremendous bangs, causing masses of birds to fly out of the surrounding trees. The flying ball was enveloped in a black cloud of rooks, crows and pigeons, while a thwarted fielder looked skyward in dismay and stood forlornly as the ball grounded and rolled over the boundary line.

Those runs spelt victory for the home side, which traditionally shook hands with the Middlehurst players as they left the field. Francis congratulated Rupert who had certainly saved the day and suggested he may like to come back to the Manor House for a drink and smiled at the answer he received: 'Thank you all the same, sir, but I promised to take Jenny Briggs into Southampton to the pictures and some supper after.'

'That's all right, Rupert, you carry on as planned and I hope you have an enjoyable evening. By the way, how do you account for the success in batting today?'

'It's my sight which has always been very good. I just watched the bowler's ball hand each delivery and I knew what he was going to do.'

They talked about Rupert's family and Francis asked how his mother was. 'Very well, thank you, and always busy with the dressmaking business. Philip, my stepfather, is most supportive and manages all the finance for the firm.' Francis nodded as Rupert went on, 'On another subject, sir, the work at the Dumbarton aero engine factory is really stimulating and I'm getting on well with my diploma at evening school and hopefully will qualify in two years time. I've also had some flying lessons at the local club and as soon as I'm eighteen I'm going to join the Auxiliary Squadron of the Royal Air Force at Glasgow.'

'Well done, Rupert. Keep up the effort and I'm sure you'll get to the goal you want.' As they parted, they shook hands and Francis went, with the help of the children, to clear up after the picnic. A little later when all was packed up, Margot noticed Jenny arrive to greet Rupert with a long kiss before they wandered off arm in arm. Linking arms with Francis and kissing his cheek she made the obvious remark, 'Isn't romance a wonderful thing, darling?'

Francis stopped walking and, wrapping his arms round Margot, gave her a very big kiss.

'I couldn't agree more, my sweet, and looking at our happy little brood, I can recommend it to everybody.'

Laughingly they gathered everybody into the car and, with Margot driving, all agreed the cricket match had been super. The whole family erupted in laughter as the small voice of Constance told them all, 'Daddy's still got his pads on!' With much more laughter Grandma Fanny told her, 'Don't worry darling, Daddy will take them off before he goes to bed tonight!'

Sir Roger Vining joined Fanny, Margot and Francis for dinner that evening and an enjoyable occasion it was, as Fanny brought them up to date with all the family news from Bristol. 'Angelina is expecting their first child and Alex and her children, Bruno and Greta, are over the moon with excitement. The baby is due early next year so we await the arrival eagerly.'

She went on to tell them all about Matthew Drummond, saying she was looking forward to seeing him again when he returned from the Mediterranean in a week or two. Francis teased his mother, 'You seem to have a weakness for the chaps in navy blue. I think you ought to give the Air Force a chance as I consider the light blue a much better colour.'

At this point his grandfather, who had been very quiet, chipped in almost sternly, 'Now Francis you mustn't trivialise you mother's position. She has seen some pretty tough times during her life and deserves some happiness now.'

Francis accepted the admonishment, 'I meant no offence and the last thing I would wish to do is upset mother.' Turning to her, he added, 'I'm sorry but I was only jesting.'

Fanny told him not to worry and was, herself, a little perplexed by her father-in-law's attitude but decided to let the matter rest. Things settled to normal and it was another hour before they adjourned to the drawing room for coffee. Later when Roger said he felt it time to go home, Francis offered to drive him, but Fanny intervened: 'You've had a very tiring day, Francis, so you stay with Margot and I'll run him home. My car is outside already.'

In a matter of ten minutes they arrived at Sir Roger's place.

'Will you come in for a few moments Fanny?' he said, 'there is something I wish to say to you.' Once inside the large drawing room he offered a seat on a settee and immediately sat next to her. Fanny felt mystified as he started to talk.

'Fanny I have to say I have admired you from the first time we met prior to your marrying Norman and subsequently the intelligent inspiration you brought into our family. You showed great courage after Norman's death and brought Francis up to be a fine husband and father.

'I have grown so very fond of you and ask you now if you will consider me as a possible partner. I know I'm no "chicken" at eighty and you are some thirty years younger, but I'm fit and very active as you well know. You may recall we walked down to the harbour in Whitby after Francis and Margot were married in 1919 and then I almost asked you the very same question I'm asking now, but felt in Whitby it wasn't the right time or place.'

Fanny sat quietly, quite astonished that her father-in-law was offering marriage, something she had never contemplated in all the years she had known him. She felt utterly bewildered by his approach. Collecting her thoughts she realised he was expecting an answer so decided to give herself time to weigh up the situation.

Taking his hand gently, Fanny spoke in a voice charged with emotion, 'Roger, I deeply appreciate all you have said about the past years; I say to you now I felt you were my friend from the start and always treated me with the utmost courtesy and respect, particularly during the difficult time when your son Algy attacked me. I am very fond of you and appreciate your offer is made with great sincerity and I'm flattered, as any woman would be. It is an enormous step we both contemplate and I need time to give it full consideration.'

Roger was smiling, 'But of course you need time Fanny. I'm just relieved you haven't turned me down outright!' They both laughed as they stood and walked to the front door where they paused as Fanny kissed his cheek. 'I promise I'll let you know very soon and thank you again, Roger, for one of the most wonderful moments in my life.' He closed the door as her car pulled away into the night.

Fanny felt bewildered as she parked her car at the Manor House and kept turning over the events at Sir Roger's house. Bertie the butler answered the door and showed her into the drawing room where Margot and Francis were enjoying a night cap. Bertie produced a whisky and water which Fanny sipped gratefully.

As soon as they were alone she put the glass down and started to sob quietly. Margot, sensing something was amiss, put her arms round Fanny to comfort her.

'Whatever is the matter, Mama?'

A tear-stained face looked at Margot and Francis and they both knew Fanny was deeply distressed. After a pause she recovered enough to tell them the whole saga in detail.

Francis was the first to react. 'Mother, frankly I think the whole situation is preposterous! What on earth has entered into Grandpa's head to imagine he could marry you at his age? You deserve more of a future than he can possibly offer!'

Fanny listened and came to Roger's defence, 'Don't think too harshly about your grandfather. He was perfectly sincere in his proposal. To be perfectly honest with both of you, I don't know that I want to remarry, as my life is full and I'm so lucky with the love and support I receive from my family.' She turned to Margot, 'What do you think my dear?'

'It's a knotty problem, Mama, and no mistake. In all my legal experience I've never come across a similar case. However, the proposal is "on the table" and marriage is the consequence if you say yes. But look at the prospects for the next few years. It is highly likely Sir Roger's health will deteriorate and you will end up as nurse, possibly pushing a bath chair. The essential ingredient of a successful union is love. Do you really love this man? Or are you just fond of him? The test of your affection is to determine whether there is true love or not.'

Fanny was still stressed, but calmer and she took Margot's hands as she spoke, 'You'll never know how much you have helped me with those words. You're right – the test is one of love and I know deep down I don't love the man but have great affection for him. That cannot be enough for us to marry. Having said that, what on earth am I going to say to him? I just don't want to hurt him.'

Francis, who had been listening to all that Margot had said, turned to Fanny, 'Mother, we understand you have made a decision and Margot and I agree and will stand by you. Let's leave the position there for tonight and sort things out in the morning. They all agreed and after goodnight kisses made their way to bed.

Chapter 24

Sunday morning, 29th July, was another beautiful day and at breakfast nobody mentioned Fanny's 'problem'. Margot had arranged to go to the morning service at St Paul's and she and Francis were taking Juliet and Norman with them.

'Mama, would you like to come to the service with us?' Fanny said she would, and hurried to get ready.

Margot went to see Juliet's hair having a good brush ready for church and Nanny stopped for a moment to say she would be very happy to take the three youngest down to the river to feed the swans and ducks. 'We always have lots of fun as Bruce and Clara try to count them but they swim around too quickly. Cook has been saving lots of crusts and thankfully our local ducks seem always to be hungry!'

Nanny departed with the three little ones, each clutching a large bag of bread Cook had provided, telling them, 'Make sure you give the swans some as they have cygnets to feed.' Fanny, Margot, Francis and the elder twins arrived in good time for the eleven o'clock matins, nodding and smiling to several people they recognised in the congregation as they were shown to a pew.

On the stroke of the hour a small choir entered followed by the Rev. Shadwell Legion who genuflected deeply to the altar. After two hymns and readings the rector ascended the pulpit to give his address.

'For my sermon this morning I wish to speak of love. Our Lord told us to love one another and that includes not only our family and friends but all our neighbours.' Here he paused, gazing up at the roof timbers as though looking for inspiration from on high.

At that moment Toddy Brantwith, a huge farmer, walked up to the pulpit and, pointing a finger at the rector, spoke vehemently, 'You can talk of love alright, you bugger! My wife Pat has told me you have been "having it off" with her in the vestry after she finished bell practice each week.'

This verbal bombshell stunned the congregation into a hushed silence as the two churchwardens grabbed Toddy's arms and attempted to remove him, but he shook them off.

'I'll go as soon as I've finished with that bastard in the pulpit.' Pointing at the Rev. Legion he almost spat the words, 'You've wrecked my marriage and I intend to see the Bishop to have you removed from this parish you adulterous swine,' then he turned and, with tears streaming down his face, walked slowly back down the aisle.

Several members of the congregation, including Fanny, Margot, Francis and the two youngsters, followed him out of the west door. Once out in the fresh air Margot took the initiative and looking up at the church clock made a suggestion: 'It's only twenty past eleven and we've lots of time before lunch so why don't we walk up to the airfield and watch the flying? There are always crowds of members there on Sundays.'

Juliet agreed, 'What a super idea, Mummy and perhaps Norman and I can have a flight?'

At this point Francis stepped in, 'I don't think there will be enough time for that today, Juliet, but I promise I'll take you both up during the summer holidays.' Both the youngsters felt a bit downhearted until Grandma Fanny produced some toffees from her handbag.

About half an hour later all five of them watched as many planes took off and landed and they were thrilled by the chief instructor who performed aerobatics including picking up a small flag with a hook on the end of a wing while flying a few feet above the ground.

Back home Margot, Francis and Fanny enjoyed lunch with the children who were all in high spirits, particularly Norman who asked, 'Does that man who shouted at the rector come to church every Sunday?'

Avoiding eye contact with Francis, Margot replied quickly, 'No, darling, he was just upset today.'

There was a decided lull in the conversation until Juliet piped up, 'I expect he forgot to bring some collection,' and here she stopped, realising there hadn't been a collection. 'Ooh! I've still got my collection in my coat pocket! Will God know, Mummy?' Margot put her mind at rest, 'That's all right, Juliet, we'll take two lots next week and I'm sure God will be pleased.'

After lunch Nanny collected the children together and took them off for some games and stories as Fanny, Margot and Francis settled in the drawing room for coffee. Here Fanny was eager to talk about the interruption at church, 'I've never seen anything like it before in my life! What do you think happened after we left?'

'We'll hear all about it from Miss Rhoda Pinkney, the Postmistress who was sitting in front of us. She doesn't miss anything and knows everything about everybody in Farndene. When Digby Fletcher was rector here he swore she read all his postcards and used to steam his letters open, so he instructed his bank manager to seal all correspondence with sealing wax!'

They all had a good laugh but Margot was soon serious, 'I felt so sorry for Toddy Brantwith, he looked a broken man as he left.'

'What will happen to the rector? Surely he can't stay after that public accusation?' She and Fanny looked at Francis as he gave an immediate answer.

'The matter will rest with the Bishop and if there is sufficient evidence, Shadwell Legion will be brought before a Consistory Court and tried. Personally I hope we see the back of him. He's a most unpopular man and many dislike the way he conducts the services. Can you believe it? The man introduced the burning of incense at communion in a church that has stood the test of time for hundreds of years without need of fumigation!'

They talked for a good hour about the family, especially the children's education after leaving the prep school in Farndene. Francis said he would like to see them in a good grammar school as day pupils but the nearest possibility was in Southampton which meant travelling each day by train. 'Frankly I think it would put too much strain on them. So you see our quandary, Mother.'

Fanny agreed and said straight away she was pleased to learn that both Francis and Margot had ruled out public schools, making the point with vigour: 'You had an excellent education at a grammar school Francis, so why not the same for my grandchildren?'

As they discussed the subject at length, Fanny suddenly made a helpful suggestion neither Margot or Francis had contemplated. She then explained her idea, 'I have to tell you there are several excellent grammar schools with day pupils in Bristol. The Royal Bristol Grammar School for boys has a fine record, while the Dame Alwyn High School for girls produces students of quality regularly taking places at Oxbridge colleges. The children could live with me and be in regular contact with the family in Bristol. I'm sure Alex and Angelina and his sisters would be delighted to have your family in Bristol.'

Margot was looking wide eyed as she reacted, 'Mama, you're an angel! You have given us such a simple solution to what has been a nagging problem. I think your suggestion is just wonderful! What do you think, Francis?'

'I have to be honest, I like the plan but it puts a lot of burden on you, Mother, and may restrict your lifestyle. Do you really think you can cope with what will be five bouncy youngsters in due course?'

'Francis the way you talk, anyone would think I'm an old and decrepit woman! You know I'm only fifty-four and in good health and quite capable of handling my own grandchildren. At any rate I have a good house staff and we can employ another nanny if necessary.'

Francis nodded as he replied, 'Mother you're a genius. For my part, I'm convinced; so how do we get in touch with the schools?'

'The boys' school isn't a problem as Robert Oulton is chairman of the governors and I'm sure he will be delighted to help. However, the Dame Alwyn School isn't so straightforward as I don't know any of the governors. The headmistress is Miss Gladys Rollo, an excellent academic and wonderful organiser. She was at the ball we recently had in Bristol accompanied by her brother Mike and his wife.'

Francis could hardly contain his exuberance: 'Good Lord! Mike Rollo! I can't believe it! Mike and I were on the same Royal Flying Corps squadron during the war and he often spoke of his sister Gladys. He told me she had always been the brainy one in the family. I don't have his address but if we can get in touch with him, I'm sure he would help us with his sister.'

And so the plans for the grandchildren's education were formulated, but it would be a matter of time before they would take effect.

Monday morning brought the usual routine to the Vining household with the children going to school, but this time they had a special escort: Grandma Fanny told them she would enjoy the walk and perhaps look at the shops on the way back.

On returning home, Bertie let her in and with his usual smile enquired, 'I hope you enjoyed your walk, Lady Dewar. Mr Francis and madam are in his study and would like you to join them.'

He knocked and opened the study door for her and as she entered it was apparent they were both distressed.

'Come in, Mother,' Francis drew a chair up for her. 'I'm afraid we have received some very bad news. About half an hour ago Dr Strickland telephoned to tell us Grandpa Vining has suffered a massive heart attack and was still unconscious. A consulting specialist is coming to see him in about an hour's time. Dr Strickland will call here later this morning to bring us up to date.'

Fanny sat stunned with the gravity of all her son had told her and Margot, realising her mother-in-law was severely shaken and had started to weep, went over to comfort her.

Fanny looked up at both of them as she poured out her heart, 'I just can't believe it! He was so full of life and quite vibrant when we talked the other night.' Then looking down at her hands she went on, 'If he is likely to be paralysed or unable to speak I hope he won't survive. I couldn't bear seeing him in that condition knowing the mental torment he would be suffering. From the beginning he has been a wonderful father-in-law and friend. I am very fond of him but it seems now any hopes for the future years are unlikely to materialise.'

Nobody said a word for some moments until Francis broke the silence, 'Mother, I think we should wait until we know more from Dr Strickland but we understand and respect your feelings about his survival.' Margot stood up and, going to the door, told them, 'I think we could do with some hot coffee so I'll tell Bertie.' As she left, Francis called, 'Tell him to bring some brandy as well.'

Dr Strickland arrived just before midday and explained the situation in some detail, 'Dr Pomery, the specialist, examined Sir Roger and took blood samples and is of the opinion he is likely to have another attack very soon. The blood will be analysed today and I will be informed of the findings. Talking to the specialist I gained the feeling Sir Roger is unlikely to live for more than twelve hours or even less.' Francis thanked the doctor who declined an invitation to stay for lunch as he had several outstanding calls to make.

Lunch was served at one o'clock but none of them felt much like eating and Fanny only nibbled a little before leaving the table to go to her room.

Margot spoke as soon as they were on their own, 'Your Mother is taking it very badly darling, and I think she feels, as we do, he is going to die very soon. We must just be on hand to support her when that time comes.'

Francis nodded his agreement, 'You're right – she is very upset but I know my Mother is made of sterner stuff than a lot of people and will stand up to the test when it comes, have no fear.'

Sitting in the office on the first floor of Madame Baume's dress-making salon in the High Street, Exeter, Nellie Ranft and Janine Kirkwood were enjoying a quiet afternoon cup of tea on a hot day at the beginning of August. The windows were open and the street noises invaded the room to such an extent that they were forced to close them in order to carry on a normal conversation.

The subject was the progress the business had made from the beginning of 1928.

'Janine, we have almost doubled our turnover this year, in the main from personal recommendations and I have to tell you much of the custom has resulted from your contact with our clients. They love the way you deal with them and the fact you are French gives our business an authentic flavour.'

Janine had started to thank Nellie when there was a knock at the door and a seamstress told them there was a foreign man downstairs asking to speak to Mrs Tupper, 'I think he means you, Mrs Kirkwood.'

Janine went down to the salon where to her astonishment her younger brother was waiting. Overcome with tearful emotion, her voice was almost inaudible, 'My dearest René, what a wonderful surprise!'

Immediately they were locked in a tight embrace for some moments. Eventually he stood back, still holding her hands to explain why he had come.

'I need to tell you all the news from Plonéour Lanvern; is there somewhere we can talk?'

'Let's go up to the office,' and, taking him by the hand, she walked to the stairway.

After polite introduction to Nellie Ranft, René began what was to be a long story about the family and local happenings in France.

'One of the main reasons for my visit, apart from seeing you, Janine, is to ask if you can possibly come over to Plonéour Lanvern to help with the annual horse fair which is for three days next week.'

Janine was about to reply when Nellie interrupted, 'My dear, of course you must go! It'll be a chance to see your family and help your brother. Business is very quiet during the August holiday month and the break will do you good.'

Janine was grateful for the offer and accepted, 'Thank you very much Nellie.' Turning to René she asked about their elder brother.

There was a notable change in his expression as he shook his head and replied, 'I'm afraid this is not good news; Alain is in deep trouble and is in prison in Quimper.'

'What trouble?' there was urgency in her question and Janine looked distressed but before he could answer, Nellie interrupted, 'This is a family matter and perhaps I should leave so you can talk privately.'

As she rose to leave, Janine caught her arm, 'No, please stay, – I would like you to.'

René continued, telling them how Alain and his wife Natalie had been living apart for some time.

'My brother desperately wanted an heir, a son to carry on the family name but his wife unfortunately couldn't bear children and the marriage came apart. Natalie asked for a divorce but Alain bluntly refused.

'Last Easter she met Bernard Carpentier, a local farmer, and left the family home to live with him. My brother was furious and felt humiliated and told his wife to stop seeing the other man. She refused and at the beginning of July Alain went to the Carpentier farm and shot Natalie with a double barrelled gun. She was critically injured and may recover, but if she dies he will be a murderer. After appearing before the magistrate he was charged with attempted murder and causing grievous harm to his wife and remanded in custody pending trial.'

Janine and Nellie were aghast at the terrible news and moments passed before anyone spoke.

'As you know, I'm on my own and although our neighbours have been very supportive, the organisation of the horse fair will be too much for me. So you see, Janine, why I need your help.'

Her sharp mind had already reached a conclusion and grasping her brother's hand she replied, 'René of course I'll help. As Rupert is on leave from his apprenticeship he can come too. He's a big strong lad, an excellent horseman and his French is pretty good, which will be an added asset.'

Plans were made for the trip to France without delay.

General Sir Roger Vining died peacefully, without regaining consciousness on 1st August having reached the age of eighty years. His passing cast a cloud over the family and to some extent over Farndene where he had lived most of his life. The funeral for a man of outstanding military and public service would inevitably be a large one. The main difficulty facing Francis was the fact the local church had no incumbent as the Rev. Shadwell Legion had had his licence withdrawn by the Bishop, pending a trial before the Consistory Court. A telephone call to London soon solved that problem and the Rev. Canon Digby Fletcher, the former rector, willingly agreed to officiate.

On the chosen day, 9th August, a large crowd assembled in the old church of Saint Paul. Conspicuous in his wheelchair was Sir Roger's son Algy, pushed by Father Vincent Logan the Abbot of Broadbeck Abbey, North Yorkshire, and accompanied by the Vining family. Among those attending were many well-known figures including Members of Parliament, senior officers from the three services and officers from France and Belgium who had served with Sir Roger during the Great War.

The coffin – borne by six officers from his old regiment, the South Hampshire Fusiliers – entered the church to the strains of his favourite hymn, 'Praise my Soul the King of Heaven' and placed in front of the rood screen.

In his address, Canon Digby Fletcher spoke from the heart, without notes, and illuminating the outstanding character of a remarkable man said, 'We will all miss him but must never forget the wonderful example he gave to us all and try to draw on that in our own lives. He wrote to me regularly and with a certain amount of humour. In his last letter he asked me not to predecease him as he needed me at his funeral! His very words were "just give them one of your friendly chats but don't go on too long or you'll bore them to tears". So now I'll close with the comment: Rest in peace Roger my dear friend, you've certainly earned it.'

There followed the final committal at the family grave where he was laid alongside his wife and son Norman.

Six soldiers from the Hampshire Fusiliers, resplendent in full dress uniform, comprised the firing party and were ready to salute their old commander. As Fanny stood supported by Francis and Margot the first volley crashed out, causing masses of birds from the surrounding trees to take to the air, wheeling and screeching in their agitation.

Suddenly her mind went back to the fateful day in 1904 when her husband Norman was buried and she felt the whirling display above again a sinister warning. Everything in her head was now reeling from the noise of the birds and further volleys of the guns as she collapsed into the arms of Francis.

Chapter 25

René, Janine and Rupert left for France on 10th August, travelling by ferry to St Malo and from there to Plonéour Lanvern, in Brittany, by rail. As there was so much family news to catch up on, they talked endlessly during the journey.

Rupert enjoyed his uncle's company and enthusiastically explained all about the engineering course he was undertaking with particular emphasis on aero engine design and construction. 'You see, Uncle, air transport will be the great leap forward in the next few years and bigger aircraft need larger engines, so that's where I come in.'

Janine listened with pride as her son enthused about the future of aviation and then pulled his leg with her question, 'Surely Rupert, if God had intended us to fly, wouldn't he have given us wings?'

They all enjoyed the joke but René struck a more sombre note by adding, 'Your idea of larger aeroplanes carrying people is all right but never forget the military men may not want people but bombs.'

Settling in the old Plonéour Lanvern farmhouse brought Janine many memories of her youth as she recalled the happy days of her earlier life there. She found the whole place much smaller, particularly her bedroom where she was sleeping but the familiar smell of the ancient timbers had not gone away.

The kitchen was exactly as she remembered it, with the large cooking range comprising four ovens with an open fire in the centre, over which hung a large spit for roasting meat, while above were rows of copper pans of all sizes. Along one wall stood a large Breton dresser housing all types of china plates, cups and saucers, much of it colourful local crockery made in Quimper. With René's help, Janine set about planning the meals for the next few days and she was soon preparing the first batch of bread to go in the large oven, enough to cover their needs for the coming week.

With pleasure, René watched his sister kneading the dough with her sleeves rolled up, remarking with emotion, 'You haven't forgotten bread making after all these years. I remember how much you used to help mother with the cooking.' He was thoughtful for a moment, 'She was devastated when you went away to marry Charlie Tupper and I don't think she ever forgave father for the way he treated you. But that's all history now.'

He looked so miserable, Janine went round the table and after giving him a big hug and a kiss, both burst out laughing as they realised he was covered in flour and tiny bits of dough.

'You'd better be off or I'll pop you in the oven with the next batch of loaves!' was her parting remark as he scampered out of the kitchen.

The preparations for the horse fair were well advanced and René and Rupert directed the setting up of the many temporary pens to accommodate some 400 horses, while Janine took over the running of the house and directed the daily women who came in to do various jobs; she also kept the accounts for her brother. In the town centre, booths were being set up for the sale of all kinds of food and drink as well as clothing and equestrian equipment. On the edge of the town a large funfair appeared with swings and roundabouts together with side shows and a coconut shy.

Fortunately the weather was fine and warm when the fair opened on 15th August and for the next three days hundreds of people were drawn to watch the auction of horses and to enjoy all the fun of the fair. They came from surrounding towns and villages and, to the delight of the local people, spent freely in Plonéour Lanvern. On 18th August – the last day – all who had taken part felt satisfaction with another successful fair and René was particularly pleased as all the horses he had put up for auction had sold well.

In the town all the booths were dismantled and were gone by Saturday evening. Sunday morning saw the faithful coming along the streets in their best clothes, summoned by the bell to early mass in the church.

That afternoon Janine visited Natalie in the local hospital and found her much improved. They talked for over an hour during which Natalie told her visitor the awful history of the latter years of her marriage to Alain. She mentioned that the priest had been to see her: 'He impressed upon me the need for forgiveness.' Natalie was clearly not in the mood to overlook what her husband had done to her: 'I told him I would think about it, but at present I would not take such a step.' She shrugged her shoulders. 'It's all right for the priest to make such suggestions but if we're going down that road, Alain is the one who must ask me for forgiveness'

Janine took her hand and gently suggested it was early days to consider pardons, 'Natalie, my dear, the most important thing for you at present is to get well. If the priest calls again, just tell him you will consider all he suggests when you have fully recovered.'

Before she left, Janine promised to visit each day while she was staying in Plonéour Lanvern.

That evening Janine prepared supper for René and Rupert and afterwards they sat quietly chatting in the cool of the farmhouse.

'I shall miss you when you return next week Janine.' René appeared a little sad as he looked across the room at his sister, 'Although I am kept busy all day every day with the work to do with the horses and guiding the staff, it is in the evenings when I'm on my own I feel very lonely.'

Janine suddenly felt compassion for her brother and wanted desperately to help him, but was at a loss as to where to start,

'René, you're thirty-seven next birthday and still unmarried. Have you considered getting married? A wife would be wonderful company, particularly as you get on in years.'

René's gaze dropped and he was clearly uncomfortable as he struggled to answer his sister,

'I'd better explain, Janine, you see in 1911 I had a wonderful friend and we got on well together but when war broke out he was conscripted into the army and killed in a battle at Arras. I still miss him dreadfully and have never met anyone to take his place.'

There were tears in his eyes as he continued, 'So you see I'm not the marrying type.'

Janine moved across the room to sit beside him and, putting her arms round her brother, spoke softly to him, 'I'm so sorry dearest René and I completely understand your situation.' She was quiet for some moments before making a suggestion, 'Would it be possible to have a permanent housekeeper? Perhaps a married woman with a husband who could undertake routine maintenance jobs you need attending to? There's plenty of room in this house and they would provide some company for you.'

'There you go Janine – always looking for ways to help me. I'll talk to my foreman to see if he can help me find someone.' He put his hands in hers and gently kissed her cheek, 'You're a wonderful sister and I love you very much.'

They talked for some time during which Janine promised she and her family would try to visit Plonéour Lanvern regularly, so her children could meet and get to know their uncle.

Janine and Rupert left by train and en route the discussed all that had happened during their stay with René.

Janine explained about her brother and his friend who was killed and was surprised at Rupert's reply: 'I knew what he was as I talked and worked with him, but does that matter? He's a very caring person who has suffered a great deal of bullying from his older brother. I've never met Uncle Alain and, frankly, I don't want to.'

Janine was taken aback by her son's forthright response but not really surprised as she realised he had matured well over the past couple of years. 'Rupert, please don't think too harshly about your uncle. After all, you've no idea what he's really like.' And then she surprised him, saying 'I intend going to the prison in Quimper to see my brother as I want to speak to him personally. Will you come with me?'

Rupert's reply was straight to the point and, looking hard at his mother, he made it clear to her what he thought of her suggestion.

'Mother, I am willing to come with you as far as the prison but I do not wish to go inside. In any event I think it will be better if you see your brother alone.'

Janine smiled and told him that arrangement would be perhaps the best.

Following the funeral of Sir Roger Vining, Fanny was confined to her bed for two weeks suffering from stress and exhaustion. In the care of Margot and Francis, she stayed at the Manor House and had recovered sufficiently to return to Bristol at the end of August. Her first thoughts were to complete arrangements for the secondary education of her five grandchildren and by October she had accomplished a great deal, as places were confirmed for the boys at the Royal Bristol Grammar School. Her meeting with Miss Gladys Rollo, the headmistress of the Dame Alwyn High School, was entirely fruitful as she agreed to admit Fanny's three granddaughters in due course. The occasion was a particularly happy one as the introduction had come about through her brother Captain Mike Rollo and the conversation centred naturally on Gladys's war time meeting with Francis.

The months slipped by and, once again, a huge family party was planned for Christmas and the New Year at the Manor House. The Bristol contingent came two days before Christmas Eve and stayed until 27th December. Margot's parents and her sister Madeline and family arrived on 29th December to join in the Hogmanay celebrations. Madeline's son, Sam, now eighteen, a tall, good-looking young man had decided on an army career. He applied to the Woolwich headquarters of the Royal Artillery and had been accepted to train as a commissioned gunnery officer. Talking to his Uncle Francis he explained, 'I have no wish to follow my dear father's lead as an infantry officer; such a role cost him his life in the Great War.'

Francis related the story of his rescue in no man's land by Captain Edgar Shelley, the boy's father: 'Your father was a man of extreme courage and without his help I wouldn't be sitting here today. I'm sure he'd have been very proud of you.'

Sadly Madeline was not so enthusiastic and told them she would like to see Sam going to university rather than embarking in a military career: 'Once he's in the regular forces he would be in the front line if there's another war.'

Sam looked at his mother with sympathy and told her not to worry, 'Now come on, Mother, there's not likely to be another war after the terrible effect of the last one, so stop worrying.'

'That's easy for you to say, Sam, but the Great War was a surprise to many people and you can never tell what the future holds. Conflicts spring up when least expected.'

The celebrations went well and 1929 was welcomed in time-honoured fashion. They saw the dawn breaking before retiring to snatch a few hours' sleep.

In Exeter, Janine and Philip had enjoyed having Mollie, Rupert and Tom home for Christmas and the New Year. Mollie told her two brothers about the visit she made to see her Uncle René in Brittany in October: 'He's such a nice person and we got on really well from the word go! Uncle has taken Mother's advice and has a live-in housekeeper, Madame Monique Savin, with her husband Pierre who is a really wonderful handyman. She is from a Rennes family and is a splendid cook. Uncle is very happy with the arrangement.'

Janine also told them about her visit to see her brother in the Quimper prison in August: 'The prison governor let me see Alain as a special favour, explaining normally no visitors are allowed for a remand prisoner, with the exception of the legal representative. Sadly, I found my brother still full of hatred towards Natalie and I couldn't persuade him to be forgiving. Privately I asked the governor if a priest could see Alain regularly and he agreed.'

On 2nd January 1929, Janine, Philip and Mollie saw Rupert and Tom off at the railway station. As she hugged and kissed them both, Janine told them, 'Look after yourselves and come back again soon!' They all waved until the train puffed its way along the line and out of sight.

PART TWO

1938-1945

BY FORTITUDE TO FULFILMENT

Chapter 26

The 1930s witnessed many interesting events in the lives of the families at Farndene, Bristol and Exeter, some happy occasions but others tinged with sadness.

At the Manor House the Vinings had prospered and by 1938 the children were mature; the twins, Juliet and Norman almost eighteen, Bruce sixteen and the other twins, Clara and Constance, nearly fourteen. The two eldest had decided views about their further education, Norman going to Oxford to read engineering while his sister, who was very artistic, elected to attend the Wimbledon School of Art. Both twins had qualified as pilots and it was Norman's intention to join the University Auxiliary Squadron of the RAF.

Bruce, who was not academic, suffered a permanent injury having been hit in his left eye by a cricket ball. The result was defective sight in the one eye but also psychological reaction which affected his school performance. Fortunately he was gifted musically and hoped to make a career in that direction.

Clara and Constance both had ambition and were 'pushy' in their approach to everything they did. Constance, the more intelligent of the two, had already decided she wanted to be a solicitor while her sister wished to teach science.

Margot and Francis, both in their early forties, had coped well during the past years and as Margot put it to her husband, 'We're just growing older gracefully!'

The Farndene Flying School had expanded and additional buildings and hangars made it a sizeable operation. With constant use, the grass airfield had become a problem, particularly in bad weather, and in 1934 a concrete runway had been added which proved invaluable.

Margot's father, David Morton, suffered a minor stroke in 1935 with the result he had difficulty in walking unaided. Her mother

Lorna fortunately enjoyed good health and coped patiently with her husband's infirmity.

Fanny, still fit and well at sixty-four, enjoyed having her grandchildren staying during term times while they attended the local schools in Bristol. Her parents, David and Ruth Edwards – both in their eighties – were still active in their retirement; David kept a friendly eye on their store which prospered under separate management.

In Exeter Janine and Philip Kirkwood worked hard at the 'Madame Baume' dress salon and in 1930, when the proprietor Nellie Ranft died she left her entire estate to Janine. Mollie, now twenty-nine, had developed into a first class business woman and was capable of running the establishment when Janine was away.

Rupert finished his apprenticeship in 1930 and went on to qualify as an engineer. In 1937, as a skilled pilot he had fulfilled another ambition to fly by joining the Glasgow Auxiliary Squadron of the Royal Air Force and had just started a conversion course flying the new Spitfire fighter with which his unit was being equipped. At twenty-seven he had had a number of 'relationships', but nothing permanent.

His brother Tom, just twenty-five, had left the Farndene Flying School and was now working for a Midlands company on aircraft design.

During the early thirties the family visited Plonéour Lanvern from time to time and all had enjoyed the wonderful atmosphere of the Brittany countryside. Mollie, in particular, got on well with her uncle René and she and her mother were the ones who went to see him, more than the two boys.

Politically there was a feeling of unease in Europe after 1933 when Adolf Hitler was appointed German Chancellor and the Nazis started to come to power in Germany. In 1934 Hitler became dictator [Führer] of all Germany. The subsequent annexing of adjacent territories finally led to the famous trip Neville Chamberlain, the Prime Minister, made to Munich in 1938. Landing at

Croydon airport on 29th September, he waved aloft a worthless piece of paper signed by the Führer, stating there would be peace between the United Kingdom and the German 3rd Reich. The Prime Minister honestly believed he had achieved the impossible, but sadly he had been hoodwinked by Adolf Hitler.

Having watched the annexation and invasion of the Sudetenland, Austria and Czechoslovakia, many Parliamentarians in Great Britain, including Winston Churchill, were sceptical about the value of the Nazi's word and their anxieties increased as Hitler berated the world and pushed ahead with a vast re-armament programme.

The tension increased into 1939 and on 1st September Mussolini, Dictator of Italy, invaded Albania.

Great Britain had given a guarantee to Poland and on 3rd September Germany invaded that country. At eleven o'clock that day Neville Chamberlain broadcast to the British nation telling them a state of war existed with Germany.

In homes throughout the United Kingdom the news was received with quiet resolution but some dismay, particularly among parents and grandparents who had experienced the horror of the Great War.

In the Manor House in Farndene, Margot, Francis and her children, as well as Fanny, gathered in the drawing room to listen to the Prime Minister's broadcast on the wireless. When it finished there was a stunned silence for several minute until Francis spoke.

'I never thought it would end like this. We are far from being prepared.' He knew what he was saying was true as his Manufacturing Group had just received large orders from the War Office.

Fanny moved across the room to Margot who was very upset. Putting her arms round her daughter-in-law she spoke quietly, 'I understand exactly how you feel. I suffered when Francis went away in 1915 and remember the words Aunt Lotte said to me at that time, 'but we have to be brave like our soldiers and all will be well!'; thankfully we are a united family and whatever the future holds for us in this dreadful war, we must support each other until peace returns.'

Margot looked at Fanny and nodded, 'You're right Mama, whatever we say, our young people will answer the call in one way or another and we must support them,' she was shaking her head, with tears in her eyes as she finished, 'but it isn't going to be easy for any of us.'

Just at that moment the air raid siren sounded and Francis hurried his family and his staff down to the cellars. Here a shelter had been prepared by reinforcing the cellar roof with steel beams and equipping the place with camp beds, blankets and tinned food. Luckily the alert was a false alarm and everyone was relieved there hadn't been a bombing raid so soon after war was declared.

The first months of the war saw a British Expeditionary Force [BEF] deployed in France and all was 'Quiet on the Western Front' – a period referred to as the 'Phoney War'. Meanwhile German and Russian armies overran Poland which fought valiantly until overcome by vastly superior forces.

One major British Naval success was the cornering of the German battleship *Graff Spee* in a sea battle during which the German ship was severely damaged and forced to seek refuge in Montevideo harbour in the river Plate delta. As the vessel was beyond immediate repair, the Captain scuttled it in the harbour and committed suicide.

At Exeter, Janine had kept her word and over the past years she and her family had become regular visitors to Plonéour Lanvern. Mollie was particularly attracted to the French way of life and often stayed two or three weeks with her uncle René, with the result she became fluent in the local patois. The Exeter dress salon 'Madame Baume' was very busy in the early months of 1940 and Janine concluded women with money were stocking up with clothes as many people thought materials were likely to become short; already she had experienced difficulty in deliveries from France and there were firm rumours of rationing. In June the previous year, there had been an important addition to the household when her two brothers had given Mollie a beautiful black kitten for her birthday present. She was 'over the moon' with the tiny cat which she called Othello.

Janine worried about her two sons as Rupert had been mobilised with the Auxiliary Squadron and was now on active service training with the Royal Air Force, while Tom was reserved in his job working on secret aircraft design.

Janine wrote regularly to her brother René and he always replied promptly, keeping his sister up to date on all that was happening at the farm. His last letter at the beginning of April told a desperate story about the amount of vermin being experienced, owing to a previous mild winter. Mollie, who was due to visit her uncle in the coming weeks talked to her mother, 'Why don't I take Othello with me when I go? He's a wonderful mouser and it may help uncle to clear his house of intruders.'

And so it was arranged at the beginning of May for Mollie to go over to France taking Othello, now a large beautiful specimen, to stay at Plonéour Lanvern for a week or two.

Francis and Margot were faced with the surrender of a wing of the Manor House to the Royal Air Force for use as an officers' mess. The Farndene Flying School airfield had also been taken over as a Spitfire Fighter Station and already a huge expansion was underway.

Margot became fully involved organising the local Red Cross and worked long hours supervising the preparations for Air Raid Precautions. She missed the children as Norman was at Oxford and Juliet was thoroughly settled at Wimbledon. However, Margot worried about her daughter who in a letter to her mother was 'seeing a tutor'! Suggestions to Juliet for her to bring the tutor down for a weekend had not borne fruit.

Arriving home on a fine evening in May, Margot let herself in to be greeted by Bertie in the entrance hall.

'Good evening, madam, when would you like dinner? Oh, and

your sister telephoned late this afternoon and would like you to ring back at your convenience.'

'Thank you Bertie. Dinner in about half an hour please and by the way is my husband home?'

'Yes, madam, he's in the study and would like you to look in for a moment.'

'Thank you.'

She went to the study and opening the door stood still, amazed at what she saw. Standing by the window was Norman in the uniform of a pilot officer in the Royal Air Force!

Margot rushed across the room to wrap her arms round her son, giving him a huge kiss and almost exploding with joy, 'My darling Norman, it's just wonderful to have you home! I can't tell you how much you have done for me this evening as I was feeling a bit down in the dumps as I came home.' She gave him another hug as she spoke.

'Hey! Steady on mother or you'll crease my nice new uniform!' Grinning, Norman took his mother's hands and kissed her cheek, 'Well, tell me, do you like my glad rags?'

Margot sized him up and down and turned to Francis with a grin, 'I think he's just too super for words, don't you darling?'

Smiling, Francis nodded, 'Your mother's absolutely right, Norman, we're terribly proud of you.'

A tap at the door and Bertie's smiling face appeared, 'Sir, madam, Mr Norman – dinner is ready.'

As they trooped off to the dining room, Margot linked her arm through Norman's, 'Now you must tell us all about yourself while we eat.'

During the meal Norman told them about his activities over the past months, 'We have been training hard and it's on the cards: our squadron may be going to France shortly to give cover to the BEF. I look forward to some action in the Spitfire, a perfectly wonderful fighter. But enough of that, I'm on a week's leave and just want to relax and be with the family.'

After dinner, Margot telephoned her sister Madeline in Whitby and they had along chat about their respective families. Madeline told her sister she and her husband Grant were well but very busy doing 'their bit' for the war effort. She went on to say that Sam was now a captain in the artillery, in command of a battery of mobile heavy anti-aircraft guns with the BEF in France. Marion, his sister, had joined the WRNS [Women's Royal Naval Service] and was stationed in Bath working on cipher duties.

'But the best bit of news is that Marion has met a very handsome Commander and they have been seeing each other, off duty, for the last six months. I really think it's serious!'

Margot told her sister how pleased she was to hear how well her niece and nephew were getting on.

The following morning Norman was enjoying a leisurely breakfast with his parents when Bertie returned from the kitchen to tell them the news he had just heard on the wireless.

'The Germans invaded the Low Countries at dawn this morning and are pouring over the borders into Holland and Belgium. Many towns have been bombed by the Luftwaffe.'

At first his words were met with astonishment and disbelief but slowly it dawned on them the import of this action and Francis gave vent to his feelings.

'This is the action of the man who gave an assurance to Neville Chamberlain in Munich last year but now we see Hitler in his true colours. I think this is the beginning of the real war which will be a tough, hard fight but a fight we must win or we will be subjected to an appalling existence under the Nazis.'

They all agreed with his comments and at that point Norman left the room to telephone his unit as he expected to be recalled immediately.

Chapter 27

Plonéour Lanvern, a sleepy Breton town in the early morning of 10th May 1940 found Mollie and her uncle René cantering through empty streets back to the farm; both felt exhilarated by the freshness of the air having ridden through surrounding forest and open countryside for the past hour.

Soon, sitting down to enjoy a breakfast of fruit, croissant and hot coffee, they enjoyed talking endlessly about the family and, of course, the breeding of horses. At seven o'clock René turned the wireless on and for the next fifteen minutes, both were astounded as they listened to the reports of a German attack on the Low Countries, during which the Nazi army had swept over neutral borders, following bombing raids by the Luftwaffe.

Mollie was clearly alarmed and looked to her uncle for comfort, 'Are we in danger here?'

René reassured his niece, 'No, we're quite safe Mollie. You see we have the Maginot Line to protect us.' She looked puzzled so he continued.

'Perhaps I'd better explain. The Maginot Line is an enormously strong defensive shield along the whole of our frontier with Germany. It was the brainchild of a previous war minister Andre Maginot. Our military commanders believe it to be impregnable so please stop worrying.'

'Thank you, Uncle, I feel reassured now you've explained it to me.'

There was a scurrying noise at the far end of the room and seconds later a large black cat came into view carrying a fat mouse in his mouth.

'Oh look! Othello's caught another mouse! So that's twelve since we came to stay.'

They both laughed as the victor moved out of the room quickly, possibly fearing someone would rob him of his prey.

Still listening to the wireless they heard Winston Churchill had succeeded Neville Chamberlain as Prime Minister that morning in England.

The news worsened during the coming days and Mollie decided to return to England without delay.

Collecting her belongings into a travelling bag and with Othello in his wickerwork basket complete with lid, she was taken to the railway station to catch a northbound train to the coast and the ferry at Roscoff.

In England, Janine got more and more worried each day and despite all her efforts to telephone her brother at Plonéour Lanvern, she could not make contact as all the lines were constantly engaged. However, at last she got through and Mollie told her mother, she and René had been to the railway station two days running, only to be told all the trains were commandeered by the French army to move troops east in an endeavour to halt the German advance. 'Tomorrow we will go again to the station and understand there is likely to be room on a train for civilians, so please don't worry, Mother, I'll soon be back with you in England; Uncle and I send you our love.'

The German advance seemed unstoppable and when their tanks broke through at Sedan, thereby outflanking the Maginot Line, the major part of the British Army was soon encircled, with no option but to retreat to the coast.

The only course now open to the British was a phased falling back to the port of Dunkirk; several defensive rings were formed as an outer protection.

The Hampshire Fusiliers were responsible for a sector on the outermost ring and Lieutenant Bruno Kunz – Alex Henshaw's stepson from Bristol – received orders to take a section of men and set up an advanced observation post reporting enemy troop movements to Headquarters. He was issued with signal pads, pencils and rubbers, a clip board, binoculars and one bicycle, for which, in true British Army fashion, he was obliged to sign. Unfortunately there was no food or drink due to acute shortages and he was told to 'forage' for whatever he could find.

He set off towards the enemy with his men, comprising Corporal Len Brocks, Privates Wally Toms, Charlie Washer, Andy Law and Ted Sutton, all stout fellows but none too keen on the job entrusted to them. After walking for around half an hour Lt Kunz identified the map reference he'd been given. The location was a small deserted farmhouse set in a shallow valley which was to be their HQ.

The corporal was given his orders: 'Go up to the top of the rise by the road and dig a slit trench from which you can observe enemy activity. Take Private Washer and send a written message back each hour. Sign for the signal pad, pencil, rubber and binoculars as well as the bicycle.'

The orders were carried out diligently and the outpost relieved every two hours but nothing of note happened until nightfall when all they heard was distant gunfire.

As dawn broke, Corporal Brocks scanned the long valley on the opposite side of the road and, as it got lighter, was astonished to see a stationary mass of German tanks with the crews making breakfast alongside their vehicles. He hastily scribbled a note and Private Toms jumped on the bike and pedalled like mad with it to the farmhouse HQ. As no reply came back within half an hour and seeing the Germans mounting their tanks, Corporal Brocks abandoned his trench and ran to the farmhouse.

There he found the rest of them enjoying hot milk into which they had melted some chocolate. Wally Toms had worked on a farm in Hampshire and, seeing a cow in an adjacent meadow, milked the poor beast and heated the liquid in a billy can.

They sat listening to Andy Law, who had produced his mouth organ, playing quietly in one corner from his repertoire which comprised 'Abide with me', 'Pack up your Troubles in your Old Kit Bag' and 'Cockles and Mussels' but no more!

Bruno told them he had received instructions to make their own way to Dunkirk as best they could.

'So, chaps, we're on our own and I'll do my utmost to get you to the port. We've got a good map and compass so I've worked out a route across country for the first two or three miles.'

Their little group set off walking through lush fields, heady with the scent of wild flowers, and covered about two miles in the first hour, striking a road shortly after. They joined other groups of soldiers all bound for the port and were glad of their company as they trudged along. The sound of distant gunfire was getting fainter but several times during the morning they had to jump into the dry drainage ditch running alongside the road, as attacking German fighters roared overhead; luckily none of their number was hit by Luftwaffe gunfire. En route, the road was littered with abandoned vehicles of all types, some burnt out, but all immobilised; a pitiful scene of utmost destruction and desolation.

Although Bruno made regular stops for rest, all were feeling the effects of the long march with no food or water and tiredness began to have an effect. At that moment they saw a fifteen hundredweight van which had been dumped by the side of the road but not damaged. The ignition key was in place and, to their delight, Corporal Brocks started the vehicle. Climbing aboard with several others they were soon moving and the next two miles went quickly until a checkpoint was reached manned by military police. No vehicles were allowed past the point and they were back on foot for the last four miles.

Reaching the port, all troops were diverted along the coast to the sand dunes for protection to await further instructions. Exhausted, hungry and thirsty they lay down in the dunes alongside hundreds of others, some with minor wounds but all at the end of their tether and still under frequent attack by Luftwaffe fighters.

Bruno decided to look for some food and drink for his men so, taking Pte Charlie Washer with him, he walked inland for a short while to a deserted farm. A chaotic scene greeted them inside the farmhouse indicating the occupants had left very hurriedly; upturned chairs and smashed crockery littered the floor. He looked in various cupboards and searched the larder but found nothing to eat.

However, Charlie Washer had found a small orchard where

there were plenty of apples for the taking. They gathered gingerly as there were swarms of wasps feeding on the fallen fruit. A water pump in the yard was working and an old wooden bucket soon filled.

Making their way back to the dunes they passed through the fields in which several dead cows were lying, inflated like balloons and swarming with wasps and bluebottles.

As they got near the sand dunes it was apparent many more soldiers had arrived since they left and Charlie told his officer, 'It's going to be difficult finding our chaps among this lot! There are hundreds up there and the dunes look the same all the way along.'

Bruno reassured him, 'Don't worry, I took a bearing before we set out but in any case we've only to listen for Law with his mouth organ and we'll be home and dry.' Ten minutes later they reached the dunes and, sure enough, were met with the harmonica strains of 'Abide with Me'.

They enjoyed the apples and drink which they shared with other soldiers nearby, the first food they had eaten that day.

Sleeping fitfully in the sand with a constant booming of the distant guns and frequent air raids on the port, the night passed slowly. The first streaks of dawn appeared to the east over a dead calm sea giving the appearance of a massive sheet of pale green glass.

Bruno woke his men and told them quietly to come with him down to the water's edge where earlier he had seen an upturned rowing boat. With the aid of three other soldiers the boat was soon righted. Apart from a hole in one side into which the remains of an army shirt, found among the vast amount of litter on the beach, was rammed with a large stone, the boat appeared to be reasonably watertight. Empty tins were collected for bailers and using their rifles for paddles the nine men pushed off from the shore towards a warship anchored about a mile out.

Hot and weary they reached the destroyer and the welcoming arms of the Royal Navy.

Given two sets of oars, Bruno and Corporal Brocks rowed

back to the shore to rescue more men. However, the scene there had changed as great crowds of soldiers now stood in the shallow water all clamouring to board a few small motor boats ferrying out to the warship. Discipline had evaporated for some and Bruno and corporal Brocks were overwhelmed and the boat almost sunk. Drawing his revolver, Bruno fired into the air and then ordered the men back at gunpoint.

With a full load of ten, Bruno told his Corporal to pull away for the warship, telling him, 'You carry on and I'll make my own way to the ship.'

Left on the beach, Bruno watched the destroyer edge nearer the shore and realised the tide was rising. Having been a strong swimmer all his life, he then made a quick decision and, stripping down to his underpants, dived in and struck out for the warship. Swimming steadily, Bruno became aware he was not alone and there was an occasional shout from others in the water. The going against the tide began to tire many and sadly a number disappeared below the waves.

Forty minutes later Bruno experienced cramp in one leg and a feeling of exhaustion began to overtake him. Although the destroyer was now very close, his eyes had difficulty in focusing and he started to lose consciousness.

By good fortune the crew of a motor boat spotted his condition and pulled him out of the sea, passing his unconscious body to the waiting seamen aboard the warship.

As he lay on the lower deck Bruno was covered with blankets and with the warmth began to come round slowly. Opening his eyes he gazed at the eager faces of the sailors.

Leading Seaman Dick Dodson spoke, 'You'll be all right mate, just lie still and we'll get you a hot drink.'

With his mind still dazed, Bruno muttered, 'Danke, ich bin …,' and lapsed into a coma again.

The two sailors, astonished at what they had heard, looked at each other as Dick Dodson shouted, 'He's a bloody German! We're spending our time and energy rescuing a fucking Crout! I'm all for chucking the bastard back in the drink!'

At that moment the duty Chief Petty Officer arrived on the scene and, hearing the leading seaman, soon put him right: 'You'll certainly not chuck him in the sea! He is a prisoner of war and we're bound by the Geneva Convention. See that he's kept warm and given a hot drink while I report to the Duty Officer.'

Captain Sam Shelley, in command of a battery of heavy mobile anti-aircraft guns had crossed to France to join the BEF in November 1939 and had seen little action during the 'Phoney' war.

His guns protected a RAF airfield, operating Hurricane fighters, near Reims. After the German invasion of Holland and Belgium and the subsequent breakthrough at Sedan, the airfield was constantly attacked by the Luftwaffe and subsequently abandoned.

Shelley's battery and others were cut off south of the German thrust at Sedan and were ordered to retreat across France to Brest to embark on a troopship for England. Their passage westward on roads choked with refugees was slow and subject to frequent attacks by the Luftwaffe. He was able to get fresh supplies of petrol from the French Army at Le Mans and made better progress to Rennes by travelling at night and parking the guns under wooded areas by day.

Four days later they arrived at the town of Chateaulin, only to be told the troopship they would have boarded at Brest had been sunk by Stuka bombers. Captain Shelley was ordered to proceed to Lorient where hopefully shipping would be available. Weary and dispirited they were stuck in the town for some time by the most enormous traffic jam.

After a two-day wait, the Plonéour Lanvern railway station was crowded as Mollie and her uncle pushed their way through to the platform for the ten o'clock train for Quimper and the north. When it arrived there was a mad scramble to get aboard but with René's help, Mollie got into a carriage and settled by the window with Othello in his basket. Already in the carriage were a number of French soldiers who, eyeing Mollie with her cat, started making wolf whistles and suggestive comments.

One, bolder than the others, asked in a cheeky way, 'Can I stroke your pussy, mademoiselle?' This caused a burst of raucous laughter.

At that moment an officer accompanied by his sergeant entered and, sizing up the situation, promptly ordered the troops out: 'See they travel in the last carriage, sergeant, and ask any civilians there to move forward.'

After a delay the train pulled away and made slow progress as far as Quimper where a number alighted, but more got on so that some had to sit on their luggage between seats.

Half an hour out of Quimper the train was suddenly attacked by two German Messerschmitt fighters and the engine stopped immediately. A scene of chaos followed as the attack continued with bullets smashing windows and killing and injuring many. At the rear the French soldiers detrained and with rifle and automatic weapons fired on the Germans. People left the train, jumping down by the track, some scattering into wooded areas alongside as best they could.

Out of the train Mollie managed well with Othello's basket just as the driver ran along telling all to take cover as the engine boiler was about to explode. Hardly had he given the warning than there followed a tremendous explosion tearing the engine apart and sending huge pieces of metal high in the air. Mollie was blown down and, luckily, not injured but the basket fell from her grasp and Othello bolted into the woods. She had no option but to go after him, running into the trees and bushes and calling is name. She heard the sound of aeroplanes and machine gunning again but continued to look for the cat.

Pushing her way through thick bushes and undergrowth for a while she eventually sat in a small clearing utterly exhausted. Covering her face with both hands, she started to cry and shiver uncontrollably – the result of recent shock. Suddenly she felt something brush against her leg and looked down to see Othello. Overjoyed Mollie gathered him up in her arms and hugged her warm furry friend, 'Oh, you beautiful, beautiful little cat! You will never know how delighted I am to see you and how much good you have done me!' Holding him tightly she picked her way back to the train and, emerging from the woods, stopped, aghast at the scene before her.

Dozens of the passengers were lying beside the track either dead or dying – among them many women and children. The distraught train driver came over to Mollie shaking his head as he spoke, 'The German planes came back and deliberately machine-gunned these poor helpless people; they were butchered mercilessly.' He wiped tears away with an oily rag which left little black smears under his eyes but quite quickly realised there were wounded needing medical attention.

'We must go to Chateaulin as soon as we can. It's about twenty minutes' walk and they will send help.' Mollie and about twenty other survivors, including some soldiers, set off for the town about one kilometre away and as she walked she suddenly realised, quite possibly, she would have been killed had she not run into the woods after Othello.

Lifting the lid of his basket she spoke softly to him, 'You are the most wonderful and beautiful pussycat I've ever known and I love you very much!'

Chapter 28

Margot answered the telephone and was glad to hear Norman's voice on a very clear line.

'Are you and father all right? I meant to ring a day or two ago but we were on standby to go to France after Hitler attacked the Low Countries, although it seems the powers that be decided we had to stay in England. Now, believe it or not, our squadron has been moved as far away as possible to a station near Dunbar, East Lothian; it's a bleak and dreary place. There is absolutely nothing happening here and nothing to look at except the North Sea!'

At last there was a pause and Margot took the opportunity to say something: 'Darling, I'm so pleased to hear from you but first of all, how are you? Your father and I have been anxious not hearing and wondering whether you were in the thick of it. I'm relieved to know you are still in Britain.'

'I'm fit and well, thank you, and I do understand what you are saying, mother, but you have to admit our present situation is frustrating. Having spent months training we're now shunted into a backwater and perhaps forgotten about.'

'Norman, don't be too downhearted; I feel there must be a reason for keeping you in England! After all none of us know what the future holds, but I'm sure Mr Churchill is in close touch with his commanders and will make the right decisions for our protection.'

'Okay, mother, you have a point but I hope we'll see a bit more action soon.' At that moment the 'pips' went: 'I haven't any more change and there's a queue outside the call box, so I'll ring off; my love to you both.'

Putting the telephone down, Margot realised how much she missed him and said to herself 'now come on, just pull yourself together and remember there are thousands of mothers with husbands, sons and daughters away in the forces', some already

209

in the thick of the fighting, and she recalled Aunt Lotte's words, 'we have to be brave like our soldiers and all will be well.'

At that moment Francis came into the room and she was pleased to tell him about Norman's call.

Aboard the destroyer HMS *Foxhound*, Bruno Kunz, still draped in a blanket, was brought before the duty officer, Lieutenant Anthony Whicher, a good looking man with light brown hair brushed back and deep blue eyes that seemed to penetrate the onlooker. He studied Bruno, standing between the armed escort, a petty officer and a leading seaman. Picking up his pen he asked,

'What is your full name?'

Bruno replied giving his first and second names.

Lt Whicher raised his eyebrows, 'and where were you born?'

'In the village of Hubschdorf, near Koblenz, sir.'

'And you told the petty officer you are serving with the British Army.'

'That's correct, sir. Actually, I'm commissioned with the ...' he was interrupted abruptly.

'Shut up! I've heard enough to suggest you are a German, possibly a deserter or a spy, trying to hoodwink us with a cock and bull story! I haven't the time or the inclination to waste on you at present. You will be treated as a prisoner of war and held in custody on board until we reach England when you will be handed over to the appropriate authorities.' To the petty officer he said, 'See this man gets some dry clothing and some food. He's to be held securely, you know what to do.'

Bruno was taken down several gangways to a lower deck where he was locked in a small room with a bench along one side. In the dim light he noticed the door had an aperture about a foot square covered by iron bars.

Sitting on the bench he was aware the ship was under way as the engine vibration had increased considerably. It was very warm and stretching out full length he was soon sound asleep.

The ship's crew did all they could to help the army survivors, including the many wounded, and moved among them handing out cigarettes, food and drink; they also helped to keep up morale.

Inevitably the news about Bruno went round the ship and the story was embellished by some sailors, particularly one cockney seaman who told a very good yarn: 'This 'ere Jerry come up from a submarine dressed as a WRNS orficer but when he gets on board the chiefy [petty officer] saw "she" had hairy legs, five 'er clock shadder an' a flat chest, so it was a fair cop, warn' it?' The gathering of soldiers urged him to go on. 'Well, this 'ere Jerry told me 'is name wus Erman Goring an' a mate of 'itler. Nah 'itler wants ter know the secret of yer NAFFI [Navy, Army, Air Force Institutes] "wad" [a very solid bun] which all you lot live on in Ingland, so he kern give his squaddies the same smashin' grub!'

Bursts of laughter followed but suddenly an air attack started and the ship violently altered course several times as Stuka dive bombers came screaming down towards the destroyer. With a roar the ship's air defences, pom-poms and light AA guns put up a massive barrage through which the attackers had to fly. Several bombs fell wide but one exploded very near the ship, sending up a vast fountain of water and soaking the gun crews. Two Stukas were badly damaged and flew away streaming smoke while a third exploded in mid-air, spraying flaming pieces in all directions.

As quickly as it had started the raid was over and, apart from a small fire started by a flaming piece of the stricken German bomber hitting the foredeck, the ship suffered only slight damage.

Down below in the cell, Bruno was aware the destroyer was under attack by the way it swung from side to side and audibly from the thunderous noise of the anti-aircraft guns. He prayed that the ship would survive; trapped in a locked room he appreciated that if the destroyer sunk he would probably go down with it. After a while, a petty officer and a leading seaman opened the door bringing a sailor's suit of dry clothes, a plate on which was a large bully beef sandwich and a tin mug of hot ship's cocoa.

Thanking the petty officer he enquired, 'I'm worried about the chaps in my section: would it be possible to tell them I'm on board?'

The PO's response was swift, 'You must be joking! There are upwards of 150 survivors on board and I haven't a clue which fellows are "yours", as you put it!'

Bruno was about to say thanks and leave it at that when he had a brainwave, 'I've just remembered Private Andy Law; there can't be another like him on board. You see he has a mouth organ but can only play three tunes, "Abide with Me", "Pack up Your Troubles in your Old Kit Bag" and "Cockles and Mussels". I just thought you might come across him.'

The PO looked hard at Bruno for a moment before speaking.

'To be quite honest you puzzle me and deep down I think what you're doing is just a pose. It doesn't cut any ice with me.' With that comment he locked the door and departed.

Mounting the gangway to the next deck his arm was suddenly grabbed by the leading seaman,

'Listen Chiefy? D'you hear that? It's "Pack up your Troubles"!' Sure enough, the strains of the famous Great War song, played on a mouth organ, were audible.

The PO, obviously shaken, stopped in his tracks. 'Strewth! I think we've got a big problem – we'd better find out who the musician is.'

Walking into the seaman's mess they found a large group of soldiers listening to the soft harmonica music.

The PO went over to the player, 'Are you Private Law?' The soldier stood up and saluted 'Yes, sir.'

'And who's your officer?'

'Lieutenant Kunz, sir.'

The PO stood still, shaking his head and muttering, 'Oh my God.' Then turning to Pte Law: 'You'd better come with me, it's urgent.'

Just south of Chateaulin, the mobile guns with the transports carrying stores and petrol, stopped on the road beside a railway track.

The heat from the late afternoon sun caused a shimmering effect and as Captain Sam Shelley sipped a mug of hot tea one of the gunners had brought him, he was aware, in the distance, a group of people were walking slowly between the rails. Turning to his number two, Lieutenant Danny Brunch, he pointed to the group as he spoke, 'Can you see what I see, Danny?'

Putting a pair of binoculars to his eyes, Danny scanned the rail track. 'It's a party of men, women and some children and by what I can see they look in a pretty bad way. Do you think we should offer help?'

'Yes, I do! Get some of the NCOs and go over to them.' He looked through the binoculars. 'It looks as though some are wounded so take medical kit.'

The group, numbering about thirty, had been on the track for about two hours having had to stop several times to tend the wounded, some of which were being carried pickaback by the stronger men, and all in a state of delayed shock after the bloody attack by the Germans.

Down on the railway track the group stopped and Mollie's heart gave an extra beat as she realised the approaching soldiers were British. Soon the wounded were receiving help and gunners handed round biscuits and hot tea.

Sam Shelley went across and having spoken to them in French was surprised when a young woman replied in perfect English.

'Good Lord! You must be one of us! What on earth are you doing here?'

'I've been staying with my uncle in Plonéour Lanvern but now I'm trying to get back to England.' Mollie went on to tell him about the attack by German Messerschmitt fighters and so many still awaiting help back down the line.

'If you'll write a note I'll send one of our dispatch riders into town to the Marie.' This done, he went on to tell her the battery was going south in the hope of shipping to get us home at either Lorient or St Nazaire.

Mollie asked if there was, by chance, some milk for her cat and opened the basket to produce Othello who was immediately the centre of attention. A gunner soon produced a tin of condensed milk which the cat lapped up amid an adoring crowd of soldiers.

As one gunner put it, 'He's just what we want – a black cat to bring us some luck, and to be bloody well honest, we need it!'

Talking to Lt Brunch, she asked if she could possibly travel with them, as there was no chance of her getting to Roscoff.

'If I stay in France I'll probably be interned by the Germans as I'm a British subject, so please help me if you can.'

After discussion with Captain Shelley he agreed on the understanding she should travel in a van with Lt Brunch and the Battery Warrant Officer.

Three quarters of an hour later the dispatch rider returned having delivered the message and Mollie tearfully said goodbye to the little gathering of survivors of the train massacre that afternoon.

The convoy lumbered away amid clouds of dust, leaving the train driver, a dejected figure, gazing after them and muttering, 'There goes our only hope. All we have to look forward to now is an existence under the Bosche; after this afternoon's treatment we know what to expect.'

In the English Channel the destroyer HMS *Foxhound* survived several more attacks from the Luftwaffe but as the ship drew further away from France, she came within the range of RAF fighter protection and the Stukas were no match for Hurricanes and Spitfires.

On board, Lt Bruno Kunz appeared again before the duty officer, Lt Anthony Whicher, but on this occasion he was invited to sit down. Corporal Brocks and Private Law had both 'vouched' for their officer and Bruno was given a formal apology, which he accepted unreservedly.

Talking with Lt Whicher he remarked, 'I never, in my life, expected to be held a prisoner on board one of His Majesty's Ships, dressed as a naval rating, put in the ship's prison and treated as a German prisoner of war when, in fact, I'm a naturalised British subject, having lived with my English mother and step-father in England for the last twenty-one years!' Adding with a grin, 'It's the stuff for a novel, don't you agree? I reckon I can 'dine out" on my experience for many months to come.' They had a good laugh and Lt Whicher added his comments: 'I have to tell you I much appreciate the way you have taken the whole business and accepted we had little option but to treat you as we did. In a moment I finish my tour of duty when I'll be delighted to introduce you to fellow officers in the ward room.'

Captain Sam Shelley's battery made good progress the night they left Chateaulin and, acting on information obtained from a French Army Unit, he decided to bypass Lorient and proceed directly to St Nazaire. As a continued precaution against the frequent German air attacks the battery parked by day in wooded areas and travelled by night when they were impeded less by fleeing refugees packing the roads.

Sam Shelley called his officers and NCOs together to discuss the situation regarding the guns and explained his line of reasoning.

'We have practically no ammunition for the three-point-sevens and towing them is using up fuel unnecessarily. It is highly unlikely we will get shipping to take them back to England. I'm suggesting we dump them now. What are your reactions?'

The group of officers were taken aback with this suggestion; the warrant officer was first to reply.

'I see your reasoning, sir, and agree it makes sense to reduce the weight our transports have to pull. However, what will be the position if we reach St Nazaire and find a large troopship waiting for us? Dumping the guns without Headquarters' permission would be a Court Martial offence.'

Several others followed this line of argument until Lt Brunch put forward a solution.

'We're about an hour and a half's journey from St Nazaire so why not send a dispatch rider there now to "spy out the land" and see what information he comes back with. If there's no shipping I agree we dump the guns.'

This course agreed, the dispatch rider set off without delay only to return about three hours later with the news there was absolutely nothing by way of shipping at the port. The locals there told him a large British troopship had been sunk a little offshore by the Luftwaffe and hundreds of soldiers drowned.

Consequently the guns, minus the breech blocks, were taken to a nearby quarry and blown up.

It was decided to carry on south to La Rochelle and, travelling much lighter and faster, they reached the ancient port early the following morning.

Sam Shelley and two of his officers walked along to the harbour to sum up the shipping position. They stood at the town end of the huge basin looking towards the sea and the old fortifications at the harbour entrance. Two massive stone towers stood like sentinels at the mouth of the basin, between which in days gone by a huge chain was stretched preventing access to any hostile ships.

Scanning the harbour they saw only a few small fishing boats moored against the fish quay; opposite were two large colliers discharging coal onto the dockside and a sizeable freighter unloading sacks of grain into wagons for transport elsewhere.

'We'll need the freighter and at least one collier to move our battery,' Sam spoke quietly as though he didn't want the local population to hear what he was saying. 'We must act carefully and try to negotiate a peaceful "take over", but we'll take them by force if necessary.'

The three moved back to the rest of the battery and instructions were given to have two fully armed groups to accompany the officers when they returned to the basin.

Meanwhile, Mollie had found a public telephone box and, after a short wait, had spoken to her uncle René in Plonéour Lanvern, telling him she was safe and hoped to be leaving shortly by ship from La Rochelle. He told her German troops were starting to occupy the area.

Returning to the harbour she met Lt Danny Brunch who was less than impressed when she told him about the telephone conversation she'd had with her uncle.

'That was a stupid thing to do! Don't you realise the Germans tap telephone calls? You may have alerted the Luftwaffe and put the whole battery at risk!' He continued berating Mollie who, by now, was reduced to tears.

Sam Shelley, hearing his number two shouting at Mollie, came across to see what the fuss was about.

'Now what's going on?' Turning to Danny Brunch, he said, 'Kindly keep your voice down and explain why you were speaking to Miss Tupper in that manner.'

Danny outlined what had happened and why he had spoken so sharply.

Sam realised he had to calm the situation: 'You carry on, Danny, and I'll deal with this matter.' Then, looking at Mollie, whose tear-stained face told everything, he said, 'Please don't think too harshly of Lt Brunch – he was only doing his duty as he considered the consequences of your call.' With a smile, he handed her a khaki handkerchief: 'Now wipe your eyes and put the whole matter behind you.'

A little later Monsieur Claude Ponfect, a short, fat and greasy looking man with a drooping moustache, the owner of the two coal boats, flatly refused to allow the British soldiers to use his vessels and threatened to call the gendarmerie if Sam Shelley interfered. However, the engineer on one of the boats took Sam to one side to tell him he'd be willing to take his to England with the condition his wife and two children were allowed to come as well.

The captain of the freighter was most cooperative on the understanding he would be paid handsomely in due course and told Sam the ship would be ready before midnight, providing the unloading of the cargo was complete.

After meeting his officers and NCOs, Sam Shelley told them it was his intention to block the entrance to the harbour quay where the three ships were lying and refuse access to anyone else until the ships sailed.

At 23:00 hours, the four large army transports conveying the whole battery personnel, moved to the harbour and formed a massive barrier. All the gunners and Mollie moved quickly along the dockside to the ships, leaving a fully armed group to stop any interference.

The owner of the coal boats, suspecting Sam Kelley's motives, had summoned the police and a strong force arrived, walking towards the barrier with their guns drawn. They called on the soldiers to stand aside.

The vehicles had previously been soaked in petrol and with the advancing police only yards away, Lt Brunch set fire to them. Within minutes the four transports were well alight and the gunners and their officer moved quickly along the dock, dodging between stacks of crates and other cargo as a hail of bullets came from the French police. One soldier, Gunner Stoppard, fell mortally wounded and two others received flesh wounds but then the boxes of ammunition and hand grenades started exploding in the four transports, causing the police to run for cover.

Once all the soldiers, including the body of the fallen comrade were onboard, the freighter drew away from the quayside and soon passed through the two massive towers, heading for the open sea. Looking back they could see the coal boat following as they watched the basin, illuminated by the enormous fire, slowly get smaller and smaller.

Sam Shelley, shaking his head as he spoke, said what they all felt, 'The tragedy of Gunner Stoppard, a fine soldier, is that having survived countless attacks by the Germans he was shot finally by our own allies, the French.'

Chapter 29

On 18th June 1940, following the capitulation of the French Army, Prime Minister Winston Churchill spoke to the British Nation. In stirring words he set out the gravity of the situation, as he knew the Allies were in a perilous position.

'What General Weygand called the Battle of France is over. I expect that the Battle of Britain is about to begin ... Let us therefore brace ourselves to our duties and so bear ourselves that if the British Empire and its Commonwealth last for a thousand years men will still say, This was their finest hour!'

Around the country his message was received with due reverence as the population knew what Mr Churchill had told them didn't understate the gravity of the threat now facing the British Isles.

At the Manor House in Farndene Margot and Francis listened to the broadcast on their wireless and accepted it was only a matter of time before the Germans attempted an invasion. In that situation they also realised they lived near the south coast and next door to an RAF station operating on their land. Having talked matters over, both were adamant they would stay in the Manor House as it was the family dwelling and the children must be able to come home as and when they could.

Francis worked long hours, travelling to and from Dumbarton to ensure production at the aircraft factory was being expanded on schedule and the aero engine division was being re-jigged to produce Rolls Royce engines under licence for the RAF.

Norman telephoned from time to time, always saying how bored they all were with no action and the desolate part of Scotland they occupied.

Juliet decided to abandon her Arts course, joining the WRNS and ending up at the Admiralty. With her experience she was soon engaged on chart work for the planning department.

Bruce was not fit for military duty owing to his damaged eye but was now doing secret work on aircraft design on a new four-engine bomber for AVRO. He had lodgings in the Midlands and wrote regularly to his parents.

The two youngest, Clara and Constance, continued at school in Bristol and stayed with their Grandma Fanny during term time, returning home for the school holidays. Both were bright students and their future looked good. At sixteen years old they had lost a lot of their bounce and pushiness and were developing into good looking young ladies. For their sixteenth birthday, Margot and Francis had travelled to Bristol and Fanny arranged a special dinner party for the two girls which turned out to be a thoroughly family occasion. Alex, Angelina and their youngest Thomas, Fanny's parents David and Ruth Edwards and Miss Gladys Rollo, the girls' headmistress, made an interesting gathering. Clara and her sister had new party dresses and in spite of the dreadful war situation all tried to make the occasion a happy one.

In the evening Gladys Rollo kindly took the two girls back to school thus enabling the rest to have the time together catching up on family activities and news.

At Exeter Janine and Philip Kirkwood worried for weeks having no news of Mollie trapped in France and had almost given up hope when on a bright June morning they received a telephone call from their daughter in Cardiff.

'It's Mollie, Mother,' and then a pause, 'I'm all right and so is Othello. We're in Cardiff and I hope to be with you very soon.'

Janine was overcome and could hardly speak to answer her daughter, 'Mollie, my love, I'm so overjoyed and can't wait to see you again. Come home quickly darling.' And the call was over.

Two days later Mollie arrived and her mother almost collapsed with joy, hugging and kissing Mollie over and over again. Then Janine stood looking at her daughter and realised the state Mollie was in. Her clothes were in a dreadful condition, her shoes worn out, her arms and hands cut and bruised and she looked very thin and weary.

Mollie sat taking in the surroundings of her home and then, typical of her nature she told her mother, 'I'll have a good bath and put on some fresh clothes and when I've eaten we must get on with the work at the salon.'

Philip stood up and made it clear to his stepdaughter, 'You'll do no such thing, Mollie. What you need are some days' rest and by the look of you plenty of good food. So forget about working for the time being and we'll sort things out later on.'

Mollie thanked him and reluctantly agreed. She picked up her things and she made for the door where she stopped, 'I wouldn't be here but for my dear Othello. He saved my life without any doubt whatever.'

With a smile she left the room but Othello was unmoved by her comments; in fact he was fast asleep in his favourite place, on the hearth rug.

That evening Janine prepared dinner for Philip and Mollie and they sat over the meal talking endlessly about all that had happened during the past weeks. Philip and Janine wanted to hear how their daughter had managed to escape from France after the German invasion.

Mollie told them how terrified she and the other passengers were when the train was attacked by Messerschmitt fighters, 'But for my darling Othello I would almost certainly have been killed.' Explaining about massive explosion of the steam engine, she recalled 'It just frightened him and he bolted into the woods.

'As I was searching for him, the German planes came back and machine-gunned the crowds of passengers, including women and children, who were standing beside the train. After I caught Othello I went back and ...' here she broke down and her mother comforted her. A few minutes later Mollie recovered enough to continue.

'The scene was terrible with dozens killed and wounded and the survivors stunned with what had happened. The engine driver and about thirty of us started to walk to Chateaulin along the track and two hours later we were almost there when some British soldiers gave us help. They were wonderful and their commander, Captain Sam Shelley, gave me permission to travel with them all the way to La Rochelle.'

Here she stopped and in a slightly panicky way held her hands to her face

'Oh, I was going to write a letter of thanks to him but I forgot to ask for his address; I think his home is on the coast in North Yorkshire, but I don't know for certain.'

Philip told her, 'It may be possible to contact him through the Army Post Office. Do you know his regiment details?'

'No, I only know his battery had three-point-seven anti-aircraft guns as I heard the soldiers mention it.'

Whilst Mollie was talking, Janine had been studying her and realised it was helping her daughter to unburden herself of the terrible ordeal she'd been through.

'Tell us more about the escape from La Rochelle, darling.'

'Well, mother, the final departure late that evening nearly ended in tragedy as the owner of the two coal boats reported to the police and they came armed to the docks to stop us. Had it not been for Captain Shelley's brilliant plan, to block the entrance to the quay with four huge transports, the police would have prevented us going on board. As we ran along the dockside the lorries were set alight and nobody could pass them to chase us. Sadly one gunner was shot dead by the police but his comrades brought his body to the ship. Once we had pulled away from the harbour, Captain Shelley would not allow the soldiers to machine-gun the police in case innocent civilians crowding the basin-side were injured.'

Janine nodded as she listened and wanted to hear more, 'How did you get on after the ship left La Rochelle?'

'Thank goodness it was very dark as the freighter, which was called MV *Rodrigo*, was very slow and it seemed an age before the light from the fire in the basin disappeared over the horizon. Out in the Atlantic the next day we had to put the dead soldier, Gunner Stoppard, into hessian sacks and sew them up with lots of weights ready for the funeral. Captain Shelley wrote out a burial service from memory as well as a verse of the hymn "Eternal Father, strong to save," which finishes, "Oh hear us when we cry to thee, for those in peril on the sea," and everyone gathered at the ship's side as he said the last rites when the body slipped down two planks into the sea.

'Some of the younger soldiers were very upset and in tears but the officers comforted them very well.'

Philip, who had been listening quietly up to that point, said he thought the role Captain Shelley had played showed clearly he was an excellent commander: 'It's in the best interests of all the soldiers to be present at the burial of a comrade and to say farewell to a friend. The soldiers often need comforting and, from what you have told us, the officers did what was necessary; but do please go on.'

Mollie sat back in her chair for some moments, as though trying to place the events in the right order in her mind, and then continued.

'The captain of the ship, Juan Placido, took the vessel well out into the Atlantic away from the French coast before turning in the direction of the English Channel. On the third day we saw the coal boat that escaped with us in the distance and by midday were close enough to hear all was well on board with them.

'I talked with many of the soldiers and their officers but mostly with Captain Shelley who I found a most interesting man.

'He told me his father, Captain Edgar Shelley, had served with the East Yorkshire Rifles in the Great War and had rescued Captain Francis Vining, a badly injured Royal Flying Corps pilot, carrying him back to Allied lines and thus saving his life. Sadly his father was subsequently killed in 1917. He also spoke of his sister Marion who is in the WRNS and works at the Admiralty in Bath. If only I could remember I'd tell you more about the journey in the Atlantic.'

Philip was eager to hear the rest of the story and prompted Mollie, 'Take your time my dear and it will all come back to you. By the way, did the soldiers have any duties on board?'

'Yes, I remember now. Captain Shelley and his officers kept a routine parade each morning and evening and duties were allocated. Two of the soldiers volunteered to help the cook prepare what food they had, which wasn't much, so everyone was rationed. Four lookouts were on each side of the ship, watching for other vessels but particularly for U-boats, and they wore waterproof clothing loaned by the ship's crew. As we sailed into the Western Approaches in the English Channel, we all nearly had a heart attack as a submarine surfaced about one hundred yards away and signalled us to stop. Luckily it was a British boat and the boarding party got the surprise of their lives finding the soldiers and me on the ship. One cheeky sailor said to me "if you like, love, you can come back with us, we're a friendly lot and it's very cosy down below!" Needless to say I didn't go but the sailors were wonderful and returned with tins of cigarettes and some chocolate for the soldiers.

'The next morning we saw the coast of England and a feeling of great relief went through all on board. I sat down on a coil of rope on the deck just crying with relief at the wonderful sight and it was then Sam Shelley came over and put his arm round to comfort me.'

She sat motionless looking at her hands in her lap and saying nothing for several moments.

'I found being with him so comforting and I know I like him an awful lot!'

Philip and Janine both looked at each other and smiled as her mother spoke, 'Darling, are we to understand there is a silver lining to the terrible ordeal you have gone through?'

Mollie's face coloured up but the sparkle in her eyes gave them the answer before she replied.

'When I said I like him a great deal I know it's a lot more than that. I suppose I've fallen in love for the first time in my life and it's strange it all came about in such terrible circumstances.'

Janine was naturally elated and pressed her daughter, 'Mollie, I'm absolutely delighted with your news! But do you know if your love is reciprocated?'

Mollie hesitated before answering, 'I honestly don't know but I had the feeling he was very attracted to me in the way he cared for me throughout the time I was with his battery. He always made a point of watching over and protecting me on every occasion. I so want to see him again but don't know how I can contact him.'

Janine sat next to her daughter and put both arms round her, 'My darling, we will do everything we can to trace Captain Shelley and I'm sure we'll find him eventually, so stop worrying.

'My dear, you said his home was on the coast of North Yorkshire but did he talk about any special features in his area?'

Philip was doing his best to help, 'You know, something like his local church or a river, harbour or docks. You see something of the sort will help us decide where he lives. Maybe if I mention a few names you will possibly know one.' He thought for a few seconds and then reeled off a few, 'Bridlington, Flamborough, Scarborough, Filey, Whitby, Saltburn, Redcar.'

Mollie, looking more desperate than ever, just shook her head, 'I'm sorry, I don't recognise any of those as he never mentioned a place. He did say he had a marvellous view from his house on a hill and could see the huge ruins of an abbey on the other side of the river but he didn't say where it was.'

Philip could hardly contain himself as he almost shouted, 'I've got it! He lives in Whitby or I'll eat my hat! When you said he looks across the river at huge ruins he would be looking at the ruined abbey of St Hilda on the hill on the opposite side of the river Esk and next to the ruin is the wonderful old church of St Mary. Do you know to get from the harbour up to the church the faithful have to climb a flight of 199 stairs – so they have to be fit and dedicated.'

Mollie jumped up and put her arms round her stepfather and gave him a hug and a kiss. 'Oh, you are so clever solving what seemed an impossible puzzle, thank you very much. Now I can write to him,' and here she stopped and her mother intervened.

'Why not write care of, say, the police station, I'm sure they will know where he lives.'

Philip wasn't so sure, 'If he's a law-abiding person they

possibly wouldn't know him.'

Janine would not be put off so easily and laughingly challenged her husband, 'I bet you a pound to a pinch of jellyfish the police will know Captain Shelley and his family. So are you on?'

Philip knew when he was in a corner and responded with good grace, 'All right, it's on and I hope with all my heart I have to pay you, as it'll mean Mollie has found her man. But where I can get the jellyfish, heaven knows! On another point, do you know if he's single?'

'Well, he never at any time mentioned a wife or children and I'm sure he would have told me about them if he'd been married.'

For a while longer they talked about Mollie's brothers. Rupert was with a Spitfire squadron on the south coast and her mother said he'd telephoned once to tell her they were in action a lot during the Dunkirk rescue. Janine produced several letters from Tom which she handed to Mollie as they said goodnight and moments later her daughter went up to bed carrying her faithful friend Othello with her.

Chapter 30

The country was in a sombre mood following the tragedy of Dunkirk and with the subsequent collapse of France, increased attacks by the Luftwaffe were a warning of the things to come. Throughout July the German aircraft stepped up their bombing of shipping in the English Channel also carrying out sporadic raids on the south coast in an effort to tempt the RAF fighters into combat, though in the process they lost valuable pilots.

British intelligence surveillance intercepting radio traffic reported that Hitler, on 1st August, ordered the Luftwaffe to destroy the Royal Air Force without delay. Consequently full scale bombing attacks commenced against Fighter Command airfields and radar installations along the south coast and Spitfire and Hurricane Squadrons were constantly in action. Huge formations of Heinkel and Dornier bombers with massive fighter escort were met head on by the defenders who severely mauled the enemy. The German plan to knock out our airfields was not achieved and the battle raged throughout August into September when the climax was reached and hordes of defeated Nazi squadrons retreated to their bases in France and Belgium. The hard fought Battle of Britain was won but in the process Britain had lost many of brave young pilots, as acknowledged by the inspiring words of Winston Churchill, 'Never in the field of human conflict was so much owed by so many to so few'

As the air battle unfolded, the Commander-in-Chief of Fighter Command, Air Chief Marshall Sir Hugh Dowding, rotated his squadrons so that the burden of the fighting in the south east fell equally on all pilots as far as it was possible.

In the last week of August, Norman Vining's squadron was moved south and was at once in action over Kent and Sussex. They lost some aircraft but gave a good account of themselves shooting down a total of eleven German raiders by the first week in September, Norman claiming three Messerschmitt 109 Fighters. During their second week, on an overcast day with showers and some bright periods, they were given a vector late morning to intercept a large enemy force over the Thames Estuary. The Germans took advantage of cloud as far as they could but had to break cover to make bombing runs.

Norman caught a Dornier as it emerged from the clouds, already damaged with smoke streaming from one engine, and promptly fired a long burst into the port wing of the stricken bomber which burst into flames as it dived to earth.

Listening to the RT [radio telephone] ground control he was alerted and shortly after saw a large formation of enemy bombers and fighters flying in the direction of London. His reaction was to get above them to attack and to make height he started a rapid climb through broken cloud at the same time turning in the enemy's direction.

Some minutes later he broke cloud cover and, with absolutely no time for evasive action, flew straight into the side of a Messerschmitt 109 fighter. As the Spitfire ploughed into the German plane Norman was knocked unconscious by the enormous impact.

Locked together the two planes rolled over and over, spiralling down in flames, leaving behind a black twisted smoke trail as the only evidence of the terrible collision.

Later that afternoon at Fighter Command 11 Group Headquarters, Wing Commander Felix Beaumont was checking squadron losses of pilots and aircraft and learnt that Norman Vining was missing. In the previous year Felix had spent a short time at RAF Farndene and, while using part of the Manor House as the officers mess, had got to know Francis and Margot Vining very well. In the circumstances he immediately offered to telephone the Vinings direct to tell them the news.

Shortly after noon that day, in the quiet south London suburb of Merton Park, groups of local friends were taking their lunch break in the Old Toby Jug public house, enjoying a sandwich and chat over a pint of beer, when the air raid sirens sounded the alert. The publican told all his customers to come away from the windows, across which strips of white material had been stuck for safety. He explained to his customers they should listen for any further developments.

Opposite the pub on the main road were situated a small petrol garage and motor workshop, behind which a group of old, ivy-covered, cottages occupied the island site. To one side a parade of shops was busy with midday shoppers; away to the right stood the Nelson Memorial Hospital.

A steel-helmeted policeman going off duty and looking forward to a refreshing pint was just propping his bicycle against the pub wall and removing his cycle clips when he saw a brilliant light breaking through the clouds above. To his horror he immediately realised it was an aeroplane on fire. Dashing into the pub he shouted a warning for everyone to lie flat on the floor at the same time diving under a table. What seemed only seconds later the whole building was shaken by an immense explosion and the pub windows were shattered sending showers of broken glass and timber across the bar room. Stunned people crawled from under the tables to gaze at the wreckage around them; miraculously nobody was injured.

Not realising the door had been blown away the policeman walked outside and looked across the road. He couldn't believe his eyes as the garage and workshop had all but disappeared, replaced by a blazing mass of twisted wreckage while the roadway was covered with smouldering debris including pieces of aircraft.

Another cycle rider a short way up the road had seen the whole thing and told the constable, 'I watched two flaming planes come spiralling down, landing smack bang opposite the pub. I sheltered in a shop doorway as bits of burning garage came down like rain after the explosion.'

Shortly after, more police and the Fire Service arrived and the area was immediately cleared in view of the danger of further explosions from underground petrol storage tanks.

Luckily the garage owner and his assistant had gone across to the Old Toby Jug for their lunch break otherwise both would have been killed. Sadly the only casualty was the garage cat, Groucho, a great friend to many in the area.

At the Manor House, Farndene later that evening Margot answered the telephone and recognised Felix Beaumont's voice.

'How nice to hear from you Felix; how are things with you?' Margot had always liked him and his wife and they met many times in the autumn of the previous year.

'Margot, I'll come straight to the point. I'm very sorry indeed to tell you Norman didn't return to base today and is presumed missing.'

Suddenly drained of all feeling and with a cold perspiration gripping her body, Margot was unable to speak for some moments.

Felix became very worried and spoke very quietly again, 'Margot, are you all right?'

'Yes, yes, thank you. I'm sorry I didn't answer but the news was such a shock. Oh Felix, I've dreaded hearing this message and have had a feeling we'd lose Norman sooner or later.'

'I'm not going to raise your hopes but there is always a possibility he may have made a forced landing in a remote area and not been able to contact base.'

'Felix it's kind of you to put that suggestion to me but I think I know the possibility of that happening is very remote indeed.'

She thanked him for his consideration and they talked for a few minutes before hanging up.

Margot went straight to the study to tell Francis and as she entered he spoke, with tears in his eyes, before she had uttered a word.

'Darling, I heard the whole conversation and the terrible news on this extension.' Moving across the room he was just quick enough to support Margot as she collapsed into his arms.

In Exeter the Madame Baume dress salon had almost entirely turned over to production of uniforms for the Government and, with some of the younger women going into the forces, Janine and Mollie worked long hours with their depleted staff to keep pace with orders. After work in the evening Mollie, her mother and Philip were glad to have a quiet meal together and try to relax before listening to the nine o'clock news on the wireless. At half past eight the September sun illuminated their living room with pale yellow light giving a feeling of comfort to all three of them.

Philip, who was reading, put his book down remarking, 'What a lovely evening. We're fortunate to be able to enjoy it but tragically many are suffering in this country and in Europe as the result of this terrible war.' He sighed and shook his head, 'And the news is as bad as ever, we never seem to be able to win against the Nazis.'

Janine who listened patiently put her hand on his arm, 'Now you must not get so downhearted. That's exactly what Hitler wants, a demoralised population so he can walk over here and occupy us!'

Mollie smiled as she joined the conversation, 'Well done, Mother. We must keep our spirits up and no doubt we'll win eventually. But I must correct one small point you mentioned. I don't think Hitler is the Messiah so he couldn't walk over here!'

They all had a good laugh as Mollie turned the wireless on for the news at nine.

After the wonderful chimes of Big Ben, the announcer gave the detail of the latest bulletin from the Air Ministry, 'during operations today the Royal Air Force shot down eighty-five enemy aircraft with the loss of twenty-two planes,' and he went on to give details of several of our pilots who had been saved.

Janine's reaction to Philip was immediate, 'There you are darling! What did I tell you? And Mollie's right, if we keep up our spirits we'll definitely win, you'll see.'

Philip had certainly cheered up and agreed he had to keep his pecker up!

He then asked Mollie if she had received a reply to the letter she sent to Captain Shelley a few weeks earlier.

Before replying she was very subdued for a moment, 'No I

haven't, and to be honest I don't think I will now. I suppose I got carried away believing he was attracted to me, so that's that!'

Janine and Philip looked up and motioned to each other not to continue the subject.

At 11 Group Headquarters, Fighter Command, information concerning the incident at Merton Park, south London, was filtering through and it was confirmed a Spitfire had crashed with a German plane. Part of the Spitfire's fuselage had blown some distance from the crash site and been recovered later. From this piece of wreckage the serial number had been identified as Norman Vining's aircraft.

With the irrefutable evidence now to hand, Wing Commander Felix Beaumont decided reluctantly to telephone Norman's parents.

The number rang for a few moments before contact was made with Francis Vining.

'Hello Francis, this is Felix Beaumont. I'm afraid I'm not the bearer of good news but I promised to keep you and Margot informed when we had further information about Norman. We now know his plane crashed in south London last Wednesday and as a huge fire followed, we must presume he hasn't survived. I'm so desperately sorry for you and Margot and hope the next thing I have to tell you will mitigate the loss of your boy in a small way. The Air Ministry have awarded Norman the Distinguished Flying Cross for outstanding devotion to duty. Unfortunately the award will now have to be posthumous and I'll write with more details as soon as I can.'

Francis thanked Felix for his personal interest in Norman's case and asked for details of the place where the crash took place, which were promised in due course.

He put the handset down and with a heavy heart left the study to tell Margot their son was no more and there could never be a funeral to see him laid to rest.

The loss of Norman Vining hit the family hard and as they received the news, each decided to come home to comfort their parents and to be together. Juliet and Bruce both arranged to return at the weekend but the two youngest, who were still at school, remained with their Grandma Fanny in Bristol.

Derek Norland and his wife Nancy lived in an Edwardian terraced house in Acacia Road, Balham, south London, with their two children, Jennie, aged seventeen, and her brother Murray who was two years younger. Last but not least was the dominant member of the family, Patch, a black and white Jack Russell terrier.

Derek, who was wounded in the final months of the Great War, worked in the Air Raid Headquarters on communication duties, while his wife did war work with the Women's Institute. Jennie travelled to London each day where she was employed in a city bank.

Murray and his best friend Geoffrey White were boy scouts and carried out 'Runners' duties for the local ARP post and the police every day after school.

A short distance from the Norland's home stood Garton House, a large mid-Victorian residence, built with the familiar pale yellow London bricks, which had stood empty since the elderly owner died in 1938. The house, situated on the corner of two roads, Garton Street and Lonsdale Avenue, had an extensive garden, enclosed by a high brick wall, at the end of which were outbuildings comprising a stable with a hay loft above and a large double coach house facing Lonsdale Avenue, all in a similar dilapidated condition to the residence.

On Saturday 15th September, a bright morning, Murray and his friend Geoffrey set out with Patch, ostensibly to run the dog but also to have a secret rendezvous.

Reaching Garton House they turned into the side avenue which ran parallel to the long garden and, a little way along, stopped until there was nobody about. In a matter of seconds they were both over the wall with Patch, all landing safely the other side.

Here was the secret rendezvous in the shape of an old world garden which had grown wild over a period of two years. Beautiful roses almost choked by masses of brambles which also grew in profusion covering ornamental trees and shrubs, creating a wilderness effect. To one side a brick built store and potting shed had become almost engulfed by ivy and blackberry growth now laden with masses of ripe glistening fruit. Further down, amid waist high grass and weeds, a small orchard of apples, pears and plums was dominated by a massive mulberry tree, the dark red fruit of which offered countless birds their daily food and the evidence after their feasting was visible by the mass of purple droppings beneath the tree. The objective of the two boys was fruit from the pear and apple trees and they lost no time in filling the hessian bags they had brought with them.

Meanwhile Patch spent his time ferreting round the garden chasing the occasional rat or bird for amusement. Reaching the outbuildings the dog started to bark at the open door of the stable and continued after Murray had shouted, 'Shut up, Patch, or you'll wake the neighbours! Patch, come here!' But he continued barking with no let up, so much so Murray climbed down from an apple tree to put the dog on his lead.

As he reached the stable door he could see someone was lying on the floor but not moving or reacting to the ferocious barking. Murray, by now completely unnerved, shouted to his friend, 'Geoff, come here quickly.'

The two boys gave each other confidence, and Murray ventured into the stable to take a closer look. He realised immediately the body lying on the floor was that of an airman. Glancing at the legs saw a lot of blood had oozed out onto the floor attracting masses of flies and wasps.

'Geoff, I think he's dead. We better tell the police when we go back so they can come to collect him. Let's go now.'

Geoff was not so certain and suggested, 'I think we should feel for a pulse before we push off; if he's still alive he might have a chance if he gets to hospital soon. What do you say?'

Murray hesitated but deep down knew from all their first aid training it was imperative to ascertain whether the heart was still functioning.

'Okay, I try the neck for signs of life,' and putting his fingers on the neck artery stood quite still for a moment before almost shouting, 'There's a pulse! I'm sure there's a faint throbbing! You feel Geoff.'

Within a few moments Geoff was away and over the wall, running for all his worth to the local police station.

Meanwhile, Murray stood outside the stable puzzling how the airman had got into the old building. Inevitably he was tempted to feel for the pulse again and relieved to find the airman was still alive. Looking at the pilot's clothes he became aware the front of the uniform was stained with the purple bird droppings which spread like a carpet under the Mulberry tree.

Murray reasoned the airman had been under the tree and went out to investigate.

Looking round nothing suggested an answer until he glanced up and there was the solution he was seeking.

Harness straps were hanging through the branches about seven feet from the ground and way above, at the top of the massive tree, the silk folds of a parachute were just visible.

Incredibly, Murray thought, the tree had probably saved the airman's life by giving him a soft landing.

Not too soon for Murray, the police, fire service and an ambulance arrived and in minutes the large doors of the coach house were forced open admitting the doctor and nurse. After giving the airman an injection the doctor told the ambulance driver to go straight to St George's Hospital without delay, 'Every minute counts as the patient is in a desperate condition!'

With bells ringing, the ambulance escorted by a police car left at high speed for the hospital at Hyde Park Corner.

Chapter 31

About the third week of September, Philip Kirkwood left Exeter by an early train to stay in Worcester with an old army friend who had been ill following wounds he received in the Great War.

As it was a beautiful early autumn day, Janine and Mollie decided to finish work at lunchtime, giving the staff of the Madame Baume Salon the afternoon off.

With the time free, Mollie and her mother intended going to Teignmouth for the rest of the day hoping to see Ellery Hales, the old friend who kept riding stables and bred donkeys for children's rides on the local beach.

Arriving at Exeter railway station they entered the concourse crowded with travellers, including a large number of soldiers, sailors and airmen on draft, standing and smoking in groups with their kit and guns, awaiting announcements about the departure of trains.

While her mother went to the booking office for tickets, Mollie checked the departure lists at one side of the station for their train details.

Arrivals from a London train were streaming off a nearby platform and looking at these people she suddenly gave a sharp gasp. Walking towards Mollie was an army captain she recognised immediately as none other than Sam Shelley. With a beaming smile he came up and grasped both her hands.

'It's lovely to see you again, Mollie, and good of you to come and meet me. But how did you know which train I'd be on?'

Completely taken aback, she withdrew her hands quickly as she spoke in a very direct manner: 'I'd no idea what train you were coming on! I'd no idea you were coming at all! How could I have any idea what you were doing when you hadn't the courtesy to answer my letter for all these weeks! You have disappointed me to say the least, so please don't pester me!' With those words she turned to make her way back to the booking office.

Sam was stunned by the sharpness of Mollie's tone and took a moment to recover from her verbal broadside but ran after her to remonstrate.

Grasping her arm he forced Mollie to stop as he explained the situation, 'I received your letter just two days ago. When you wrote care of the police station they didn't deliver it for very good reasons. Will you please give me a chance to tell you?'

Mollie stopped, somewhat reluctantly at first, but looking at Sam and taking in what he had said, she realised she had been hasty. 'I'm sorry, Sam, but I had no idea you hadn't got my letter, so what you are going to tell me will I hope put matters right. I was just going to see where mother's got to so why don't you wait until you meet her to explain what has happened?'

Sam fell in with Mollie's suggestion and after meeting Janine, who thought he looked very attractive, he invited them to the Royal Hotel, a short distance from the station where they could eat and talk in comfort.

Once in the hotel dining room Sam went to great pains to outline all that had happened after landing at Cardiff back in June. 'Foolishly I didn't make a note of your address, Mollie, and for the life of me I couldn't remember which town you lived in. I'd given up all hope of seeing you again when a policeman called at my mother's house in Whitby and produced the missing letter. He told me a colleague had put the letter in his pocket to deliver on the beat but most unfortunately the chap went down with acute appendicitis before he left the station. The poor fellow almost died with peritonitis and was off work for weeks and it was only when he returned the letter was discovered, still in his pocket!'

Janine watched her daughter's reaction and was aware how much Mollie's face had softened and her eyes shone as she listened to Sam's explanation. It looked as though Cupid had done his work and as a mother she felt sure it spelt happiness for her daughter.

As they left the hotel two hours later Janine suddenly remembered the train tickets she had bought, 'Oh my goodness! I've two tickets for Teignmouth and we can't use them now so it looks as though I've lost my money.'

Sam's reaction was instant: 'Here, give me the tickets and I'll see what I can do to charm the booking clerk.'

Returning ten minutes later he handed Janine the money refund and said with a smile, 'I told the clerk my fiancée and I had double booked so he gave me the cash back without batting an eyelid,' and to Mollie, 'and I hope one day soon what I've just said will be true.'

Mollie's smiling face coloured and deep down she too hoped one day it would be true.

Wing Commander Felix Beaumont finished writing a personal letter of condolence to Francis and Margot Vining on the Sunday after Norman's crash and sat back sipping a mug of hot coffee an orderly had just delivered, when the Signals Flight Sergeant entered the room.

'Sir, I've just received a telephone message from St George's Hospital in London, and here is the gist of it.' He handed his officer a signals message form.

Scanning the form, Felix suddenly sat bolt upright as he took in the import of the contents.

'Good God! I can hardly believe what I'm reading! I've never believed in miracles but this is most surely one!' Turning to the Flight Sergeant, he said, 'It's the best bloody news I've had for years; I'm absolutely delighted to learn Norman Vining is alive!'

Shortly after, he spoke with the surgeon at St George's Hospital who said Norman was in a sorry state on arrival at the hospital, suffering from very severe wounds including burns. 'We've patched him up as best we could and the miracle is that he's alive in spite of lying in a stable for nearly three days. But for the boy scouts he would have died.'

Felix decided, there and then, to fly down to RAF Farndene to tell Margot and Francis the wonderful news and half an hour later his Spitfire was airborne flying west.

Sitting in the Manor House drawing room the Vining family was taking coffee on that Sunday afternoon, with Bertie the butler moved quietly offering second cups all round. Juliet and her brother Bruce had arranged a few days leave and had done their best to comfort Margot and Francis but it was clear their mother hadn't recovered from the shock of Norman's death. Conversation was limited and Juliet felt it was one sided and a bit forced by Bruce and her.

Looking out of the French doors Juliet saw a figure walking across the lawns towards the house,

'Look, Mummy, there's an airman coming to the door.'

Margot recognised the visitor immediately. 'Why, it's Felix. Bertie, please let the Wing Commander in.'

After formal introductions Felix said he had something most important to tell them. 'I feel like a herald as I give you the most wonderful news. Norman is alive and in St George's Hospital, Hyde Park Corner.'

At this point Margot almost leapt from her chair to put her arms round Felix. 'Oh, Felix, what an incredibly wonderful, marvellous thing you have told us.' She stopped out of breath and with tears streaming down her face just as Juliet joined in the hugging with her mother.

Gently Felix broke free, 'Now be careful both of you or the herald will be crushed and you won't hear the rest of what I have to say.'

The elation subsided and he went on to give all the information he could, suggesting they visit their son the next day.

Time was short, so Felix had to be on his way and as he said farewell suggested they wave him off. Fifteen minutes later they stood on the lawn at the back of the house as the Spitfire thundered over in a low pass before making two victory rolls and climbing away to the east.

With a lighter spring in his step, Francis went to the study to telephone the good news to his mother and the rest of the family in Bristol, as well as Margot's parents in Whitby.

Back in the Drawing room Margot was quiet as she recalled

the words Fanny had spoken at the beginning of the war, 'but we have to be brave like our soldiers and all will be well.'

She had suffered the supreme test of bereavement and now, by what seemed a miracle, their son had, as it were, come back from the dead; suddenly Margot felt a remarkable sense of calm.

Standing up, she turned to Francis, Juliet and Bruce to say what she thought was now necessary. 'You have all been wonderful giving me support during the past few days and I appreciate how much it has helped me but I feel perhaps I should have helped myself more than I did and I'm sorry. I know I have been guilty of self pity, which I fought desperately to overcome, but losing a first-born child is a terrible thing. Please forgive me and try to understand the turmoil in my mind which, thank God, is now at rest.'

As he was joined by the two children, Francis came across the room quickly to take his wife in his arms and kiss her, but it was Juliet who said what they all felt about Margot. 'We understand exactly what you have gone through, Mummy, and the last thing you must have is a feeling of guilt. You have been the most wonderful mother always giving so much to us children and now it's our turn to give back some of that love and care you gave us.'

Francis agreed, 'Juliet, you have said exactly what I was thinking. Now we must look ahead to the time when Norman has recovered and is back with us. I suggest we make a firm resolution to have a family party of parties hopefully in the next few months.'

The same Sunday afternoon in Balham, the Norland family were still talking about yesterday's events when there was a rat-tat at the front door. Derek Norland answered the call and moments later he returned with Sergeant Fred Wallace from the local police station.

Fred Wallace was a huge man with a florid complexion and a waxed moustache, worn since his army days as a Sergeant Major in the Middlesex Regiment. Casting his eye round the room, he noted how neat and tidy it appeared with bent cane chairs around a long oak table covered with a green cloth, in the centre of which stood a large brass bowl containing an equally large maidenhair fern.

Pretty chintz curtains at the window blended well with the patterned paper on the walls upon which several family photographs were hung. The brown lino on the floor shone, reflecting the various pieces of furniture standing on it, while a pale fawn woollen rug in front of the hearth was the resting place of the family dog, Patch. On the mantelpiece an eight-day chiming clock occupied the middle between two well-polished brass candle sticks, the whole backed by a long mirror. The room brought back pleasant childhood memories of his parent's cottage in Mitcham, Surrey.

'Please sit down, sergeant,' Derek offered a seat and Fred Wallace made himself comfortable in an easy chair, planting his enormous, well-polished boots firmly on the floor.

'Thank you, Mr Norland. Now I've come to see your son and his friend and, as they are both here, may I talk to them direct?' Derek Norland nodded his approval.

'Well,' the sergeant went on, addressing Murray and his friend Geoff, 'I understand you two young fellows were trespassing in the garden of Garton House, Garton Street, yesterday and at the same time taking fruit without the owner's permission. What have you got to say for yourselves?'

At this point he turned to Derek Norland giving him a huge wink.

The two boys were obviously worried by the accusation of trespass and Murray spoke up for both of them, 'We hadn't any idea we were trespassing and thought the place was derelict as nobody seemed to own it. We didn't take any fruit as we forgot all about it when we found the injured airman.'

The sergeant got up and went out of the room, returning immediately with the two hessian bags of fruit the boys had left behind and, with a broad grin on his face, handed them to Murray.

'These belong to you and your friend and, I have to tell you, at the station we are all impressed with you two boy scouts. That airman would have died in the stable if you two hadn't gone scrumping. I was pulling your leg when I spoke of trespass as no owner has been traced for the past two years. Our Chief Inspector will be writing to you shortly congratulating you both on your action and presence of mind. Well done both of you!'

At this point Nancy Norland suggested a cup of tea and shortly after Fred Wallace joined them for what he called his favourite refreshment, 'a cuppa tea and a slice of fruit cake.'

Francis and Margot reached St George's Hospital late on Monday morning – their train being delayed by an air raid alert – and were shown into a private room to meet the surgeon Mr Patrick Wilson who explained Norman's injuries in detail.

'Your son has a number of broken ribs, torn arm muscles, scorched skin on his upper body and various small cuts to his face and hands. However, these are not life threatening and, given time, he'll recover. He also received severe injury to his left lower leg and foot which were crushed. I regret I had no alternative but to amputate below the knee to save his life. I wish I could give you better news and can only add that if your boy hadn't been extremely fit to start with he wouldn't have survived lying in a stable for three days.'

Margot sat gripping her husband's arm as she assimilated all the surgeon had said and burying her head against his shoulder wept for some moments as Francis comforted her.

'Mrs Vining, I do understand your feelings. To hear your son has lost part of his leg is, without doubt, a tremendous shock but I have great faith he will recover in time and with an artificial appliance will have a normal lifestyle.' The surgeon spoke quietly and with sincerity.

Margot looked up and, accepting the handkerchief Francis offered, answered Patrick Wilson without hesitation, 'I'm sorry. I was overcome by the whole situation but feel much better now. We appreciate all you have done for Norman and are just thankful he is alive. I'm sure what you said about an artificial limb is perfectly true and knowing our son, he'll get on with his life.'

Patrick Wilson stood up and invited them to join him, 'Shall we go now to see Norman? He is a short way along the corridor.'

Margot and Francis entered the room after the surgeon and immediately their eyes focused on Norman, propped up in bed with several pillows. At first sight he appeared to be swathed in bandages, on his hands and arms and around his head, while there were several small patches on his face and neck and one eye covered by a large pad.

Norman spoke first, smiling with the visible part of his face, 'Hello Mother, Father, thanks for coming up. I bet you never reckoned on seeing me in this state, looking like Nelson!' His humour broke the ice with his parents and Margot went to the bed and stopped, 'Darling, where do I kiss you? I might hurt you.'

Norman's reply was typical, 'There may be a square inch somewhere on my face but why don't I kiss you both? I can't shake hands at present!'

After a few moments laughing, the surgeon left them to continue his rounds and they talked for a while about the family and it was then Norman sprang a surprise.

'I want you to know I have been seeing a young lady for some time and I think I've fallen for her completely.' Margot sat up and was about to say something but he continued.

'Please let me tell you all about her before you comment. Her name is Helen Dauntsey. She's the daughter of Sir Charles and Lady Violet Dauntsey of Framley Park, Oxford, and she's a cipher officer in the WAAF [Women's Auxiliary Air Force] at Group Headquarters. She is very good looking with blue eyes and auburn hair and is about your height mother. Before the crash I hoped to get some leave to bring her down to meet you and the rest of the family but it will have to wait until I'm back on my feet.' He stopped suddenly realising what he had said and typically made a joke about his condition, 'I mean back on my foot!'

His parents were delighted to hear about the young lady and Francis wanted to know more: 'Is it really serious, Norman? Are we likely to hear wedding bells shortly?

Norman nodded, 'Yes, Father, the sooner the better as far as I'm concerned!'

Margot's eyes were shining at this news. 'Norman darling, we'll look forward to meeting Helen soon and a family wedding is just what we want, so buck up and get well as quickly as you can.'

They chatted for a little while longer and Norman made two requests before they left.

'I want to thank the two boy scouts who found me if they can come up here to visit me. Please also telephone Helen at Group Headquarters and tell her where I am and ask her to come to see me.'

Francis and Margot left the hospital and, arm in arm, walked through Green Park chatting about the future for Norman and the family. Reaching Piccadilly, Francis decided he was hungry and suggested lunch at a good restaurant in Lower Regent Street, 'I think we need some food and while we eat we can make some definite plans for the family homecoming party for Norman which I hope won't be too long now.'

Chapter 32

Norman Vining made a good recovery and, after being fitted with an artificial leg and foot at a special unit at Roehampton, South London, was granted extended leave by the Royal Air Force.

In mid-November he arrived at the Manor House, Farndene, driven down from London by his girlfriend Helen Dauntsey who had also been given leave. It was a very emotive homecoming for him but he and Helen soon settled in and relaxed in the country atmosphere.

From the word go, Helen hit it off with Margot and Francis and each enjoyed the other's company. She was a delightful character, an intelligent person who had read Modern Languages at Cambridge, obtaining a first class degree. Her incisive mind was admirably suited for the duties she performed in the RAF. Very much in love with Norman, she looked forward to a wedded future with him.

However, during the second week at the Manor House, Norman suddenly had cold feet about their future.

'Helen, darling, since being down here on leave I've been turning over the question of our being engaged and subsequently married and find I'm uncertain about the whole business.'

Helen felt uneasy and was on the point of saying something when he stopped her.

'Darling, please let me finish what I want to tell you. You know I'm absolutely in love with you and find you a wonderful person to be with. Am I being fair to you expecting a healthy young woman to marry a part cripple with no hope of ever being one hundred per cent again? I want you to understand I'd be terribly upset should I lose you but if you want to end our relationship, I'll understand.'

With her eyes misted with tears, Helen sat looking at him for a moment before speaking and then, taking his hands, spoke from her heart: 'My poor dearest Norman, whatever put such ideas into your head? I have never, for one moment, ever considered you a cripple because you've lost a foot! I love you as you are and would be devastated if we broke up, so please put all those thoughts out of your mind.'

It was Norman's turn to have misted eyes! And, putting his arms round Helen, drew her to him in a long embrace before replying, 'Sweetheart, you are the most wonderful person I have ever known and I've loved all you've said. Thank you for dispelling my doubts and telling me how much you love me.' He sat holding hands and looking into her eyes for minutes before going on, 'Now that's settled there's one other question I have to ask you: when will it be convenient for you to marry me?'

Helen's answer was immediate and without hesitation, 'Darling Norman, the sooner the better!' And, giggling after a slight pause, 'I can then share your bed legally, sweetheart!'

After much hugging and kissing, he suggested, 'Let's tell our parents and then decide on a date for the wedding.'

On 15th November, Janine and Philip sat listening to the nine o'clock news on the wireless, glad to be indoors on a very cold evening, and the announcer spoke of heavy raids in the Midlands the previous night. Philip felt uneasy as his sister Kitty lived in Coventry with her elderly Aunt Phoebe, and leaving the room went to telephone them. Returning minutes later he told Janine, 'I can't understand it, the operator said the line was out of action. I hope Kitty's all right.'

Janine looked up from her sewing and made a suggestion: 'Darling, why not ask the operator to put you in touch with the Coventry Police Station? They will know the local situation and be able to set you mind at rest.'

'Thank you Janine, that's a splendid idea; I'll do that now.'

A quarter of an hour passed before he came back to the room looking shaken, 'Janine, the news isn't good. The police were very helpful but told me there was a massive raid on Coventry last night during which the wonderful cathedral was gutted and a large part of the town severely damaged. Conduit Street, where Kitty lives, had several direct hits but they couldn't tell me if her house, number seven, was one of those demolished. The officer took our telephone number and will let us know as soon as he gets more information.

'I'm so sorry, darling. It sounds as though Coventry has suffered one of the terror raids Hitler promised when Mr Churchill refuse to contemplate peace talks with the Nazis. But take heart, Philip, Kitty may be safe and we'll know soon now the police are looking into the situation.'

As she picked up her hand work again she told Philip of her own anxieties, 'I worry about Tom in the Midlands working in an aircraft factory which will be an obvious target for the Germans.' She paused in thought for a moment, 'And Rupert, who went through those terrible dog fights with the Luftwaffe; it seems ages since we saw him.'

Philip spoke comforting words, 'Now, my dearest, we must not worry, as worry will get us nowhere. By the way, what time is Mollie's London train due?

'She said she'd catch the fast train which I think gets in at about ten fifteen.'

Looking at his watch, Philip noted it was just five minutes to ten, 'I'll go along to the station to meet her in a few minutes. I could do with a walk and it'll be company for her coming home.'

'That's very thoughtful of you, Philip, but mind you wrap up well and take a torch.'

Janine just finished speaking when the front door bell gave a long ring.

As Philip stood, he looked puzzled, 'Who can that be at this time of night? You stay put, Janine, and I'll answer the door.'

Janine could hear voices in the hall way and was curious until the door opened and in strode Rupert and Mollie followed by Philip grinning broadly.

Dropping her handwork Janine jumped up to greet her son, 'Rupert darling, what a wonderful, wonderful surprise!'

Rupert picked his mother up and swung her round before kissing her and only after gazing at him for a moment or so did she sit down again, followed by the rest of the family.

Mollie explained, 'Sam came with me to Paddington to see me off and as we had nearly three quarters of an hour to wait, we went into the station snack bar for a hot drink. There, would you believe it, sat Rupert having a sandwich; I just couldn't believe my eyes at first! We sat talking and it was so fortunate he and Sam met and got on well together.'

Rupert chipped in with a grin, 'I did rather well as Sam paid for the drinks. But seriously he's a straightforward fellow and will be all right for our Mollie.'

They enjoyed the cocoa Philip made and caught up with all the news, with Rupert telling them, 'I've been recommended for the distinguished Flying Cross and when my leave finishes I am posted to an Operational Training Unit in Lincolnshire with the rank of Flight Lieutenant as Assistant Chief Instructor. You see our squadron has been pulled out of the front line for rest.

Philip was interested and asked where he would be going, 'Do you know the location of your posting, Rupert?'

'Yes, it's at Sutton Bridge in Lincolnshire. My CO trained there before the war and told me the air field is practically on the Wash north of Wisbech. By all accounts a pretty bleak place and, according to him, inhabited by a hardy race of farming folk, many of whom are related to their Dutch forebears who came over here during the seventeenth and eighteenth centuries to help drain the Fens.

'I report back to my squadron in Hereford before my new job starts in January. All being well, I'll be home for Christmas for a few days, so keep your fingers crossed.'

'I know the area very well indeed and remember King's Lynn particularly – there are some excellent taverns!' Philip was thoughtful as he continued, 'We gunners practised on ranges south of Hunstanton, firing over the Wash with our howitzers before the Great War. It seems just like yesterday when I think back to those times.'

At this point Janine interrupted, 'Now you two, stop talking war and let's hear how Mollie got on today.'

'I had a lovely time with Sam, he's so attentive thank goodness, and we had an early lunch at a restaurant in Northumberland Avenue after which he took me to the National Gallery where Myra Hess gave a piano recital at one o'clock; she was marvellous and the place was packed. It was really thrilling as afterwards she talked with many in the audience and, of course, to Sam who had met her before at the Royal Academy of Music. As it was a lovely sunny afternoon we walked through St James's Park to Westminster Abbey where we spent nearly two hours. We had supper in Piccadilly and you know the rest when we met Rupert at Paddington.'

'Any sign of a date for wedding bells, darling?' Janine was, as ever, curious.

Mollie smiled, 'Well no, Mother, but Sam has some leave shortly and wants to come down to see you and Philip to ask your permission for us to wed! After that, we'll go to Whitby to see his mother and Grant, her second husband, and hopefully also meet Sam's sister Marion who is in the WRNS in Bath.'

'That sounds very good to me, Mollie, and I hope we'll see Sam quite soon.'

Janine turned to her son, who had sat quietly while his sister was talking, 'And how are things with you and Jenny Briggs?'

Rupert looked a little glum but answered his mother straight away, 'Oh, so, so,' and, after a pause, 'I don't think there's much future in that direction. To be perfectly honest I reckon it's all over between us. You see, I went on a short leave to see her and it appears she was going out with a soldier regularly, so that was that. I have to tell you I never felt I'd really fallen in love with Jessica, as the affection I had for her was like a brother and sister.'

'Rupert, I'm sorry but if it wasn't to be, it's better to be honest now rather than later after marriage. There's an old saying "there are fish in the sea no doubt of it, as good as ever came out of it", so don't despair.'

'I'm alright, Mother, and I'll start looking for another girlfriend in the local fish and chip shop.'

This had them all laughing for a few minutes. Rupert suddenly remembered his holdall and, unzipping it, produced a large package of greaseproof paper, 'Here you are mother, a present from a local Kent farmer.'

Janine took the heavy bundle and, placing it on the table unravelled the paper, astonished as she looked at the contents.

'Rupert, wherever did you get this? And as she, Mollie and Philip gazed at the 'present', Rupert just grinned.

'I told you, Mother, it's a present from a grateful farmer whose land was near our airfield. He said I had to bring it home and enjoy it with my family. So now you know all that remains is for us to eat it!'

Janine was certainly delighted and, hugging Rupert, had the last word, 'I've seen many legs of pork in my life but this one must have come from a jumbo pig! I only hope it'll go in our oven.'

Philip chipped in, 'Don't worry, my dear, if it's too big for the oven just cut it into rashers and we can fry it!'

They sat talking until well after midnight when it was time to say goodnight. As they went to bed, Janine recalled lines from one of her favourite poems she thought most fitting, 'Thus stories told to bed they creep, by whispering winds soon lulled asleep'. As Philip kissed her before putting the light out she gave a little sigh of contented happiness before speaking, 'Darling Philip, we must always count our blessings and be thankful for the wonderful gift of our family!'

Philip nodded, 'You're right, my sweet, I absolutely agree; now no more poetry or we'll not wake in the morning.' With those words the light went out and they were soon fast asleep.

Breakfast was late the next morning and mid-morning a call came through from the Coventry police. Philip had a long conversation with the station inspector who had a lot of information to pass on. 'Major Kirkwood, first of all, let me put your mind at rest; your sister and her aunt are well and uninjured. They were extremely lucky as the house next door to theirs had a direct hit and the occupants were killed. Miss Kirkwood's property was severely damaged but may be repairable. She and her aunt were sheltering in the basement which had been reinforced and so survived. They are being cared for in an emergency centre set up at the village of Church Lawford which lies between Coventry and Rugby. I'll give you a telephone number there so you can enquire about your family direct. Finally, if you are considering coming to see your sister I suggest you travel via Rugby and not Coventry as the damage in the city is horrendous.'

Philip said how much he appreciated the trouble the police had taken and thanked the inspector before ringing off.

Helen Dauntsey's leave was up at the beginning of December and she and Norman left Farndene. After dropping her off at 11 Group Headquarters, Norman carried on to London where he had been instructed to attend a Medical Board the following day. Reaching his friend's flat in Mayfair where he was staying for a few days, he decided, there and then, to go along to St George's Hospital to see Mr Patrick Wilson, the surgeon who operated on him.

Shown into the surgeon's office he was greeted by Mr Wilson with a warm handshake and taking Norman's arm, steered him to a chair.

'Now sit down, Norman, and let me have a look at you. I mean, of course, the left leg and appliance.' Kneeling down he helped remove the artificial leg, examining the stump with great care, occasionally pressing gently and enquiring whether Norman could feel any discomfort.

Standing up, his next remark was to the point: 'That's a damn fine job, even though I say it myself! From my examination all I hoped for has taken place and the healing process is almost complete. Before you go, I'd like to have some x-rays for future reference.'

Norman agreed and went on to tell the surgeon about the Medical Board he had to attend on the morrow, 'you see, sir, I have a feeling they want to stop me flying again on the grounds that I'm not fit to handle an aircraft. What do you think?'

'I consider you to be perfectly fit to fly again. If you are opposed by the board, just quote the name Douglas Bader to them; he flies with two tin legs, as good as if not better than many! You are at liberty to tell them my opinion if you wish.'

Norman left the hospital later in a much better frame of mind and determined to face out tomorrow's interview with resolve.

The first weeks of December were busy for Fanny in Bristol as she made arrangements to take her two granddaughters, Clara and Constance, home to Farndene as soon as they broke up from school, staying on with Margot and Francis over Christmas but returning to Bristol to be with her family there for the New Year celebrations. They travelled by train on 15th December, arriving at the Manor House exhausted following delays all along the line. The girls talked endlessly and were obviously glad to be home again with their parents. One after the other related the good and the bad points about their school.

Clara declared, 'Miss Rollo our Principal is super and terribly "U", and I think I'll copy her hairstyle when I leave school.'

'Yes, that's right, I agree with Clara but on the other hand I don't think she's firm enough with some of the staff. Like Miss Stainforth who takes us for French and German who never uses nail varnish or lipstick and her clothes are, well, absolutely "non-U". Constance was about to make a further observation when Francis interrupted her.

'Now you two cheeky young things I think that will be enough school reporting for now. Have you stopped to think what the teachers think of you? After all, I imagine none of you is perfect! Try to be a bit more generous towards other people and you'll find it very rewarding.'

Margot took the girls out of the room on the pretext of checking their clothes and belongings, leaving Francis to talk with his mother.

As soon as they were alone, Francis returned to the subject of the two girls and in particular their conversation minutes earlier. 'You know, Mother, I find the sort of talk Clara and Constance were engaged in about the staff at Dame Alwyn School somewhat nauseating to say the least. I look back at my education, both at the primary and subsequently at the grammar school and realise how good they were. I mixed with all kinds of children and in so many ways it did me the world of good. My criticism of Dame Alwyn is that the girls there come from privileged families and their outlook lacks breadth. Between you and me, I've always had a slight doubt about that type of school.'

Fanny smiled a little as she listened to her son and put her point of view quite firmly.

'Francis, I think you are over-emphasising what is really young girl's chit chat about the mistresses who teach them. We all did it when we were at school, perhaps using a different kind of language, but it didn't mean a great deal. In fact, looking back after leaving school many of us realised how fortunate we'd been in having such dedicated women to teach and inspire us. Your two young ones will be alright for the simple reason the main influence in their life comes from their home. The way you, Margot and I behave generally is their example and usually some of it "rubs off" on them, so stop worrying.'

'I suppose you're right, Mother, and thanks for putting it so succinctly,' adding with a wide grin, 'I'll just have to try being a bit more "U" than "non-U" in future!'

As Christmas drew nearer the population suffering night bombing from the Luftwaffe began to feel there was no end to the war and shortages of basic things made life frustrating for many. However, food, though not plentiful, was enough and the rationing system ensured everybody had a balanced diet to suit the work they had to do. The forces, as well as miners and fishermen, had extra cheese and meat to help with the strenuous manual work they undertook.

People living in the country had an advantage over town dwellers as rabbits, pigeons and other wildfowl were plentiful and augmented the official rations. In the suburbs of many towns and cities, groups of neighbours took to pig rearing, feeding them on household scraps and an allowance of meal supplied by the government. The duty of caring for the pigs fell on the group and a rota system operated; it was tough going particularly for mucking out and feeding at six o'clock on a bitter winter morning. They well and truly earned every pound of pork they got in due course!

Flying Officer Norman Vining was shown into a waiting room at the Air Ministry on 6th December and shortly after appeared before the Medical Board. Replying to a number of questions about his health he felt confident with his answers. Two doctors examined the injured leg for some minutes before returning to the table to make notes. He was then escorted from the room to await the Board's findings. Returning about a quarter of an hour later, the Air Vice Marshal chairman gave the verdict.

'Flying Officer Vining, we have examined your case thoroughly and have come to the unanimous decision it would be premature to pass you fit for flying duties on an operational squadron. You may not be able to fly in your present condition so we feel a few months on ground duties will help, after which we can reconsider your case. Have you anything you would like to say?'

'Yes, sir, as far as flying is concerned I feel you should know I have been flying regularly each day during my sick leave.'

At this the chairman and his colleagues sat up with a jolt, hardly able to believe their ears.

'You say you've been flying each day; but where and on whose authority?' The Air Marshal was indeed curious.

'I flew one of my father's planes on his estate at Farndene, Hampshire and I can assure you, like Douglas Bader with two tin legs, I experienced no difficulty whatever.'

A look of astonishment registered on the faces behind the table and the chairman hastily asked Norman to wait outside once again. Twenty minutes passed before he reappeared in front of the Board.

'From what you have told us it is clear you are capable of handling an aircraft. Our decision is that you undergo a thorough medical examination and subject to your passing that you can undertake flying duties in Training Command for a while. We feel at this stage you shouldn't join an operational squadron. You have an excellent flying record,' the chairman smiled as he carried on, 'and a charmed life from what I've heard about your recent accident. We wish you good luck and hope to see you back on operations in the not distant future.'

They all shook hands with Norman who left the room with a feeling of success and satisfaction.

Chapter 33

In spite of the war, families came together for Christmas 1940 whenever they could. The Vining family was no exception and by good fortune all the children managed to get home, if only for a few days in some cases, and the Manor House once again buzzed with activity. There were some surprises: Juliet for example came with her boyfriend, Lieutenant Commander Freddie Washbrook, who was also her boss at the Admiralty but nevertheless turned out to be great company as well as an excellent pianist. Norman, still on sick leave until January, collected Helen from Group Headquarters as she had managed Christmas leave. Bruce astonished everybody when he arrived home with a gorgeous blonde with blue eyes – a young actress and dancer known on the stage as 'Dainty Duvall' but whose real name was Dorcas Smith! She proved to be an excellent bridge and poker player.

The Christmas Eve dinner party went with a swing and, as it was a fine night, they all walked to St Paul's, which was packed for the midnight service taken by the Rev. Canon Horatio Hulbert. He had settled in the parish with his wife Dorothy and their two young sons in 1929, following the sacking of the Rev. Shadwell Legion who had been found guilty of an adulterous liaison with a parishioner on the church premises! Over the years, Canon Hulbert revitalised the expanding parish and both he and his wife were very popular with the local community.

Breakfast on Christmas Day was a drawn out affair and Bertie, taking the numerous late arrivals in his stride, always greeted them with a smile. Norman, having settled for an enormous plate of porridge, whispered to Helen, 'Bertie's an amazing fellow and in all the years I've known him, I cannot remember him being anything but cheerful. He's an absolute gem and he and his staff run the house like clockwork for my parents.'

Helen's reply had a touch of envy in it, 'We could do with

Bertie at home. My parents are in despair having had one butler after another in the last few years since our dear old Jenkins died.'

The large Vining family gathered round the table for Christmas dinner – including herself, Clara counted eleven. By tradition, Francis carved a large turkey and ducks and luckily there were several wishbones to satisfy demand. After the meal everyone, including the staff, adjourned to the drawing room for the Christmas tree with presents. Margot had thoughtfully found several little jewellery gifts for the girls and a lovely Scottish brooch for Fanny. For the men she provided handkerchiefs, while Francis produced a small bottle of brandy and cigarettes for each. There followed half an hour of carols with Freddie Washbrook at the piano.

Later in the day and during the evening the carpet was rolled back, exposing the parquet floor, and dancing carried on to a late hour to gramophone records and, from time to time, Freddie playing jazz on the piano.

With long walks for some on Boxing Day, the family made the most of a wonderful break away from the war, enabling all to catch up on the news of their siblings. All too soon the brief 'oasis of time' came to an end and inevitably there were tears as they took leave of one another.

At the start of January 1941, after a tedious train journey, Rupert finally arrived at RAF Sutton Bridge, Lincolnshire, and soon gained the impression he had landed in the back of beyond, set in a most desolate part of England. Waiting for transport at the railway station he looked east across the river Nene to the airfield beyond. Through a veil of light rain being driven by a persistent northerly wind he thought, 'I've seen some bleak places in my time but this is surely the most inhospitable looking RAF station anywhere.'

An hour later, after settling in his quarters, Rupert met the Station Commander, Group Captain Rodney Stanmore, a well-built man of forty-five who had an infectious smile. He was a popular extrovert whose rapid rise through the ranks told its own story.

Rupert felt his welcome genuine and sincere and when they were joined shortly after by Squadron Leader Barry Groombridge, the Chief Instructor, he quickly gained the impression they were glad to have him on the staff.

Rodney Stanmore explained the problems experienced during the past two months. 'We've had no fewer than five fatal crashes, two of which closed the airfield for hours, thus losing vital flying time. Barry and I have tightened up procedures as some of the young fellows arriving here are desperately short of experience and the conversion to Spitfires and Hurricanes proves too much for them. So you see our dilemma and hope with your assistance we can put a stop to the needless waste of life.'

A long discussion followed after which Rupert was introduced to the other members of the training staff.

At a later meeting, Barry Groombridge put Rupert in the picture regarding the training routines at present in force and the Chief Instructor explained in detail, 'The pilots alternate between lectures and practical flying, the latter including mock attack procedures at our bombing range at Holbeach, on the Wash. We have a flight of aged, single engine, Fairey Battle Bombers. At the end of a length of fine steel cable they tow a drogue providing an airborne target for gunnery practice on the range.'

They also discussed the fatal accidents in detail; the short runway was a contributory factor in three of the crashes. The pilots didn't get airborne quick enough and the planes just ploughed into the embankment carrying the Sutton Bridge to King's Lynn road. Barry also mentioned plans to extend the runway south-eastwards on land being taken over by the RAF.

'We expect the Air Ministry surveyors shortly and they will do the preliminary investigation prior to a construction company getting the work done.

Rupert found the appointment demanding but enjoyed the challenge during the next few weeks.

The January weather didn't help the flying programme as

snow and ice grounded aircraft for days on end. In mid-February conditions improved and every effort was made to catch up on the backlog.

The 14th of the month, although cold, turned out to be a beautiful sunny day and a number of trainee pilots were airborne late morning with the Chief Instructor for air-to-air gunnery practice at the Holbeach range.

Rupert finished lecturing at midday and joined the Station Commander in the officers mess for an early lunch. Halfway through their meal, a steward informed the Group Captain there was an urgent telephone call for him. Returning moments later Rodney looked shaken as he told Rupert the news.

'I've just had the most terrible message from the Holbeach range. It appears Barry Groombridge has been involved in an accident there and crashed out on the Wash. It's a high spring tide and his plane disappeared below the surface within minutes; Barry can't have survived.'

After speaking to Group Headquarters the Station Commander informed all courses of the tragedy telling them, 'We have lost an excellent pilot and a good friend to many. Group will investigate immediately; meanwhile, flying is suspended until tomorrow. Extra lectures will be arranged so watch the noticeboards for details.'

The following day the investigation was completed and it was found Squadron Leader Groombridge took evasive action away from one of the trainee pilot's aircraft and misjudged the height of the Fairey Battle. His port wing hit the drogue towing steel cable severing about two feet of the wingtip. The plane flew into a deep trough and sank beneath the water in minutes.

Headquarters were unable to replace the Chief Instructor for the present and asked Rupert to take over his duties.

Mid-December Philip Kirkwood had travelled to Church Lawford, near Rugby, to see his sister and aunt and found them in good health and quite happy with the emergency accommodation. The Coventry Council were making excellent progress with temporary repairs to the damaged houses in Conduit Street and number seven would be habitable once more by the middle of January. Kitty Kirkwood thanked her brother for the kind invitation Janine had sent but she and her Aunt Phoebe decided to stay in the centre for the time being.

However, by the first week in February the repair work on Kitty's house was far from complete for many reasons, mainly lack of materials. The conditions at the centre were also not entirely satisfactory, so they accepted the invitation to stay with Janine and Philip for a short while.

Arriving in Exeter mid-February they were met at the railway station by Philip and soon settled in. A week later they were all awakened by the sirens late in the evening and a large number of enemy bombers passed over the city en route for the Midlands. A later wave of German planes bound for Bristol were confronted by thick fog over the target area and consequently returned to Exeter dropping a large tonnage of bombs indiscriminately. A big estate of council houses, built in the early twenties for returning ex-service men, was severely damaged and the occupants sustained a large number of casualties; the city itself was also bombed but didn't suffer so many killed and injured. Janine, Mollie, Kitty and Phoebe were naturally frightened and Philip did his best to comfort them. To their great relief the all-clear sounded around midnight, but it was well into the early morning before they managed to get to sleep.

After breakfast, Janine, Mollie and Philip went into town and found many streets blocked by piles of debris from smashed buildings and some unexploded bombs. Reaching the High Street they had to negotiate rubble which had cascaded across the road from collapsed shops and offices.

Number 58, Madame Baume's salon, was a sorry sight resulting from a direct hit on the premises next door. All the front windows were broken, tiles were missing from one side of the roof and guttering had been blown into the street.

A policeman on duty outside the building told them to take great care over broken glass as they went into the ground floor.

Everywhere was covered in thick dust and pieces of ceiling plaster; upstairs in the workrooms the machines were enveloped in similar debris and work in progress severely damaged. Philip decided to contact the city council for assistance to get the business working again.

In the afternoon he, Janine, Mollie, Kitty and Phoebe were finishing a late lunch when Ida Windsor, a senior seamstress at the salon, called at the house. She was in a distressed state and Janine took her into the drawing room to talk privately. Hearing the voices, Mollie joined them as well.

Ida started to speak but broke down weeping for several minutes until, comforted by Janine, she recovered.

'It's my dear mother. She was killed last night.' Ida stopped for some minutes, and continued with one or two breaks, 'Oh, Mrs Kirkwood it was so terrible. We all went down the garden into our Anderson shelter and suddenly Mum noticed our cat Nobby wasn't with us. She went straight back into the house and then ...,' she broke down again before finishing with the words, 'then there was this awful explosion and the earth shook and we were covered in dust.

'When we looked out, Dad and I knew it was our house, as there was only a great heap of rubble where our home had been,' she paused and, shaking her head in disbelief, told Janine the final outcome, 'About ten minutes later Nobby turned up unharmed!'

While Janine did her best to console Ida, Mollie went into the kitchen, returning with some hot sweet tea for their visitor. Ida thanked them for their offer of accommodation but explained she and her father were going to stay with her aunt who also lived on the estate.

Later in the afternoon Philip drew up plans to reinforce the cellar making it an air raid shelter.

Towards the end of the third week of March, Air Ministry Surveyors arrived to look at a large area of farmland to the east of the RAF station at Sutton Bridge. Group Captain Stanmore asked Rupert to join him as they met the surveyors on the land in question. Several cars and a fifteen hundredweight van drove onto the area which had been planted with winter sown wheat now showing as a green haze on the earth. A windmill was situated about eighty yards to one side by a large drainage dyke.

After measurements were taken and checked, it was decided to remove the mill which could prove a hazard to flying.

As they were talking, an old Ford tractor pulled up on the road and a figure came across to them. Rupert realised the approaching person was a woman dressed in a thick tweed skirt over which she wore a heavy old waterproof jacket and wellington boots, while on her head sat a broad-brimmed leather hat. She stopped a short way away to stare at all of them individually before opening the conversation with a verbal broadside.

'Who the hell are you lot? And what in God's name are you doing on my family's land? She glared as she capped her first remarks with, 'Have you taken leave of your senses? Do you realise you have ruined a substantial area of winter sown wheat? As nobody replied immediately she slapped in a further enquiry, 'Well, I want an answer! Can none of you speak?'

The senior surveyor did his best, 'Madam, we are here on official business to measure this area to be incorporated into Sutton Bridge airfield. This is in fact Air Ministry property.'

The reply was prompt, 'We must get the facts straight! First I'm not madam but Miss Catherina van Houten and second the land you stand on does not belong to the Air Ministry as the conveyance documents arrived only this morning and have not yet been signed. Furthermore, I overheard someone suggesting removing the mill. Well, for your information that mill was built by my forebears at the end of the seventeenth century and pumps water from beneath the very land you are standing on. If it's removed it will only be a matter of months before this whole area is once again a bog.'

The surveyor tried again, 'I'm very sorry Miss van Houten but I venture to tell you we are here to make safe the training of pilots for your defence by extending the runway of the airfield.'

Her reply was immediate and pointed, 'I hear what you say

but I'm here in the business of producing food for the nation including your pilots, without which they may starve. Now get off our land and take your cars with you.'

She turned and striding to the road she mounted the tractor. After several attempts the engine wouldn't start so Rupert went over to offer assistance. Miss van Houten asked if he knew anything about tractors, to which he replied, 'I stripped one of these down when I was fourteen and it went when I put it together again.' It took him a short time to find the fault, a blocked fuel lead, and after a few turns of the starting handle the engine burst into life.

She thanked Rupert and added, 'I'm sorry if perhaps I was a bit abrupt with your colleagues but it's very painful for our family to lose land – farms we have cultivated for over two hundred years.' She was thoughtful for moment or two. 'If you and your colleagues care to come over to our house I can show you the original drawings and plans prepared by my forebear Bram van Houten in 1798. Follow this road towards King's Lynn for about two miles and take the first right turn and in about five minutes you'll see our property along a drive to the left. Come any time during daylight and thanks again for your personal help.' The tractor roared into life carrying Miss van Houten away from the group of onlookers who were still completely taken aback.

Rodney Stanmore was the first to speak, 'Phew! What a woman!' And to Rupert, 'You certainly saved the day by fixing her ancient tractor. I reckon she took a shine for you, you lucky man!'

They had a good laugh and Rupert went on to tell them about her invitation to see the original plans for the area which the surveyors thought an excellent idea. Rodney suggested going back to the officers mess for lunch after which they could all go to the van Houten house. At this point none of them had any idea of the surprise awaiting them.

Shortly after two, on what turned out to be a fine March afternoon, a small convoy of cars and a van left the airfield and fifteen minutes later arrived at the van Houten house.

The beautifully proportioned brick and stone Dutch residence stood some two hundred yards from the road amid extensive gardens which set off mature elms, oaks, hollies and several large bay trees.

As they walked from the parked vehicles, the huge oak front door opened and an elderly manservant smiled as he invited them in. A flight of seven steps reached the entrance and Rupert realised this allowed for garden level rooms in the house below the ground floor. Once inside they were greeted by Miss van Houten and her father Jan, a sturdy middle-aged man who spoke with a slight Dutch accent. 'I'm pleased to welcome you to my house so please come in and make yourselves at home," he said, 'My daughter Catherina told me all about you but you mustn't take her too seriously. You see, she is very protective and looks after me, our home and the farms very well.'

Entering the panelled library, Jan and Catherina lifted a large oak box onto the table and unlocking it withdrew sheaves of documents tied with leather thongs. The appropriate deeds and plans were sorted and unrolled for inspection. Jan explained how his family had reclaimed marsh and bog over many years by digging drainage channels that drained water from the surrounding area. Alongside the drainage dykes were windmills constructed to pump the water through a series of increasing levels and finally into the sea at low tide.

'These mills still do their job adequately some two hundred years later. Not a bad bit of engineering when you consider the primitive tools available in their day. Can I suggest we leave the surveyors to pore over the deeds?' Turning to the Group Captain and Rupert, he added, 'Meanwhile, perhaps you would care to see our house?'

A guided tour took them all over the remarkable building during which Jan explained the various materials his forebears had used, 'Bricks were made in Bedfordshire, stone brought from Portland; the main stairway and banisters are of English oak but the handrails are Honduras mahogany replacing a temporary staircase in July 1805 just before your famous Admiral Nelson's victory at the

Battle of Trafalgar.' He went on to tell them, 'My one concern is what happens to the house when I and my two unmarried daughters pass on; sadly, it will possibly go out of our family.'

Tea had been organised by Catherina and her younger sister Bep, served in a splendid drawing room with two sets of double French doors giving access to the rear garden via stone stairs. During tea, Rupert was conscious a number of times that Catherina was looking at him in an inquisitive way and, to be sociable, she took a seat next to him to make conversation. 'You were very kind this morning and I really am sorry I was so abrupt to you all.'

Rupert smiled as he replied, 'Never mind being abrupt. What you need is a new tractor!'

She also smiled and he noticed for the first time she was a fine looking woman with penetrating hazel eyes and auburn hair. Sensing his gaze, she withdrew her hands with the comment, 'Please don't look at my hands as they suffer with the farm work I need to do.'

'Please don't worry. I know all about dirty hands as I used to help my father in the stables when I was very young.' He went on to tell her about his French mother and the loss of his father in the Great War and how he enjoyed working with horses on the family farm in Brittany.

Catherina told him the sadness they suffered, 'My mother Lies, was trapped in Holland in May last year when the Germans invaded and we have no idea where she is at present. She went to visit our family in March a year ago and if she is caught by the Nazis she'll be interned.' Rupert commiserated and hoped better news would come soon.

As they said goodbye, Jan gave an open invitation for them to come at any time in the future. Catherina's words to Rupert were similar, 'I so enjoyed talking to you about your family life and your knowledge and experience with horses. Please come again soon.'

Smiling, Rupert nodded, 'Thanks, I certainly will when I can.'

He got into the car with a grinning Rodney Stanmore who couldn't contain himself.

'Rupert, this morning I said that young lady had taken a shine for you but having watched her this afternoon I'm convinced she's after you in a big way! You'd better look out!'

Rupert shrugged his shoulders as he spoke, 'Maybe you're right but what is to be will be!' During the ride back to the airfield he found she was very much in his thoughts.

An hour later Group Captain Stanmore informed Rupert he had been appointed Chief Instructor with promotion to the rank of Squadron Leader backdated to 14th February. 'Congratulations, Rupert. A well-deserved promotion!'

Chapter 34

Norman Vining had, as he put it to his mother, been kicking his heels on sick leave until mid-March when he received another call for a Medical Board examination. The result was the green light to fly again but not on operations and he was told to report to Training Command the following week.

He telephoned Helen to tell her the good news and she told him she was free for three days at the weekend and would love to come down to Farndene for a break. Norman's reply was typical, 'Absolutely no problem, darling. I'll meet you at the station Friday afternoon, so just tell me which train you'll be on.'

True to his word, Norman collected Helen and both were soon enjoying tea with Margot and Francis in the comfort of the Manor House.

Francis then broke his great news to them: 'I'm to receive a Knighthood in the Birthday Honours List for services rendered. To be perfectly honest, all I've done is increase production of engines and aircraft parts under licence and give Lord Beaverbrook, who heads the Ministry of Aircraft Production, assistance and advice whenever he needs it.'

Norman's response was sincere: 'That's wonderful, Father, and I bet Mother can't wait to go to the palace to meet the King,' and to his mother, 'You'll need brand new clothes – I can spare some clothing coupons if you want them'

'Thank you, Norman, but as the King hasn't seen any of my wardrobe I'll manage with what I've got! On another subject, your father and I are going to the theatre in Southampton tonight to see the D'Oyly Carte production of "The Mikado", would you like to join us?'

'Thanks all the same, Mother, but I think Helen and I will stay put as we have a lot to catch up with.'

That evening, Bertie served dinner for Helen and Norman and brought them coffee in the drawing room.

After he left them alone, Helen appeared a little subdued which prompted Norman to ask, 'You're very quiet, darling. Is anything the matter?'

She turned to face him before replying, 'No, but I've something to tell you and I'm not sure how you will take it.'

Norman was about to say something when she went on, 'Darling, I went to see our doctor today and she confirmed I'm pregnant. You see I've missed two months now and I started what they call morning sickness last week.'

For a moment or two, Norman sat gazing at Helen and then slowly he gathered her into his arms as he spoke softly, 'My dearest Helen, whatever made you think I'd not want to hear all you have said? It's the most wonderful thing you've told me and it makes me want you more and more.'

After a very long embrace she smiled and reminded him the next important issue was the date of the wedding. 'I would like it to be as soon as possible so we can tell our parents the good news.'

Norman looked at his pocket diary, 'Darling, I see 13th April is Easter Sunday in about a month's time so we'd better decide between say 29th March or 6th April but not necessarily on a Saturday; what do you think?'

Helen pondered for a short while, 'Norman, I don't want our marriage to be an enormous occasion; after all there is a war on! So why not consider 28th or 29th March?' adding, with a puckish smile, 'Are you aware you'll get a whole year's refund of marriage allowance if we get spliced before the end of the tax year on 5th April? So you see, darling, I'm well worth marrying!'

They had a good laugh before finally deciding on 29th March. However, the next problem was the venue and on this point Helen had no definite view, 'It's up to you, Norman, to choose where we are married.'

'I have to be honest, Helen, my sweet, I'd prefer to go to our local church where, in fact, I was christened and many of my forebears have been married. The rector is a thoroughly good character and I'm sure you'll like his style; so what do you say?'

'I'd love that, Norman, but we want only our immediate family and perhaps one or two very close friends.

Norman agreed but also explained the need to have special leave, 'I shall have to wait until I get to Training Command next week to apply for compassionate leave for the wedding, which I'm sure I'll get.'

Helen's sense of humour surfaced again, 'Darling, don't you think passionate leave would be more appropriate?'

They sat for a long time compiling lists of prospective guests only to prune them over and over again until deciding to shelve any further decision just as Margot and Francis returned from the theatre.

'Hello, you two look very tired.'

Francis flopped down in a chair near the fire, 'You missed a splendid show and Darrel Fancourt was magnificent as the Mikado. He's very impressive and put the fear of God into some elderly ladies in the front stalls. Now what about you two; have you enjoyed your evening?'

Helen smiled as she replied, 'Yes, we've also had a good show tonight and decided on the date of our wedding.'

Here Norman chipped in, 'Now don't worry, Father, you and mother are included in the guest list but we're both clear we don't want a large gathering, just immediate family and a few very close friends. Oh, and we'll be married in St Paul's church in the village.'

While all this was going on Margot was contemplating the event and joined the conversation, 'I'm absolutely delighted with your news,' and to Helen especially, 'Francis and I look forward to welcoming you into our family and if you and Norman would like to have the reception here we'll be only too happy.'

Francis organised a bottle of champagne and after drinking a toast they sat talking for the next hour, mostly about the wedding of course.

During the last week in March the good early spring weather helped the flying programme at RAF Sutton Bridge. By careful selection Rupert filtered out the slower student pilots and arranged extra instruction on aircraft handling, with the result that serious accidents were avoided. He also introduced white markers on the cables towing drogues on the bombing range.

An unpopular move was physical training for all pilots in the form of a three-mile run round the airfield perimeter track each morning before breakfast. Rupert told them, 'When you get to operational squadrons in a matter of weeks now, fitness will be vital. You'll be more alert than the Germans and if you think and react quicker than them you'll live longer, make no mistake about it!'

A few days later cold weather returned bringing banks of fog that persisted all day, at times blotting out the airfield completely. With all aircraft grounded, Rupert decided to accept Jan van Houten's invitation to visit.

Arriving at the house mid-afternoon he was welcomed by Jan, 'Catherina's in the stables as a mare is giving trouble. I understand you know a bit about horses, Squadron Leader. Would you be kind enough to have a look at the mare for us?'

Accompanying his host, Rupert walked to the long outbuildings at the end of which were several stables. As they entered, Jan called to his daughter, 'Catherina, we've a visitor – the Squadron Leader from Sutton Bridge.'

Catherina greeted Rupert and explained that the mare had become lame in the last few days. 'Would you mind looking at her?'

After a few minutes' examination Rupert told them he thought it was fetlock infection in the left leg and added, 'You need to have a vet look at her without delay. I think she needs injections to clear up the problem.'

Returning to the house, Jan telephoned for the vet who promised to come out later that afternoon. He then asked Rupert if he would like to join them for tea, 'After all I think you've earned it.'

Shortly after, Catherina entered the room and Rupert noticed she'd changed into a dress and had brushed her hair back with a velvet band. She smiled as she sat down and immediately opened the conversation, 'Squadron Leader ...', Rupert interrupted, 'Squadron Leader sounds so formal, so please call me Rupert.'

'Well in that case I insist you address me as Catherina and my sister is Bep.' At this point her father joined in, 'Please feel able to call me Jan, it will give me great pleasure if you do.'

During tea, Rupert was able to tell them that work on the runway extension would be starting within a week or so, 'It all depends on the contractor who has been told to prioritise the work. As far as the mill is concerned I believe the idea is to paint it white to make it conspicuous to aircraft.'

'That's a pity. You see it was built in the late eighteenth century with special bricks from a brickfield at Brogborough, Bedfordshire, ' Jan was obviously moved as he spoke, 'You see, if you put paint on the brick surface it may destroy its weatherproof quality and once that's done it will start to crumble.'

Rupert nodded, 'I understand the point you make, but how can we make the mill more conspicuous?'

'It takes a woman to give you the answer,' Catherina was enjoying the situation, 'all you need to do is wrap the mill in white cloth. I'm sure your Barrage Balloon people could make something to fit the situation.'

Catherina left the room to answer the telephone returning a few minutes later with bad news, 'That was the vet telling us he cannot come out now as the fog is very dense but will come first thing tomorrow morning.' She crossed to look out of the window, 'I'm afraid it's very thick here and as the light is fading fast it may be unsafe for you to drive back to the airfield Rupert. The road is narrow with dykes on each side for about two miles.'

He too went to the window and could see nothing for the heavy grey bank of fog and realised it would be folly to attempt driving in such conditions.

Jan came to the rescue, 'Rupert I'd rather you didn't travel tonight. We can offer to put you up until the morning when, hopefully, it will be clearer.'

'That's very generous and yes I'd like to accept your hospitality but may I use your telephone to let them know at the airfield I'm safe for the night?'

With a telephone message passed to the duty officer at RAF Sutton Bridge, Rupert had an early dinner with the van Houten family and then spent the evening talking with Jan and his two daughters. Their manservant, Johan, served hot chocolate at ten o'clock after which Jan said goodnight. Bep followed him shortly after leaving Catherina and Rupert still chatting, mainly about their families and farming.

Rupert described his mother's farm in Brittany and wonderful coastline near Plonéour Lanvern where the Atlantic rollers give plenty of scope for surfing.

'I tried it there with my uncle René before the war and it's very exciting. I swallowed too much sea water and was quite sick when we got to the beach. Do you ever go to the seaside Catherina?'

She smiled as she recalled the family trips to Holland, 'our family farms were in the north at Winsum, the Groningen area and yes, I used to swim when we went on holiday to the Friesian Islands where there are miles of sand dunes by the coast,' she looked pensive before resuming, 'but that was long ago and none of us has had a break away from the farm since 1939.' Again she paused as tears welled in her eyes, 'That is excepting Mama of course, who is trapped by the Germans.' She buried her face in her hands and wept.

Crossing the room, Rupert sat next to her on the sofa and putting his arm round her shoulders tried to comfort her.

'Catherina, I'm so sorry you are upset and perhaps I shouldn't have talked so much about our families. Please don't give up hope for your mother and always, when you think of her just say a little prayer; it'll do both of you a world of good!'

She turned a tear-stained face to him, 'Rupert you are the loveliest person I've ever met and, strangely, I felt you were so different the moment you came to my rescue with that awful tractor. There's something in your make up I find fascinating, perhaps you get it from your French mother. You're a very attractive man, not just in your good looks, but your outgoing character and I like you very much!' And with that she kissed him on the cheek.

He was quite taken aback but realised the import of all she'd said. Rupert found her very attractive but wondered if her remarks were just superficial or meaning something more profound? He determined to find out.

'Catherina, you are a very sweet person and I appreciate the more than generous things you've said to me. I, too, find you a very attractive woman and want you to know I believe I'm falling in love with you!'

She turned with her face very close to his, 'Oh, Rupert I so wanted to hear those words because I know I've fallen in love with you but was scared my love would be unrequited.'

No more was said as they came together in a long embrace and after several minutes they sat with arms around each other just looking at the dying embers of the fire until he spoke.

'Catherina, I know I've only known you a very short time but I want to marry you and will ask your father for his blessing if that's the correct course in your family.'

'My answer is yes I want to be your wife. It is customary for a man to ask permission for a daughter's hand in marriage in Holland but in our case it will be only a formality.'

After another kiss she said how fate played an enormous part in people's lives, 'Do you realise we may never have declared our love for each other had it not been for the dense fog tonight. For once something so bright and clear has come out of the thickest mist.'

They kissed goodnight and Johan showed Rupert to his room; looking out of the bedroom window he saw the faint rays of the moon indicating the fog was starting to clear slowly and thought 'It's beginning to clear but not before it brought Catherina and me together!'

The household was on the go just after dawn and as soon as breakfast was over Rupert and Catherina asked to see her father.

Jan expressed his great joy at the prospect of his daughter's marriage and expressed it very simply.

'To be honest I half expected the news as I've noticed a lovely change in Catherina lately and concluded she was in love. In addition, I also became aware you two were looking at each other with what I'd call lover's eyes! I have to tell you I'm delighted she has chosen you, Rupert, and I'm sure you will be a good husband for her.'

After fond farewells and feeling on top of the world, Rupert drove back to the airfield as the sun rose dispelling the remaining morning mist.

Flying Officer Norman Vining arrived at the RAF Training Command Headquarters on Tuesday 18th March and was informed immediately of his posting to RAF Sutton Bridge, as Assistant Chief Instructor and his promotion to the rank of Flight Lieutenant. In reply to his request for compassionate leave he was told to apply for that as soon as he got to his new RAF Station.

Arriving at RAF Sutton Bridge, Norman felt as Rupert had done as he looked at the airfield shrouded in banks of mist. The transport picking him up at the railway station was driven by an attractive WAAF corporal who helped him with his baggage. Once en route he couldn't help remarking, 'This place is a bit of a dump, isn't it?'

'Well yes, sir, but you'll find it grows on you! When the fog clears and the sun shines you can see for miles across the flat fen farms and the locals are very hospitable, you'll soon see.'

'Thanks, corporal, I'm here for some time so I hope you're right.'

After identity check at the airfield entrance, he was taken to the headquarters building to meet the chief instructor and the commanding officer.

On meeting Norman, Rupert's welcome was a natural reaction and shaking hands expressed his pleasure, 'Norman, I'm delighted to have you with us and congratulate you on an amazing recovery. We've all heard about your incredible luck after the crash. How are your parents? You may know your father was very good to me arranging an apprenticeship which started my whole career.'

Norman responded by telling the good news of his father's knighthood.

The following morning Rupert explained in detail the training procedures and told Norman the current course finished at the end of the week and there would be a gap of a week or two before the next intake: 'It gives us a chance to freshen up all round and work on the aircraft inspection programmes.'

At this point Norman thought it opportune to ask for leave to get married. 'You see, Rupert, we'd like to have the wedding on 29th March if at all possible.'

Rupert smiled, 'It's a bit short notice but I can't see any difficulty if it's urgent!'

'Well, yes, my fiancée has just discovered she's expecting so it'll be nice to make haste with the ceremony before things become too obvious!'

'That's all right, Norman, I can spare you for, say, ten days so we'll talk about it nearer the time.

'Meanwhile, there is a lot of work to be done, reporting on each pilot individually prior to their posting to operational squadrons so your help will be invaluable. Oh, I must warn you there will be one heck of a party on Friday night before they leave and we are expected to be in attendance for some of the time. A tip is to watch the CO and as soon as he takes his leave, so do we.'

At the end of the week, Rupert drove to Catherina's home and they had a long talk about the timing of their wedding; she explained the difficulty of an early date.

'You see Rupert, my love, it will have to be later in the summer or the autumn as the demands of our farms are intense with spring preparation for planting, followed by cultivation and then harvest, which covers nearly three months. We're shorthanded after four of our younger men were called up so a greater burden falls on the remaining family.'

Rupert looked a bit down in the mouth as he listened but was generous enough to accept what she had said, 'I understand, dearest, but I really hadn't thought about a delay of so long.'

'My poor darling, you look so sad and I wish it could be much sooner but it would be unfair to my father and sister as well as the staff. Even if it had to be September that would only be in six months' time and as there's so much to decide, those months will be valuable.'

'Very well, we will have to wait as I agree there isn't an alternative, but we must be formally engaged now!' Adding, with a cheeky smile, 'I don't want someone coming along and stealing you from under my nose!'

They laughed and a long kiss followed but Rupert meant what he said, 'I want you to fix a day soon so we can go into Cambridge to choose an engagement ring and put an announcement in the papers. I hope to visit my mother and stepfather in Exeter to tell them our news before any publicity.'

Catherina checked her diary and suggested the following Wednesday 26th March which also suited Rupert, so they made plans to leave the farm at ten o'clock that day.

As he kissed her goodbye he said with a smile, 'I'll pick you up on the dot of ten next week, so mind you're ready!'

'You know I'll be ready, dearest, so don't worry, but I love you when you put on your commanding voice, it makes you sound very important!' They both dissolved into a spate of laughter.

Chapter 35

After Rupert's car arrived at the van Houten house, he was admitted by Johan and shown into the drawing room to wait for Catherina. The polished oak boards shone, setting off the various rugs and beautiful Dutch furniture. He browsed looking at several oil paintings of Netherland scenes of the seventeenth and eighteenth centuries and liked the coast and sea pictures the best. He smiled to himself as a bracket clock struck ten.

The door opened and Catherina came into the room causing Rupert to gasp with astonishment as he looked at her. She wore a beautifully tailored overcoat of dark green tweed with black fur trimmings which matched her fur hat. Tall black leather boots were complimentary to similar gloves and handbag.

'Catherina, my darling, you look just ravishing!' Stepping forward he took her in his arms and they kissed several times.

Offering his arm in an exaggerated way and with a grin on his face, he said, 'I'm delighted to have the pleasure of your company Miss van Houten and I think you look the absolute tops! So shall we get cracking without delay?'

Their car sped to Cambridge arriving a little after eleven as Rupert made for King's Parade. 'There's a special jeweller there called "Marcel Plouvier" recommended by Rodney Stanmore. He asked me to give Marcel his good wishes.'

The jeweller was in fact a very high class business and on entering Catherina and Rupert were met at the door by an assistant and shown to easy chairs set around low tables. Trays of rings were then produced and Catherina's eyes were a study as she tried various gems until at last a diamond and sapphire cluster was her choice. Marcel then greeted them and was delighted to receive the message from Rodney Stanmore.

'Do I understand this is an engagement ring, Squadron Leader?

'Absolutely, we're engaged officially as soon as I put the ring on Catherina's finger.' And with that he slid it onto the third finger of Catherina's left hand.'

With a smile Marcel said, 'And now may I suggest you kiss your fiancée.'

Rupert didn't need second bidding and he and Catherina embraced, much to the pleasure of the jeweller's staff who gave a little round of applause.

As they were leaving, Rupert asked Marcel if he could recommend a good restaurant for lunch.

'Yes indeed I can. Try Turks across Jesus Green by the river, the food is excellent.' He gave Rupert directions and they said goodbye.

Strolling through Cambridge, Catherina linked arms with Rupert, holding him close and squeezing his hand, 'Rupert, darling, I love you very much and just want to be with you more and more. I'm so very happy and never realised being in love could be so wonderful!'

'You already know I'm over the moon loving you, Catherina, and I'm just longing for that super day in a few months' time when we get married.'

As they reached Lower Park Street they stopped to kiss, much to the amusement of a passing postman who quipped, 'That's just the job, guv, Postman's Knock! I used to play it myself but always indoors.' And with a smile was on his way.

A delight to the eye, Lower Park Street was a haven of tranquillity with a number of beautiful houses and an outstanding terrace of period cottages built of yellow bricks. These had mellowed over the years to a pale colour which offset the lattice windows and dark slate roofs. Small front gardens were divided by low brick walls on which sat short black iron railings, giving an air of neat completeness.

'What a pretty street and how quiet it is away from the traffic,' Catherina stopped to enjoy the scene, 'There's wisteria with twisted trunks along the front of several cottages; it'll be a beautiful sight in a week or so and just look at the tubs of mixed tulips! They're such pretty flowers and remind me of trips to Holland when I was young.'

Walking across Jesus Green they passed crowds of people old and young, some walking, some riding bicycles, nannies with small children, courting couples sauntering arm in arm like Catherina and Rupert, and riders on horseback trotting along the bridle track. Here was a cross section of humanity enjoying the ambience of a beautiful open space bordering the river Cam.

The greeting at Turks Restaurant was welcoming and the head waiter showed them to a table for two with a view both ways along the river.

Having ordered, Catherina sat admiring her new ring which shone as she moved her hand.

'Rupert, dearest, it really is beautiful and the stones glitter and sparkle. I could just sit contemplating what it all means now and for us in the future. I feel the ring has encircled my heart binding it to yours.'

'Golly, that's very romantic, darling, but truthfully I feel as you do and thankful I have met you and fallen in love.'

When the main course arrived at the table, so did the head waiter who asked if the lunch was a celebration.

'Well, yes it is we've just got engaged today!'

'I thought as much when I saw the ring on your lady's hand, so will you accept your wine as a gift with our good wishes for your future happiness.'

Rupert thanked the head waiter who poured for both of them.

During lunch they chatted about their future and watched the various boats rowing up and down the river.

Leaving Turks a couple of hours later Rupert suggested they walk along by the river to the next bridge before collecting the car to go home. About half way Catherina wanted to stop, to enjoy the wonderful view across the gently flowing water to the willow trees bordering the opposite bank. They sat on a vacant seat admiring the skill of the coxed fours and eights as they passed.

Shortly after, the park attendant, resplendent in a smart green uniform with matching peaked cap, stopped to chat, glad of an opportunity to break the monotonous beat he had to accomplish every hour. His conversation revealed a man of considerable experience.

'You'll see from my medal ribbons I served my country in the Great War but my left hand was damaged by a faulty shell fuse, so when I was demobbed I could no longer work as a carpenter at Kings College. The governors, God bless them, offered me this job at the same wages.'

Catherina noticed he wore a leather glove on the left hand but admired the way he accepted his injury.

'It must have been very sad to give up such a skilled job,' Catherina felt very sorry for him, 'Do you enjoy your present job?'

'I do, miss, but I count my blessings. Don't forget there were many thousands who didn't come back, poor devils, and apart from this hand I'm in good fettle and the exercise has done me the world of good.' He grinned as he looked down, 'And I've shortened my belt by four holes and my missus had to take my trousers in about six inches.'

Rupert was interested and asked, 'What unit were you with?'

'The Royal Artillery, as fine a regiment as any I can tell you and it was a grand sight to see the columns of guns and limbers, each pulled by four horses as they moved forward.'

'My late father served with the Artillery but sadly was killed in Belgium in 1918.'

The old man looked very interested, 'What was your dad's name?'

'Sergeant Charlie Tupper; he was an expert with horses!'

The attendant looked astonished and shaking his head as he spoke, surprised Rupert and Catherina.

'Sergeant Tupper! Good Lord, I knew him well! A fine man and, as you say, an expert with horses. He knew more about equinal matters than any with our regiment. Well, who'd have thought I'd be talking to his son today. You know that's what I like about this job 'cause every day I meet new people, some sad and some cheery like you, miss. We talk and they go on their way.

I often wonder what happens to them but I'll never know. But here am I talking to someone whose father I did know and I have to say it's brought back memories.'

'What else can you tell me about my father Mr ... I'm sorry I don't know your name!'

'Begging your pardon, Squadron Leader, I'm Vernon Grubb, Lance Bombardier of the 43 Field Artillery Regiment.' Executing a smart salute, he continued, 'You ask what I remember about your father, well I can honestly say a better man you couldn't find in the regiment; he cared for his men who looked up to him with affection and he was a wonder with our horses and knew just how to deal with sickness and injuries. It was a sad day for us all when he was lost.'

'Do you remember where my father was killed?'

'I can: it was in July 1918 when we were ordered up the line to a village called Ruillemont in Belgium, to support a large attack to take place later that week. In the convoy there were eight field guns and limbers together with the ammunition and cooks transports with their field kitchens. At around midday some Gerry planes came over dropping bombs on us and three guns and crews were knocked out, killing the horses and men together. I tell you it was a massacre and your Dad was with the leading gun crew that got a direct hit. The Belgian army ambulances came very soon and took the wounded away but, to this day, I do not know what happened to Sergeant Tupper's remains.'

Rupert sat quietly for a moment or two. 'Thank you very much Mr Grubb, it has been a great help to know in detail exactly what happened. I'm sure my mother will be most interested when I tell her. She may like to write to you so will you be kind enough to let me have your address?'

After writing the details in his diary, Rupert and Catherina shook hands with the Park Attendant and walked back to King's Parade to collect the car.

On the journey home Catherina told Rupert her feelings about all that had happened.

'It's been a perfectly wonderful day in my life; one that I'll never forget with so many splendid things happening. First my beautiful ring, then our celebration lunch at Turks, and then meeting Mr Grubb who knew your father so well. But the best thing of all was having you with me all day long. That was "the icing on the cake" as you say.' With that she put her arm round Rupert's neck and kissed his cheek.

'Hey, steady on, don't you know it's dangerous to kiss the driver when in motion!' He promptly pulled the car over, stopping at the side of the road and putting his arms round Catherina, gave her several kisses which she obviously enjoyed.

Special leave having been arranged, Norman arrived home in Farndene on 25th March in time to make arrangements for his wedding. The occasion brought together the family from the various parts of the country and Francis and Margot worked wonders finding accommodation for all of them.

The family contingent from Bristol included Alex, Angelina and their youngest son Thomas now almost twelve. Alex's sister Mildred turned up but not Jessica and her husband. Fanny brought her parents David and Ruth, both now very frail but still determined to come to their great grandson's wedding.

Helen's parents, Sir Charles and Lady Violet Dauntsey arrived with Helen's brother Cuthbert on leave from the army.

Margot's family party travelled together from Whitby and included David and Lorna Morton and Grant and Madeline Sheldon.

On 29th March in the ancient church of St Paul's, Farndene, Helen and Norman were married in front of a congregation of close family and friends together with a mass of local people who came along to wish the couple well. The rector, Canon Horatio Hulbert gave a short homily and apologised for the lack of a peal of bells – currently prohibited as they were only to be used in the event of invasion.

'I realise,' he said, 'how disappointed you are so I've arranged for a recording of the bells of St Paul's Cathedral, London, to liven up the proceedings.' He bent down and lifted a small portable windup gramophone onto the pulpit ledge and proceeded to play a beautiful peal much to the amusement of everyone. After the laughter died down he continued.

'This is Helen and Norman's day and you have all shown your affection for these two young people setting out on their married life together in very difficult times. They go with our blessing and my advice for happiness. Treat every morning as a new day full of promise and put into life a little more than you expect to receive from it and never ever let the sun go down on a grievance. It reminds me of a couple in a previous parish who were always arguing and when I enquired who was to blame, the wife told me, "It's him, he always says I'm not always right but I'm never wrong", so beware of infallibility, it may be your undoing!'

As it was a fine March day photographs were taken outside the church and as usual the photographer fussed and diddled about for almost half an hour. Helen looked quite beautiful in a cream silk dress which had been made from her late grandmother's wedding dress. With Norman in uniform they looked a splendid couple. Norman's two younger sisters, Clara and Constance, were bridesmaids and both were dressed in pale blue silk which Fanny had been lucky enough to buy in Bristol. Sadly his twin sister Juliet was unable to get leave to be at the wedding.

Back at the Manor House the family and a few friends were served sherry in the drawing room before the wedding breakfast in the dining room. The gathered company numbered twenty-two and Bertie's staff worked wonders decorating the tables with masses of spring flowers they had collected on the estate.

Sir Charles Dauntsey toasted the happy couple with a witty speech, pulling Norman's leg about Helen's extravagant ways, 'My wife and I will be paying off the resulting overdraft for the next ten years!' And after a few more cheeky comments he became serious, 'Norman, although I say it myself, you have the most lovable and competent wife who will be a wonderful support in the coming years and my wife and I are sure you will look after her.' Then, his features showing a little sadness, he turned to his daughter, 'Darling Helen, we will miss you but are delighted you have chosen a quite splendid partner and know you will have great happiness together.'

Norman replied, thanking everybody and picking up the joke in his father-in-law's speech added his own fun, 'It was good of you to tell me about your overdraft and I can only offer to take it over, adding it to mine which will take the rest of my life to pay off!' He continued thanking everyone for coming, many for long distances, and for the many lovely presents he and Helen would acknowledge in person in due course.

The bridal pair left at four o'clock to go to Southampton for the night before travelling to Cornwall on the morrow for a short honeymoon.

Chapter 36

April 1941 found Great Britain still recovering from the humiliating defeat at Dunkirk but the Prime Minister Winston Churchill, heading a Coalition Government, spoke with candour when he told Parliament that victories were not won by retreats. His rhetoric stirred the nation to arms and promised the military debacle of the previous year in France would be avenged. Plans studied by the War Council, of which he was chairman, were positive and the build up of RAF Bomber Command proceeded apace as a means of hitting back at Nazi Germany until Britain's land forces were stronger.

In Exeter Philip had worked hard pressing the local authority to repair the air raid damage to the Madame Baume premises at 58 High Street and, with the help of the War Office, the work was completed the week before Easter. While the structural work was going on, Janine and her staff had stripped down all the machines, cleaning and oiling them in readiness. Consequently on 8th April the business commenced operations, again making uniforms and some equipment for the Government. All the staff came back and Janine and Philip celebrated with cake and cider before work got under way again.

The area procurement officer for the War Office called to congratulate them and make a plea. 'The re-equipping and expansion of our forces is proceeding apace and we need all you can turn out during this year. Would it be possible for you to increase production, possibly by working shifts, and if so I'll give an order for local labour to be drafted into your business.'

Janine said she would give his request full consideration and promised to let him know very soon.

That evening after their supper, Janine, Mollie and Philip discussed the request for increased output and they decided to divide the workforce, making two shifts. The first working from 7am until 2pm and the second from 2pm to 9pm, both groups to be given suitable breaks for refreshment and paid for eight hours as neither had a dinner hour. Janine and Mollie would each head a shift when the new arrangement commenced after Easter Monday 14th April.

Rather than employ unknown staff, Janine suggested asking existing staff to see if any had relatives who would like to join the firm.

Immediately before Easter, Captain Sam Shelley made a surprise visit on two weeks' leave prior to a posting to Scotland as part of the Royal Artillery re-grouping. The necessary reorganisation was taking place following the loss of personnel and equipment in France the previous year.

Mollie just couldn't believe her eyes as she welcomed him, 'Darling Sam, what a wonderful surprise present for Easter!' and with that both were wrapped in a tight embrace for some moments.

'I've fourteen days' leave before I go to a place near Edinburgh to form a fresh group of batteries with brand new guns. The good news is that I am to be promoted to Major but the downside is that I'll be away for three months in Scotland.'

Mollie was a bit crestfallen with the latter news but congratulated him, 'Well done, Sam! I expect you to get lots more promotion before long as I want to be a General's wife!' They had a laugh as Sam suggested a plan for the coming week.

'Shall we announce our engagement and when I go north next week will you come with me to Whitby to meet my mother and stepfather? It would mean, of course, you'd have to travel back to Exeter on your own but I'm sure you could cope with that all right. And darling, I want you to choose a ring this week and perhaps we should also think about a date for our wedding.

'Dearest Sam, you have the most wonderful ideas and I love every one of them! Yes, let's announce our engagement and I'd love to choose a ring but as far as the suggestion to travel to Whitby is concerned, I don't think that will be possible at present. I'd love to meet your folks but I'll explain why I can't do that now.'

'Mollie darling, that's a pity. However, from what you've said there must be a very good reason.' Sam looked very crestfallen as he realised the plans he'd thought about were not going to be possible.

She went on to explained in detail what was happening at the Madame Baume business and he understood.

'Sam, once the shift arrangements are working in a few weeks time, why don't I come up to Whitby and meet you there for a long weekend? I could see your folks and better still have a weekend with you. It's no distance from Edinburgh to Whitby. So what do you say?'

'Darling, that's a brilliant idea and I should be able to wangle a long weekend once we're settled. I can telephone my mother, before you travel, to make sure they'll be at home to greet you.'

Mollie knew Mr Gavin Stotesbury, the best jeweller in the High Street, Exeter, and later that day, with his help, the special ring of diamonds and rubies was chosen. Sam slipped it on her third left-hand finger and they kissed several times. Mr Stotesbury congratulated the happy couple, adding, 'A kiss is exactly the right thing to seal the engagement!'

Janine had prepared special meal that evening and just as she, Philip, Mollie and Sam sat down there came a long ring at the front door.

Philip's reaction was natural, 'Now that's tiresome and just as we're about to eat!'

Mollie came to the rescue, 'Don't worry, I'll answer the door. If I'm delayed too long please put my food back in the oven,' and with that she left the room.

Those at the table were mystified as they heard whoops and laughter in the entrance hall but when the door burst open all was revealed! In came Rupert followed by Mollie who was glowing with happiness.

'Hello Mother, Philip, Sam, I was just passing so I thought I'd look in!'

Janine hugged and kissed her son before drawing up a chair for him at the table.

'Sit down Rupert and we'll all have supper together, unless you've eaten already.'

'To be honest Mother, the last meal I had was breakfast at Training Command Headquarters. You see I was lucky enough to get a lift in a communications Anson flying to Bristol and I'll go back with it next week, so there you have it.'

The buzz of conversation naturally about Mollie's engagement to Sam and Philip produced one of his hidden bottles of wine to toast them.

In the general chatter that followed Rupert asked, 'what's happened to aunts Kitty and Phoebe?'

'The bomb damage to their house was completed at the beginning of March, and as they were anxious to go home I took them back without delay,' Philip paused momentarily, 'but Coventry is still in a terrible mess and the damage has to be seen to be believed. I hope it won't be long before our bombers can put an end to the Nazis once and for all.'

After the meal was over, Janine and Mollie said they would serve coffee in the sitting room when suddenly Rupert said he also had an announcement to make. Conversation stopped.

'I'm delighted to be home again and particularly to be here for Mollie and Sam's sake. I've kept my news until now as I didn't want to steal their thunder. The fact is, I also have just become engaged to an adorable girl in Lincolnshire. She's Catherina and comes from a long line of a Dutch family. I've brought her photograph for you all to see. She would have loved to come to meet you, but as her family are farmers it was not possible at the moment.'

Janine could hardly believe her ears and like all mothers was delighted to have the news but felt a slight tinge of sadness as she realised her 'chicks were about to fly the nest', leaving only Tom still unattached.

Putting her arms round Rupert and kissing him she said, 'My darling boy, I so very happy for you and hope we'll all meet

Catherina soon. From her photograph she is certainly an attractive young woman.'

Rupert thanked them all and suddenly remembered the holdall he left in the hall. Bringing it into the room, he told his mother, 'Mr van Houten, Catherina's father, has sent you a present,' and produced a large package wrapped in layers of greaseproof paper.

'Rupert, is it another jumbo leg of pork?'

'No, Mother, just undo the wrapping and you'll get a surprise.'

Minutes later there were gasps as Janine uncovered a very large goose.

'Johan, Mr van Houten's manservant, plucked and prepared the bird for the oven and took the liberty of suggesting various types of stuffing to accompany the goose when it's cooked.'

Janine was indeed touched by the generosity of the gift and said she would write to Catherina's father to thank him, 'I'll tell him how much we appreciate his kind thought, especially at the Easter weekend,' and with a smile added, 'as Mr Dickens might have said "there never was such a goose"!'

Rupert also wanted to know if his mother had any news from Tom.

'I get regular letters from Tom, unlike my other son who has lost his notepaper!' Janine had a little dig at Rupert, a notorious 'non-writer', 'and he's well but very busy in the drawing office working on a new generation of bombers. He has a girlfriend, a school teacher from Halesowen, and they meet whenever they can. He is hoping to get some leave shortly so he can bring her home to meet us. I think it's quite serious between them, so "watch this space" as the advertisers say. His last letters are on my desk, so help yourself, Rupert, if you wish.'

Rupert mentioned the autumn was the likely time when Catherina could leave the farm to be married, 'So it looks like a September or October wedding for us, Mother, I hope you and Philip will be able to come up to Lincolnshire during the summer to meet Catherina and her father. Mr van Houten said he'll be delighted if you'll stay with him for as long as you feel able.'

Janine said she and Philip would see what could be done about a visit, 'And hopefully a date can be set before I write.'

Mollie and Sam had also discussed their pending marriage but it was apparent no decision was possible until Sam finished his course. With a pert smile Mollie made her point, 'It's not fair! I'll have to remain a spinster for months and months!'

Rupert couldn't resist a leg pull, 'Well why not write to Mr Churchill? I'm sure he'd be only too pleased to arrange a suitable posting for Sam!'

Sam's response was immediate, 'You're too darn right – he'd post me, most probably to the Middle East, if I know anything about it!'

'Now Rupert stop teasing your sister there's a good boy. By the way, a letter came for you this morning, it's on my desk.'

After some minutes, Rupert returned with the letter in his hand, 'It's not very good news from Jenny, Mother. Here read it for yourself.'

Janine unfolded the sheet of pale blue notepaper and began to read.

Crofters Cottage,
The Manor House Estate,
Farndene,
Hampshire
9th April 1941

Dear Rupert,

It is so long since I wrote to you and I find I haven't got your RAF address so I'll send this to your mother and perhaps she'll forward it to you. I do hope you are well and were able to get some leave after the Battle of Britain was over. I'd love to see you again to talk to you about life in general and particularly us. My boyfriend Grant was sent to Egypt last November but I heard from his father on 4th April telling me Grant had been posted missing believed killed on 26th March.

I'm devastated and still find it hard to believe and keep hoping he'll turn up as a prisoner of war.

*It makes it doubly sad for me as I'm expecting his baby and
he'll never see it; and Rupert, I just don't know what I'm going to
do. Mum is very good about my condition and is helping me but
Dad is exactly the opposite, telling me I should have had more
sense and won't talk to me about it. Please write to me as soon
as you can and if you are able to come to Farndene I'd love to
see you.*

    My love to you Rupert,
      Jenny

Janine sat pondering the import of Jenny's letter and became
aware Rupert was upset by the sad news.

'Rupert I know how you feel getting this awful message
from someone you regard as a sister and what makes it harder
is knowing there isn't much you can do except write now and
regularly in future. I'm aware writing is not one of your strong
points but you'll have to make an effort.'

'I agree with all you've said, Mother, and I know Jenny's in
a tough spot. It's a pity her father can't be more helpful and just
snap out of feeling embarrassed; it's a case of self pity.'

'You're right but remember Mr Briggs is from an older
generation and regards the situation his daughter's in as one that
could have been avoided. Jenny and her boyfriend were enjoying
an extramarital relationship and should have married before he
went abroad, for the simple reason that, as his widow she would
be eligible for a pension whereas now she gets nothing from the
army.'

'So Mother, had I better write to her?' Rupert was uncertain
about what to say and was fishing for help.

'I'll help you draft a letter, Rupert, one that is sympathetic
but doesn't give her any false hopes as far as you are concerned.
You must tell her about your own engagement and pending
marriage.'

Rupert was relieved and, putting is arm round his mother, kissed
her several times as he spoke from his heart: 'You've always been a
most wonderful person in my life, even when I was away all those

years living with the Briggs family I knew I would be coming back to you. When I felt homesick I used to shut my eyes and just imagine I was sitting next to you. Although I'm getting married in a few months' time and will be Catherina's husband, never forget I'll still be your son who will always love his mother.'

Janine's eyes were wet with tears as she kissed him, 'Rupert that was the loveliest thing you've ever said to me! I have no doubt you'll be a good husband and I look forward to having Catherina in our family.' Standing up, she linked her arm with his: 'We must join the others in the sitting room and I'll make some coffee for us all.'

Easter passed and better weather ushered in May with longer days and shorter nights which meant there were fewer hours for the German bombers to harass the population. The RAF became stronger as hundreds of new air crews started arriving in Great Britain from Rhodesia, South Africa, Canada and the USA. The result meant the Luftwaffe daylight attacks diminished and the Allies' own fighters began to penetrate the continent on a daily basis.

At RAF Sutton Bridge the operations expanded with the introduction of an AFU [Advanced Flying Unit] to train navigators and bomb aimers. Work on the runway extension started in April and was to be completed in three months in time for the arrival of old Whitley Bombers to be used for training purposes.

On 11th May the startling news from Scotland revealed Rudolph Hess, Adolf Hitler's deputy, flying his own plane, had landed in Scotland and had been taken into custody. It was the topic of conversation in the officers mess where one wag suggested, 'They say Rudolph is a bit kinky, like Herman Goering the other fat queer, so I reckon he chose Scotland as the men up there wear skirts!'

Howls of laughter followed until one Scots lad remarked, 'Aye, laugh your silly heads off. We may wear kilts but the Jocks put the fear of God into the Jerrys in the Great War and they'll do it again in this one, you'll see! In any case you Sassenachs can't wear a kilt as it would show off your pink knees!'

With a fresh course of fighter pilots due the last week of May, Rupert decided to check the airfield and adjacent bombing range at Holbeach. His Spitfire took off on a calm May morning and, climbing to around three thousand feet, he cruised round the whole area, checking landmarks and noting the windmill to the east of the airfield had not been covered with white cloth as directed. Losing height he approached the Holbeach range from the Wash which showed large areas of mud as the tide was a very low neap. Suddenly his eye caught part of the tail plane of a Spitfire sticking out of the mud; his immediately concluded it was the wreck of Squadron Leader Barry Groombridge's plane and, making a tight turn, he quickly returned to Sutton Bridge airfield.

A recovery team, including a Royal Engineers Unit stationed nearby, managed to pull the plane out with a huge mechanical winch and it was brought to the airfield for further examination. However, the cockpit canopy had been torn off and Barry Groombridge's remains were not with the wreckage.

As month succeeded month the intense training continued and fortunately there were no further fatalities although a number of planes were damaged, some beyond repair.

As her pregnancy became very obvious Helen Dauntsey resigned her WAAF commission and spent a lot of time with her parents at Framley Park, Oxfordshire. Norman managed several weekend breaks to see her and the family doctor favoured September rather than October for the birth.

In early August Helen became ill and was admitted to the local hospital in Oxford in the care of a specialist gynaecologist who was very worried about her patient's condition. A week later a miscarriage occurred leaving Helen desperately ill. Norman obtained compassionate leave and stayed with his wife for several days until she began to recover. Ten days later she was well enough for him to return to Sutton Bridge to resume his duties although Norman worried constantly about her.

Helen went home to her parents and Lady Dauntsey gave her daughter the loving care she needed.

At the start of September Helen developed acute post-natal depression and was convinced the death of her child was an ill omen, telling her mother, 'I know it's a warning for me that Norman is going to die flying for the RAF. He tells me he's only training but I think he is fighting the Germans and will be shot down again but this time he'll die.'

Sir Charles and Lady Dauntsey called in Sir Leonard Freemantle, a specialist psychiatrist who examined Helen on several occasions and concluded her mind was deteriorating and recommended her husband be sent for.

Norman arrived the next day and was alarmed at Helen's condition – so much so he asked the specialist to see him at once. At the meeting, the psychiatrist explained the root of Helen's condition, 'I have examined your wife a number of times and her fixation is that you are going to die in action. She is convinced the death of her baby foretold just that. She can recover but it will be a long and difficult process.'

Norman sat taking in all the doctor had told him, 'In view of all you've told me what, then, is the remedy?'

'You must be with your wife for some months until she is well enough to understand the situation clearly. My advice is you must resign your commission and leave the RAF to give your wife the chance she needs. Failing that I fear she will become totally deranged very soon.'

Norman felt completed shattered by the doctor's advice and it took some minutes for him to collect his thoughts. 'Your recommendation is profound to say the least but deep down I know I'll have act quickly if I'm to save my dearest wife. It's really a question of whether the RAF will let me go.'

'They'll let you go alright; I heard all about your leg injury and miraculous escape from my colleague, Mr Patrick Wilson who operated on you at St George's Hospital. If you resign your commission you will never be fit for any military service thereafter.'

Shortly after, Norman sat with Helen and her parents and told them he intended to leave the Royal Air Force as soon as he could and look after his wife for as long as was necessary.

Helen's reaction was very weepy, 'My darling, don't fly any more please and come home now to be with me.'

Norman decided he would return to Sutton Bridge to see his Commanding Officer, Group Captain Rodney Stanmore. Leaving Helen he also felt the need to tell his parents and discuss the whole situation with them and after a tedious train journey he arrived at the Manor House, Farndene, late that evening.

Margot and Francis were delighted to see their son but quickly realised all was not well with him.

They sat listening as Norman told them the grim truth about Helen and all that the psychiatrist had concluded after examining her.

'You can see the outlook is particularly bleak for Helen and me if I don't leave the RAF immediately and in these circumstances I've no option but to resign my commission.'

Both Francis and Margot agreed and they did their best to comfort their son, talking to him for most of the evening.

Francis suggested, 'When you are free of the RAF I can offer a worthwhile job assisting me as I visit various aircraft factories in my capacity as adviser to Lord Beaverbrook, the Minister for Aircraft Production. At least you would be assisting the war effort.'

Norman thanked his parents and told them he would go to see his commanding officer the next day. 'I'll stay the night and leave by an early train in the morning.'

'No need to do that Norman. I'll give you a lift as I'm flying to Rugby to a large aero engine factory tomorrow – I can drop you off at Sutton Bridge.' Francis had permission to fly his own plane to various parts of the British Isles on duty.

After dinner they spent the rest of the night talking about the other members of the family.

Chapter 37

Janine's two teams worked well during the summer of 1941 and production of service uniforms and other items of military equipment increased dramatically. Several additional members of the staff came from friends and family of existing workers and these older women brought plenty of experience into the business. Although Exeter had only sneak air raids from time to time, Philip had installed a basement shelter for the staff and insisted they all went down to it during alerts.

In July, he and Janine had been to Lincolnshire for a few days to meet Jan van Houten, Catherina and her sister Bep and were delighted with the wonderful welcome they received. During their stay, Rupert managed to join them for a short while and he and Catherina announced that Saturday 18th October was to be their wedding day. They also decided only family and a few friends would be invited. The marriage to be held in the local church followed by a reception at Mr van Houten's house and he very kindly offered Janine and Philip accommodation for a day or two for the wedding.

At RAF Sutton Bridge the new runway and taxi tracks were completed by late June and became fully operational at the start of July. Several new anti-aircraft guns were sited to protect the airfield.

During August the Whitley bombers arrived and the first courses of navigators commenced.

On the morning of 2nd September, Norman and his father flew into RAF Sutton Bridge and after a brief stay Francis took off again for Rugby, having met Rupert briefly.

Norman explained his dilemma to Rupert and they decided to see Group Captain Stanmore there and then.

Rodney Stanmore listened patiently and commiserated with Norman. 'My dear fellow I'm so very sorry to hear about your wife's ill health and have to tell you I'd take the same line you're suggesting and would resign my commission to save my wife from insanity.' He was thoughtful for a couple of minutes, 'However, let me talk to Headquarters before you make any further moves and see if they can help in any other way.'

He had barely finished talking when the whole place started to shake with violent explosions and the most enormous noise as ack-ack guns opened up a distance away around the airfield.

'Good God, we're being attacked! Get down!' Rodney shouted to Rupert and Norman as they dived on the floor for cover. Further bombs were exploding sending huge vibrations through the building, causing books and other items to tumble to the floor.

As quickly as it had started, suddenly all went quiet and the three of them got up cautiously to look out of the windows. Several fires burnt in hangars and workshops and a number of craters were visible on the airfield. The station fire crews were in action putting out several planes which were ablaze.

The duty officer in the control tower had a narrow escape when one of the raiders machine gunned the building, smashing most of the windows. He reported three Dornier 'flying pencil' bombers had carried out the attack of which one was shot down by ground defences and crashed in the Wash; the other two got away but one had an engine out of action and was losing height as it departed.

For the next hour or two everyone on the station gave a hand to sort out the damage and a report was made immediately to Group Headquarters who promised assistance without delay. By good fortune there were no fatalities but several airmen had minor injuries and were dealt with in the station sick bay. The below surface air raid shelters had done their job and during the coming weeks additional shelters were constructed, particularly at the dispersal areas where many of the aircraft were serviced during the day.

As soon as things quietened down, Rupert telephoned Catherina to reassure her he was alright and her response was natural.

'Rupert, darling, I was so worried that I wanted to come to the airfield to see that you weren't hurt but Papa told me not to. I do hope nobody was hurt.'

Rupert put her mind at rest and promised to look in on her as soon as he could.

The frenzied activity by repair gangs making good the damage caused by the attack saw most of the minor restoration complete in a few days. However the major damage to some buildings and one large hangar would take a lot longer and entailed bringing in a building contractor.

Meanwhile Norman worried about Helen and tried to speak to her on the telephone each day. On 6th September he was asked to report to the Commanding Officer.

Group Captain Stanmore was smiling as Norman entered the office, 'Come in and take a seat.'

As soon as he was settled the CO went on, 'I have some very interesting news for you. I explained your situation to Air Vice-Marshal Mike Rollo who told me he has been asked by the Air Minister to find a suitable fighter pilot, who has served with Fighter Command during the Battle of Britain, for special duties with our Air Attache in Washington USA. Since the signing of the United States Lend Lease Act in March this year, Mr Roosevelt, the president, is keen for the American people to meet our airmen who have fought the Nazis. Duties would entail visiting factories and giving lectures about the British war effort and your own story about the air battle.

'As a matter of interest Air Vice Marshal Rollo was a fellow pilot with your father in the Royal Flying Corps during the Great War.'

Norman was completely taken aback and realised the offer was indeed a Godsend but his thoughts returned to Helen's ill health. 'The job sounds unbelievably good but what about my wife? Can she come with me?'

'Mike Rollo fully appreciates your problem and made it perfectly clear Mrs Vining would accompany you and travel with you wherever you go in the States. May I suggest you go home and talk it over with your wife; just take your time, there is no immediate hurry as you will not be required to leave this country until the end of November. Oh, there is one other sweetener with the job; you will be promoted to Squadron Leader if you accept!'

Norman thanked his CO and went straight to the Chief Instructor's office to tell him the news.

Rupert listened to Norman's story and then told him in no uncertain terms, 'If you want my advice, Norman, don't hesitate, take the job with both hands. Hopefully it will be a wonderful chance for Helen to recover in peaceful surroundings. Go down to Oxford now and tell her the marvellous news.'

They shook hands and Norman went to his quarters to collect some things prior to travelling to Framley Park.

The same day, Francis had flown back from his visit to the enormous aero engine factory at Rugby, where he had met Lord Beaverbrook in an effort to speed up the development of new Rolls Royce engines for the RAF. He was glad to be back with Margot and they enjoyed a quiet dinner together during which he told her something quite startling.

'A couple of days ago we were joined at lunch by two Royal Air Force Air Marshalls, one being no other but Mike Rollo. We had a nostalgic chat about old times and then he asked how Norman was getting on. At the time of his accident, Norman was hot news at the Air Ministry and much admired for his resilient attitude to his injuries. I told Mike Norman was flying again as an instructor but went on to explain the terrible problem facing him about Helen. The incredible fact is, Mike had been asked by the Air Minister to find a Battle of Britain pilot for special duties in America and, after talking to me, has decided to offer the job to Norman.'

Margot was quite excited but immediately asked, 'but what about Helen? Will she be able to go with him and more importantly, will she be fit enough?'

'That remains to be seen but so long as her health permits, yes she can go and it will be a wonderful opportunity for both of them. This is strictly in confidence, so when Norman tells us, we must appear not to know anything!'

'Of course I'll keep it confidential, darling, but what a marvellous thing to happen for our boy, just at the right moment.' Margot naturally worried about her son and felt the offer would be a wonderful help for both him and his wife.

Norman's news bought hope to Sir Charles and Lady Violet Dauntsey and Helen seemed to be helped almost immediately and her response was natural, 'Darling Rupert, I just want to be with you always and it will be lovely to get away from this terrible war and live in peace. Can we go now and not wait until November?'

Norman explained to Helen there were formalities to attend to but he would be able to see her each day until they sailed for America, 'I understand I'll be at the Air Ministry and see Foreign Office Officials for various briefings in London. I really feel this is a wonderful opportunity for you and me to be together and can only be beneficial to your recovery. I have decided I must take the job and will tell my CO as soon as possible.'

Norman went straight to Farndene from Framley Park to tell his parents about the job he'd been offered in Washington. Naturally Francis and Margot feigned surprise and listened to their son outlining what the posting meant.

'As far as I'm aware at present, I'll be on a kind of roaming brief in the United States telling all manner of people how we in Britain are fighting the war. The Air Minister apparently asked me as I'd been in action in the Battle of Britain and survived an unusual crash. The great joy is that Helen can come with me and I hope desperately it will help her to recover fully.'

His mother agreed, 'Norman that's wonderful! You two will be completely away from this dreadful conflict for a long time, hopefully until the end of the war and I find that very comforting.'

Norman was quietly thoughtful before replying, 'Mother, I understand your feelings but I'm torn between my desire to do all I can for my darling wife and my duty as a serving officer, flying to defend my country and all that means to my family, to my friends and everything I hold dear.

'You will understand, Father. You fought as a fighter pilot in the Great War and can appreciate my position at present. By taking the American job I feel I'm opting for a cushy number while others are doing the difficult work and risking their lives.'

Francis, looking hard at his son, didn't reply immediately and a silent vacuum ensued for a minute or so.

'Norman, of course I understand all you've said and readily admit my recollection of air to air combat was an exhilarating experience I'll never forget. The surge of adrenaline that accompanies the challenge of fear is personal to the fighter pilot as he enters a fight to the death and winning is the result he seeks. You, having been through that ordeal, have acquitted yourself without any shadow of doubt! To go on serving your country, you have been selected to represent "The Few" to the American nation with, I understand, the approval of the President himself, and that is not in my opinion a cushy number.' Norman was about to reply but Francis held his hand up and continued, 'Your mother and I are so very proud of all you have achieved in your short existence and want you to fulfil yourself in your future life. That fulfilment can only be based on a happy and successful marriage. As I see it, the priority for you now is the wellbeing of Helen and you are the only person who can bring her back to full health. If you go to America with Helen I'm certain you'll never regret taking that step and you go with our blessing.'

Norman hugged both his parents and thanked them for the wonderful support they'd given him.

The early September weather was a typical 'Indian Summer' and people were glad of the warm sunshine to ease the harshness of war. In Exeter, Janine, Mollie and the staff at Madame Baume's workshops found the heat in the workrooms somewhat a disadvantage and they decided to change the pattern of shifts. By starting very early in the morning at sunrise, work commenced at five am until midday when the establishment closed during the strongest heat of the day. The second shift started at three o'clock and finished at ten pm and as a result output was maintained for the War Office.

On the Sunday of the first weekend of September, Major Sam Shelley arrived with news that came as a bombshell to Janine and Philip but most of all to Mollie, as he told them, 'I have two weeks' embarkation leave as my batteries are going to the Mediterranean area. We believe we're required to help defend Malta as it has been subjected to intense air attack recently.'

He put his arms round Mollie who was in tears and then continued, 'Mollie, darling, we must be married while I'm on leave and get a special licence if necessary.'

Mollie's tear-stained face brightened and, looking into his eyes, she said, 'Darling Sam, yes we must be married before you go overseas and we'll see the vicar at St Martin's, our local church, to see what has to be done.'

Janine then made a revelation which surprised them all, 'Mollie, you want to have a white wedding, don't you? Well when war broke out I decided to buy white silk from France sufficient to make you a wedding dress as and when the need arose. I still have the material and I'd love to make your dress my dearest girl.'

Mollie could hardly believe her ears, 'Mother, you wonderful person for being so clever. Yes, I'd love a white wedding. But will there be enough time?'

'Even if I have to work night and day to get it done in time, I'll do it for you Mollie and it'll be ready.'

The vicar of St Martin's church, the Rev. Julian Chesil was most helpful and the application for the special licence was made with his help: 'in wartime conditions the licence is usually issued within a day or two, so we can plan on a wedding day at the beginning of next week.' True to his forecast, the licence arrived in record time and Mollie and Sam decided on Monday September

15th at midday and the preparations began.

'The sad thing is. Sam, you will have gone abroad when Rupert is married next month but that cannot be helped. We'll make it up to you when you return by having a wonderful family get together.' Janine meant every word and talked positively about the time when the whole family could be together again.

On a beautiful autumn day, Mollie and Sam were married in front of their family and some very dear friends. Philip gave her away and she looked a picture in the exquisite dress Janine had made for her, setting off her lovely complexion and dark hair; she was indeed a beautiful bride.

Madeline and Grant, Sam's mother and stepfather came with Grant's son Matthew who acted as best man for the groom. Sam's grandparents, David and Lorna Morton made the journey from St Andrews to see their grandson married.

Rupert and Catherina, Tom and his girlfriend Hazel, and the whole Madame Baume staff as well as a number of local friends made up the congregation.

Marion, Sam's sister, also managed special leave and arrived just in time for the ceremony.

The reception back at the family home was just what Mollie and Sam wanted and as the weather was sunny and warm, the guests wandered around the garden before sitting down to a buffet breakfast.

Philip toasted the happy couple and mentioned the occasion he discussed marriage with Mollie at Easter time in 1928.

'It all came about when I asked her what her ambitions were and her replies were as follows.

'To excel at her work, which she has done; to travel to Europe – and she has been to France a number of times to see Janine's family; to go to America and Canada which she hasn't yet achieved.

'My final question was whether she intended marrying and her answer I can remember clearly, "I've decided to remain single for the foreseeable future but perhaps I'll wed if the right man comes along"! Dear Mollie we all know now "he" has come along and it does us all the world of good to see you and Sam so much in love and now happily married; the fulfilment of your dreams!'

There were other short speeches before the newlyweds departed for a short honeymoon in Teignmouth, where they were guests of Ellery Hales and his wife Beryl, still running the riding school but prohibited from taking their donkeys on the beach by the defence regulations.

Sam and Mollie spent many hours walking beside the sea and he was fascinated as Mollie told him the thrill of her first visit to Teignmouth with her mother and two brothers in 1920. 'We came on the excursion train from Exeter and it was the most wonderful day I'd ever had in my life. I remember the sun shone, the sea was calm and it was the time we met Ellery Hales who had the donkey rides on the beach. As we had very little money in those days, mother was wonderful as she had saved enough from her wages at Madame Baume's to give us children a few treats on our holidays. I knew when I eventually married I just had to come back here for my honeymoon; you see it's the most special place for me with many happy memories and from now on it will be even more special as I'm your wife, my dearest Sam.'

'That's the loveliest story I've ever heard and I'm just so happy we met in France and fell in love. We'll keep coming back to Teignmouth over and over again in the years ahead; it's now a very special place for me as well, darling.'

They sat on a low wall overlooking the sea and as they kissed the seagulls wheeled overhead, mewing and calling to each other and for that moment the sun shone on everything.

Chapter 38

Saturday 18th October, a day of great promise, dawned with a typical early Fenland mist shrouding the Lincolnshire countryside which slowly cleared later in the morning.

The families and friends gathered during the past twenty-four hours were staying in and around the village of Walpole St Peter, a mile or two from RAF Sutton Bridge. The little church, dating back to the thirteenth century, looked hardly large enough to accommodate the congregation made up of the Tupper family headed by Janine and Philip with Mollie, now of course Mrs Shelley, the van Houtens including cousins from King's Lynn and many local farmers and their children all squeezed into the very ancient seating.

Sitting in the front pews were the close family members and, waiting on the opposite side, Rupert in RAF uniform and his brother Tom who was best man.

Everyone chatted happily until the organist pumped out the Bridal March on his harmonium, the signal for all to stand. Turning their heads many hoped to get a glimpse of the bride as she moved slowly down the aisle on the arm of her father, Jan.

As they stopped at the chancel step all eyes were on Catherina who wore a beautiful gown of pale cream silk and in her lovely auburn hair she had an orange blossom headdress holding a veil. A single string of natural pearls with matching earrings was her choice of jewellery. Bep, her sister was the only bridesmaid and over her dress of burgundy-coloured velvet she wore a double fine gold chain, a fitting contrast to her sister.

As soon as the bridal party were settled, the rector Canon Spencer Tollard proceeded with the marriage service and joined in the hymns with gusto almost outdoing the organist who pedalled as fast as he could on the harmonium to keep up with the singers.

Having pronounced Rupert and Catherina man and wife, the rector gave a short homily, addressing his remarks to the whole congregation.

'It has been a great pleasure to see Catherina and Rupert take their vows in this very old church and as a matter of interest I looked in the marriage register one hundred years ago. An entry on 18th October 1841 reads as follows: "Rudolf van Houten, bachelor, married to Marjolein Weisman, spinster" and I understand that that couple are the great, great grandparents of our bride today. Since that time every member of the van Houten family has been baptised and married in this wonderful old building.

'We all face untold dangers at present and none of us knows when we'll see peaceful times again. So, when you go from this place today, think about it as a haven which has stood for centuries through good and bad times and will always be here to offer spiritual comfort.

'Before I give a blessing I must apologise for the tone of our organ. During our harvest festival last month it seems a family of mice made their home in the harmonium and appear to have eaten two of the stops! They are still in residence causing our organist to play with bicycle clips on, in case they decide to run up his trouser legs!' The gathered company enjoyed the fun, laughing when the organist stood beside the organ revealing he wore bicycle clips.

After the blessing the bride and groom walked down the aisle past many smiling faces and nods of goodwill. Outside, an RAF photographer took a picture of the happy couple followed by various groups of family and friends.

Everyone was invited back to the van Houten residence to drink the bride and groom's health. A marquee had been erected on the lawn at the back of the house and here a barrel of beer and other lighter refreshments were provided. Catherina and Rupert mingled with the well wishers for about an hour until the family and close friends retired to the house for the wedding breakfast.

The celebrations went on for the afternoon and it was almost four o'clock when Catherina and Rupert left the house in his car, bound for Keswick in the Lake District, for a week's honeymoon, the longest both could be spared from the RAF and the farm.

The party at the van Houten house went on for the rest of the evening and as Janine, Philip, Mollie and her brother Tom were guests of Jan until the next day, they all enjoyed the opportunity of getting to know each other better – a true family bonding.

By late November Norman and Helen had completed most of their preparations for America and were due to sail on Monday 8th December from Southampton. Helen had recovered considerably in the past weeks and was pronounced fit enough to travel by the specialist. At Margot's suggestion, Sir Charles and Lady Violet Dauntsey came to stay for a few days at the Manor House, prior to their daughter and son-in-law's departure for the USA. A family party, to see them off, was arranged and the family gathered at Farndene on Sunday the 7th.

Robert and Edith Oulton drove over from Bristol bringing Fanny, Alex and Angelina in one car to save petrol. Everyone was delighted to see the Rev. Digby Fletcher, now in his eighty-seventh year, who had come down from London to stay with Francis and Margot for a couple of weeks.

Fanny was particularly delighted and sat talking to Digby about past times. 'It seems only a year or two ago that you presided at Norman's funeral in 1904 and here you are as spritely as ever. To be honest you don't look a day over sixty!'

Digby was flattered and amused. 'Fanny, how kind of you but I'm eighty and a little bit over! I have to say you have always been kind in all you've done over the very many years I've known you. Now that's more than I can say about some of the parishioners in Farndene in the past. I recall one such, whom I'll call "Farmer Giles" whose pet aversion was any sermon over ten minutes in length and he told me so, as soon as I arrived in the parish all those years ago. You may imagine I was an enthusiastic preacher, wishing to convey the great message of the bible to my flock, with the result I "took root" on occasions in the pulpit.

'Farmer Giles, who always sat in the front pew, had a ready

remedy to my lengthy addresses. He placed his collection in six neat piles of coins on the pew shelf in my full view. If my sermon exceeded ten minutes, glancing at his watch he proceeded to remove one pile of coins every extra minute, putting the collection back in his pocket. He thought he was smart but I outwitted him by taking the collection during the hymn before the sermon. He was certainly a character but is sadly no longer with us. Who knows,' he continued with a chuckle, 'perhaps he's doing the same thing to St Peter above!'

Madeline and Grant arrived from Whitby after an exhausting journey during which the train was diverted twice due to bomb damage the previous night.

Francis and Margot took great trouble preparing the guest list for dinner on the Sunday night which included, in addition to the family, the Rev. Horatio and Mrs Dorothy Hulbert, Wing Commander Felix and Mrs Daisy Beaumont and one or two local friends, making a total of twenty-two for the farewell dinner.

During drinks before the meal the conversation moved to shortages of all kinds especially for the ladies who had great difficulty in finding simple things, like silk stockings, so Norman came to their rescue.

'I've an idea we can help. Why not give your foot size to Helen and once we get to America we can send not only silk but some of their famous nylon stockings to each of you.' The ladies applauded the idea but drew the line when Felix Beaumont suggested he could help with the measuring!

Digby Fletcher asked about their journey, 'do you know which ship you'll be travelling in?'

'Yes, we sail from Southampton in the liner *Pretoria*, a twenty thousand tonner.' Norman thought for a moment, 'I believe she used to belong to the Cape Line but was commandeered at the outbreak of war.'

Digby looked surprised, 'Oh, not from Liverpool? I thought all convoys sailed from that port.'

'The *Pretoria* doesn't sail in convoy as it's a very fast vessel. Apparently it cruises at thirty knots or more which means it's almost impossible for a U-boat to hit her. So it ploughs the oceans entirely alone like the great Cunard liners.'

Settled in the dining room, chatter ceased as Digby stood to say grace and turning to Fanny who sat next to him, whispered with a grin, 'I promise it'll not be more than ten minutes!' followed by his booming baritone delivery, 'Let us be thankful for the food before us to nourish our mind and body and the family and the friends to cherish and support us. Let us think of others less fortunate living under Nazi occupation in Europe and pray for their early release. We ask for God's blessing on those we know and love. Amen'

Digby's words were the signal for the meal to start and the accompanying buzz of conversation and laughter made it a joyful occasion. It was almost ten when dinner finished and the ladies went to the drawing room leaving the men to smoke. Margot had been quiet during the meal and now welcomed the opportunity to chat with Fanny.

'Mama, first of all a very big thank you for all you've done and are still doing for the children. It's been a tremendous help for Francis and me and I know the young ones enjoyed being with you in Bristol.'

Fanny took Margot's hand and smiled, 'It has done me the world of good and I'll miss their lively activity when Clara and Constance leave school. I expect I'll feel quite lost for a while but I've many other interests so I shan't be at a loose end. But tell me Margot have you something on your mind? I thought you looked very thoughtful at dinner.'

Margot didn't reply at once as if she felt uncertainty about what she was going to say. 'Mama, you're right, I feel apprehensive about Norman and Helen in only one way. I wonder if she's fit enough to undertake all that is being asked of her. From what Norman has told us he will be on a pretty gruelling schedule of travelling and lecturing throughout the United States. If she can't cope it may cause a relapse in her mental health.'

'Margot, I understand your feelings but remember this, she and Norman are going away from this awful war into a land where there is plenty and that satisfies her one big problem. Norman is no longer flying and will be with her every day. We can only trust all will be well and she will recover fully in time. One other point, Helen is an intelligent young woman and I suspect there may be a lot more good qualities none of us have seen as yet.'

Margot thanked her and was soon drawn into the general conversation about Norman's wonderful idea about sending stockings from America. Lady Violet said she would be glad to have things like dried fruit, adding, 'I've heard the Americans have a wonderful cooking aid called "dried egg" which can be reconstituted to make anything from scrambled egg to fruit cakes. If Helen can send parcels over we can put the money into their bank account here.'

Further deliberations were halted as the men joined them for coffee and Felix greeted them all with, 'I hope all you ladies have measured your feet and legs. Personally I think you all have smashing legs with or without stockings!'

Daisy chided him, 'Now Felix, behave yourself or you'll have to stand in the corner and miss some of Francis's lovely cognac.'

And so the evening passed happily until the party guests who were travelling, departed at half past eleven. The family staying over with Margot and Francis at the Manor House, were still talking until well after midnight as though each was loath to break up a wonderfully happy occasion.

Francis decided to offer them a nightcap and as soon as the glasses were charged gave a toast.

'To Helen and Norman, you go with all our good wishes and fondest love for your journey across the water.' Glasses clinked and there were many hugs and kisses before Daisy and Felix started singing the popular Vera Lynn song, 'We'll meet again' and they all joined in the merry salute.

In that happy state, goodnights were said as they drifted off to bed in ones and twos.

The 9th December was typical of that month, low drifting clouds accompanied by frequent sharp showers of rain and hail with blustering winds from the west. In these conditions the liner *Pretoria* cut a course through turbulent white capped seas of the Atlantic en route for America.

An entirely different world existed on board as the 190 passengers lived cocooned in the splendid opulence of pre-war luxury sailing. Comfortable lounges were panelled in oak or rosewood with easy chairs dressed in various fabrics or leather, there was a 2,000-book library and the dining rooms' walls were lined with maple wood and large ornamental tinted mirrors. For relaxation a cinema showed films each afternoon and evening and a theatre put on a smart show every night. A palm court café equipped with a dance floor and a rhythm quintet, offered tea and after-dinner dances. Most of the staff aboard were no longer young, but they provided a splendid service.

Sitting in their spacious cabin Helen and Norman relaxed and chatted about all that had happened during the past day or so.

'Norman, darling, I never believed we could be whisked from the terrible war in England to this wonderful ship with practically no restrictions and pure comfort everywhere one looks. I'm going to enjoy every minute of our journey especially as I'll be with you!' Smiling, she added, 'I wouldn't mind if the ship went on and on for the rest of our lives.'

'I couldn't agree more, my sweet, but don't forget we're bound for the land of plenty and from what I've been given to understand, the Americans are a most hospitable crowd so we've a lot to look forward to when we get there.'

It was soon time for dinner and Helen, wearing a pretty cocktail dress of aquamarine silk with slingback shoes and a crystal necklace with matching earrings, produced a whistle from Norman, 'Darling, you look absolutely wonderful!' Hugging her, he gave her a passionate kiss which left them both breathless.

'Gosh, darling, you are certainly intense! But I love every minute of it.'

She straightened his tie and brushed a little face powder from the lapel of his lounge suit. With a smile she took his arm as they made their way to dinner.

Entering the dining room they were escorted to a table for four by the head waiter who explained, 'You will be joined by Mr and Mrs Amos Zachary; he's an industrialist travelling to the States with a buying mission for the Government. You may rotate to other tables during the voyage if you wish.'

Norman thanked him and, as an aside to Helen, 'To be honest I'm more interested in the food than the people; frankly, I'm famished so I hope they won't be long.'

Almost as he spoke, the couple arrived and after introducing his wife Beulah, Mr Zachary chatted easily, giving the impression he was a person who led from the front.

There were choices on the menu and all four expressed surprise and delight at having 'pre-war food in pre-war surroundings'.

'Tell me Mr Vining, why are you travelling to the USA?'

Norman replied in a relaxed fashion, 'I'm going on a lecture tour of the States, a sort of fact-finding mission, and fortunately my wife is able to accompany me for the whole time.'

Mr Zachary nodded but was clearly not impressed, 'Oh, I see, but as a young man have you considered offering your services by staying in England?'

Norman was completely taken aback and looking at Helen, frowned and shook his head, indicating she should say nothing.

'Mr Zachary, I hear what you say but I don't intend making any comment other than to say I'm going to the United States at the invitation of Mr Churchill and with the approval of Mr Roosevelt, the President.' With that riposte, Norman carried on a normal friendly conversation until the meal was over.

A little later he and Helen spent the rest of the evening dancing which Norman enjoyed, holding her close and whispering loving things in her ear, making her giggle.

Back in their cabin both were ready for bed when Helen suddenly remembered the dinner table conversation, 'Darling, I was very put out by that pompous little man insinuating you ought to be fighting for your country! I'd have given him something to think about but realised you didn't want a scene at the table.'

Norman was grinning as he told her what he had in mind,

'Dearest, you're correct I didn't want to make an issue of his remarks there and then. You see I've a more subtle way of dealing with that type of person; I shall wear my uniform to dinner tomorrow night!'

'You naughty boy. I can't wait to see his face when he realises he's made a colossal faux pas!'

Chapter 39

For once the war news in December 1941 was uplifting as the German pocket battleship *Bismarck*, engaged by the Royal Navy and finally sunk in the Atlantic saw the removal of an enormous threat to British shipping. Sadly the battleship HMS *Hood* was lost with most of her crew during the encounter. Another capital warship HMS *Ark Royal* was sunk in the early part of the month.

The other startling news that broke in December was the appalling Japanese attack on the American Fleet at Pearl Harbour, Hawaii, bringing the United States into the war against both Japan and Germany. Mr Churchill declared the outcome of the war was determined at that point, as the biggest army and arsenal in the world would be fighting side by side with the British Allies and providing the arms to finish the job.

Air raids continued nightly and the population gradually became hardened to seeing swathes of their cities reduced to smouldering piles of rubble each morning with the loss of family and friends often leaving evacuated children orphans. The British spirit was undaunted and as one London East Ender remarked, 'If 'itler finks he kern knock us darn 'e dunnow wot 'e's up erginst. As Ole Winney told im, yer gonner git wot for wen ar Raff boys git goin! Jus yoo wate Adoolf 'itler, jus yoo wate! An as fer yer lord Haw-Haw, 'e's gotit cumin to im wen we win, weoll ave is guts fer garhers!' [Lord Haw-Haw was the nickname given to William Joyce, an English traitor broadcasting propaganda to Britain for the Nazis].

The remarkable resilience of the people was acknowledged by regular visits by the King and Queen and Mr Churchill and Ministers to the worst-hit towns and cities and morale was boosted accordingly.

At RAF Sutton Bridge training had continued during the autumn without any serious mishap and with the new runway extension proving invaluable. Rupert and Catherina were settled, as Jan had offered them part of the house for their sole use, solving their problem of accommodation. Naturally, Catherina continued working on the farm with her sister Bep and the other members of the staff, mostly older men and women. Rupert came home to Catherina most evenings unless there were late lectures, in which case he stayed in his quarters on the airfield.

Towards mid-December Mollie came up for a few days to see her brother and sister-in-law and to bring Christmas presents.

After dinner on the first evening she told them about Sam, 'I've had several letters from him and his guns are defending Malta against constant air attacks. If you like I'll read you the last one,' taking the envelope from her handbag, she withdrew a long screed.

Rupert winked at Catherina before pulling his sister's leg, 'Just read the news, Mollie, and not the lovey dovey parts!'

Mollie blushed as Catherina came to her defence, 'Rupert, stop being a bore by teasing your sister; you should know better by now! Just ignore him, dear, and tell us all about Sam.'

Mollie spread the letter on the table and began to read the bits she thought would be interesting.

'"We've been in action every day since we arrived and are attacked by a succession of Italian and German aircraft. The local population go into the hundreds of caves on the island as soon as the alert is sounded and as a result there are fewer casualties. It can be very hot at the middle of the day compared with England and we are all pretty brown as we only wear shorts, boots and of course a tin helmet. The RAF has done its best with three ancient Gloucester Gladiator biplanes, nicknamed Faith, Hope and Charity, shooting down a number of far superior attackers. Replacement fighters will be Spitfires and Hurricanes, so they tell us, and we await developments. Our food is acceptable but monotonous. However, the local farmers often bring oranges and figs for us to buy which is a Godsend. When the raids ease off I intend having a look at some of the very old buildings and churches as many have wonderful mosaic interiors dating back to before the Crusades."' Folding the letter, Mollie put it back in her bag and sighed, 'I miss him every day and worry he is in so much danger but like so many other wives I'll have to be brave.'

Catherina put a comforting arm round her sister-in-law's shoulder, 'Mollie, take heart and say a little prayer for Sam each day; it'll help both of you until he returns safely.'

She leant across to kiss Mollie's cheek and hold her hand. 'Thank you, Catherina, I'll do just that and will tell Sam what time every evening the little prayer will be said.'

The days passed quickly but there was time for Mollie and Catherina to get to know each other more and it was a tearful farewell when it was time to part. Jan gave Mollie a brace of pheasant and some wine to take home to Janine and Philip with his good wishes.

Meanwhile, on 10th December aboard the liner *Pretoria*, now well into the Atlantic, Helen and Norman were enjoying the luxury. The purser asked them to join him at his table for dinner that evening, the other guests being an American diplomat and his wife and a United States army chaplain.

Assuming they would be sitting with Mr and Mrs Zachary, Norman had put on his uniform much to the pleasure of the Americans. However, glancing across the dining room Norman noticed Mr Zachary looked thoroughly embarrassed, so much so he sent a short note of apology to Norman via the waiter. Showing it to Helen he told her, 'I'll go over later on and put the chap at ease.'

The table conversation was lively and Helen asked the chaplain, 'Is God really on our side? Or is the Almighty impartial?

The Chaplain smiled, 'A good question! Personally I don't think our Maker is on any side but he will give us the courage and determination to overcome the Devil. We all know Satan has entered the minds of the Nazis and that will eventually be their downfall.'

A number of passengers had noticed extra vibration from the ship's engines and the Diplomat's wife was curious, 'tell me Mr Purser, why is the ship vibrating more?'

The purser answered carefully, 'It's a technical point, madam. We've increased our speed as the ship is in mid-Atlantic and consequently away from possible air cover, in an area where U-boats may be present. I'd say it's almost impossible for a U-boat to attack a vessel travelling at our high speed.'

The Americans were eager to hear Norman's experience as a fighter pilot in the Battle of Britain but naturally he was diffident about 'shooting a line' in RAF parlance.

In the early afternoon of the following day the engine vibration ceased and the liner appeared to be going slower, so much so an announcement was made telling the passengers a fault had occurred in one of the engines which was being repaired. Meanwhile the ship would proceed on one engine.

Norman met the purser a little later and asked him, 'What's the real problem in the engine room?'

The purser was quite frank, 'I can tell you but keep it to yourself: we've bearing trouble and I don't think there are spares on board. We can make a steady eighteen knots or so on the remaining engine which will put about another day and a half on our journey time.'

Norman thanked him, 'Frankly, I don't mind at all if it takes another day or two; I'm thoroughly enjoying the cruise.'

After an early cup of tea in the Palm Court restaurant, with a pianist playing popular tunes, Helen decided to go to their cabin for a rest before dinner: 'I'll have a little nap before dinner, darling. Are you staying here?'

Norman stood to escort her to the door, 'I think I'll go to the library for a while,' adding with a smile, 'I just need to "gen" up on all the funny little sayings the Americans seem to use. See you honey!' As both giggled he kissed her on both cheeks.

He found the library quiet and comforting with beautifully pro-portioned bookcases in walnut with ebony tracings, comfortable wine-coloured arm chairs with adjustable reading lamps and several writing tables all standing on a patterned Wilton carpet. The librarian, an elderly grey-haired man with soft grey eyes and sharp features, took off his pince-nez as Norman enquired, 'I'm looking for something that'll give me a broad idea of American day-to-day conversation and jargon.'

The librarian smiled, 'It's a funny thing I'm often asked for just those publications by English people going to the United States, but from the many contacts I've had over the years with Americans, I remember that most of them just love to hear English being spoken by Englishmen.'

He moved across the room and returned a few minutes later with two books: 'These will give you an insight into the way the Americans converse and, in addition, the odd way they spell many of our words.'

As he handed the volumes to Norman the whole ship shook with a violent vibration and a rumbling explosion. All the lights went out for about half a minute but came on again although much dimmer.

Norman and the librarian looked at each other before the latter spoke, 'Good God, what on earth was that?

Norman shook his head and suggested, 'Maybe it's trouble with the faulty engine the purser told me about.' At that moment the lights became brighter and the librarian said he would investigate and let Norman know the result in due course.

Left alone, Norman settled in a comfy chair and started reading the foreword in the first book but some moments later was interrupted by the ship's fog horn blasting out 'boat stations'.

His first thought was to go to Helen and, dumping the books, he moved quickly out to the central area of the ship which was already a mass of frightened people being directed to the various upper decks for their boat stations. With great difficulty he managed to push against the throng as far as the main stairway where four crew members were directing passengers. They refused Norman access to the lower cabin deck, simply saying that all passengers had to go up to the boat decks. He pleaded with them but in vain and then he remembered the side stairs behind the lift shaft.

Pushing hard through the crowd he eventually reached the side exit and to his relief was not prevented from going down. Several people passed him on their way up but he ignored them as he rushed along. Reaching his cabin he flung the door open but to his horror the place was empty. Shouting Helen's name he checked the bathroom to no avail. He stood for a minute out of breath as he realised she had gone to the upper decks for the lifeboats. At that minute he also realised the ship was tilting slightly which meant only one thing: the explosion must have been a torpedo!

Stumbling up the stairs again Norman came to the main area and joined the stragglers being herded up to the lifeboats by the crew. Quite exhausted he reached the top decks now packed with passengers, faces registering fear, some shivering in the cold Atlantic breeze, some weeping, all watching apprehensively as the crew struggled with the lifeboat launching operations now being made more difficult by the increasing list. A distribution of life jackets proceeded and crew members ensured everyone was fitted correctly. The late afternoon light was sufficient to illuminate the sea area around the ship and beyond for two or three hundred yards like a vast dark grey sheet of glass with an occasional white fleck here and there.

Suddenly a shout went up from an observant passenger, 'Look over there! It's the bloody U-boat!'

The waiting throng now looked in horror as they watched the surfaced submarine a couple of hundred yards away. From the conning tower German sailors were jumping out to man a large gun on the gleaming deck.

'They're going to shoot at us!' a woman screamed, 'We haven't got a chance, we'll all be killed by those Nazis. I know, I saw them in Austria before I escaped; Nazis are a pack of murderers!'

Two of the crew did their best to calm her down as her fear started to 'infect' several other women.

By this time the twilight was almost spent as a powerful searchlight suddenly stabbed the darkness, illuminating the U-boat in clear silhouette. A split second after came an immense boom of gunfire followed by an explosion as a shell hit the conning tower of the submarine, producing an enormous hole. Immediately a second shell hit the base of the tower which all but disintegrated while a third hit the hull sending an immense column of water into the air. As the sea settled there was no sign of the German sailors previously on the U-boat hull.

The passengers cheered but at the same time the liner lurched to an impossible angle and many of those left on deck started to slide down towards the sea.

A fire in the stern added to the confusion as black smoke poured from the stricken vessel and a stream of burning oil burst out onto the surface of the sea, like lava from an active volcano.

The British destroyer HMS *Damocles* now moved closer, flooding the area with further searchlights that picked out the shattered U-boat now sinking stern first, and dozens of people in the sea, as well as many in lifeboats and on Carley floats it had been possible to launch. The sea was also littered by flotsam floating away from the liner

The warship moved in cautiously and lowered a pinnace and two motor launches to pick up survivors but kept a safe distance from the *Pretoria* which was now alight from end to end, spewing burning oil onto the surface of the sea and illuminating the whole scene with a dull red glow.

Norman slid into the sea with a dozen or so fellow passengers and after the initial shock of the cold water, decided to swim away from the large patches of burning oil fuel leaking from the doomed liner. Hampered by the lifejacket he made slow progress and twenty minutes later was suffering from the intense cold which pervaded his body. Hypothermia took over and slowly his consciousness ebbed away. In his delirious state he suddenly felt a stinging in his leg, 'it's a wasp sting', he thought, 'but my mother will look after it'. Moments later he heard Helen's voice calling 'Norman, darling, just hold on and I'll help you' but the blurred scene around him gradually faded as he felt and knew no more.

For the next two hours the destroyer picked up a considerable number of the survivors and only gave up the search after the liner finally capsized, disappearing below the waves following an immense explosion which ripped the vessel apart.

In Britain the next day news of the disaster hit the headlines of all the papers and the first reports of the number of lives lost was startling. One daily had half the passengers and crew missing while another stated the loss of life was considerable. The Ministry of Information announced it was early days to make any firm announcement but hoped soon to give lists of survivors.

At Farndene, Francis and Margot listened to the news on the wireless and were stunned by its import. However, after long conversations with Fanny in Bristol and with Helen's parents in Oxford, they agreed to wait and hope that Norman and Helen had survived.

Margot sat quietly at the breakfast table trying hard to focus her mind on the reality of the situation and only when Bertie spoke did she concentrate on what he'd said.

'Thank you, Bertie, but I don't feel like eating at the moment, I'll just have black coffee, thank you.'

The butler brought the coffee and said gently, 'Don't despair, madam, just have faith and hopefully all will be well.'

Margot was touched by his concern, 'That was a most kind thought, Bertie, and I really appreciate you saying we must have faith.' Once more, her mind went back to Aunt Lotte's comments, 'but we have to be brave like our soldiers and all will be well'.

Up to that point Francis had said little but now he became aware Margot was under great stress and going round the table, he sat next to her and put his comforting arms round her shoulders, 'Margot my darling, don't give up hope; it's only hours since the liner sunk and from what we've heard one of our warships was at the scene.'

Margot wiped her eyes and kissed Francis on the cheek, 'You're right and, as Bertie said, we must have faith. I've been thinking, why don't we go along to St Paul's? The walk will do us good and one can be reflective there. And when we get back perhaps you will be able to get up-to-date news from Juliet at the Admiralty.'

A quarter of an hour later they emerged from the Manor House, Margot in a heavy coat of dark red tweed with fur trimmings matching her fur hat and Francis in a long brown overcoat and a deerstalker with the flaps turned down to keep his ears warm. As they walked arm in arm Margot relaxed and jokingly said, 'Darling, you look just like Sherlock Holmes in that hat.'

'Alright, have a laugh at my expense, my dearest, but you know I'm getting a little thin on top and this hat keeps my head warm.'

They enjoyed the joke and chatted as they walked along the lanes in hazy December sunshine glinting on the frosty fields and hedgerows making them sparkle like diamonds. The slight mist on the fields yielded slowly to the persistent sun, giving the countryside an ethereal look. Reaching Toddy Brantwith's farm they stopped to watch as a woman pitchforked hay out of a large trailer into metal feeders for the cattle coming across the field to eat.

'Francis, I don't recognise the lady, do you?'

'No, but I think I recognise the uniform; I think she's a Land Girl, one of the new organisations set up by the Government to help farmers. Poor old Toddy has been on his own since he divorced his wife – you know, the lady who had an affair with the Rev. Shadwell Legion, who was subsequently "unfrocked" by the Bishop.'

Having completed her job, the Land Girl started the tractor and came alongside the boundary fence to speak to Francis and Norman.

'Hello, I'm Natalie Booker and I've come to help Farmer Brantwith around the farm.'

Margot noticed she was a much older person than the majority of the girls being recruited by the Government but nevertheless her smile denoted a pleasant disposition. She looked attractive in her uniform and the hat contained a mass of fair wavy hair.

Francis introduced Margot and himself and they listened as Natalie told them about herself.

'I was brought up at a place called Copdock outside Ipswich on the Colchester road and my parents had a mixed farm with cattle, horses, pigs and a lot of poultry. I married a tax inspector whose promotion took us to Coventry where I lived for the past fifteen years. My husband died in 1935 and I was on my own after that. During the terrible Blitz raid on 14th November 1940 my house was badly damaged and I couldn't live in it until the war damage people had repaired it. It took them six months so in the meantime I decided to make myself useful and joined the Land Army.

'After training I was offered a choice of North Wales or Hampshire so I chose the latter and was sent here.'

As Natalie paused for breath, Margot spoke quickly, 'What an interesting story and are you enjoying helping Toddy Brantwith?'

'Well, yes and no; yes, I like working for him and looking after the milking herd but no – because he doesn't keep horses I'm not able to ride in my spare time.'

Francis nodded understanding, 'I'm sure my wife and I would like to welcome you at the Manor House and offer the occasional use of one of our hunters if you wish.'

Natalie's eyes shone with her answer, 'You're very kind indeed and perhaps I can come along after Christmas at a time convenient to you?'

Margot nodded and with that she and Francis took their leave.

A little further on both had fits of the giggles as Margot declared, 'If only you'd asked her whether or not she had any designs on Toddy Brantwith, we could have spent the rest of the day listening to a splendid story of romance!'

The church clock struck ten as they went in the south door away from the bitterly cold air and into the relative warmth of the nave.

'I'd like to sit in that pew at the back,' Margot pointed to the one with the names carved along the hymn book shelf, 'It is significant for a particular reason and I'll tell you why when we sit down.'

Francis was curious and as soon as they were seated asked,

'Well, what's the special reason my love?'

Smiling as she looked at him, Margot took his hand and related her reason.

'Darling Francis, the incident took place way back in 1919 not long after we arrived at the Manor House and you made a comment at which I took umbrage and stormed out. I was extremely foolish and, in a huff, I walked to this church and sat here. Looking around I saw the plaque in memory of your father and I came to my senses and prayed for strength to be able to forgive. Being in this church and in this particular pew had a remarkable effect on me because when I looked at the pew shelf I saw all those boys names carved along its length and I knew many of them were lost in the Great War and I felt humbled. And now we're here together because we have no idea whether Norman and Helen have survived this dreadful calamity.'

Francis held her hands tightly as he spoke, 'My dearest Margot you are a most wonderful person and I understand all you've said, particularly about our son and his wife. We know the risks and the chances everyone is up against in wartime but like you I have great faith and that will carry us through. I'm glad we came here today as I look upon this church as our family's spiritual home, a place we have entered for many generations past for blessing on our triumphs and tragedies. We'll go home in a moment knowing the outcome of our present problem is in the safe hands of our Maker!'

Margot and Francis stood in a long embrace, then arm in arm walked out into the pale December sunshine.

Chapter 40

The sick bay aboard the destroyer HMS *Damocles* was sufficient for the needs of her crew in normal circumstances but following the rescue of so many passengers of the ill-fated liner *Pretoria* the facilities were stretched to the limit. The severely injured were made as comfortable as possible, lying on stretchers along the floor with just enough space between them to permit the doctor, Lieutenant Surgeon Wimpole and his assistants to pass as they checked each casualty.

As he regained consciousness slowly, Norman became aware of the whiteness of his surroundings and for a while was too weak to keep awake. He roused as someone held his wrist and opening his eyes looked up at the doctor taking his pulse.

'That's better old chap, I think you're on the mend but only just.'

Norman's mind was still blurred as he watched the doctor check his temperature. 'You're warming up nicely and in a little while we will give you something hot to drink which will help you recover. You've been damned lucky as you nearly snuffed it in the sea.' The doctor moved away and Norman closed his eyes again at the same time trying to ascertain where he was.

Shortly after, an orderly gently touched his shoulder rousing Norman from his comatose state. Upon opening his eyes he beheld a bearded figure kneeling beside the stretcher with a large mug in his hand. 'I'll help you sit up, matey, so you can take this nourishment,' the big fellow eased Norman to the sitting position and helped him sip the steaming hot cocoa laced with rum.

The first mouthfuls created a burning sensation in his stomach but as he drank more he could feel the warmth spreading through his body.

Norman, still supported by the orderly, began to focus his mind and he suddenly needed answers to his questions, 'Where am I? Where's Helen?' and after a slight pause, 'Tell me please, what on earth's happened?'

'Now keep calm, matey, and I'll tell you. You are in the sick bay of HMS *Damocles*; you were fished out of the sea by one of our launches in an advanced state of hypothermia. You were as near a gonner as you could be but are now recovering. I don't know who Helen is though.'

'She's my wife, Mrs Helen Vining, she was with me on board.'

'We rescued many from the water after the liner was torpedoed so she may be on board, I'll make enquires.'

Norman sank back, still bewildered and unable to grasp the full meaning of what had been said to him. He no longer ached and the blankets gave comforting warmth which induced sleep once more.

HMS *Damocles* had alerted the Canadian and American Maritime Agencies following the sinking of the *Pretoria* and as a consequence all shipping and aircraft in the area were on the lookout for survivors.

On the morning of 14th December the destroyer put in at Halifax, Nova Scotia, the main western terminal for Atlantic convoys and the severely injured casualties and the 'walking wounded' were taken to the local hospitals by the Canadian authorities for check ups and treatment where necessary.

Norman found himself in a pleasant ward of the General Hospital with several others all cared for by a group of attentive nurses. He was desperately worried about Helen and the ward sister promised to enquire at the other hospital. Meanwhile he had steadily regained strength and was able to walk up and down the ward with the aid of two crutches, the strapping of his artificial leg having to be repaired following damage by sea water. Looking out of the window he could see the sea and was aware the buildings had a light covering of snow on the windward side. Commenting on this to another patient, a local Canadian, he was given a rundown about the usual weather in December.

'This is nothing to what we have had! I remember two years ago the whole place was blanketed with four-foot drifts, which lasted for seven weeks. But don't worry it'll probably arrive in a day or two.'

Mollie arrived back in Exeter after a harrowing journey during which the train to London ran two hours late. She told Janine and Philip, 'Crossing London by the Tube was a nightmare; the trains were packed and the awful smell of the people using the stations as air raid shelters each night is overpowering. It was about four o'clock when I got to Waterloo and the people were already putting out their bedding for the night – whole families with many children, poor things.'

Janine listened to all the news about Rupert and Catherina and said she would write to Jan to thank him for the splendid presents. She also brought Mollie up-to-date with the Madame Baume work.

'We have a new order from the War Office which means an increase in staff to cope with the volume and Philip suggests we try working round the clock by creating a third shift. It'll mean finding another supervisor and more experienced seamstresses but it could work; what do you think?'

Mollie appeared somewhat taken aback by the news and could not give an immediate answer.

'Mother, my first reaction is that we're being pressurised and, bearing in mind we're only a small firm, there's a limit to what we can reasonably produce.' She was thoughtful for a while: 'if you push the staff too much they'll leave and as many are over the conscription age limit there's nothing to stop them going. And if that happens we'll be a lot worse off and unable to match the present production.'

Philip replied, 'Thank you, Mollie, you've made a very good case for turning down the new order but we must do all we can to help.'

Janine added her thoughts, 'We can accept the new order but it'll take longer to produce that's all and I agree with Mollie about the possibility of the older women leaving, particularly if they are asked to work at night.'

After a meal they sat chatting and Janine told Mollie the good news that Tom was coming home for Christmas and bringing his lady friend Hazel Newson. 'It seems her parents are going to Scotland to stay with relatives and Hazel didn't want to go. I believe we may be in for some good news when they get here.'

'Now you two, stop scheming! Just let Tom and his girlfriend come to their own decisions without your help.'

Janine had a giggle at Philip's admonishment and Mollie added the last word, 'We just want Tom to feel we're one hundred per cent behind Hazel and him, that's all.'

The rest of the evening was spent planning Christmas and the New Year celebrations.

On 16th December Francis and Margot had come to the conclusion Norman and Helen may not have survived and as they sat at breakfast it was Bertie who, once again, gave them hope, 'If I may be permitted to make a point madam, the *Pretoria* was sunk on 11th December and we know one of our warships was in the vicinity most probably picking up survivors. There must have been a number of lifeboats launched, each carrying, maybe thirty people or more. Those boats would make for the North American mainland. It could be some time before the lifeboats get to land, if you follow my reasoning. Therefore, no news could be good news.'

'Bertie, that's very good advice and we'll wait a little longer hoping for good news.'

Margot left the table as she spoke and, with Francis, went to the study. Once there he added his view to Margot's.

'I agree with Bertie's comments and we'll have to be patient.' And as he spoke the telephone rang.

Lifting the receiver he answered, 'Hello, the Manor House,' and as he listened, Margot watched his face break into a warm smile, 'Thank you, Juliet, it's most kind of you to let us know and I do understand your message has to be brief. Our love from both of us; hope to see you soon, bye darling.'

Francis went straight to Margot, put his arms round her and gave her the message, 'That was Juliet bless her. Norman is safe in hospital in Nova Scotia, but so far there is no news of Helen. She said the Admiralty Signals Unit receives everything in code and it takes time to decipher each message. As soon as she has further information she'll ring again. We must tell Bertie how right he was.' With tears running down their faces they stood hugging each other.

'What a wonderful present for Christmas and to think a few moments ago we'd all but given up hope.' As she continued Margot wiped Francis's tears away with a small handkerchief, 'We must contact Fanny who can tell the family in Bristol the wonderful news, but telling Helen's parents will be a delicate subject. You ring your mother and I'll speak to Charles and Violet about Helen.'

Early on the morning of 16th December a Boston aircraft of the Royal Canadian Air Force took off from Nova Scotia on a routine coastal patrol, mainly to check shipping and to keep a lookout for enemy submarines. At 08.00 hours, in poor visibility the navigator spotted two lifeboats about fifteen miles from the coast and the plane went down to investigate. What they observed was one boat towing another and one or two people waving as the aircraft passed over. A signal was sent immediately to base giving the exact location of the lifeboats and on a second very low pass a buoyancy pack containing emergency food and water was dropped and picked up by the survivors.

In Halifax the destroyer *Damocles*, now refuelled, put to sea with a Canadian destroyer and a fast coastguard launch and all three vessels made for the lifeboats at top speed as the weather was deteriorating.

The subsequent rescue operation was effected in the nick of time as heavy snow showers accompanied by strengthening winds swept the whole area. The survivors were landed at Halifax not long after midday and immediately rushed to the hospitals.

News of the rescue passed through the hospitals like wildfire and Norman again asked the ward sister to check if Helen was among those rescued.

'Mr Vining, I'll do all I can to find your wife but it'll take time to treat the injured and then find out who they are. Luckily most of them have been brought here which will make it easier and I promise I'll let you know the moment I get news.'

At about five o'clock when Norman was playing chess with another patient, the ward doors opened and the Sister called to him, 'Mr Vining, you have a visitor.'

Through the door came an orderly pushing a wheelchair in which sat a small female figure wrapped in a heavy dressing gown, her hands, forearms and feet heavily bandaged and her face covered with a thick layer of white ointment.

Norman knew immediately it was Helen and hobbling towards her, with tears running down his cheeks, he just shouted, 'Helen, darling, thank God you're safe!'

Helen smiled, in spite of the gooey state of her face and putting her bandaged hand in his said what he'd longed to hear, 'Norman, my dearest, dearest Norman, I prayed all the time in the boat and I just knew we would meet again. I thought I saw you in the water and called to you to hold on but there was so much smoke coming from the fire I lost sight of you.'

They sat for a little longer but the sister said gently Helen must go to her bed and get as much sleep as possible, promising to bring her again in the morning.

After a tender farewell Helen left and Norman just sat unable to take in the remarkable fact that he and his wife had survived against almost impossible odds and were together, being cared for by the wonderful Canadian nurses.

The staff nurse came to tell Norman about clothes, 'Mr Vining, our local tailor will be coming a little later this afternoon to measure you for a suit and a complete outfit, so if you can remember your own sizes for socks, gloves etc., it'll help.'

'Thank you very much nurse, I shall be glad to get out of these pyjamas. But will the tailor be able to make me a uniform as I'll need it when I get to Washington.'

'A uniform? I don't quite follow you!'

'I need a new RAF uniform; perhaps I'd better explain. I lost my leg flying with Fighter Command in the Battle of Britain and as a result I was sent to America to tell them all about the way the people in Great Britain stood up to the air attacks. As a serving Squadron Leader I expect to return to operations in England after my spell in the States.'

The staff nurse was wide eyed as she replied, 'I had no idea you are a fighter pilot! In Canada we heard all about the terrible air battles in Britain and knew you were having a difficult time. In the States I don't think they fully appreciate what England has done by standing alone against the Nazis, so your presence there will put them in the picture. Squadron Leader it is our great pleasure to help you.' And with those words she shook Norman's hand.

'You're very kind nurse,' he smiled as he went on, 'but please call me Norman, Squadron Leader sounds a bit over the top.'

News of Helen's rescue brought heartfelt relief to her parents and at Francis's invitation they decided to go to Farndene for Christmas and the New Year celebrations, arriving at the Manor House on 23rd December. Fanny came the same day bringing Clara and Constance who had broken up from school the week before.

The family gathering was increased when Bruce arrived with his actress lady friend Dorcas on Christmas Eve and Juliet and Freddie Washbrook early on Christmas Day.

Many of them went to the morning service at St Paul's and joined in the singing of plenty of carols. The rector Canon Horatio Hulbert also asked them to remember the many men and women away on active service and included a list by name of all the local people, mentioning Norman and Helen Vining who had been rescued that week from the Atlantic after the liner *Pretoria* was torpedoed.

Francis and Margot sat down for their Christmas dinner and, as usual, Francis carved the ducks and pheasant. He invited them all to drink a toast to absent friends and family and naturally there were a few tears here and there.

Sir Charles told them how touched he and Violet were by the genuine friendship extended by Francis and Margot, 'It augers well for the future. When Norman and Helen return home they will come to one loving family and after the terrible events they have experienced we know they will have the support of us all.' He raised his glass, 'To the Vining and Dauntsey collaboration and long may it prosper!'

Glasses were raised followed by applause and Freddie Washbrook added, 'I think it would be a good idea if the names were amalgamated; you might call the new joint family either Vinsey or Dauntsing! Whatever you choose I think both families are splendid.'

As in previous years everyone, including staff went to the drawing room for the Christmas tree and presents followed by carol singing with Juliet playing the piano. Later she and Freddie played duets and during the evening the carpet was rolled back for dancing with jazz pianist Freddie doing his stuff.

They all enjoyed the get together with their family, away from the rigours of war and Margot, particularly, spent a lot of time with Juliet, Bruce, Clara and Constance in what she called 'the bonding', making sure they had the opportunity to talk about their hopes and heartbreaks with her.

Juliet and Freddie had to return home the day after Boxing Day but everyone else stayed on to see the New Year in when Francis 'first footed' for Margot and the family.

In Nova Scotia the hospital authorities did all they could to make the survivors feel at home for Christmas and many local inhabitants came to see the patients bringing little personal gifts and goodies to eat. The Royal Canadian Air Force sent a Christmas tree and decorations and called daily to chat with Norman and many others. On Christmas Day turkey dinner was on the menu followed by Christmas pudding, while in the afternoon the local choir came to sing carols and entertain.

Since the rescue the weather had closed in and it had snowed on and off for several days resulting in some local drifts.

By special arrangement the hospital permitted the patients to see in the New Year, 1942 and Helen and Norman were together for the special moment. Helen, still in a wheelchair and with bandages on her hands and arms, wished Norman, 'A Happy New Year, dearest, and soon we'll be getting on with our lives in America.'

'I'd love to give you kisses, sweetheart, but I can't see even the tiniest bit of your face without that gooey white stuff covering it! So I'll just have to wait and save them up.' Norman was holding both her hands as he spoke but with great care in case he hurt her.

They talked about their family and their expectations for 1942, looking forward to the time when they would all meet again.

Chapter 41

Great Britain suffered further setbacks as early in 1942 Singapore fell to the Japanese. The Atlantic continued to be a most dangerous place with U-boats operating in packs sinking an enormous tonnage each month. However, by the end of that year with America now in the war, the balance of power in the Atlantic shifted in the Allies' favour enabling vast convoys to come to Britain unmolested.

Again on the credit side a daring and successful combined commando and naval attack was made on St Nazaire, destroying the port operating mechanism thus rendering the dry dock unusable for submarines; the RAF carried out the first 1,000-bomber raid on Cologne – a forerunner of what was to come.

Following a meeting between the Prime Minister Winston Churchill and President Roosevelt with their combined chiefs of staff, Operation Bolero was set up: a code name for the vast build-up of American armed forces in Britain. These included infantry, tanks, artillery and aircraft, and the undertaking of training in preparation for the invasion of Europe. The 8th and 9th United States Army Air Force set up bases here and started daylight raids on Nazi occupied territory as well as Germany.

To the quiet town of Farndene in Hampshire the peaceful invasion of American forces came as a rude awakening. The sudden arrival of the United States Army Construction Corps saw prefabricated buildings, workshops, temporary roads and airfields produced with incredible speed and soon Farndene was ringed with what looked small towns to be occupied by soldiers and airmen.

The population got used to seeing large numbers of GIs of all ranks walking in the area and children soon found the soldiers friendly with lots of chewing gum and candy to give away. The young women were also attracted to the Americans who had plenty of nylon stockings on offer for favours!

Again in Cambridgeshire, Lincolnshire and Yorkshire the creation of large American Air Force stations was now completed and they were operating.

At RAF Sutton Bridge, Lincolnshire, the airmen saw huge formations of two or three hundred bombers daily, flying over with fighter escorts bound for occupied Europe and Germany.

'The sight of the Yanks make one's heart feel good and is a morale booster for everyone here,' Rupert was talking to Group Captain Rodney Stanmore over lunch, 'but to be honest with you, I long to get back at the sharp end.'

'Be patient, Rupert, and you'll get your opportunity soon enough; mind you, I'll miss your presence with us. You've done a sterling job here and, above all, you've reduced the accident rate which had reached alarming proportions. Apart from all that, I'll miss both your own and your charming wife's company; you're a lucky dog, Rupert, but you deserve it!'

Accepting the compliments Rupert smiled, 'Thanks, I've grown to love this part of England and as you know it's brought me great happiness. After this lot is over you must come back to stay with us and you'll probably find me sitting on a five-barred gate in an old pair of corduroys, chewing a wheat straw and watching the world go by!' They both enjoyed the joke but Rodney had the last word.

'I can't believe that, Rupert, more likely you'll be sitting astride a hunter accompanied by Catherina and your six children; you're a family man and lots of children will make your day!'

In June Rupert's long-awaited move came with promotion, when he was posted to RAF Farndene as Wing Commander, joining new squadrons being formed and equipped with the Mustang fighter. This aircraft, now fitted with the updated Rolls Royce Merlin engine, was at that time a most powerful and formidable warplane, heavily armed and capable of flying deep into Europe.

Naturally, Catherina was very upset and tearful with the news but deep down knew Rupert had to go as he was now an experienced commander. Comforting her, Rupert promised to telephone regularly and put his arms round her as he said, 'My darling Catherina, say a little prayer for me each night and I'll do so for you. And so at ten o'clock every evening our thoughts will be one.'

Leaving Sutton Bridge on 10th June, he took over with the new squadrons straight away and after five weeks' training the wing took part in the first operation over France, attacking German airfields and rail centres and photographing selected coastal areas in Normandy. Two Messerschmitt fighters were shot down and the raid was considered a success.

Throughout the summer and autumn thousands of Americans arrived in Britain and the build up in the south of England gave a picture of one vast military camp.

On 4th November 1942 the War Office informed the chairman of the Devon County Council that a large area of land in his control was being requisitioned for defence purposes and thousands of acres, complete villages and coastline including Slapton Sands were to be evacuated by 20th December. Everything moveable was to be taken including all livestock and root crops. About three thousand people were affected and all was accomplished on time; within a week or so the American forces took over and training for the invasion of France commenced. The effect on the Devonshire people was devastating and a number never got over the ordeal; with the arrival of the US Army there was understandably a lot of bad feeling towards the Americans.

Janine, Mollie, Philip and the staff of the Madame Baume workshops had worked hard and willingly throughout the year and had met the increased orders from the War Office without extra people being recruited. Consequently, the establishment closed for ten days over Christmas and New Year to give everyone time to recover. On 23rd December Philip arranged a little party in the main workroom and managed to find some gin and sherry to go with sandwiches and cake. Janine thanked them all and told them to have a good rest before wishing them all a happy Christmas and New Year.

The same evening after supper, as the three of them sat reading with their coffee, Mollie saw a notice in their local paper and read it out, 'This is interesting with the heading "You Can Help the War Effort", the War Office is looking for linguists who would be willing to act as interpreters on a voluntary basis. "If you can speak German, French, Dutch or Italian and are willing to help, please get in touch with the local representative" and it gives a telephone number. Well I can speak French and I've a good working knowledge of German so I may give this rep a ring to see what it's all about.'

'That sounds interesting, Mollie, and as I'm French by birth maybe I can be of some help too,' Janine was keen to be in on the idea if possible, 'but i wonder where the interpreters are required?'

Philip then put forward his theory, 'I expect the interpreters will be used for liaison duties, possibly with General De Gaulle's crowd, the Free French Army. The only snag is the Free French are at the Carlton House Terrace in London and Ribbesford in Worcestershire by the river Severn; I don't know of any of the French in this area.'

Mollie cut the notice from the newspaper and with a giggle spoke to her cat Othello, 'You understand English and French, don't you, my beauty? So you could catch English mice for the Free French couldn't you?'

'Well, now that's settled, perhaps we can put our minds to Christmas,' Janine was keen to sort out the Christmas fare needed as Tom and his lady friend Hazel were coming home on Christmas Eve for five days but would be going to her family for the New Year celebrations. So she and Mollie put their heads together and soon had the menu mapped out for the holiday.

After nearly six months at RAF Farndene, the Mustang squadrons had acquitted themselves well over the continent and were much feared by the Luftwaffe.

Leave was alternated for all pilots, some away for Christmas and the rest for New Year and Rupert decided to take the former, arriving home to Catherina on 22nd December for seven days.

As he entered the van Houten house, Catherina rushed into his arms and they were locked in a long embrace, kissing over and over again until both were almost out of breath.

'Darling Rupert, I've missed you so very much and I know I love you more than ever before.'

Rupert was also overcome with the emotion of their meeting, 'My dearest, I too have missed you and as I promised I said a little prayer for you every night, saying I knew I loved you more each day!'

Jan and Bep were also delighted to see Rupert and as soon as Johan, the manservant, had brought Rupert's holdall in from the car, they settled down to hear all the news from Farndene.

He explained, 'The RAF Base is on the old Farndene Flying School airfield but is now about three times the size, with several huge hangars, workshops and accommodation for all the ground staff.

'The officers mess is in part of the Manor House and I've been invited to dine with Sir Francis and Lady Margot Vining on several occasions. They're lovely people and always considerate to the needs of all our pilots. Of course, you'll remember their eldest son Norman was my number two instructor at Sutton Bridge and went to America on the air attache staff at the British Embassy in Washington.

'I've also been back a number of times to see Alec and Beatty Briggs, the family I was fostered with until I left school; of their three children, there's only Jenny at home. She had a baby last August and she's managing very well on her own as the father was posted missing believed killed in the Middle East last year. She still hopes he's a prisoner of war and will turn up one day.

'Well that's enough of my news, what's happened here since last June?'

'Oh, nothing like as exciting as your news, but when I've told you about the horses, Papa will tell you how the farms have fared.' Catherina stopped as though uncertain whether or not to go on.

'Well, what about the horses, Catherina? Has something happened to them that you don't want to tell me?' Rupert was puzzled and waited for the answer.

'No, it's not the horses, Rupert, but what has happened in the stables,' Catherina smiled as she went on, 'You see, in August we had a mare with a viral infection and the vet was called. It was not the old man but his new assistant Mr Toby Sutton and, as I was out harvesting, Bep looked after him and thankfully the mare recovered quickly. However, Toby Sutton insisted on returning two or three times to check the horses and on each occasion Bep was on hand to see him. Now there is something magic about those stables! If you remember it was on a foggy evening in November last year when you called and kindly looked at a mare for us, after which we found we were in love,' here she got a fit of giggling, 'well, history has repeated itself and the magic has worked: Bep and Toby have fallen in love and Papa is very pleased for her.' Still laughing, she concluded, 'Those stables will be very famous as Eros lives there!'

'What a wonderful story and what a happy ending for Bep.' Rupert thought about Jan whose wife was missing in Holland and was losing both his daughters within two years. Turning to Jan he asked him, 'Won't you be lonely when both your girls move away?'

Jan expected a question of the sort and made a prompt reply, 'Rupert, I've had the pleasure of both my daughters with me for all their lives until now and if they wish to leave here I'll help them to find happiness in their own home. I'm sure they will come to see me regularly and I'll visit them if they want me to. I have many interests and a good staff so I'll manage but, who knows, one of my sons-in-law may decide to live here permanently with his wife. If so, I wouldn't mind. My only worry is my dear wife Lies who you know is trapped in Holland and my hope is that she has managed to evade capture by the Nazis. We must never give up hope and pray for her safe return.'

Rupert and Catherina enjoyed each other's company and the week passed quickly; soon both only had their memories of a happy Christmas together.

In July 1942, Grandma Fanny brought her two granddaughters Clara and Constance home to Farndene from Bristol, as they had finished school for good. Both had done well in their final exams, Clara winning a place at Oxford to read maths and chemistry, while Constance decided to delay going to university by applying to the Ordnance Survey of Great Britain. She passed the entrance exam with flying colours and was accepted.

On 1st September she started training for the preparation of maps and charts for the armed forces at the heavily guarded establishment at Chessington, Surrey. Accommodation was found for her locally with a Mr and Mrs Larry Burchall. Larry and his wife Rhoda had both come out of retirement to run the only bakery in that area and they made their young lodger feel at home from the start.

Constance came home for Christmas and she, with Clara down from Oxford, were delighted when Bruce arrived with his lady friend Dorcas and Juliet and Freddie Washbrook turned up on Christmas Eve.

On Christmas Day Francis and Margot invited four American soldiers to dinner and, once again, Freddie playing jazz on the piano was the hit with everyone.

All enjoyed dancing with the Americans, particularly Dorcas who put on a splendid display with a young sergeant, and it was well after midnight when the four soldiers left, expressing their profound thanks to Margot and Francis.

'Gee, sir, lady, it's sure been a swell night for me and my buddies. I guess I've never seen a Sir or Lady before and you're both great. Good guys and dames like you should be Dooks and Dookesses not just what you are. Thanks a million!'

Keeping a straight face they said goodnight to the Americans and Margot added, 'We've enjoyed your company very much and you must come again sometime.'

Clara and Constance thought their mother was brilliant asking the GIs to visit again, 'The sooner the better as far as I'm concerned Mummy,' Clara gushed, while her sister nodded agreement.

The following afternoon Francis and Freddie had taken Clara

and Constance, well wrapped in thick coats, scarves and gum boots, for what the family called a Boxing Day jaunt, usually a two-hour walk through the estate with the dogs. Juliet, Dorcas and Bruce stayed behind in the drawing room with Margot, enjoying the chance to chat over their coffee with the comfort of a roaring log fire, when Bertie announced to Margot there were four American soldiers waiting in the hall, 'They asked if you could spare them a few moments, madam?'

They all had a giggle but Juliet couldn't contain herself, 'Ooh, now you've done it, Mummy! As they left last night I remember you told them to come again sometime. Well, they've taken you at your word!'

Margot just smiled at the leg pull as she rose to leave the room, 'I'll see them in the study, Bertie, in a few minutes,' and to Juliet, 'you can come if you wish.' But Juliet, still grinning, just shook her head.

They settled down to more coffee, the ladies discussing the ever present problem for women, the question of clothes and lack of any fashion during the war, while Bruce, who had picked up a book, gave up trying to read and dozed off near the fire.

About twenty minutes later Margot returned carrying a large cardboard box which she put on a side table and sat down with the request, 'I think I'd like more coffee; would you mind, Bruce?'

She thanked her son and sipped her coffee, deliberately saying nothing else but watching three eager faces. Margot prolonged their agony by asking Bruce what he was reading.

'Oh, nothing in particular, Mother, in fact I was so comfortable I just had a little nap while you were out of the room,' and then unable to restrain himself any longer, 'How did you get on with the Yanks?'

'Very well indeed, Bruce, they called to bring a little present to show their gratitude for the marvellous time they had yesterday. They're nice boys and two of them from California are desperately homesick. It's the first time they've been outside their state since birth and they had always been led to believe the British were an unfriendly and stuck up lot. They all thought we, as a family,

were so friendly and like their folk back home. I have their details
and told them I'd invite them again in due course.'

Juliet listened patiently to her mother but questioned eagerly,
'Well, what's in the box, Mummy?'

Margot smiled as she told them, 'Goodies for us all: chocolate,
candy, cigarettes, large tins of pineapple, peaches and blueberries
… and some nylon stockings!'

A vacuum of astounded silence followed with Juliet and
Dorcas eyeing the prospect of American nylons. Juliet broke the
spell.

'Nylons, Mummy, that's fantastic, I just can't wait to try them
on.'

'You'll have to wait, darling. We'll open the box as soon as
the girls come back with Freddie and Daddy. That'll be nice,
don't you agree?'

When the walking party returned, there were whoops of joy
from Clara and Constance when the box of goodies was opened
and they all said how much they'd enjoyed the American boys.

'Can we ask them for New Year's Eve, Mummy?' Clara hung
on hopefully for her mother's reply.

'I don't see why not.' Margot turned to Francis, 'What do you
think, darling?'

'Yes, let's have a super party to see 1943 arrive in style! Let's
try to forget the war for a few hours and enjoy being together with
our allies from across the water.'

On New Year's Day 1943, Norman and Helen, having spent
the past year based in Washington D.C., looked back on all
that had happened to them during the previous twelve months.
Although both had suffered physically and mentally from the
terrible experience following the torpedoing in December 1941,
Helen had come through the ordeal remarkably well. During the
five days survivors were adrift in the Atlantic, she encouraged
the other occupants of the lifeboat, assisting with the rowing,
comforting others when a number died from exposure and
tending the wounded with sparse medical kit, although suffering

from exposure and frostbite herself.

Norman was astonished at her resilience and concluded the ordeal had shaken her out of her original depression.

Each month they'd travelled to different states and attended a wide variety of functions, during which Helen also made a major contribution by speaking about her role at Fighter Command Headquarters during the Battle of Britain.

As guests at a special reception at the White House they were introduced to Mr Roosevelt, the President, who thanked them personally for all they'd done. Norman remained on the staff of the Air Attache at the British Embassy, continuing the lecturing duties.

Chapter 42

January 1943 brought new hope to the Allies now amassing a huge army in Great Britain as every month fresh arrivals of American troops, arms and ammunition swelled the gigantic war machine being assembled. The US Army Air Force also expanded and, equipped with more powerful bombers and long range fighters, continued by day the devastation of the German war machine being wrought by RAF Bomber Command each night, the latter led by the expert Pathfinder Group using new radar devices to mark specific targets accurately.

Against this positive achievement the problem of U-boats, surface raiders and mines continued and the Battle of the Atlantic was fought out by many an unsung hero who perished in the icy waters of that ocean. However, with the coordination of escorting warships and complete air cover for convoys, there was nowhere for the U-boats to surface safely to recharge batteries, and gradually the number of enemy submarines sunk increased beyond a level that could be sustained; slowly the Allies won skirmish after skirmish to rid the Atlantic of the enemy.

Shortly after the beginning of the New Year, Mollie came across the newspaper notice she'd cut out of the *Exeter Gazette* at Christmas time and decided to telephone for information. After a couple of attempts she spoke to a very efficient secretary who made an appointment for the next day, Thursday 7th January.

She told her mother, 'I have to see someone about the interpreting work tomorrow at eleven o'clock, so I'll leave work about ten minutes before. The place is further down the High Street so I shouldn't be long.'

She found the office the next day and, going up to the first floor, knocked and went into a small reception area where she was greeted by the secretary, a tall, good looking ATS officer. The

344

secretary recorded the answers Mollie gave to many question about her qualifications, family and knowledge of foreign languages. She was then shown into an inner office and introduced to a Major Leon de Marne, a solid, handsome man with dark brown hair and smiling eyes, who had the insignia of the Free French on his uniform. 'A typical rugby player,' Mollie thought.

'Do come in and make yourself comfortable.' He drew up a chair for her at his desk, 'Now if you give me a couple of minutes I'll scan through the report my secretary has given me and then we can have a chat.'

As good as his word, in a very short time he put the form down and for the next ten minutes addressed her in fluent French, followed by a further questioning in perfect German and then with a broad smile spoke again in English.

'My, your knowledge of French is extraordinary, Mrs Shelley, how come?'

'My mother is a Breton woman and my father English, though sadly killed in the Great War. All my life my mother insisted my two brothers and I were bilingual. I also learnt German at school and subsequently a little Italian at evening school. I also know the local patois in Brittany where my mother's family still live.'

'Mrs Shelley, what I'm about to tell you please treat as highly confidential. I've interviewed many applicants in the past week or so but you are the first one with the foreign language skill which I find quite superb and the exact individual we're looking for. If you decide to accept the offer I'm going to outline, you will be doing much more than fighting in the front line. You will, in fact, be in a different kind of front line but producing information of untold value to the war effort.'

'It sounds quite mysterious, Major, but what exactly is it?' At this point Mollie felt baffled.

'The duties you'll be asked to perform will include translation, interpreting and assessing highly classified information in a secret establishment in Buckinghamshire. It will of course require your living at that place continuously but with reasonable breaks similar to military leave only more generous. Your starting pay will be equivalent to that of a regular army captain and your living accommodation similar to a commissioned officer's quarters. May I ask you to consider this proposition very carefully before you reach a decision and hopefully in reasonable time you'll accept my invitation to join our organisation.'

Mollie sat completely bewildered for some minutes, weighing up all the major had told her and trying to imagine the secret establishment he'd mentioned. Deep down she realised the invitation was no ordinary offer but instead something extremely important but the thought of leaving the Madame Baume business and her mother weighed heavily on her thinking.

'Major, I really have to go away to think over all you've said and discuss it with my mother. At present we run the Madame Baume business just along the High Street and I play a vital role there supervising the production of uniforms and equipment for the War Office, so it's not an easy decision for me; I hope you understand my dilemma.'

'Of course, Mrs Shelley, I do appreciate your situation, so please go away and talk it over with your mother and let me know your decision in due course.'

Smiling, he rose to escort Mollie to the door, shaking her hand as she left.

Back in the High Street she buttoned her coat against the cold wind and decided she needed time to mull over the events of the last hour before discussing the major's proposition with her mother. She walked to St Martin's church where she and Sam were married and inside joined a number of others sitting quietly, away from the bustle of the city just a few steps away.

Mollie's thoughts went back to her wedding and to her husband Sam and, as she focused her mind, it became clearer that she should do more to help the war effort; she felt suddenly a compulsion to make the bold decision to go to Buckinghamshire. She knelt to say a prayer for Sam and her family and to ask for guidance in the future. As she finished she noticed the vicar had entered and, moving quietly among those present, offered comfort to all. Reaching Mollie his face lit up, 'Ah, Mrs Shelley, how good it is to see you again. I hope you and your family are all well and your husband, of course, who I know is in Malta.'

Mollie thanked him and after a chat she left the peace of the church to make her way back to Madame Baume's workshops.

At RAF Farndene the Mustang squadrons were active in good weather, joining up with other fighters in what Douglas Bader called the 'Big Wings' to penetrate deep into occupied Europe, striking at communication centres such as railway marshalling yards, bridges, signal boxes, as well as dock installations and oil storage facilities. The Luftwaffe suffered considerably, losing valuable pilots and was unable to prevent the RAF wreaking havoc on an enormous number of military targets. This style of attack was to continue with even larger groups of aircraft making offensive sweeps to target the enemy.

As the months passed, the Mustangs carried out reconnaissance of specific areas of the coast and hinterland of the Pas de Calais, Normandy and Brittany recording the details of all coastal defences.

In Farndene town and surrounding farmland the ever-increasing numbers of Americans with their tanks and armoured vehicles made the original Farndene people feel a minority population and, while they made the GIs welcome at first, friction began to appear as time went on.

Problems arose with some local women becoming involved with Americans, causing intense jealousy among the Farndene men who often picked fights with the GIs, so adding to the problem. A number of teenage girls became pregnant, as well as one or two married women. Husbands serving abroad with the British Forces were in for a tragic shock when they returned to Britain.

Realising the looming problem of illegitimate children to be born to local women and fathered by Americans, Margot and Francis, assisted by a number of friends, set up a home for unmarried mothers by financing the purchase of a local house which could take up to twenty women.

They appealed for financial support to the local US Army commander, General Shaun D. Goodhew who provided generous funds, but drew the line when Francis jokingly suggested the Home be called Little Washington Haven. They finally agreed to name it St Andrews Home, after Margot's birthplace in Scotland.

Francis and Margot also did their best to support the Americans stationed locally and frequently invited groups to the Manor House for a meal and relaxation and these gestures were very well received by the visitors.

A committee, set up to liaise with the American Commanders to ensure good relationships and to iron out problems, was chaired by Francis, and Margot often attended meetings.

They heard regularly from Norman and Helen in the United States where the couple were still in demand and were likely to remain there for the foreseeable future. In a long letter, Norman told his parents Helen had completely recovered from the breakdown she suffered after her miscarriage: 'It's a great joy seeing my darling wife fully fit again. She has been an inspiration telling the Americans how steadfast the British people are, standing up to Hitler's onslaught of the mass bombing of our towns and cities with great courage. At the lecture in Washington, before an audience of nearly one thousand, Helen followed my speech with a rousing oration and finished by singing both verses of William Blake's 'Jerusalem'! The place erupted with a standing ovation lasting nearly eight minutes.'

Following the meeting Mollie had with Major de Marne in Exeter, she and her mother agreed not to discuss it at the workshops but wait until the evening. Consequently, as soon as dinner was over that night, Mollie told Janine and Philip all that had happened during the morning interview.

While Philip was somewhat indecisive, her mother was firm in her assessment and told Mollie, 'My darling, it's not easy for you to make the decision. You and you alone must make it, but what you must not do is hold back on my account or because of your present commitment to the salon. If you take the post in Buckinghamshire you will go with my complete support and we'll make changes at the workshops to deal with the situation. I'd be lying if I said I'd not miss you! Of course I would, but you're not going abroad to another country and you say you'll have holiday breaks, so we'll see you regularly.'

Mollie put her arms round her mother and kissed her.

'Mother, you are and always have been my wisest council and what you've said to me makes it easier to respond to my inner feeling that I should accept the job. I love you very much and now know I go with your loving support.'

They talked at great length about Mollie's departure and with Philip they worked out a new staff structure for the shifts at the Madame Baume workshops.

The die was cast and they knew life would change for them all in the coming weeks.

As the months passed, bringing warmer weather and longer days the Allies' offensive grew more intense, so much so that their combined forces made their re-entry into Europe in July with the invasion of Sicily under the command of General Dwight Eisenhower. The conquest of the island was the springboard for an attack on the Italian mainland.

In Britain, towns and cities were still taking punishment from Luftwaffe bombers at night but the population stood up to the onslaught with remarkable fortitude, bolstered by the knowledge the Nazis were on the receiving end of massive bombing raids round the clock by the RAF and the US Army Air Force.

By July Mollie was fully trained and integrated in the Bletchley Park operation and enjoyed the challenge of code breaking. The highly secret organisation intercepted messages sent by the Germans using their Enigma machine and often within hours the information had been decoded and passed to the Prime Minister and chiefs of staff.

In early August she was given two weeks' leave of absence, arriving home to a wonderful welcome.

Janine and Philip were delighted to have her with them again and Mollie relaxed with the family, making a tremendous fuss of Othello. She sat stroking and talking to him to the amusement of her mother who suggested, 'Why don't you take him back with you? He's very clever and would probably catch any German mice or rats trying to spy!'

'I'm sure he'd catch any Nazi rodents but he wouldn't like the enormous Alsatian dogs the police have – they patrol the surrounding parkland and buildings night and day. They look very fierce and my darling Othello is only a little pussy cat! So I'll have to leave him in your care for the present.'

As the weather became hot and sunny Janine suggested a long weekend at Teignmouth where they stayed with Ellery and Beryl Hales who made them most welcome. Many happy memories were recalled and with horse riding each day the break did them all the world of good.

Back home in the middle weekend, Tom and Hazel came home for a few days and Janine had fun talking about the day excursion she and the children had, way back in 1920.

'Do you remember when you got lost Tom? Mollie was terribly upset and thought you had gone for good.

'Well yes I do, but you'd read the lovely story of the baby donkey that was lost until his mother found him and there was a little baby donkey on the beach so I went to find out if it was the one in the story; don't forget I was only seven then.'

Hazel wanted to know more about the story, 'It sounds just the sort of thing my little people at school would enjoy. The children love story time and stop being naughty if they think I'll not read to them at the end of classes.'

'I've a number of stories which I think you'd like but they're in French so I need to translate them for you, Hazel.' Janine had a bookshelf full of French literature.

'I could translate them if necessary, Mrs Kirkwood, as I specialised in French and music at training college; perhaps I could borrow the little books for a short while?'

Janine agreed and, as supper had finished, suggested they have coffee in the drawing room where Tom and Philip were soon in deep conversation about the conduct of the war, while the three ladies discussed the problem of clothes.

A little later Tom told them he and Hazel had decided to become engaged and her parents were in agreement and happy for their daughter. He continued by asking Janine and Philip if they would also be agreeable, 'You see, mother, it's very important because I'm the last one of your children planning to leave home permanently and I know it'll be a little bit sad for you. Although I love Hazel I'll still love you as I always have done.'

Janine put her arms round Tom and kissed him as she told him plainly, 'My dearest Tom, Philip and I are delighted to hear your news and we wish Hazel and you great happiness in your lives. You have our love and support and look forward to the not distant future when you can be married.'

The rest of Mollie's leave went quickly and on the day she left for Bletchley Park, Janine and Philip saw her off at the station, waving until the train disappeared from sight.

Philip, aware Janine was upset, put a comforting arm round her shoulder as they walked across the station forecourt, 'My dearest Janine, I still love you with all my heart!' He stopped to kiss her gently which brought a smile to her tearful face. 'Now dry those pretty eyes and I'll take you to a nice little restaurant where we can have some lunch and time to talk.'

Janine squeezed his arm, 'Thank you, Philip, you're a darling and I'd love to have some lunch.'

And, arm in arm, away they strolled along the High Street, chatting happily about the family.

On 25th September Francis and Margot received the sad news that Harry Bradshaw, the former head gamekeeper on the estate had died, aged ninety-five years. The following week the funeral, held in St Paul's church, was attended by almost one hundred family and friends.

In his address the Rev. Horatio Hulbert told the congregation about this remarkable man.

'Harry, son of a blacksmith, was born in Portsmouth in 1848 and apprenticed to his father. He decided at the age of sixteen that the blacksmith's trade was not for him and joined the Royal Navy during the reign of Queen Victoria. He served thirty-five years and retired as Master at Arms in 1901 when he became the late General Sir Roger Vining's head gamekeeper. He was a good hearted man loved by many,' then, with a smile, 'poachers excluded! He supported this church and rang the bells here for many years: in essence a true Christian, a man of many parts. He was always punctual for the start of bell practice and for the finish. He told me we must always stop on the stroke of nine so he and his mates could get to the Fox and Grapes in time for a jar or two before closing time. Well where he's gone there's no closing time and he'll be well looked after.'

Francis and Margot arranged for refreshments for those attending in the church hall.

Fanny came from Bristol for the funeral and to stay for a few days, enjoying the opportunity of talking to her son and daughter-in-law. Over dinner on the first evening the conversation inevitably touched on family matters and Fanny told them how she felt now all the grandchildren had finished school.

'It was great fun all those years the youngsters were with me and although I admit I got pretty tired at times, I enjoyed every minute of their company. Since Clara and Constance departed I've somehow been at a loose end and unable to concentrate on my other activities. I suppose I'm getting old and it's a sign of old age when one doesn't want to do much. The children stimulated my life and alas now I'm in a sort of vacuum.'

'Mother, I'm sure we understand what you're going through and Margot and I feel we've contributed to your present condition! After all, it was our children you took for all those years, and without your help I'm not sure how we would have coped with the situation. We'll do everything possible to help you and we must try to find ways to achieve this.'

At this point Margot had a brainwave, 'Mama, would you consider coming back to Farndene? Not permanently but while the war is on. We'd be delighted to have you here and, believe me, there's plenty of room and a tremendous amount happening with all the Americans literally on our doorstep. You know the RAF still occupy part of the house for the officers mess and they're great company and a pretty lively lot. Take your time to think it over. There's no hurry at all.'

Fanny was quite overcome, 'Margot, my dear, what you've offered is extremely generous and a wonderful proposition and I'm so very grateful. But what about your family? When they come home won't they want to stay here? I wouldn't want to be in the way and feel I'd taken their rooms.'

'Now then, let's get this clear once and for all. You are our family and a very precious part indeed and we've loads of room to put you up. As Margot said, we'd be delighted to have you and for as long as you wish. So it's up to you, Mother – you don't have to make a hasty decision.' Francis patted her arm as he finished.

'You are both dears and I'm touched you have offered me a home without any hesitation. Let me think it over and I promise I'll give you my answer as soon as I can.'

As the months passed at Bletchley Park the autumn revealed itself with a spectacular display of colour, the trees slowly shedding their leaves to cover the ground with a carpet reminiscent of Joseph's coat of many hues. During off duty hours Mollie frequently wandered through the park surrounding the Headquarters Mansion with several friends she had made since joining the organisation. One very close to her was Antonia Boer, a good linguist who spoke French and Dutch and was a brilliantly quick keyboard operator capable of sending and receiving Morse messages. Antonia's Dutch father Bert, a silversmith, came to England in 1905, married her mother Denise in 1910, and settled in her home town of Bedford. Denise was also a designer of silverware and they set up a showroom and workshop in Tavistock Street, which became a huge success over the years.

Antonia was their only child and she became bilingual in

Dutch and English from an early age, adding French during her school days. She joined the WRNS as soon as she was eighteen in January 1942, working in a signals unit and then agreed to transfer to Bletchley Park early in 1943.

During a long weekend break Mollie was invited home with Antonia to her parent's house, a large Victorian residence in De Pary's Avenue, Bedford, where she was made most welcome. Mollie enjoyed exploring the old buildings and churches in the town and she and Antonia went for long walks by the river, watching the local school boys practising in single skulls, coxed fours and eights as they skimmed past on the water; and of course there were always swans and ducks to feed.

And so a close bond developed between Mollie and Antonia which was to become more important as time passed.

Chapter 43

Towards the end of October a lull in operations gave Rupert an opportunity for a few days leave so he flew over to RAF Sutton Bridge en route to the van Houten farm. To his surprise the airfield dispersal areas were packed with Horsa gliders and a number of Stirling bombers obviously used for towing. The Station Commander Group Captain Rodney Stanmore was delighted to see Rupert and after a long chat offered to drive him to the van Houten house.

Catherina, over the moon with joy, held on to Rupert tightly, 'In case you run away before I've had time to talk to you, my darling,' she told him, 'I've so much to tell you, but first of all the most important thing to say is I love you more than ever and I've missed you every day since you went back.'

Rupert responded with lots of hugs and kisses, assuring her of his undying love.

Rodney Stanmore was invited to stay for dinner with Toby Sutton, the vet now engaged to Catherina's sister Bep; this made a lively group which discussed many aspects of farming, particularly horses.

'Rupert, I understand from Catherina you're an authority on horses and your late father ran a stud near Exeter before the Great War. When this war is over will you breed horses?'

Rupert smiled, 'Toby, first let's get this war over and then, yes, probably I will look at that kind of business, provided people still want to ride.'

Catherina joined the discussion, 'I'd love to breed horses, you know the really big ones, the Shire or better still the Percheron, that wonderful draught horse of a breed originating in La Perche in Southern Normandy. I can just see Rupert sitting on the seat of a large farm wagon driving two of those beasts at the annual horse show in King's Lynn!'

They all chuckled, but Rupert had the last laugh: 'A good idea, my love, but what if we do away with the cars and travel wherever we go in Britain with a large caravan pulled by two horses. It'll be most enjoyable and jogging down to Exeter will only take about a fortnight! Just think of all the books you'll be able to read en route.'

They sat talking until quite late and it was after eleven o'clock when goodnights were said and the guests departed, leaving Catherina and Rupert alone, sitting by the fire with their arms round each other. Suddenly Catherina remembered, 'I've written a little poem for you, darling, would you like to hear it?'

He was intrigued, 'I had no idea you're a poet, my sweet, but please go on.'

She took a small book from her bag and, selecting the page, read:

If I may look inside your heart
It will not hurt or make you start.
I'd peep within and hope to see
the signs of all your love for me.

Within my heart, I have to tell
I've wrapped your name and wrapped it well.
With warmth sincere I'll play my part,
just loving you, with all my heart.

And when our hearts with love entwine
Like fragrant, twisting columbine.
We'll tell the world and have such fun,
because our hearts will beat as one.

'That's a sweet little poem, my darling, and it sums us up exactly! I'd love to have a copy to keep in my wallet and when I get lonely for you, I can read it and think how much we love each other.'

'I'll write it out for you before breakfast but now we must be getting to bed as it's nearly midnight.'

Once abed Catherina cuddled up to Rupert and they made passionate love until sleep overtook two happy but exhausted lovebirds.

During the year Mollie had received fewer letters from her husband Sam and in his last one, at the end of November, the reason was clear. After leaving Malta the batteries took part in the invasion of Sicily and the Italian mainland, culminating in the surrender of Italy. Sam said he hoped for a posting back to Britain but for the present they were halted near Rome.

Mollie re-read the letter several times particularly the part in which he told her he still loved and missed her very much. Putting the letter to one side she also realised how much she needed him but made up her mind to get on with her duties, thinking, 'the more I can do to bring this dreadful war to an end, the quicker my daring Sam will come back to me'.

In December she and her friend Antonia were allowed two weeks' leave covering Christmas and the New Year. In high spirits Mollie arrived home on the 22nd to receive a wonderful welcome from Janine and Philip, not forgetting Othello, the apple of her eye.

The workshops at Madame Baume closed for five days over Christmas giving Janine and her staff a welcome break after an intense period making reserve uniforms and equipment for the Second Front, which was expected some time the following year.

With just the three of them at home, they decided to go to St Martin's church for the Christmas Day service. Once settled in a pew and glancing round, Janine was delighted to see many of their friends and acquaintances and much enjoyed returning many smiling greetings.

The vicar, the Rev. Julian Chesil, was in good form starting his address, 'Elsie, my wife told me at breakfast time to "cut it short" when I got into the pulpit, otherwise there'll be a burnt offering for Christmas dinner! So as always, nearly always, well sometimes, I do as Elsie tells me, I've decided to entitle my sermon, "The Short Cut".

'When Joseph realised the birth of Mary's baby was imminent, he spurred on the donkey, on which she rode, no doubt taking a short cut to the inn where he hoped to get accommodation. His request for a room was cut short by the innkeeper who told him the only place he could offer was under the building in the stables.

'For the birth of a baby these days we expect the presence of a doctor or a midwife and the support of the family both before and after the event. And when the little one arrives, the mother and baby are showered with gifts by a loving family.

'Mary had none of these things and was alone having her baby in a stable, a stuffy, smelly, unhygienic place for a mother and her newborn child. No family to support her but only the arrival of a group of adoring shepherds, hard-working men who had possibly never seen a bath adding to the stable aroma!

'From the stable scene, picture that young woman overcome with the joy of her firstborn, without any comfort save straw to lie on, no cradle for the infant but a manger in which she laid the tiny bundle on hay, surrounded by cattle and the ass she had ridden on, all dimly lit by a primitive oil lamp.

'With that picture I want to take a short cut to your hearts! I want you to receive the message of Christmas, the joy of the newborn Jesus, that tiny child who gives us all the hope of peace among men.' The vicar looked at his watch and smiled as he nodded his head thinking, 'I don't need to worry about a burnt offering for dinner'!

After the service he stood at the west door greeting the congregation and wishing each a Happy Christmas. As Janine, Philip and Mollie left, he shook hands and made an unusual remark, 'I have a feeling we'll all be together this time next year and I'm positive the terrible evil of the Nazis will be destroyed by then.' To Mollie he said, 'Take heart: Sam will be home then and you'll be together. I pray each day for all our men and women serving in the forces.'

As they walked home, Janine commented on his prediction, 'The vicar's words were unusual but he spoke with such conviction I'm sure he really feels the war is nearing its end.'

In Farndene the numbers of American soldiers had increased and the countryside seemed at bursting point with tanks and armoured vehicles lining the roads and lanes. These moved in and around the area on training exercises and daily columns of tanks could be seen moving across the downs, often silhouetted against the sky.

Over Christmas and the New Year the military activity almost ceased as the troops relaxed and enjoyed the hospitality of many local families.

At the Manor House, Francis and Margot entertained a group of Americans and as Juliet with her fiancé Freddie Washbrook had managed some leave and Clara was down from Oxford, the party was a lively one. Unfortunately Constance couldn't get home for Christmas, due to the intense pressure at the Ordnance Survey but hoped for leave early in the New Year.

On Boxing Day the Americans put on a huge entertainment and dance and all the Vinings were invited. Margot couldn't believe her eyes as she gazed at the wonderful buffet provided: mouth-watering things not seen since the beginning of the war and sandwiches made with white bread, very acceptable after years of the 'National Loaf', which many believed contained the sweepings of the flour mill!

Dancing went on until well after midnight to a Glen Miller style dance orchestra and many of the Yanks were excellent dancers, much to Clara's delight.

Liquid refreshment was confined to Coca-Cola and fruit juice as no alcohol was permitted on the American military establishment.

Fanny arrived from Bristol after Christmas to join Francis and Margot in seeing in the New Year and told them she had at last decided to accept their kind offer to live at the Manor House for the rest of the war.

'I took my time as it's a momentous decision. I talked it over with Edith and Robert Oulton in Bristol and they considered it a sensible move to make. Robert, bless him, will arrange to let my house and keep an eye on it while I'm here. They're wonderful friends and I'll miss seeing them so much but let's hope it'll not be for long.'

Margot was thrilled, 'Mama, that's splendid news and Francis and I will love having you here for as long as you wish to stay. Your must choose your room and if you want to bring your own furniture that'll be alright. We'll work out details after the New Year's celebration.'

As soon as 1944 arrived, the US Army started intense training and often the exercises went on night and day for weeks on end, including support from their air force.

At RAF Farndene the Mustang squadrons' operations against Nazi-occupied Europe intensified early in January and the raids into France included constant photo-reconnaissance of coastal areas in preparation for the Second Front.

After a relaxing Christmas and New Year break at home, Mollie soon settled back at Bletchley Park to the never-ending task of code work. Off duty, she and Antonia spent a lot of time together, going to a small restaurant in Bletchley and then to the local cinema if the film of the week was worth seeing.

On 12th February Mollie was interviewed by the Bletchley Park Unit Principal, Joshua Swatridge, a heavily built man in his sixties, whose smiling face greeted her as she entered the room.

'Come and have a seat, Mrs Shelley.' As soon as she was settled, he continued, 'I expect you're wondering why I asked you to look in, so I'll tell you. I wanted you to know personally how impressed we are with your standard of work and the accuracy of your translations; they have been consistently excellent and I congratulate you.' Mollie was pleased to hear his comments but said nothing as he went on.

'There's another reason I wished to talk to you and it's this. I have been requested by a higher authority to ask you to consider taking part in a more secret operation in which your knowledge of French would be vital. I'm not able to elaborate further as to the style of the operation, other than to say it is of the utmost value and importance to the conduct of the war.'

Mollie sat quietly, somewhat bemused by Mr Swatridge's words. Wondering what he was driving at, she asked outright: 'Thank you, Mr Swatridge, but I need to know a little more about the invitation. What is the higher authority and where is the secret operation?'

'Mrs Shelley, I regret I cannot tell you more about the secret location but be assured the authority is the highest.'

'I understand the secrecy, but I need to have a hint to enable me to give the request consideration. If I agree, would I possibly go abroad to perform the duties?

Although he obviously wanted to help her he was thoughtful before responding, 'That is a distinct possibility, Mrs Shelley, but I'm not permitted to say more than that. Now I want you to think it over but on no account discuss what I've said with anyone else.'

Mollie nodded her agreement and thanked him before leaving the office.

Back at her translating desk, where she worked opposite her friend Antonia, Mollie sat quietly turning over the proposition which at that stage was a complete mystery to her.

On the other side Antonia sat equally sombre in her manner, quite the contrary to her usual ebullient character and looking up put a pertinent question to Mollie.

'Have you had an interview with Mr Swatridge?'

Mollie nodded, unsure whether to elaborate when her friend continued.

'So have I, and if yours was about an offer of more secret work, it looks as though we're both in the same boat!'

Mollie felt very relieved but realised it would be unwise to continue their conversation there for all to hear. 'Antonia, why don't we take a walk in the park at lunch time? We can talk and perhaps help each other make a decision. What do you say?'

That agreed, the two friends had a quick snack at noon then walked for half an hour away from the house. Mollie started the conversation: 'Have you any idea what the secret operation is that Mr Swatridge was on about?'

Antonia, having weighed up the possibilities replied, 'Yes, I have an idea he was inviting us to join the SOE [Special Operations Executive]. I deduced that when he said it meant going abroad. Do you think that's a possibility?'

'Well, if it is, I want someone to say so before I'd commit myself. I think I'd be willing to go to France if you were coming with me but not otherwise.'

Antonia felt flattered by her friend's remark and responded, 'That's very kind of you, Mollie, and exactly the same condition was going through my mind. Yes, I'd be willing to go to France but only in company with you.'

They chatted as they returned to the house and decided to have a further discussion that evening before making a final decision.

After dinner that night they had a long deliberation in Antonia's room and eventually decided to accept the invitation. Realising they would not be able to write to their parents, Mollie suggested sending a long letter home saying special training would take them away for a short time during which it would be difficult to correspond.

'That's a splendid idea, Mollie, and if we put our heads together I'm sure we can produce a convincing narrative to satisfy our folk.'

'We'll do that tonight and in the morning let's both go to see Mr Swatridge together.'

The die was cast and the two friends knew they were embarking on a very important mission.

Chapter 44

On 2nd April 1944, a week before Easter, Mollie and Antonia started training at a secret establishment in southern England having been interviewed a fortnight earlier at an address in Carlton House Terrace just off Pall Mall in the West End of London. They were told that relief for Brittany was required urgently and they were most likely to go there towards the end of April.

To establish their military status in case of capture both were commissioned, Mollie with the rank of Captain and Antonia as a Lieutenant.

The training course covered the use of pistols and explosives, map reading, ways to escape custody, etc., No parachute training was required as they were to be flown in during the next full moon.

In Lincolnshire during March, Catherina saw her doctor who confirmed pregnancy; from then on she had a special ration book entitling her to extra food, milk, butter and eggs as well as oranges and bananas if and when they were available.

Catherina wrote a long letter to Rupert telling him the wonderful news and how thrilled her father and sister were and asking if he could come home for a few days.

At Easter the American infantry forces in Farndene stated moving towards Devon where a full-scale invasion exercise was to take place later in the month. In December the previous year an area of about 30,000 acres of southern Devon, with some eight villages and coast including Slapton beach had been completely evacuated of all livestock, domestic animals and people. The Americans used the sea and land to rehearse for the forthcoming landings on Utah beach in Normandy, the Slapton beach being identical to the one in France.

At the Manor House the Easter holiday was very quiet with just Clara down from Oxford and Constance from Chessington, where the Ordnance Survey Authority had told her she would be living in special accommodation in the Survey building from the middle of May; Bruce also came home with Dorcas for two or three days.

Fanny, now settled in the Manor House, enjoyed seeing and talking to her grandchildren and they to her. Bruce particularly remembered the happy times they had in Bristol during their school days and remarked, 'Thanks to you, Grandma Fanny, we never felt homesick and on occasions when we got into trouble at school you always managed to deal with our problems; best of all we used to have wonderful desserts such as treacle pudding, spotted dick, apple pie and jam roly-poly all with loads of custard.' Turning to Dorcas, he said, 'So you see that's what you'll have to give me when we're married!'

Dorcas enjoyed the fun but her reply was to the point, 'If I ate that kind of food every day I'd soon put on weight making it impossible to dance.'

Margot listened with pleasure as she realised how much Fanny had done for the five children during their time at Bristol and watched the easy manner her young ones had with their grandmother. She also realised why Fanny had elected to move to Farndene, as it gave her the opportunity of seeing her grandchildren much more.

On Easter Sunday the family went to St Paul's church and met a number of the villagers they knew; after a light lunch most of the youngsters went walking with the dogs, enjoying the fine sunny weather.

After dinner on Easter Monday Clara and Constance went into the village to a dance with Bruce while Dorcas stayed behind to make up a foursome for bridge with Fanny, Margot and Francis.

Bruce and Constance returned home about eleven fifteen, joking that Clara had decided to stay a little longer with a handsome American sergeant who was an excellent dancer; he said he'd see her home when the dance ended.

Shortly after midnight, Bertie the butler answered the doorbell and urgently called Francis and Margot who came into the hall. To their horror they saw their daughter in a terrible state, her clothing torn, her face and arms scratched and bruised and with no shoes on.

Clara went forward and collapsed into her mother's arms in a semi-conscious state.

As soon as Bruce and Francis had carried Clara up to her bed, Margot talked to her daughter softly.

'Tell me darling, whatever happened?'

Clara stared at her mother for a moment and then, with tears streaming down her face, whispered, 'An American raped me.' She then broke down completely.

Francis moved quickly downstairs to the study followed by Bruce and, once inside, told his son, 'Use the other line and call our doctor to come immediately to examine Clara. I'll use this line to inform the police.'

Within the hour a locum Dr Belinda Crabtree had arrived and examined Clara, confirming she had been raped in a particularly brutal way, evidenced by extensive bruising and lacerations to the lower abdomen and thighs; she administered a sedative and told Margot she would call again in the morning.

Francis had been astute by calling the Southampton Police Headquarters before the local station and in response Superintendent Freddie Gaskin – who had succeeded Superintendent Jack Snapper – arrived with his sergeant at one fifteen.

As it was impossible to speak to Clara, Margot told the police all she had gathered from her daughter as they waited for the doctor. 'The American sergeant she'd been dancing with, saw her to the drive gates and said goodnight. As she walked towards the house past the rhododendron bushes she was suddenly grabbed from behind. Clara screamed but the attacker put a hand over her mouth as he dragged her into the bushes. She fought but was overpowered by a very large man. In the dim light of the waning moon she saw her assailant was white and was wearing an American soldier's uniform. When he spoke he told her to shut up or he'd kill her; he spoke with a drawling American accent.

'Clara remembered he stank of alcohol and the hand that covered her mouth had the tops of two fingers missing; she thought it was the right hand.'

The superintendent listened carefully and replied straight away, 'Lady Vining you have given us a tremendous amount of help by talking to your daughter. I'd like to interview Miss Vining tomorrow when it's convenient. Meanwhile I'll contact the American Military Police when I leave here and expect to have their cooperation.'

During the last week of April, Mollie and Antonia finished their training and were taken to a safe house near Tangmere, Sussex, where a final briefing took place and their equipment and clothing checked to ensure all labels and other means of identification were removed. Each had to give up their wristwatch.

They were told, 'The code name of your Group Leader in Plonéour Lanvern, Brittany, is Dominic and his base is at the Abbey of Our Lady on the outskirts of the town. Your code names are as follows, Mrs Shelley to be known as Marie and Miss Boer as Thérèse. You must use only these code names and never in any circumstances reveal your true identity.'

As they waited, Mollie realised by a twist of fate she was bound for Plonéour Lanvern. She hoped she didn't meet her uncle René in case he recognised her and 'blew her cover'.

That night, one of a full moon with a cloudless sky, they were driven to RAF Tangmere where they were helped to board their aircraft. The small group of well wishers waved them off as the jet black Lysander took off for France.

Huddled in the small compartment with the constant roar of the engine, Mollie and Antonia sat, just able to see the outline of the Sussex coast as the plane headed across the Channel.

Mollie, grinning, shouted to her friend, 'This is it, "Thérèse", but don't ever tell anyone you're anyone else!'

'Okay, "Marie", we're in it together and I predict we're going to win,' and taking out a small hip flask Antonia took a swig and then offered it to Mollie.

Two weeks after Easter, Superintendent Freddie Gaskin called at the Manor House, Farndene, to tell Francis and Margot the current situation regarding the rape of their daughter. Seated in the drawing room he explained the result of investigation by the American Military Police.

'I received a telephone call from General Shaun D. Goodhew commanding this area, and he told me his police have identified the soldier they believe responsible for the rape, helped by the information you, Lady Vining and your daughter gave us. The suspect is serving with the 88th Heavy Tank Regiment, which unit is presently involved in a major operation in the west of England. Consequently, the General has decided to defer arresting the man until the exercise is completed. He asked me to convey his apologies again and will call to see you very shortly.'

Francis thanked the superintendent and after a further short discussion the policeman left.

After a conference in Devon, General Goodhew flew back to RAF Farndene and the following day visited the Manor House with gifts for Clara and her mother.

The General, a tall fair-haired man with an easy manner but piercing blue eyes, sat with his long legs crossed admiring the elegance of the drawing room before speaking with a Southern States drawl.

'Sir Francis, Lady Margot, having been your guest on more than one occasion and knowing how much you've done for our guys, I feel kinda embarrassed coming here today. When I consider what one of our goddam GIs did to your dear daughter my blood boils. But have no fear I intend to nail this guy and I'll make it my duty to see he gets the maximum sentence. I'll let you know as and when the suspect is tried and the outcome.'

Francis thanked him and went on to say, 'Clara is still recovering from her ordeal and hopes to be fit enough to return to Oxford very shortly. She asked me to thank you for all you've done to find the culprit. She also said she couldn't appear as a witness in any court action.'

'I understand completely, Sir Francis, and we'll do everything we can to save your daughter any further embarrassment.'

As he stood to take his leave, Margot thanked him for the beautiful flowers and chocolates, 'They'll help Clara along the road to fitness again.'

Two hours after leaving England, Mollie and Antonia sat tired and cold in the cramped compartment of the Lysander and, although both had dozed a little, the lack of comfort and the very low temperature made their journey anything but comfortable. Quite suddenly the roar of the engine became less oppressive and they were conscious the plane was banking steeply, so much so the field below was clearly visible on the left. Antonia was the first to see the landing sign, 'Mollie, look at the four lights in the form of a cross, they're the indicator for the pilot to land.'

'I can see them so we must have arrived. Oh golly, I'm scared! Are you Antonia?'

'You're too right I am! But we've come into this with our eyes open and we're going to make it work so, Mollie, keep your chin up, I'm with you all the way!'

In a matter of minutes the Lysander was bumping along the field, turning quickly to taxi back to where a group of shadowy figures were waiting. Immediately it stopped, with the engine ticking over, Mollie and Antonia were helped down with their bags and two people replaced them in the cabin. The plane then swung round to start the takeoff run down the field and in a matter of minutes had roared away into the night sky.

The quietness that followed was overwhelming and the resistance party greeting them did so in hushed voices. Helped into an open farm wagon with their belongings, both women were wrapped in a blanket against the cold and were soon moving along lanes pulled by a large draught horse. They were conscious of the faint fragrant scent of wild flowers in the fields and hedgerows and the damp earthy smell of the night air as the huge cart moved slowly in the light of the setting moon. After half an hour the wagon left the road to cross a large field full of cattle and some horses, arriving at the rear of the Abbey of Our Lady, a huge stone building dating from the thirteenth century. In the shadow of the building Mollie and Antonia were guided down steps to a solid oak door.

They were admitted immediately by an armed guard and walked along a corridor to a large fully lit room; here several partisans sat around smoking and talking but stopped as the two women came in. A tall, bearded figure came forward to greet them, 'I'm delighted to see you've arrived safely. I'm Dominic.' To Mollie he said, 'I think you must be Marie,' and to Antonia, 'That makes you Thérèse.' They both nodded agreement.

'I expect you're tired and hungry so let me offer you something to eat and drink, after which you'll be able to get some sleep.' Dominic then introduced the whole group before inviting them back to the huge table, 'Now come and sit down and we'll join you.' The food consisted of several baguettes, cheese, sausage and ham with plates of chopped onion and tomatoes, and there was local red wine or hot strong coffee. While they ate, Dominic outlined the current situation in the area and told them he would brief them in more detail in the morning. With the meal finished, he took Mollie and Antonia to a room in which there were a couple of wooden chairs and a chest of drawers between two camp beds.

There were no windows and a single low-powered bulb provided barely enough light.

As he said goodnight, Dominic apologised, 'I'm sorry the "necessarium" is at the other end of the building but you'll find the "necessary" under each bed; sleep well, I'll see you in the morning.'

Once the door shut Mollie couldn't restrain herself any longer and in a hushed voice told her friend.

'I know who Dominic is! I recognised him in spite of the whiskers.' Antonia was all ears as the story unfolded. 'His name is Leon de Marne and he's with the Free French Forces; he interviewed me in Exeter before I joined Bletchley Park!'

'Are you sure, Mollie? He's certainly very French and good looking. I could go for him in a big way if he hadn't got all that horrid fungus on his face!'

They both had a good giggle and Mollie, yawning, suddenly felt very tired. She looked at her wrist and sighed, 'Drat, they took our watches at Tangmere, so we don't know what the time is but I reckon it's two or three in the morning.'

A few moments later all talking stopped and they were both fast asleep.

Francis and Margot attended a meeting of the 'Liaison Committee' at the local American Headquarters on the morning of Friday 28th April and had started a short agenda when a rather agitated senior officer entered and spoke hurriedly to Francis who was acting as chairman.

'Sir Francis, due to extreme circumstances I regret I have to ask you to terminate the meeting immediately. We expect the return of some of our forces to this area very shortly and the instruction from our Commander in Chief is that all civilians should leave US Army Establishments.'

Slightly bemused, Francis closed the meeting and as requested left the Headquarters building with other members straight away.

As they walked back to the Manor House, Margot and Francis discussed the unusual turn of events.

'Why on earth was it so important to end our meeting so abruptly? And the exclusion of all civilians suggests something is happening or has happened the Americans don't wish the public to know about. What do you think Francis?'

'You're right darling, the whole business sounds fishy. However, I imagine we'll get to know what's going on when the troops return. They'll talk, just you wait and see.'

And talk they did. After noon the next day the first armoured units passed through Farndene en route for the camps on the town outskirts. None stopped and each group was escorted by Military Police on motorcycles and in jeeps.

But although all American personnel were confined to the camps, some managed to sneak out to meet girlfriends and some startling news leaked to the public.

Several GIs talked of a disaster at Slapton Sands in Devon, and stories, some embellished, told of hundreds of casualties with dead bodies floating in the sea and washed up on the sands. One young tank driver on a landing craft said it was torpedoed along with others which caught fire; he'd been rescued after hours in the sea.

And so the stories trickled to the Manor House by various routes and Margot and Francis realised the truth of such rumours.

Chapter 45

May 1944 opened with some wonderful spring weather and within a few days the trees and hedgerows took on their early covering of new leaf encouraged by a warm sun and frequent showers. At RAF Farndene, Rupert was able to take a break after continuous daily operations and flew over to RAF Sutton Bridge where, once again, Group Captain Rodney Stanmore welcomed him.

Rupert explained, 'Rodney, I've only got twenty-four hours so I'll have to look slippy. Can you give me a lift home?'

'No problem, just give me about half an hour while I clear my desk and I'll run you over to the farm.'

Catherina, her father and sister gave Rupert a rapturous welcome and invited Rodney to stay for the evening meal. Catherina was beside herself with joy and, hugging Rupert, bubbled with excited chatter, 'My darling I've missed you every day,' adding laughingly, 'I'm going to hold you tight forever so you can't leave me again!' They kissed several times and then turning to her father, 'Tell Rupert your good news, Papa.'

Jan too was smiling, 'We received a wonderful message from a member of the Dutch Resistance who had escaped across France to Spain. He told us my wife Lies is alive and in hiding with a farming family in the north of Holland; she lives under an assumed name. So, please God, it will not be long when we are together again!'

The news of their mother's survival dominated the conversation for the rest of the evening and both Catherina and her sister were clearly overjoyed not only for their own sakes but mainly for their father. Bep summed it up, 'Papa was sad for so long but now he's taken on a new lease of life; Catherina and I are so happy for him.'

Rodney added his view about the possible end of the war, 'It can't be very long before we invade Europe, bearing in mind the enormous number of Americans we have here in Britain. I see the US Air Force going into action most days and the size of their bomber forces is enormous.'

Rupert agreed, 'That's true and around Farndene there are masses of tanks, armoured troop carriers, and trucks. Flying over the tops of the South Downs I've seen ammunition stacked as high as houses stretching for miles, with more tanks, parked aircraft – both fighters and bombers – guarded by a small army living in whole villages of tents. The Americans seem to have recovered from the disaster in Devon at the end of April when whole units were lost at sea.' He went on to tell them, 'The Yanks have played the cards very close to their chests and all ranks are forbidden to talk about it, particularly with civilians. One assumes all was not well down in Devon.'

His twenty-four hour break came to an end all too quickly and, after taking off from RAF Sutton Bridge, he made a low pass over the farm house where the family gathered to wave as Rupert thundered away after two victory rolls.

In the crypt of the Abbey of Our Lady, Mollie and Antonia slept soundly until ten o'clock when a little woman brought them some hot coffee. 'When you are ready I'll show you where the ablutions are so you can wash and clean your teeth. There is no hurry, so please take your time; I'll be in the room just along the passage.'

They sat in bed sipping the beverage and trying to take stock of all that had happened the previous day.

'It seems like a fantastic dream and I actually pinched myself to see if it was,' Antonia looked across to Mollie as she went on, 'What is frightening is I actually had a dream in England, during which I was in a room just like this one but without any furniture.'

Mollie smiled, 'You probably had a dream last night because you had too much cheese to eat before bed, so don't worry any more. I still find it had to believe I'm in Plonéour Lanvern of all places in Brittany; it's a curious stroke of fate! We'd better hurry because Dominic said he'd brief us this morning.'

A little later Dominic greeted them and said, with a smile to Marie [Mollie], 'I know you know who I am but we'll keep that to ourselves,' and then outlined the immediate history of the Resistance group in that area of Brittany.

'In mid-March the group was infiltrated by the Gestapo using a traitorous Frenchman who obtained the names of all the local partisans. The Germans swooped at four in the morning, arresting half of them. By sheer chance a local farmer and his boy were driving cows along the road to the milking shed, so blocking the way to a German convoy of Gestapo and soldiers. He told his son to run across the fields to the village baker, a Resistance member, telling him to alert others as soon as possible. The boy's action saved over half of the group but twenty-five of those captured were tortured and shot the following day; others managed to escape and are living rough in the forest to the east. Tragically, many of the families, women and children, were sent to Germany to do forced labour. Unfortunately, to date, we have been unable to identify the traitor in our midst, so we must act with great care.

'I was asked to come over to re-group the whole area and prepare for armed resistance as soon as the second front starts.'

He paused momentarily and then turned to Marie, 'I specifically requested that you join us, remembering your complete command of French and of the local patois when I interviewed you in Exeter,' then to Thérèse [Antonia], 'And you, Thérèse, were recommended by Bletchley Park for your skill in receiving and transmitting wireless messages; I'll give you instructions as to where you are to transmit later on. Luckily, the nuns have several wire clotheslines which you'll be able to use as aerials.

'So you are completely in the picture I need to tell you the Abbess is my sister Celeste, who has permitted us to use this crypt. She decided to help the Resistance after two of the nuns were captured with the round up in March. When arrested they were sitting with an elderly woman who was dying from cancer but whose son was a partisan. The two sisters were tortured, beaten and burnt with cigarettes and finally dumped at the abbey door; both died a few days later.'

He opened a drawer and withdrew a large folded map, spreading it across the desk top and inviting them to pull their chairs up to watch as he pinpointed various places marked with a red circle. 'These are places of strategic importance to us and will be captured when we are instructed from London. The other points marked with black circles are German ammunition and fuel dumps as well as places where occupation forces live. Finally the place identified with a yellow spot is the Gestapo headquarters.'

During a pause, Thérèse asked, 'what exactly is our role in all this?'

Dominic smiled, 'Well I was just coming to that and what I'm going to tell you two will be a very big surprise. You are to act together as couriers and go to specific places to deliver messages from this headquarters; you will be disguised as nuns. My sister, Celeste will provide the necessary habits and give you some instruction on how to conduct yourselves. Marie, I'm aware you know this area quite well which will be helpful. The messages will be concealed in small bread rolls baked here and identified by a small cross on the underside. Finally, only speak to Germans if you are spoken to and always avoid eye contact with them. Now is there anything you'd like to ask me?'

'Yes!' Thérèse looked worried, 'Do we have any form of identity card?'

'Oh, I'm sorry I completely forgot about that. You will carry an identity form with your photograph and signature as nuns. We do all that here and our documents are very good, you see the forger once produced counterfeit franc notes which were superb.'

'And what if we meet other nuns from the abbey? Won't they be suspicious?' Thérèse was uncertain in her mind.

'A very good point, Thérèse, but don't worry. You see they're in the Convent of Saint Mary in the town and most of the nuns there have little contact with the abbey.'

During the next week, Marie and Thérèse made several trips to visit old or infirm people, delivering messages on each occasion. Marie noticed the drastic change among the population and she told her friend, 'I remember coming here with my Uncle René, meeting many friends of his; the whole place was so bright and the people happy and outgoing. But now all we see are sullen faces, etched with fear, avoiding eye contact with everyone and obviously trusting no-one; they look thin and haunted.'

Later in the week on Friday, German soldiers were stopping everyone, examining identity papers, questioning and searching many they stopped.

As Marie and Thérèse reached the checkpoint they showed their papers but the younger soldier wanted to know what was in their basket. Marie pulled back a linen cloth uncovering the rolls and the soldier, smiling, helped himself to one and was about to take a bite when Marie stopped him.

He was taken aback but her quick thinking saved the day, 'Put that one back and I'll give you a roll from underneath which will still be hot.' Taking the bread from him, she substituted a hot roll and also gave his colleague one as well, 'Ich hoffe dass sie gut schmecken, aber wir müssen fort um mehrere alten Leute, die ganz krank sind, zu besuchen [I hope you enjoy them, but we must go as we have to visit several old people who are quite sick].

The soldiers were pleased to hear their own language and their thanks were profuse; they wished Marie and Thérèse 'Guten-tag' as they departed.

Walking away Thérèse told Marie, 'My legs are like jelly but the way you dealt with those two was superb.'

Marie smiled, 'My legs nearly gave way. I knew the first roll the soldier took had the message in it and if he'd taken a mouthful that would have been that!'

Towards the end of the first week of May, General Goodhew called at the Manor House, Farndene, and immediately Francis and Margot realised the American looked distraught and very tired as he spoke to them.

'Last time I called on you two I promised to let your know when we arrested the GI who raped your daughter and the outcome of his trial. Well there isn't going to be a trial as, in my opinion, God has intervened. In a nutshell, the guy we believed to be responsible is no more; he perished along with umpteen others in the sea off the Devon coast at the end of last month.' He paused, looking at his clasped hands, 'I have to tell you I've no grief for that guy and I'm sure glad he got his comeuppance but I'm sick at heart for all those other young American boys who are now dead because of incompetence up the line.'

Francis and Margot had already heard by various means there had been a major calamity in Devon and now it was being confirmed by a senior commander.

The General accepted a drink offered by Francis and, after sipping the scotch, spoke again.

'You two have been wonderful friends to me and many of the GIs under my command and I'm eternally grateful. I came here today primarily to tell you about the rapist but I also needed to talk with very close friends who are experienced family people. What I'm about to tell you I want you to treat with the utmost confidence and on this point I know I can trust you.

'We held an exercise called Operation Tiger in Devon at the end of April: a rehearsal for the coming invasion of Europe involving thousands of troops with tanks and artillery. During the night, as they approached the Devon coast, several German E-boats torpedoed troop carriers and then the bastards machine-gunned survivors in the water.' He fell silent, tears in his eyes.

'We lost over eight hundred GIs – many only kids – due mainly to a cock-up in the higher command. Can you believe it? The various participants in the exercise were using different radio wave bands and consequently couldn't communicate with each other, so nobody knew where they were or what was going on until it was too late.'

He seemed relieved having talked about the whole affair and the drawn look left his face for the present.

'What you have told us we'll keep to ourselves have no fear.' Margot took hold of his arm, 'We understand how you feel, having been through a similar trauma when our son was missing after his plane crashed during the Battle of Britain. It's good for you to talk to someone and we feel privileged you feel able to discuss the situation with us.'

As Margot finished, Francis confirmed what she had said, adding his own thoughts, 'Shaun, war is a combination of tragedy and tribulation, of sadness and senseless waste, and I speak with my own experience in the Great War. What you have witnessed is something that shouldn't have happened due to neglect of duty somewhere in the chain of command but I am certain you'll profit from the errors before the actual invasion, when the effect of such errors would have spelt failure of the whole operation.'

The General nodded as he listened and his features lightened a little. 'Francis, all you and your good wife have said has helped to lift the burden I felt when I came to your house. Your comments about profiting from the errors are so true and, to avoid failure, we will and must put things right before the big test. There's something about you English people I've come to admire and it's this: the stoic way you handle the most incipient problems is amazing and when knocked down you have the remarkable ability of recovery with increased strength. You two fit that bill exactly and it's been a great experience getting to know you; I'll never forget the friendship you offered to many of us when we arrived in the Mother Country.' As he thanked them again, with tears on his cheeks he broke into a smile with the final comment. 'God, you Brits are the toughest and most determined folk I've ever met, which means Hitler will never get on top of you. Frankly he hasn't got a chance!

'Just one other thing which may interest you: I'll be flying to Washington next week for a President's conference so I'll try to meet up with Norman and Helen; if you have anything you'd like me to take for them I'll be delighted to be carrier.

'Now, if I may, I'd like to return to the tragedy of your daughter's rape. As we're as near certain as one can be that the culprit was a GI, I sent the file to Supreme Commander's Headquarters with a recommendation the US Army should make a gesture in the form of a payment to help mitigate the suffering of your girl. They have replied, offering a sum of US $5,000, which for legal reasons must be an ex-gratia payment. Clara may refuse the offer if she wishes, but it may help with her university expenses. Thinking back to my own vollege days, a bit of extra cash is always useful.'

Francis thanked him and promised to tell Clara when next she telephoned, 'Shaun, I'll let you know her answer in due course. Now Margot and I will be pleased if you can join us for dinner this evening; we have three RAF pilots coming along so if you can make it we eat about eight o'clock.'

'Thanks, I'd love to and I know I'll get a good meal as you have one of the greatest cooks in this land!' And with a twinkle in his eye, 'Mind I don't steal her when finally I go back home!'

That evening the guests gathered on time and General Goodhew was introduced to Wing Commander Rupert Tupper, Squadron Leader Gordon Haig and Flight Lieutenant Burton Flowers, an Australian from Hobart, Tasmania, with a sharp mind and ready wit. The party went well and Shaun Goodhew relaxed and enjoyed the lively talk at the table between the RAF boys, particularly Gordon Haig who was an art critic before joining the Air Force.

The subject of culture came up with Gordon making the point, 'The Nazis have created a police state, stripping Germany of any kind of culture!' He sounded on the pompous side as he asserted, 'However, in spite of being reduced by rationing we have kept culture in our society, unlike the Australians for example who have become somewhat uncouth and brash in their manner!' He was enjoying pulling Burton's leg, 'But one sympathises, bearing in mind they come from a long line of cockney convicts!'

Burton Flowers rose to the bait with a prompt response. 'Culture, culture you say! We know all about culture down under! We've got culture right up to our arseholes! Only down there we spell culture with a "K", not so posh as the Pommie way with a "C ",which stands for …' he stopped as he caught the General's eye and quickly changed what he intended to say, 'well, stands for anything you like. But the whole business brings to mind a little ditty that goes something like this,

379

A pretty young lady named Fay,
Was put in the family way.
By the mate of a Rigger,
Oh yes, you can snigger!
He spelt culture, tell Haig, with a "K".'

They enjoyed the fun and when the laughing subsided, Margot had a word, 'Now you young fellows just stop ribbing each other for a few moments as I want to ask you, Burton, a very direct question.'

'I'm all ears, Lady Margot, fire away.'

'I believe you're courting a local lady in Farndene and I'd like you to tell us what sort of place you will be taking her to in Australia when the war is over.'

Burton was suddenly very serious, 'I'm hoping my Daphne and I will be wed before going home to Hobart, Tasmania. My folks are fruit famers and we have orchards covering some three thousand acres, producing apples, pears, and plums. My father is experimenting with a vineyard and, if successful will extend the acreage soon. The farm is a bit remote but we all get along well together and have friends within about twenty miles each way.'

'That sounds remote but I suppose your family is a large one perhaps?'

'It's a good size, Lady Margot, I've three brothers and two sisters and my aunt and uncle live around half a mile from our house with their family, three girls and two boys, my cousins are all over eighteen years old. By the way, Daphne's folk farm outside Farndene and she's used to looking after cattle and horses so I reckon she'll be okay back home.'

At this point Shaun Goodhew added his view, 'What we've heard from this young man is similar to the thousands of American boys who have fallen for and will marry English girls. Both the GIs and their girlfriends come from all walks of life, which means there will have to be adjustments on both sides to make a success of their union. But we're all romantics at heart and know that love is a "level playing field" on which all ranks and condition meet.

I've a hunch it'll work and we'll see some very happy families as a result.'

By the middle of May the Allies had stepped up their bombardment of the German war machine (and their occupying forces in France and Belgium) with round-the-clock bombing of bridges, railway marshalling yards, power stations and fuel dumps by the RAF and the US Army Air Force, to devastating effect. The operations were, in fact, a softening-up process prior to the invasion of Europe.

At RAF Farndene the squadrons of Mustangs escorted Bomber Command in daylight raids deep into France, rarely meeting any opposition from the Luftwaffe which had suffered horrendous losses at the hands of Allied Air Power. One American General said the stage was being set for the 'show of the century' adding, 'this will be bigger than Broadway with no expense spared! I guarantee it'll be the biggest HIT ever, but probably Hitler won't like it!'

Early in the morning of 6th June 1944, Miles Pritchard, son of the late Dan Pritchard, who had succeeded his father to run the local Farndene butcher's shop as well as being churchwarden at St Paul's, was returning from the Southampton abattoir with a van load of meat, accompanied by his assistant Harry Jason. As they entered the town they passed American camps and establishments all of which were deserted. The roads and lanes, hitherto packed with tanks, armoured vehicles and transports were now empty and silent, devoid of any living soul. Miles made the first remark, 'Harry, do you see what I see? I reckon there's something big going on. Everything has disappeared during the night.'

Harry nodded, 'You're right, guv, and I couldn't sleep last night for the constant roar of aircraft passing over. They woke me just after midnight and went on for hours; my missus was awake too and we both had a feeling something big was happening, so we'll probably hear later on.'

The meat was unloaded into the cold room by eight o'clock;

Miles and Harry sat down with a mug of tea to listen to the wireless as the BBC announcer broke the startling news.

'In the early hours of today, massive Allied forces landed in Europe supported by immense naval and air force bombardment which is continuing as I speak. A foothold has been established against limited resistance and reinforcements are pouring into the substantial bridgehead. Further bulletins will be broadcast at intervals during the day.'

With a broad smile on his face, Miles looked across to Harry who was nodding as his boss spoke.

'This is it, Harry, we're at last getting to grips with those Nazi bastards! Hitler and his followers will be put to the sword and not a moment too soon. In the words of Mr Churchill "this is the beginning of the end"!'

Harry got up and, with renewed energy started cutting up a side of beef, whistling 'there'll always be an England' as he worked.

Chapter 46

Throughout Great Britain the wonderful news of the opening of the Second Front was received with enormous enthusiasm and relief, as the war-weary population realised the invasion forces were the spearhead of the gigantic army that would crush Hitler's Germany and rid the world of the most evil Nazi system.

As people went about their business that morning one detected a spring in the step, while perfect strangers acknowledged each other with greetings, as much the time of the day as the desire to speak with someone, telling them the remarkable news if they hadn't heard it.

At Stepney, in London's East End, one jubilant cockney shouted to his mate, ''E's dun it, ole Winne's dun it, mate! 'E's gawn an landid wiv 'em Frenchies! Nah 'itler, Gobbles an 'is mate fatty Gorine wanna watch art wen ar boys cetch 'em. The Naarzies wiwl geh it up their Jacksie orl rite!'

Years of terror bombing, of flying bombs, of shortages of food and clothes, of feelings of frustration, were washed away as people absorbed the import of the announcements that morning. At last 'Operation Overlord' was underway and after so many setbacks, there were spectacular scenes of thousands of ships and craft, escorted by hundreds of warships stretching across the English Channel, accompanied by a massive air armada. All this culminated in the gigantic enterprise pouring onto the shores of France. The armed forces and the civilian population were suddenly given the feeling we were at last winning; in Winston Churchill's words, 'Victory at all costs', was now not a possibility but a certainty!

To the suppressed people of Europe the arrival of allied forces in France was what they had prayed for; the hope of early deliverance from German occupation. The French Resistance fighters listened eagerly to BBC broadcasts in the early hours of 6th June 1944, as endless streams of messages from SOE [Special Operations Executive] for various parts of France went on at intervals during the night.

At the Abbey of Our Lady in Plonéour Lanvern, Thérèse, now in civilian clothes, sat throughout the night receiving and recording instructions which were passed to Dominic. There was a mood of joy and optimism among the partisans as they waited for the individual order for their group from London. At 03.00 hours, the message they all awaited came through, 'With plenty of water the mill must turn and grind the corn'. With smiles they shook each other's hands and waited as Dominic spoke.

'My friends, the hour has come to take up the sword of deliverance to rid our country of the scourge of Nazism. You all know your allotted tasks and the exact time you are to act. If you meet opposition you can't handle, report immediately and reinforcements will be sent. Go quietly and may the Almighty help our cause.'

Without further ceremony, the various groups of fighters left and filtered out into the night air, making their way to rendezvous with bands of men and women from the surrounding forests, each to his allotted operation but all with the common task, the destruction of the German enemy.

Within the hour bursts of gunfire and a series of explosions tore the peace of the area apart.

As the first light of dawn drew apart the curtain of darkness, ominous signs of fighting were apparent, with huge columns of smoke rising from burning buildings and depots in and around the town. The streets were deserted, except for one or two dead still lying where they fell, which meant the occupation forces had withdrawn from part of the town and taken up defensive positions round their army and Gestapo headquarters to the west; here they had prepared defences and were supported by tanks and light artillery. The partisans were having a difficult time trying to dislodge them.

Breakfast time at the Manor House, Farndene, took on a new dimension that June morning and Bertie appeared to be supercharged with the news. As Francis and Margot entered the dining room he could contain himself no longer, 'Sir, madam, the BBC announcement is the most wonderful news I've heard in my whole life; we've invaded Europe and a bridgehead has been established! Isn't that just marvellous?'

Francis and Margot were delighted and in reply to their questions, Bertie went on at length, 'We knew there must be something big on, because I heard the planes droning over practically all night and since daybreak the RAF have been taking off in waves from our airfield and lots of others have been landing here probably to refuel. The BBC will make further announcements during the day.'

'Thank you Bertie for such splendid news and we'll all wait for extra bulletins later. Will you be kind enough to tell Lady Dewar the news now, before Cook takes her breakfast up, as she might like to come down and join us,' Margot was keen to give Fanny the opportunity of sharing the special announcement and discussing the news over breakfast.

Bertie came back straight away to tell them, 'Lady Dewar will be with you directly and says will you please wait as she doesn't want to miss anything.' And so the day started for the Vining family as they, like so many other millions in Britain, came to grips with fresh BBC news from the 'Front' across the Channel.

Margot and Fanny both expressed their hope the war would end very soon and all the young ones return home safely. Francis agreed but added his own wish list, 'After our family is restored I hope we'll get the rest of our house and our airfield back from the RAF.' Grinning with a shrug, he added, 'Some hopes! Once the government have commandeered property they like to hang on to it like leeches for as long as they can!'

Smiling, Fanny came to the rescue, 'Francis dear, don't worry so. It may not be that way but if it is, just go into Parliament and do what Gilbert and Sullivan did; poke fun at the Air Ministry until it gives in. Whig or Tory I don't know but into Parliament you must go!'

As Bertie applauded they all had a good laugh, helped by the wonderful news of D-Day.

The conversation turned to the family and Fanny wanted to know how Clara was faring following the attack at Easter, 'I hope she's settled back at Oxford, poor dear.'

Margot explained her daughter had delayed returning to university on the advice of her doctor and the rest and treatment had worked wonders. 'You see, Francis and I helped Clara come to terms with her ordeal and the one thing our doctor insisted on was patience and we've plenty of that! The college authority has been marvellous, assisting her in every way to catch up with studies. She's coming home later this month so you'll see for yourself how much she's recovered. We're also expecting Constance who is getting leave from the Ordnance Survey at long last.'

By D+12, the bridgehead in Normandy had been considerably enlarged to over eight miles wide as fresh troops and materials poured in through the prefabricated Mulberry Harbour, towed across the Channel shortly after 6th June. The German forces were finding it difficult to bring reinforcements to the area from the adjacent parts of France due to the Allies' complete domination of the air and the action of partisans.

In Plonéour Lanvern, the battle between the Resistance and the occupation troops continued, with the Germans defending a large portion of the town from every direction. The initial surprise helped the partisans and a number of tanks were destroyed along with transports and buildings. It appeared, however, that the Germans had got prior information about the possibility of Resistance trouble and were prepared; unfortunately the leakage must have come from a French traitor.

The Resistance fighters suffered a number of casualties but were unable to get adequate medical treatment, consequently some died from their wounds; in addition, things were getting desperate as medical supplies and ammunition were running low. Dominic asked London urgently for help and a supplies drop was arranged for the following night.

The next day they heard from the Resistance at Rennes that a Panzer regiment moving north was being diverted to Plonéour Lanvern en route to Normandy. At this stage Dominic talked with his leaders and Marie to decide the best course of action.

He explained to the group, 'London Command is well aware we are holding down a large German force here, thus preventing troops moving north to reinforce their army in Normandy but we're stretched to the limit at present. I'd like to hear your views as to our next move.'

After a long discussion when several partisans gave their opinion, Marie finally put forward a suggestion that they ask for an RAF strike against the German Headquarters and preferably the Gestapo building and all agreed. To identify the building a small group planned to infiltrate the German defences at night and get onto the flat roof of the Gestapo HQ, where a large white Swastika would be painted. Others intended to create a diversion by setting fire to a number of houses nearby. In the early hours a signal from London acknowledged their request and confirmed help would come as soon as possible.

That night two RAF Liberators dropped four massive supply canisters, three of which landed in the dropping zone but the fourth drifted in the strong wind towards the German defensive position. A tremendous gunfight eventually drove the enemy back sufficiently to retrieve the canister.

A number of partisans were wounded, including Dominic who was shot in the arm and shoulder, and all were taken to their headquarters at the abbey. The news that followed was not good as the Germans had arrested the only remaining local doctor and were holding him prisoner, with a view to denying the Resistance any medical help.

RAF Farndene squadrons continued flying from dawn to dusk, supporting the army in Normandy and attacking selected targets requested by Supreme Allied Headquarters. On D+16, a bright, clear day, Rupert's squadrons were briefed early to escort nine Mosquito bombers to attack buildings and installations in Brittany.

Later in Plonéour Lanvern the distant roar of aircraft gradually got louder and the weary eyes of partisans looked skyward. Suddenly there were shouts of joy as the onlookers saw the massive formation approaching. The Germans put up a tremendous barrage of anti-aircraft fire as the Mosquito planes attacked, each selecting a target but three dealing exclusively with the Gestapo building, firing rockets in salvos which literally blew the place apart, leaving it a blazing ruin from which there appeared to be no survivors. Elsewhere the attacks were pressed home despite formidable anti-aircraft fire and a large area was devastated by rocket and machine-gun fire from the Mosquito and Mustang squadrons.

Having completed a successful raid, the planes turned for home and it was then that Squadron Leader Gordon Haig called Rupert on the radio telephone, 'Rupert, I think you've a problem – I see fuel pouring from your kite [aircraft]. You'd better check your fuel level.'

'My God, there's practically nothing left, Gordon. I'll have to make an emergency landing quickly.'

'Rupert, don't do that in case of fire, just bale out and I'll watch you down and report your position as soon as I get back.' Gordon saw his Wing Commander leave the Mustang, plummeting down until the parachute billowed in support. Ten minutes later he watched Rupert land on the sandy shore of a large lake, part of a local reservoir and then turned towards England. Some way away the pilotless plane dived into a forest and exploded in flames.

Dominic, although in great pain from his wounds, met his commanders that night and they reported the Germans were still putting up a strong defence and several new Panzers had joined them that afternoon. The partisans had captured some soldiers who, when interrogated, gave the name of the Frenchman who had passed information to the Germans.

As the name was revealed Marie felt embarrassed to hear it was her uncle, Alain Cabellou. He had been released from prison by the Germans on the understanding he collaborated with them by infiltrating the Resistance movement.

Dominic told them firmly, 'We'll deal with Monsieur Cabellou later in our own good time but our present problem is not having a doctor here to operate and tend our wounded. To provide for this, I managed to get a telephone call to a good doctor friend, Benedict Giscard who practices just south of Quimper. He's willing to come over here to help us but cannot risk travelling by road at present, so we have to make alternative arrangements for him. I know how we can achieve this.' Turning to Marie, he said, 'I'll need your help as you know the local area so well.'

In Lincolnshire the shock of receiving a telegram was too much for Catherina and she passed out into the arms of her father who gently lowered her to a couch. Bep, her sister, brought a glass of water and it was a few minutes before she was fully conscious.

Papa read the message which said Wing Commander Rupert Tupper was missing on operations. Jan's immediate thought was to telephone his friend Group Captain Rodney Stanmore at RAF Sutton Bridge, to see if further information could be obtained. Meanwhile a weepy Catherina, now six months pregnant, was comforted by her sister who told her Rupert was an excellent pilot and may have possibly gone to another airfield but been unable to tell RAF Farndene.

The telephone rang a little later and Rodney Stanmore gave them the good news, 'Rupert had to bail out and is alright. Squadron Leader Gordon Haig knows what happened but he's on operations again at present. As soon as he's available later this afternoon he'll ring you.'

The news naturally calmed Catherina who cheered up a little, 'If necessary, I'll sit by the 'phone all day until Gordon Haig rings,' and after a little thought, 'I felt something like this would happen to my darling Rupert. I hate those evil Nazis who have made war on so many innocent people and I pray God will see that those Germans are brought to justice. They have taken my dearest Mama and husband! How can I ever forgive them?'

Rupert knew roughly where he was as he sat taking stock of his position on the shore of the reservoir near Plonéour Lanvern. He stood up, quickly rolling up his parachute with a view to concealing it from prying German eyes.

The hot June sunshine was tempered by a pleasant breeze as he crossed the sandy shore, the result of two years of drought conditions lowering the water level, and entered the wooded area which ran alongside the lake. A marked coolness greeted him under the trees and he soon found a large upturned conifer showing its roots like a Peacock displaying to a mate. Stuffing the parachute and his flying helmet and gauntlets into a huge cavity with his foot, he concealed them by throwing down loose twigs and dead leaves until the camouflage was complete.

Taking a hand compass from his pocket he took a bearing and started walking along the shoreline towards the head of the reservoir where he knew there was a dam. Where possible he sought shade, keeping near the wooded area to keep cool but also to be ready to hide from the Germans if necessary.

From time to time he sat down to rest, gazing out across the lake which shimmered in the bright June sunshine and watched large dragonflies hovering above the surface of the water. On each occasion his thoughts went to Catherina and he hoped Gordon Haig had managed to telephone to put her mind at rest.

An hour later he noticed the direction of the lake turned and upon rounding the corner he saw a solitary fisherman sitting on a box with his rod propped up on a support. Unfortunately, the bank ahead was without trees for about eighty yards, too great a distance to risk crossing. Rupert edged forward very slowly watching as the man dozed in the afternoon heat, and taking two small round pebbles he lobbed them over the fisherman's head to see them plop into the lake. The man awoke with a jerk and with keen concentration started winding in his line frantically, while Rupert sprinted unseen to the trees ahead and was soon out of sight. Having got under cover he sat regaining his breath and cooling off before continuing along the woodland track. Twice he ventured to the water's edge to drink after realising he was becoming dehydrated in the June heat.

By about four o'clock that afternoon he could see the huge dam, along the top of which a narrow road ran to the far side where there was a house and several other buildings. On his side there was a large kitchen garden, complete with row upon row of all kinds of vegetables including peas, beans, cabbage and swede. Standing sentinel among his brassica charges stood a tall scarecrow, dressed in a long threadbare brown coat, topped with an old brown beret on his straw head.

'That is just what I need', thought Rupert and after looking round he walked up to the kitchen garden and undressed the scarecrow. Having shaken out the all the insects he put on the brown coat over his uniform. He decided to tie the coat with a length of stout string as there were no buttons, then having eaten two or three pods of refreshing peas, he set off across the top of the dam.

The door of the house opened when Rupert was exactly level with it and a big elderly man emerged.

'Good afternoon,' the greeting accompanied a broad smile, 'Where are you going?'

Rupert hesitated as he replied, 'Good afternoon, I go along to my family at Plonéour Lanvern.'

The man walked up to Rupert before continuing in English, 'Well if you are going there I'd advise you to change those boots!'

Rupert instinctively looked down at his flying boots, realising his disguise was not effective. He was about to speak again but the man interrupted, 'I'm certain you're the pilot of a plane that crashed over there,' motioning with his arm, 'and if you are, the sooner you are out of sight the better. So please come into my house now.'

Following closely, Rupert went indoors to be greeted by the wife, a short stout woman with a smiling rosy face, who shook him warmly by the hand. 'Bravo, monsieur, I am so pleased to welcome you as one of us. You gave the Boche what for today and the people of Plonéour are delighted. Vive la RAF!'

'Forgive me, I'm Georges Dassault and this is my wife Claudette, so please use our Christian names and we will help you if we can. Do you really have family in Plonéour Lanvern?'

'My name is Rupert Tupper so please call me Rupert. My uncle is René Cabellou who breeds horses, though it is a good many years since I have seen him; do you know him?'

'Of course I know him! I bought horses from him before the occupation but not since.'

At this point Claudette interrupted her husband, 'Here you are, going on about horses when our guest looks tired and possibly hungry,' and holding Rupert's hand again enquired, 'When was your last meal?'

'I had breakfast at seven o'clock this morning but nothing since except some of your delicious peas which I helped myself to; I hope you don't mind.'

'Well that settles it. Georges get our guest something to drink while I cook something for him; the poor man must feel exhausted.'

An hour later, Rupert felt fit for anything, having devoured a good helping of rabbit casserole with plenty of homemade bread accompanied by some local red wine.

'Claudette, that was absolutely delicious and I thank you and your husband for looking after me, but perhaps I should leave now as I don't want to endanger you with the Germans.'

'You'll be safe here until we can get you to your uncle's farm tomorrow, but if the Germans come you must hide and we'll show you where.' Getting up from the table, Georges rolled back a large carpet square revealing a trap door, 'This leads to a cellar where our children played when they were young but we haven't used it since they grew up; you'll be safe down there if the need arises.'

While he was speaking, Claudette, looking out of the window, suddenly gave a gasp as she pointed towards the town, 'There's a truck with Boche soldiers coming towards the dam! Quick, Rupert, you must go to the cellar and make no noise until we tell you to come out again.'

Chapter 47

On 27th June 1944 Major Sam Shelley and his men arrived back in the United Kingdom from the Middle East to be re-equipped; they were given two weeks leave prior to joining the Second Front as reinforcements. The following day Sam travelled to Exeter, arriving at Philip and Janine's house in the afternoon. Naturally, they were delighted to see him after so long and wanted to hear all about the invasion of Sicily and the Italian mainland and he duly obliged.

Suddenly he asked, 'Where's Mollie? I haven't heard from her for some months but as we were on the move so much. I expect her letters are still trying to catch up with me.'

Philip and Janine were quiet before she answered, 'Sam, we haven't heard from her for weeks now and in her last letter she said something about doing special work during which she may not be able to write. She told us not to worry and would be in touch as soon as possible. Philip and I think it's a bit odd to say the least.'

Sam was obviously concerned so he asked, 'Do you know if she's still at Bletchley Park?'

Janine shook her head, 'We just don't know and nobody will give us the telephone number so we haven't been able to find out; what do you think she is doing?'

'I've a shrewd suspicion she may be working for the SOE, and if so she may be anywhere at home or abroad.'

Janine looked puzzled, 'What does SOE stand for, Sam?'

'The Special Operations Executive; they organise and support the Resistance movements on the continent. They are very active at present harassing the German occupation forces, particularly in France.'

A sharp intake of breath indicated Janine's concern at the possibility of her daughter's involvement with the fighting in

France. 'Sam, is it possible she's with the Resistance fighters? Mollie would never kill anyone, so what use would she be?'

Sam was careful with his reply, 'I said she may be working for the SOE but that's one of the many possibilities connected with the invasion. I know a fellow officer who was seconded to Bletchley Park and I'll try to get some information from him; that is, if he's still there. Meanwhile please don't worry as there may be a perfectly straightforward reason for Mollie not writing.' He changed the subject, 'Tell me, how's Madame Baume these days?'

Philip sensed Sam's deliberate switch in the conversation and answered quickly, 'We're still pretty busy with a backlog of orders for uniforms and equipment and the girls have been working overtime for several weeks. Thank God we're not worried by air raids; the doodlebugs [flying bombs] are mainly directed at London and Kent, Sussex and Surrey. There are hundreds of anti-aircraft guns sighted along the south coast in those counties and a high percentage of the doodlebugs are shot down before they reach our shores. Maybe you'll end up on the cliffs of Dover with your chaps.'

Sam decided to stay with his in-laws for a few days after which he intended going to Whitby to see his mother and stepfather.

Marie, dressed in dark clothing and wearing a balaclava helmet which covered most of her face, moved cautiously along the lanes towards her uncle René's farm on the outskirts of Plonéour Lanvern, on a clear night illuminated by the moon's first quarter. As she hurried she recalled the instructions Dominic had given, 'Go to your uncle and ask him to send his man Pierre Savin, who is a partisan, with two horses to collect Dr Benedict Giscard from his place just south of Quimper. Speed is of the utmost importance as men are dying for want of surgery. Take a loaded pistol and be ready to use it if necessary'.

Marie approached the farmhouse from the rear and remembered a back entrance through outbuildings. Once inside the house and entering a passage leading to the main room she could hear raised voices; she recognised one as her uncle René's and it was clear a heated argument was taking place.

Edging forward she could see René seated but confronted by his older brother Alain who stood gesticulating and shouting, 'You think you can deny me my share of the farm, do you? I don't care what my father's will said I intend having half!'

René was calm replying, 'Whatever you say, Alain, you can't alter our father's wishes, so please go and attend to your own business.'

At this remark Alain became very angry and almost spat his words, 'Mind my own business? I will do just that! I am not accepting a share of the farm and with you out of the way I'll have the lot!' He took a gun from his pocket and raised his arm to point it at René who appeared too terrified to move.

Marie had already drawn her pistol and slipping the safety catch aimed at Alain; before she could fire, the crash of two shots rang out. To her horror she saw Alain's knees crumple as he pitched forward hitting the floor with a thud, where he lay motionless. From a doorway on the other side of the room the figure of Pierre Savin emerged holding a rifle as he shook his head.

Marie entered the room but momentarily nobody spoke; all appeared stunned gazing at the lifeless figure on the floor. Marie felt sick but relieved she hadn't performed the execution.

Taking off her balaclava helmet she greeted René, 'Uncle, I was about to shoot but Pierre did what was necessary. You see, a captured German soldier said the Resistance had been betrayed by a Frenchman whose name was Alain Cabellou. Sadly he betrayed his own countrymen and many have been killed as a result.'

René put his arms round his niece and kissed her on both cheeks, 'I'm sorry you had to witness my brother's death but from what you say it was entirely necessary. But whatever are you doing in Plonéour Lanvern?'

'I've been working with Dominic at the Resistance headquarters for a while and that's the reason for my coming here tonight.' She went on to explain the difficult situation and the need to bring Dr Benedict Giscard to help.

René listened carefully before answering, 'I'll go to Quimper and it'll help if you come with me, Mollie [he was not aware of her SOE name], that will enable Pierre to deal with the body which must be buried without delay,' and to Pierre, 'Can you get help with the task?'

Pierre nodded, 'No problem, monsieur, I can get friends and I know where we can lose the traitor so he won't be found.'

René was satisfied and half an hour later he and Mollie, leading a spare horse, rode off through the forest towards Quimper.

Having been in the cellar for nearly an hour, Rupert was beginning to give up hope of getting out that evening when he heard movement above and the trapdoor opened. He looked up at Claudette Dassault's beaming face as she spoke, 'You can come out now. The Boche searched the lakeside without success and they've gone.'

Her husband took over the story as Rupert emerged, 'I told them we'd seen nothing but would let them know if we noticed anything suspicious,' adding with a broad grin, 'The German fools believed it, so you're safe here for the present till we get you to your uncle's place.

Rupert asked how that was to be achieved and Georges said he had a simple plan to fool the Germans.

'Let me explain: I have a regular visit from a service engineer who comes in a van from Quimper. He checks the pumps with me and we go into Plonéour Lanvern, taking the readings of all the underground meters at main distribution points; it's a way of checking for leaks in the system. I'll telephone this evening and see if he can come tomorrow, then you and he can swap places and I'll drive you to your uncle's farm.

Rupert thought the plan sounded good but he was concerned for Georges if they were stopped and searched by the Germans.

'Georges, I'm protected by the Geneva Convention so long as I wear my uniform but you're not and would probably be shot for helping an enemy airman escape.'

'I'll take that risk and to be honest the chance of being found out is very small indeed, so please don't worry. You see, I'm half British as my mother married a Frenchman, and I get the "Bulldog" spirit from her!'

'How interesting, and how did your father meet his wife?'

'He went on a special engineering course at the college in Loughborough and my mother's brother joined the same course; father and he became firm friends. Father was invited to Mother's home where he met, fell in love and finally married her and they truly lived happily together for the rest of their lives.'

'What a lovely story, and that explains your command of English.'

'Well yes, and I taught Claudette after we were married and we converse in English some of the time each day to keep the language alive.'

Claudette joined in with a giggle, 'It's a good thing we did, or you might have had difficulty in making us understand when we first met.'

'That's an interesting point, Claudette, and I'll explain why. My mother was Janine Cabello before she married my father Charlie Tupper who was sadly killed in the Great War, and she insisted my sister, my brother, and I were all bilingual in French and English. From an early age we spoke some French every day and it has served me well over the years.' To her husband Rupert said, 'What makes the whole thing even more interesting is the fact you had an English mother and French father, while I had a French mother and an English father; truly an Anglo-French alliance!'

They sat talking for a while longer and Rupert noticed the living room had bookshelves along one entire wall and wanted to know what Georges read.

'We have a large selection of English literature and plays which we read regularly for relaxation as there are no other distractions in the heart of the country here; my favourites are William Shakespeare, William Wordsworth and Gilbert and Sullivan which my mother introduced me to.' Georges hummed a snatch of the policemen's song from the 'Pirates of Penzance', and beamed, 'There you are. I can remember it after all these years!'

'Commendable, to say the least! And what are your choices, Claudette?' Rupert found this unusual English library in the heart of France fascinating.

'I love Lewis Carroll's *Alice's Adventures in Wonderland* and your poets Shelley and Keats. England is fortunate having so many talented and prolific writers. I've tried writing poetry myself but I don't find it easy. I make excuses to Georges that all the good subjects have been taken by the British but he doesn't believe me, so I'll keep on trying.'

'Come, come my dear, you have produced one or two good pieces and I only criticise to help you, not to put you down.' He smiled at his wife as he made the point.

Rupert relaxed discussing *The Merchant of Venice* and *Twelfth Night* with them and almost forgot he was in hiding in a foreign country surrounded by enemy troops, but suddenly they were put on alert as the sound of an approaching motorcycle came up from the valley.

Georges reacted immediately by pushing back a table and chairs, rolling up the carpet and opening the trapdoor, 'Quick, Rupert, down in the cellar. We mustn't take chances.'

Minutes later the room was restored and Rupert safely hidden below, where he speculated who the visitor might be. He didn't have to wait long for the door opened in ten or so minutes and he emerged into the living room.

Georges introduced the visitor, a broad-shouldered man of medium height with a mop of dark hair matching his beard and moustache. 'This is Geraud Sabatier, the service engineer from Quimper who has come out to tell me his van has conked out with big end trouble and will be off the road for a while. All my bright ideas to get you to your uncle have come to naught.'

Geraud shook Rupert's hand vigorously and expressed his pleasure at their meeting, 'Georges told me why you're here and we'll see what can be done to help. I managed to get some German petrol without their knowledge and my lightweight motorcycle needs very little.'

They all sat at the dining table and Claudette produced some homemade bread and cheese and Georges some local red wine. They sat discussing and planning for an hour until it was nearly dark when they reached a final decision.

Geraud outlined what he would do, 'Once it's dark I'll take you on the pillion to your uncle's farm. Having been born and brought up here I know all the back ways in Plonéour Lanvern and I intend to use those as well as crossing open country so we're unlikely to meet any Germans. Rupert, you must wear a boiler suit to conceal your uniform and have your pistol ready in case we have to shoot.'

Half an hour later Rupert, decked out in an old black boiler suit got onto the motorcycle and having thanked Georges and Claudette, said goodbye; within minutes he and Geraud disappeared down the valley into the night.

Pierre Savin had mustered three other partisans and between them they tied the body of Alain Cabellou in an aged carpet, transporting it in a horse-drawn cart to a remote derelict cottage about a mile from René's farm. Here they removed the covering of an old well and by the light of hand torches one member was lowered into it. He pushed three sticks of dynamite into the shaft walls, with a length of fuse connected to each. Once back on the surface, the group unceremoniously dumped the corpse down the well and were about to light the fuses when they heard a motorcycle approaching across the field.

'Quick, get under cover until we see who comes.' As they hid, Pierre told them not to fire unless it was absolutely necessary.

The motorcycle drew nearer and Pierre realised the two riders were not Germans, so he called to them, 'Hey, what do you two think you're up to?'

The cycle came to an abrupt halt and Geraud replied promptly, 'We're looking for René Cabellou's farm; can you help us?'

The 'burial party' came out from hiding and Pierre immediately recognised Geraud, 'Well, well, fancy meeting you here at the dead of night! How are you, Geraud? It's a long time since we last met, but who's your passenger?'

'He's an RAF pilot whose plane crashed after the big raid today. His uncle is René Cabellou and he needs help until he can be flown back to England.'

They crowded round, eager to shake Rupert's hand and congratulate him on the devastating raid on the Germans.

Pierre took control immediately, 'We'll escort you to the farm but we need to finish a little job here before we set off,' and the fuses were promptly lit. Ten minutes later on their way, a distant muffled explosion told them the tomb had been sealed.

At the van Houten house in Lincolnshire things were more relaxed following a long telephone call to Catherina from Squadron Leader Gordon Haig, in which he described Rupert bailing out and his safe landing on the shore of a large lake near Plonéour Lanvern. He went on to assure her of his safety.

'The Resistance is very strong in that area and I've no doubt your husband will be protected until we can arrange to pick him up and return him to England.'

Catherina remembered Rupert telling her about his uncles in Brittany and felt reassured he would come back to her safely. Meanwhile, in spite of her swelling abdomen, she insisted on helping on the farm and was quite happy driving the tractor which she had christened 'Eros', reasoning to her father, 'But for that tractor I may never have met my darling Rupert.'

Jan was amused and questioned the name, 'Why the Greek god Eros? Why not the Roman love god Cupid?'

'Papa, I prefer Eros as he's Greek and I like and admire the Greeks. Cupid is Roman and therefore Italian and I don't care for them as they're fat, two-faced and their leader is that awful man Mussolini!'

Her father was thoroughly amused: 'Well, so be it, Catherina, but you must be careful with your baby and be guided by the doctor. If she tells you to take things easier then you must take her advice and not take risks in the next week or two.'

'Very well, Papa, I'll see her this week and do as she wishes for my little one.'

Jan nodded his approval and returned to the question of farm workers, 'It's going to be difficult at harvest time without your help and organisation but Bep says she'll manage and hopefully we'll get a few students to give a hand. As you know I was offered some German prisoners of war from a prison camp near Peterborough but I declined. They are a detestable race and I want nothing to do with them.'

Catherina put her arms round her father and kissed him, 'Papa, don't give up hope for Mama. I pray for her every night and I'm sure we'll all be together again sooner than we realise.'

'You're right, my dear, I'll take heart and hope all will end well.'

'Papa, Bep told me yesterday she and Toby have decided to wait to get married until he can take over the veterinary practice as his boss will retire at the end of the year. They're also hoping the war will be over by then. So you see she will organise the harvest and I'm sure she'll do it very well.'

'I appreciate your comments as you know your sister extremely well and like you I'm confident we'll cope alright. But like Bep I long for the end of this dreadful conflict and pray it'll be soon.'

It was around two in the morning when Pierre Savin and the other partisans reached René Cabellou's farm, by which time Rupert was very tired. Entering the house by the rear door they were met by Pierre's wife Monique who took one look at Rupert and was forthright with her comments, 'This poor man is nearly exhausted and we must get him to bed without delay. Pierre, get your friends to help him upstairs while I make up a bed.' Smiling at Rupert she said, 'Sir, we're honoured to have you with us and will look after you while you're here.'

About ten minutes later Rupert sunk into a soft feather mattress and within seconds was oblivious to his 'supporters', Monique, Pierre and the three partisans standing in the bedroom. Monique drew a light blanket over the sleeping figure and they left the room.

They sat in the kitchen drinking hot coffee laced with cognac waiting for René's return and at three o'clock they heard the arrival of horses at the stables. Moments later René, accompanied by his niece and Dr Benedict Giscard entered and Monique bustled to get them hot drinks.

Pierre explained all that had taken place during the previous hours and how, by chance, they had met a RAF officer whose plane had crashed after the raid on the Germans, 'He is in bed asleep upstairs!'

René's eyebrows raised, 'Good Lord, asleep in my house,' and with a grin, 'I go out for a ride for a couple of hours and you find a lonely airman in a field, bring him home and put him to bed here!'

Monique was quick to respond, 'That's about it, but I put him to bed as he was exhausted, poor fellow. But I'll tell you this, he's a tall, good looking man with dark brown hair, not unlike yours,' he nodded in Mollie's direction, 'in fact, I think he's very handsome.'

They all had a good laugh before Dr Giscard and Mollie left for the Resistance headquarters escorted by the three partisans.

Chapter 48

In the crypt of the Abbey of Our Lady, Dr Geraud Sabatier operated for over four hours, often by the light of hurricane lamps during the many power cuts, removing bullets, stitching up torn tissue and in one case, setting a broken arm with two pieces of a wooden crate acting as splints. At half past seven in the morning he packed up his instruments and sat drinking hot strong coffee as he assessed the situation with Dominic.

'You'll have to watch for infection in some of the bullet wounds and in those cases the individuals should rest for a day or two; my remarks include you, although in your case the round had not penetrated the shoulder blade and was easier to remove. Oh, and one other important point, make sure all the material stained with blood is either burnt or buried, otherwise it'll attract flies and wasps and spread infection.'

Dominic was fully aware of the magnificent job Geraud had done and told him so, 'We are so very grateful for all you've done here and at a time we were desperate for medical help. What are your plans now?'

'I thought I'd stay for a few days as I've arranged for a locum friend to look after my practice at Quimper. Have you anywhere I can stay?'

Dominic realised the abbey crypt had little comfort to offer but remembered René Cabellou had offered help, 'Why don't you go over to the Cabellou farm and stay with René while you're here?'

As Geraud nodded approval, Dominic continued, 'Marie has to go to the farm this morning to get the name of the RAF pilot so we can inform London to arrange collection and I'm sure she'll be happy to show you the way. She'll be using her disguise as a nun, so don't be surprised when she appears.'

While they were talking Thérèse, the wireless operator, arrived with some startling news, 'I've just received an important bulletin from London stating the American army has broken out from the Cotentin Peninsular area and is advancing rapidly west and south west towards Brittany, and the British and Canadian armies are also advancing away from the Normandy bridgehead.'

She handed the radio report to Dominic who continued reading the rest of the massage, '"Every effort must be made to thwart the German forces moving to reinforce areas to the north of Brittany."'

Turning to Geraud, he showed him the message sheet, adding, 'This is the big issue we've been expecting. We have the men and the arms, ammunition and explosives and we know how to use them to the greatest effect. I'm sorry to tell you there will, no doubt, be more casualties.'

About an hour later, towards nine o'clock, Dr Geraud Sabatier, escorted by Marie, arrived at the Cabellou farm where René welcomed them. Smiling he told his niece, 'You look most attractive as a nun and as a lapsed Catholic you could charm me back to the church!' To Geraud he said, 'Monique, my housekeeper, will make a comfortable bed for you; meanwhile is there anything else you need?'

Geraud shook his head, 'No, just sleep thank you.'

As he departed with Monique, René asked his niece, 'Don't you want some rest? You look just about all in.'

'Yes, I'm tired but there are more important things to do before I can sleep. I need to know the identity of the airman who arrived here last night so we can contact London and get him airlifted back to England with the full moon next week.'

René realised the truth of what she'd said: 'I understand. Why not go upstairs and ask him?' Adding in a light-hearted way, 'Monique said he's good looking so mind you don't fall for him!'

She smiled, shrugged her shoulders and made for the stairs, pausing on the landing as memories of the happy times she'd had in the farmhouse in the thirties came flooding back. Knocking the door gently, she pushed the bedroom door open so she could just see the outline of the airman, as the curtains were still covering the windows.

He was still asleep, sprawled on the bed, but was disturbed as she moved to the window to draw the curtains. As he turned on his back she recognised her brother and let out a shriek of joy, 'Rupert! My darling Rupert! It's me, your sister!'

Startled by the light and sudden noise of a woman shouting his name, Rupert sat bolt upright. Modestly pulling the blanket up to his chin, as he had slept in his underwear, he gazed at the nun quite bewildered and enquired, 'Forgive me, sister, I had no idea you were coming into the bedroom. But how did you know my name?'

'Rupert, I'm your real sister not just a nun sister!' And pulling the wimple away from her face, Mollie revealed her dark hair and full features.

They were locked in a huge hug as René appeared at the bedroom door. 'What on earth is going on, Mollie? I know I said jokingly don't fall for a good-looking airman but you seem to be doing just that!'

Mollie turned with tears of joy running down her face, 'Uncle, he's not an ordinary airman but Rupert, my darling brother and your nephew!'

The great rejoicing gripped all three as they sat talking, hardly able to believe the situation wasn't a dream, until René suggested a celebratory drink.

Standing up and glancing through the window he suddenly froze at what he saw and spoke sharply to Rupert, 'Keep down and out of sight. Colonel Wolfgang von Braustich, the local German Area Commander has just arrived in his car. Mollie, come downstairs with me now, your presence will help if the going gets tough.'

In Britain the population followed the course of the war on the Continent with avid interest and most daily newspapers issued large wall maps free with their publications. The news in July was indeed heartening as the Allied armies broke away from the Normandy bridgehead and started to surge through France, finding the German resistance was spasmodic.

At breakfast at the Manor House, Margot was so enthralled she broke the house rule of no papers at the table, 'Darling, the US army is advancing rapidly south, south west and west, away from the Normandy landings. There doesn't seem any stopping the American tanks! Isn't it marvellous? Perhaps the war will be over by Christmas.'

Francis smiled at his wife, 'Maybe and maybe not, my sweet. The way ahead for our forces will be tough and a lot will depend on the weather; but how are the British doing?'

'They're advancing as well but not as quickly as the Yanks. Let's hope they capture the flying bomb sites soon to put a stop to those dreadful things and the V2s which are nothing more than terror weapons, killing innocent civilians.'

At that moment Bertie came into the room with a letter from America, which he handed to Margot, 'Madam, I put the rest of the mail on your desks but seeing the postmark was American, I thought you'd like this one now.'

Margot was delighted, 'Thank you, Bertie, that was most thoughtful of you.'

Slitting the envelope with a knife she started to read and moments later let out an excited whoop, 'Darling, you'll never believe it, Norman and Helen have finished their tour of duty in the States and are coming home in September! What absolutely wonderful news! Here, you see for yourself.'

Taking the letter, Francis read the good news and, like Margot, was delighted, 'I see he's posted to Headquarters, 2nd Tactical Air Force with promotion to Wing Commander for Operational Planning.

'I believe that means he'll not be flying again, thank God!'

'I agree, but how splendid to think we'll have Helen back with us as well, particularly as she's now fully recovered from the terrible time she went through. We must make plans for a homecoming get together for them as it's only about six weeks away. Darling, I can't begin to tell you how happy I feel and just long for the day when our loved ones are home for good.'

Francis walked round the table, put his arms round Margot and kissed her gently. They left the dining room with their arms round each other.

René and Mollie reached the ground floor of the farmhouse in time to open the front door in response to the Colonel's knock.

Mollie still in the nun's habit was introduced to the German officer as Marie, René's niece, and the three were soon seated. Marie noted the visitor was a tall man of about sixty years, with dark brown hair greying at the temples, strong features and penetrating brown eyes. He'd large hands on which the only adornment was his wedding ring. His military bearing and experience was evidenced by the campaign medals and the Iron Cross he wore.

He smiled as he spoke, 'Monsieur Cabellou, I trust I'm not intruding on a family situation? But I couldn't leave without saying a personal farewell. You see I've been recalled to Berlin and I wanted you to know how much I and some of my officers appreciated the friendly support you have given whilst we've been stationed here. The provision of riding facilities has been immensely beneficial for us and I haven't forgotten the timely provision of horse meat you made available for my troops when our rations were cut drastically.'

René murmured his appreciation at the German's remarks as the Colonel continued.

'My only regret has been the problems your people have suffered at the hands of the Gestapo, an organisation I personally find repugnant. Luckily they were eliminated by the RAF in a daring raid.'

Marie felt the German was basically a good soldier and probably not a Nazi but wanted to find out.

'Colonel, may I ask you a very pertinent question?' He smiled and nodded.

'Do you honestly think you will lose the war?'

He looked hard at Marie before answering, 'Sister, I realise you are dedicated to peace in your role as a nun and may not appreciate a soldier's point of view. I'm a professional military commander and I was trained to defend my country. Sadly, many officers like me were caught up in the Nazi web and only found out when it was too late. To be honest, I regret not leaving the army at the beginning.

He rose to leave, bowing as he shook hands with Marie and her uncle and moments later his car drew away from the house.

René turned immediately to his niece, 'Mollie, fetch Rupert down. I can't wait to tell him what has happened during the Colonel's visit. It's hard to believe what we're involved in, more like the stuff of fiction.'

It was almost midday when Marie returned to the Resistance headquarters, reporting to Dominic all that had transpired during Colonel Braustich's visit and the plan for his capture. She also told him her brother was the RAF airman at the Cabellou farm.

Dominic was elated to hear the Germans were leaving and promised to give them a farewell present in the form of a series of ambushes on the road from Pont l'Abbe and Benodet, the route they would take to Lorient.

'As far as Colonel Braustich and his fellow officer are concerned, after capture they'll be shut in the local prison until the Americans arrive.'

Marie went to see Thérèse to tell her all the news, particularly about Rupert so a pickup could be arranged with London. That completed, she lay on her bed exhausted and within minutes was fast asleep.

Just after four in the afternoon, Marie awoke to vigorous shaking from Thérèse who spoke sharply in a half whisper and with fear in her voice, 'Get up as fast as you can! The Germans have surrounded the abbey and we have to get out immediately.'

Marie was up in a flash and, pulling her clothes on, asked where they had to go.

'Dominic wants us to collect all our personal things in these large holdalls and he'll lead us out of the abbey. God knows how he's going to do it with all those Jerries out there; I'm really scared!'

Marie put her arm round her friend as she spoke, 'We mustn't panic. I admit it's scary but we'll get out I feel sure; here goes!' And with that she piled all the bits and pieces in to the holdall and as soon as they'd finished, joined Dominic who told them to follow him.

Opening a large oak door with a very old key he motioned the six of them through, locking the door when they had passed. Hurricane lamps illuminated the huge vaulted area with a low, arched ceiling, supported by pillars which rose from the stone floor like fat cigars. They could hear running water and the cold, damp atmosphere had a musty smell.

Speaking in low tones, Dominic explained, 'Here a small river, diverted in a conduit in the thirteenth century, passes under the abbey and in days gone by provided the only source of water for the nuns. We'll go down the steps to the river which runs away from here in a tunnel about five feet high. Leave all your things here except arms and ammunition and a few grenades and take off your shoes to wade through the water. It's about a quarter of a mile to the exit which is in the wooded area on the higher ground to the west. We must keep very quiet and only talk if absolutely necessary.'

Moments later the little group stepped into the icy water, which luckily was only shin high due to the prolonged drought. With bent backs they started their long trek along the ancient brick-built tunnel; a tiny speck of light was the distant exit gave hope for escape and freedom.

Chapter 49

The six escapees emerging from the river conduit sat drying and warming their feet in the afternoon sun, after which Dominic and Marie went a short distance to higher ground at the edge of the woods where they had a clear view of the abbey. Passing the field glasses to Marie he observed, 'The blighters are still around the place with a tank and two armoured vehicles; no doubt searching every nook and cranny.'

She agreed and swinging round to the large area of heathland stretching away to the north and east towards Quimper, was puzzled by the large clouds of dust and smoke rising in the sunlight.

'There's something very odd going on over there Dominic; here have a look.'

Using the field glasses he studied the area and moments later, grinning broadly, almost shouted, 'They're tanks, masses of tanks and what's so good about them is that they're American Sherman tanks!'

Absolutely bubbling with excitement he put his arms round Marie and whirled her round, shouting at the top of his voice, 'They're here! Thank God, the Yanks have come at last!'

Hearing the shouting the others came running up to Dominic and were soon looking at the wonderful scene of massed columns of American armour bearing down on Plonéour Lanvern.

They stood, the men and women smiling with relief, shedding tears of joy as they watched the liberators getting ever nearer.

The Germans garrisoned in the old college buildings had prepared defences in depth and already anti-tank guns were firing towards the Americans, who returned fire. For half an hour the shelling went on with Dominic and his group having a grandstand view until suddenly the Sherman tanks stopped and withdrew a short distance.

From the north east came the ominous roar of approaching aircraft and squadrons of medium bombers flew over. The noise of the explosions was deafening as stick after stick of bombs blasted the German positions, leaving the whole area devastated and the college building, the German Headquarters, a blazing wreck.

The American tanks were on the move again as Dominic explained, 'That was an example of the area bombing technique which obliterates practically everything. I see the remnants of the German forces are flying white flags of surrender! Can you blame them?'

In high spirits the group made their way back to the abbey, watching with satisfaction as the Germans, very much a spent force, marched with white flags towards the town square.

In Lincolnshire at the van Houten house Catherina, now in the final stages of her pregnancy, was resting having spent the morning driving her tractor Eros unearthing early potatoes for the pickers, mostly local women, to collect into half hundredweight sacks.

She looked well with a considerable bulge, indicating the child she was expecting would be no lightweight!

After a snack lunch with her father Jan and her sister Bep she decided to rest and it was then she became very tearful about Rupert, 'Why doesn't he come back to me? I need him so very much and I've prayed for his safe return but my prayers have not been answered.'

Her sister comforted, 'Catherina, Rupert will come back, I have no doubt, and from all the news we are getting about the Americans going rapidly into France, he'll probably be flown home by them. Why don't you write him a letter to await his arrival? I'm sure he'd love to have a few lines to greet him when he arrives in England.'

Catherina cheered up a little, 'Bep, you're a wonderful sister and what you've said has a calming effect on me. Yes, I'll write to my darling now and I'll also send him a little poem to say how much I love him!' Without further ado she set about writing to her loved one.

Van Houten Farm,
Sutton Bridge,
Lincolnshire,
28th July 1944

My darling Rupert,

It seems so long since we were together and I miss you more and more each day! I hope you are well and will soon be back in England so I can tell you how much I love you still. Our little one has grown and I'm quite fat but our doctor is happy everything is going on satisfactorily and our baby should arrive in the next week or so. I've been driving Eros, my terribly old tractor, helping with the harvest but I think I'll have to take things a lot easier until our baby is born. So hurry home as fast as you can! I've written you a little poem I hope you'll enjoy so you can think of me every time you read it!

If only I had known you all those many years ago,
I would have held you in my arms and never let you go.
And whispered sweetly in your ear the things you want to
*   hear*
About the way I feel for you, because I love you dear.
The way you speak, the way you smile, just thrill me through
*   and through,*
So take me in your arms again and say you love me true.
And then we'll tell the world at large about our love affair
Life full of golden happiness and romance we both share.

It may be only a short while to the arrival of our little one so we must think of some names for either a boy or a girl. I'll start today and you must promise you'll do the same when you get this letter.

Papa, Bep and Johan have all been marvellous during the past months and I've been so lucky having such a wonderful family around me.

I had a lovely long letter from your mother telling me all the news from Exeter but she's worried about you and your sister

Mollie. I wrote back, comforting her by saying no news is so often good news and I hope it helped.

I'm going to take a little rest now so I'll send you love from Papa, Bep and me.

Come home to me soon my dearest Rupert,
With all my love with lots of kisses,
  Catherina

Catherina called Johan and handed him the letter, asking him to send it off as soon as possible. 'Please post this to my dear husband as quickly as you can, Johan.'

His reply, with a smile, was typical, 'Of course, madam, I'll get on my bicycle and take it to the post office at Sutton Bridge to catch the afternoon post.'

Catherina patted his arm and thanked the old man, 'That was a very sweet suggestion and I appreciate it very much Johan.'

By the late afternoon the American tanks had entered Plonéour Lanvern, followed shortly after by truckloads of their infantry, who quickly rounded up the German forces and placed them under armed guards, making preparations to move them in empty trucks to a large prisoner of war compound at Quimper. In a large marquee erected in the local park they also tended the many wounded, both French and German, as the local hospital had very little in the way of medicines and drugs.

Back at the abbey, Dominic and the others very soon discovered the Germans had emptied the contents of all the holdalls onto the floor and had filched anything worth stealing. They had also taken the wireless receiver and transmitter, leaving the partisans without means for communication with London. After a discussion, Dominic decided to go to the American army which had set up a temporary headquarters in the town hall.

As he set off with Marie and Thérèse they became aware of crowds of happy people swarming along the streets, all talking excitedly and gesticulating as they made their way to the town square, where a great crowd was already welcoming the

Americans. The liberators were standing in groups handing out candy and chewing gum for the children and cigarettes for the adults, and, typically, the GIs had their arms around and were kissing as many of the pretty girls as they could!

Pushing a way through the throng the three went to the town hall where they were met by several military policemen who barred entry to all civilians. Dominic explained to the guard, 'My two colleagues and I are members of the Special Operation Executive and must speak with your commander regarding the Resistance organisation.'

The policeman looked puzzled, 'I'm sorry, sir, I don't know your organisation but I'll see what can be arranged. Just wait here a moment.'

Minutes later they were escorted into the building and shown into a large room in which technicians were setting up telephone and radio equipment. A huge man greeted them, 'Good to meet you. I'm Colonel Stefan Grunweiser, how can I help?

Dominic made formal introductions and explained their mission was completed now the area had been liberated, 'May we ask you to facilitate our speedy return to England.'

The Colonel nodded, 'Okay, I'll see what can be arranged but I need proof of identity; do you have passports or something similar confirming your nationality?'

Dominic again explained they had only false French identity documents for obvious reasons while they operated with the Resistance movement.

Shaking his head the Colonel put the position quite plainly, 'Gee, I'm sorry I can't help without proof you're with the, whatever it's called, English operation, for the simple reason we're forbidden to carry civilians in our aircraft, unless specifically authorised by the Supreme Headquarters. If I send you forward to the airbase at Quimper, they wouldn't take you without the necessary documents. I really regret I can't help you at the moment.' With that they shook hands and walked back through the crowds to the abbey, feeling trapped and dejected.

Sitting together, trying to work out a solution to the problem,

Marie suddenly made clear her thoughts.

'First of all, I'm not using my cover name any more but reverting to Mollie from now on. Second, I'm going over to my uncle's farm to see my brother, Rupert. He may be able to help us.'

Dominic was impressed, 'What a brilliant idea Mollie! Why ever didn't we think of him before? Rupert is a serving officer and the Yanks will have no difficulty flying him home. He can contact SOE headquarters and ask them to get us back to England.'

Thérèse suggested they all go together adding, 'Like Mollie ,I'm dropping the French name from this very moment,' and to Dominic, 'As I'm back to being Antonia, what'll we going to call you?'

He smiled, 'You already know I'm Major Leon de Marne with de Gaulle's Free French Forces but also known as Dominic for SOE purposes over in France; so now you have it officially!' They had a good laugh before he went on, 'I want to see some of the Resistance people to decide about the stores of arms, ammunition and explosives, so they may be made secure and handed into the control of the Americans. So I suggest you two go on to René's farm and I'll join you later on when I've finished here.'

Within the hour Mollie and Antonia had reached the Cabellou farm and with René and Rupert they celebrated the arrival of the Americans with some champagne. Having listened to the account of the meeting with Colonel Grunweiser, Rupert promised to see the American Commander to get a flight back to England: 'Mollie, I'll pull all the stops out to see something is done to get you and Antonia home again; just leave it to me.'

Almost at once, Leon de Marne arrived looking exceedingly worried as he told them the latest news concerning the Resistance movement: 'A short time ago several partisans from the Quimper area arrived, saying the Communists in the organisation had started seizing stocks of armaments intending to use them to take power by force as soon as the Americans moved on into France. Apparently several local government officials in the Quimper area have already been shot and I was warned, as a Free French Officer, a de Gaulle supporter and former commander of the

Resistance, I'm in some danger. For all I know, you Mollie and Antonia may also be vulnerable. Our stocks of ordnance are safe for the moment as only a very few partisans know the location of the stores.'

To say the news put a dampener on the celebrations was an understatement and all looked very concerned until Rupert made a suggestion.

'I reckon all of you should go into hiding for your own safety until I get a rescue operation sorted out. I know the very place and the people who will, I'm sure, be only too happy to help. They are Monsieur Georges and Madame Claudette Dassault who live at the reservoir dam on the outskirts of the town; he's the engineer and both he and his wife speak good English.'

René offered help, 'It's too far to walk so I'll get Pierre to harness up a small cart.'

They agreed and Leon suggested delaying the departure until after dark, 'It'll be safer if we leave unobserved. While you're waiting, I'll slip back to the abbey to say goodbye to my sister Celeste, the abbess, as it may be some time before I see her again.'

After a further discussion, he left promising to be with them again by the time it was dusk.

Back in the town square the mood of celebration continued and many locals produced hidden bottles of wine to share with the American troops who were later seen bivouacking in the park and playing fields for the night, although some lucky ones found a welcoming bed with the comforts that went with it!

At RAF Farndene, the ceaseless activity continued, supporting the allied armies as they pushed rapidly into France. Francis and Margot continued to entertain groups of pilots in the evenings to give them a little time for relaxation in the comfort of the Manor House. Most noticeable was the upbeat attitude of the airmen, who were convinced the war was in the last phase and Germany would be completely defeated, hopefully within months. Many spoke of the massive losses suffered by the German armour, in particular the trap sprung at Falaise, where hundreds of tanks, armoured vehicles, field guns and lorries were destroyed, not to mention the horrendous loss of their troops.

Squadron Leader Gordon Haig was among the guests one evening and Francis asked him, 'Do you have any further news about Rupert?'

'We know he's safe and well through the SOE Headquarters and, as the Americans are pushing quite rapidly into Brittany, it's possible the area has been liberated as we talk. I'll let you know if we get any update on his situation.'

Margot thanked him, adding, 'It must be very worrying for his wife, particularly as she is expecting their first child very soon. At least he'll be coming back, unlike the thousands who either know they are widowed or their loved one is on the missing list. When this war is over we must do all we can to prevent a recurrence and deal with the defeated Germany with common sense and magnanimity and not repeat the stupid mistakes made after the Great War.'

Margot smiled as those present at the table called, 'Hear! Hear!' and clapped their hands in approval. Gordon Haig congratulated her, 'What you said makes eminent sense and I believe we need more women like you in Parliament.'

At René's farm the three waited until well after dark but Leon failed to return which made them concerned, particularly Antonia who became very upset.

Mollie tried to calm her but her friend was clearly extremely worried, 'I'm sure he'll come back shortly, Antonia; he's probably decided to stay with his sister a bit longer.'

It was after eleven o'clock when René suggested they made a start, going round by the abbey to see if Leon was still with his sister and they all agreed. The small trap-style cart set off at a trot and on reaching the abbey thet were told by the abbess that her brother had left: 'Leon went about an hour ago and said he'd take a short cut by the river to save time.'

Turning back to the town they reached the police headquarters where the gendarme on duty said there had been a disturbance by the river involving some American soldiers and the injured had been taken to the American field hospital in the local park.

By this time Antonia was in a very distressed condition, so much so that Mollie asked her why and was surprised with the answer she received.

'Mollie, I would have told you sooner or later but felt the present wasn't the right time. You see Leon and I fell in love not long after we arrived in France. So you'll understand how worried I am about him!'

Mollie put her arms round her friend, 'Well, I can understand what has happened and I'm so pleased for you. We'll go straight to the park to see if we can find Leon.'

Chapter 50

On Friday 21st July, Catherina's labour pains started and shortly after her father had telephoned, the doctor arrived with a midwife and nurse. After an examination the doctor concluded the birth was imminent and preparations were made accordingly.

Two hours passed before she gave birth to a boy of eight pounds. Within the hour Jan and Bep were able to see Catherina, sitting up in bed with her baby. Jan was quite overcome as he kissed his daughter, 'My darling Catherina you look so very beautiful with your lovely son and I'm very proud of you,' and then a little wistfully, 'Your mother will be so pleased and I hope it won't be too long before we see her again.'

Bep was also delighted and sat holding her sister's hand and smiling at the wonderful result of so many months' waiting. They all enjoyed the happy family feeling the little one had brought with him, and when Johan arrived with a large bunch of roses he'd picked in the garden, Catherina was delighted.

'Johan, you're so kind to take all that trouble and I'll so enjoy the perfume in my room.'

He left with Jan shortly after, saying he had many things to attend to and Bep stayed talking to her sister, 'I hope to be married just as soon as the war finishes, Catherina, and, like you, I'll want a family.'

'I hope what you say happens soon, Bep, most of all, the end of this terrible war and the sadness it has brought to so many. I long to be with Mama, to spend time with her to make up for all these lost years and help Papa and her find happiness again. But now I just want my darling Rupert to come home to me and his little son.'

Bep leaned over to wipe tears from her sister's eyes, 'He'll be here soon. I have a feeling it'll be a wonderful surprise for all of us.'

After making enquiries, Rupert, Mollie and Antonia traced Leon to the American Field Hospital and were shocked to find him quite badly injured, suffering from broken ribs, a broken arm and bruises and cuts to various parts of his body. The Military Police explained, 'It seems three of our guys took some dames for a stroll by the river, where they got involved with four Frenchmen who were beating up your buddy. He wasn't a pushover and had already downed two of his attackers when he got hit on his arm with an iron bar. Our guys went to the rescue and as two were armed with pistols, brought in the four attackers. We reckon they're Commies so we handed them over to the gendarmes who banged them up in the cells.'

The doctor in attendance confirmed the injuries but added, 'I suspect he may have a fractured skull and, as we have no X-ray equipment here, I propose sending him to our base hospital in Quimper. SHAEF [Supreme Headquarters Allied Expeditionary Force] confirmed he's a serving officer with the Free French Amy and we'll do all we can to get him back to health.'

Although heavily bandaged and in some pain, there was a touching reunion with Antonia, and Leon was able to reassure her he'd be up and about again once his arm had healed.

As it was so late, Mollie suggested they return to Uncle René's farm for the night and go to Monsieur Dassault the next day. Rupert agreed and said he'd get a flight to England once he saw them in safety at the reservoir.

All went well in the morning and by midday Rupert had been transported to the American air base at Quimper, and from there to RAF Lyneham, Wiltshire, by Dakota, arriving during the afternoon. After a long debriefing, during which he emphasised the plight of the SOE members stranded in Plonéour Lanvern, he was assured immediate action would be taken to ensure their safety.

Back at RAF Farndene, he was given a royal welcome and the Commanding Officer told him to go home for a couple of weeks to recover. Among the correspondence awaiting his return was Catherina's letter which brought a smile to his face as he read the little poem she had written.

He telephoned the van Houten house and Catherina was almost speechless with excitement hearing his voice, 'My dearest Rupert, I've missed you so, so much and I love you more than ever,' before he could reply she continued, 'and my darling I have the most wonderful news for you; you are daddy to a beautiful boy, so come home as quickly as you can to your family.'

Rupert was delighted and promised he would be with Catherina that night. He also telephoned Janine and Philip in Exeter telling them that they were grandparents and that Mollie was safe in Plonéour Lanvern and hoped to be home very soon. 'I'll try to come down to see you if I possibly can during my leave and, oh, I nearly forgot, can you tell Antonia's parents she's okay as I haven't her telephone number or address.'

At the Plonéour Lanvern dam, Georges and Claudette Dassault made Mollie and Antonia most welcome and enjoyed their company. However, Antonia became restless with worry about Leon de Marne, 'I can't find out how he's getting on and when he'll be fit enough to go back to England.'

Georges came to her rescue, 'If you write a note to him I'm sure I can get it delivered. You see, my engineer from Quimper, Geraud Sabatier, is coming here tomorrow to help me with the pumps and he'll go to visit your friend and then let you know his current condition.'

Later, after they had gone to bed, Mollie asked her friend a very pertinent question, 'Antonia, are you sure you've fallen in love with Leon?'

Her reply was unequivocal, 'I've never been so certain of anything before. We became lovers about two weeks after we landed in France.'

Mollie had more or less understood that was the case and her second question was to the point, 'What do you know about him? Is he single or married? And if the latter, had he been living with his wife before he joined the SOE?'

Antonia was taken aback and didn't answer for a few moments, her face registering her anxiety.

'Mollie, I don't know! I admit I didn't give it a thought but now you've asked me, I'm worried in case he's married.' She started to cry so Mollie put her arms round her friend and spoke comfortingly, 'Now calm yourself, Antonia, we can find out tomorrow.'

'Mollie, it's not as simple as that,. You see, I think I'm pregnant! In fact I've thought so these past two months. So you will understand my worry.'

'That puts a very different complexion on your situation and it's vital you find the answer without delay.' Mollie sat back turning the problem over in her mind and then suddenly she hit on the solution, 'Antonia, why didn't I think of it before? Our contact must be with Leon's sister Celeste, the abbess. I'm sure she'll have been in touch with the American hospital, so we must telephone the abbey first thing tomorrow morning.'

Antonia hugged her friend and said how relieved she felt at Mollie's suggestion. They turned the light out and both were sound asleep in a few minutes.

Rupert's homecoming turned into a whirlwind of excitement as soon as he entered the house at half past eleven that night. Although it was late, Jan, Catherina and Bep waited in the drawing room and as soon as Rupert entered the two women rushed to hug and kiss him, completely overwhelming him for the minute. With his arms round both he moved across to greet Jan and then suggested they all sit down. Catherina couldn't contain herself any longer, 'My dearest, I've waited so long for you to come but now you're here I can tell you I love you as much as ever,' and still smiling, 'and so does your little son who you shall see very shortly when I give him his next feed.'

Johan brought hot chocolate with some homemade biscuits and they sat talking until nearly one o'clock when Catherina said she had to feed her little one; with that signal they said goodnight.

Rupert sat with his wife as she fed the baby, coming to terms with fatherhood and loving every minute of it!

The following morning, Mollie asked Georges and Claudette if Antonia could telephone the abbey. After a long conversation with Celeste, Antonia told them the good news, 'It seems the Americans found no fracture in Leon's skull and, at his sister's request, took him to the abbey where he'll be cared for. She wants us to go to see him when we can.'

Given a lift by Geraud Sabatier, Mollie and Antonia arrived at the abbey just before midday and were welcomed by Celeste who took them directly to a quiet room overlooking the fields where Leon sat in an easy chair with his feet up.

'Hello, you two stalwarts!' Leon smiled as he greeted them, 'You must excuse my not rising to greet you but Celeste said strictly I was to rest,' and with a wink at his sister, 'I always do what she tells me.'

On the pretext of a chat, Celeste and Mollie discreetly left Leon alone with Antonia and, once in Celeste's room, she explained in detail.

'Mollie, I'm glad I have an opportunity to speak with you about my brother and Antonia; you are very close to both of them and I'd value your opinion. But first let me explain the situation in detail.

'Leon has told me he is very much in love with Antonia and hopes she feels for him in the same way as he wants to marry her. It worries him is not knowing if she's single and if there is someone else.'

Mollie half expected what she heard and in turn asked Celeste, 'Before answering, let me ask the same questions; is Leon single and has he anyone else who could be a barrier to a marriage?

The answer was unexpected but promising, 'Leon is not single but has an ex-wife; he was divorced in 1938 after ten years of marriage. I won't go into the details other than to say she was unfaithful, leaving him with two small children when she absconded with a French naval officer. The children are in the care of my younger sister Jacqueline and her husband Henri de Beaune who live in the Lot valley near Cahors. When the war is over my brother will go back to his estate there which is extensive and includes mature vineyards. That's about all I can tell you about Leon; so what about Antonia?'

Mollie smiled as she answered, 'I can tell you she is very much in love with your brother, she is single and to the best of my knowledge, has no other beau who might be a problem. The prospect of marrying Leon and taking on his two children is considerable, but it's up to her to make the decision.

'She's a caring person with a lovely nature, so bringing up the two children would be second nature to her. As a matter of interest, how old are they?'

'Rosalie the eldest is thirteen and her brother Philippe two years younger. I haven't seen them for over three years but they write to me fairly regularly.'

Going back to join Angelina and Leon they found them sitting on a sofa with their arms round each other, looking very pleased with themselves.

Leon looked so happy as he told them, 'Antonia has agreed to marry me and take on my two children.' He stood and crossed the room to Celeste. Putting his uninjured arm round her and kissing her, 'So you see my dearest sister, at long last I've found happiness again!'

Celeste told Antonia how delighted she was to welcome her into the family and a long discussion ensued during which Antonia said she wished to be married back home in England as soon as possible. In the meantime, Mollie and Antonia were invited to stay at the abbey to help look after Leon, pending their return to Britain.

The weeks passed with no word from the SOE Headquarters in London and although Leon's arm was healing, he still suffered considerable pain from his injuries. Then finally, on Monday 28th August, a warm and clear day, an American major arrived at the abbey in a jeep and informed Leon, Mollie and Antonia he had received a signal from SHAEF, stating an RAF plane would be arriving the next day at Quimper, to transport them back to England.

'I'll send a jeep to collect you early that morning and the driver will take you to the air base in good time.'

All three assured the major they'd be ready and thanked him for his help.

The following day all three breakfasted early and a little later Celeste came to say goodbye. She was a little tearful and admitted, 'I've been so happy helping you all during your days of waiting, being able to spend time with my dear brother and with you, Antonia, who will soon be my sister-in-law.' To Mollie she said, 'My talks with you have been so rewarding, listening to your life story which, in turn, gave me a view of the outside world we in the abbey are insulated from. I shall miss you all but will pray for the Almighty's blessing on you.'

And so they left, driving through the town and countryside in which, so recently, they'd fought the enemy but now thankfully was returning to a peaceful normality. They had come to France with very little beyond the clothes they stood up in and now they were departing with little else but what they wore and some incredible events and people etched in their memory. And for Mollie, an emotional farewell with Uncle René the previous night.

The base was very busy with aircraft coming and going but at midday their attention was captured by the arrival of a massive RAF Halifax bomber which they realised was their 'rescue mission'.

They were welcomed aboard by the crew, who made them as comfortable as was possible for their flight to the SOE base at RAF Tempsford in Bedfordshire.

Mollie suddenly felt the excitement gripping her as she contemplated going home to her mother and Philip and seeing Sam again after so long.

'I'm really thrilled I'll see my family in a few hours' time. What about you Antonia?'

'Like you, Mollie, I just can't wait to see mother and father again,' and then she paused for a moment, 'But I'm a bit apprehensive as I'll be taking Leon with me; I do so hope they like him! What will I do if they don't?'

Mollie reassured her friend, 'They'll like him alright, have no fear,' and in her friend's ear, 'He's a dear man and I'm so very happy for you, so buck up with the wedding in case someone else steals him under your nose!'

Further conversation became very difficult against the roar of the four engines and they were glad to snuggle down to sleep in the quilted sleeping bags provided, as it got much colder at high altitude.

By the beginning of September the Allied armies had pushed deep into France and Belgium, liberating vast tracts of both countries and the capitals Paris and Brussels. In the west the Germans were holding out in pockets at Brest, Lorient and St Nazaire, so the Americans merely contained and blockaded the three ports with a view to starving the enemy out.

In Plonéour Lanvern, Celeste had a wonderful reunion when her sister Jacqueline came to stay at the abbey with Rosalie and Philippe. Jacqueline was delighted to learn Leon would be remarrying and the two children were eager to hear all about Antonia. They talked endlessly with a feeling of complete freedom, realising the terrible yoke of the Nazis had been removed completely.

Celeste told her sister, 'Antonia came with a friend, Mollie, a simply wonderful person who is the niece of René Cabellou a local horse breeder and farmer. She and Antonia volunteered to come to France with the SOE to organise and fight with the Resistance and their dedication was an inspiration. We must never forget these very brave English women who did so much to rid France of the Germans.'

Aboard a new Liberator bomber flying from America across the north Atlantic, Norman and Helen Vining were enjoying their homeward trip on 15th September, a beautifully clear morning. To give the second pilot a break, Norman took over the controls for a spell and enjoyed being back in the 'hot seat' again. The crew had made special provision for a light meal for their passengers and Helen was at her best in conversation with them all as they dined. By special arrangement the bomber was diverted to RAF Farndene and touched down at two o'clock in the afternoon.

A rapturous welcome awaited Norman and Helen as they entered the Manor House and Margot just hung on to both; with tears of joy she kissed and hugged her son and daughter-in-law several times.

'My darlings we've waited so long for this moment and now at last you're here, safely home, thank God!'

While Bertie brought in the cases, Francis and Margot took them into the drawing room and, once seated, Francis said, 'I've so many things I wanted to tell you two and now you're here I just don't know where to start!' There were smiles all round as he scratched his head, 'Well, it'll come later but first of all we've missed you very much and hope partings will be short ones from now on.'

Helen told them she had completely recovered and she and Norman promised to tell the whole saga of the torpedoed liner.

Margot suggested they wait until dinner that evening, 'Bruce is hoping to get home tonight with Dorcas, so we can all hear the story then. Grandma Fanny is coming back from a visit to Bristol tomorrow and with luck Juliet and Freddie will be here for the weekend.'

'What about the girls, mother?'

'Oh, Clara said she will try her best to get here but Constance may have difficulty as she's still very busy at the Ordnance Survey; we'll just keep our fingers crossed.'

Norman left the room for a moment, returning with a case which he opened on the tabletop, saying with a grin, 'These we specially brought back for all the ladies in the family.' And he held up a large handful of nylons and silk stockings. We brought all sizes to fit the long, the short and the tall!'

Margot's reaction was natural, 'That's wonderful and it takes me back to the night before you left for America when you promised to get us all stockings. Thank you both very much for being so clever and remembering.'

During the next two days Norman and Helen settled in and relaxed, enjoying being back in England. An early decision they both made was to go to St Paul's where they sat quietly together, assimilating the atmosphere of the ancient building, thankful they had survived a terrible ordeal and were now back with their family.

Helen kissed Norman as she spoke, 'We've been through a desperately difficult time but now it's behind us. In all the upheaval I prayed for us and I'm sure God heard my plea. Norman, I love you more than I ever imagined I could and I'm so happy to be a small portion of the Vining heritage of which this church is so vital a part.' Putting his arms round Helen, he kissed her, 'My dearest, all you've said I feel as well and my love for you is as great as ever. I'm a most fortunate man having someone as adorable as you!'

They kissed again just as Canon Horatio Hulbert entered the church. Seeing the couple hugging, he called out, 'You can pray in here for nothing but for embracing I charge a penny a kiss!'

With a broad smile he came down the aisle to greet them, 'Helen, Norman, it's just wonderful to see you both back safely and looking so fit.' They shook hands as they exchanged greetings, after which he invited them to the rectory, 'Do come in to meet Dorothy and we can all have a drink to celebrate your return.' As they left the church, Helen, with a giggle, dropped six pennies into the collection box, 'Those are for the kisses you saw! I haven't enough change with me for the others we had before you came in, so can we have the others "on the slate" until we meet again?'

The family gathered for the weekend and Margot thoughtfully included Helen's parents, Sir Charles and Lady Violet Dauntsey, who were invited for a few days.

Alex and Angelina came from Bristol and they were joined

by Bruno on leave, having returned from France to join Military Intelligence; his knowledge of German would be valuable for interrogating prisoners to weed out the Nazis and SS men.

At dinner on Saturday night, he had the whole family in kinks as he related his experience aboard the destroyer HMS *Foxhound* when he was taken for a deserter from the German army trying to get out of the war, 'I was so overwhelmed I forgot to take off my underpants, the only thing I was wearing, to show them the label "Gunnels, men's outfitters, Bristol,' to prove I was who I was! I was jolly lucky the Navy didn't make me walk the plank!'

Talking to her mother, Helen was eager for news of her brother Cuthbert and was told, 'He's in the Parachute Regiment and although the training is hard he finds it rewarding. He's on the staff of the Brigadier and when he was home last he said they were all itching to get into action, hopefully soon.' Lady Violet was thoughtful for a moment or so, 'But Helen, I do worry for him and hope and pray they don't have to drop into Germany.'

Helen reassured her mother, 'He'll be alright, Mother, you know our Cuthbert, the boy with a charmed life! If he fell down a sewer he'd come up covered in violets!'

As they laughed, Bruno joined the conversation and in an effort to put Lady Violet's mind at rest gave her a picture of the Allies' advance towards the Rhine, 'Our group entered Brussels on 3rd September and the advanced units crossed the Albert Canal a few days later. The German resistance was minimal and among the troops captured were many elderly men glad to be out of the war. Also there were boys about sixteen years old who had been drafted in from the Hitler Youth movement and many looked very scared indeed. My hunch is that as soon as we have a big enough force at the Rhine we'll go straight into Germany and it'll be the end within weeks.'

He went on to describe the scenes as Brussels was liberated, 'The population went wild with excitement and parties went on for hours celebrating. On the down side, the Resistance took the law into their own hands, rounding up collaborators who were usually hung from the lamp posts in side streets, while the women had their heads shaved and were paraded through the city, to be jeered at and spat upon; rough justice, but not a pretty sight.'

Lady Violet's reaction was natural, 'It sounds awful and uncivilised! Surely the culprits should have been handed over to the courts for a fair trial.'

'That's true in a normal situation, Lady Violet, but we mustn't overlook the fact that those people had been occupied by a barbarous regime for four years and had suffered greatly, often as a result of betrayal by their own kinsmen. Quite rightly, the betrayers were regarded as traitors and the partisans doled out the only punishment fit for those guilty of treason – the noose.'

Chapter 51

With the autumn of 1944 came a continued mood of optimism among the British public, many of whom hoped desperately the war would be over by Christmas. The advances by the Allied armies and those of Soviet Russia were acting like giant nutcrackers with Germany being squeezed and crushed week by week. By mid-September the British and Americans had swept most of France and Belgium clear of the enemy and on 17th a massive operation, codenamed 'Market Garden', involving the Allied airborne forces, drove north into Holland taking most of the objectives but failing to capture the bridge at Arnhem, where the British Paratroopers fought a gallant battle but eventually had to withdraw with heavy losses.

However, the softening-up process of the Third Reich, continued by air where the Allied superiority was thirty to one over the Luftwaffe, and the ever increasing precision bombing on key targets – ordnance factories and communication centres – was having a crippling effect and reducing Germany's power of resistance.

In December the continental weather became extremely cold with prolonged snow and ice, and in these conditions the Germans staged their last counter-attack. On the 16th of that month they swept through the Ardennes in a campaign, later known as the 'Battle of the Bulge', catching the Americans unawares. They were unable to stem the German advance and the enemy made some progress until blocked by Allied armour brought in from the north. The attack came to an end.

Again, with massive air coverage on both sides of the Atlantic the U-boats were hunted ruthlessly and with precision. All forces being aided as the Kriegsmarine Enigma code had been broken, giving the Allies vital information about German submarine plans of attack in advance; the Battle of the Atlantic was all but won.

Christmas saw many happy reunions, none more wonderful than the family gathering in Exeter as Janine and Philip welcomed Mollie home, now released from the SOE as her task was complete.

For her outstanding performance in France she was awarded the OBE (Military Division); the investiture to be in the New Year and her mother and step-father were delighted with the prospect of accompanying Mollie to Buckingham Palace.

Janine told her daughter, 'Tom and his fiancée Hazel are coming home on Christmas Eve, staying until 2nd January in the New Year, so we can enjoy being together as there is so much to talk about and many decisions to make.'

'What's going to happen at Madame Baume's now the war's nearly over?' Mollie was aware the last contract from the War Office was nearly finished.

'That's one of the things we need to discuss; a decision will have to be made about the staff as some may have to be paid off,' Janine appeared unhappy and added, 'Dismissing people who have worked so well is the part of running a business I dislike.'

'I understand, Mother, but bear in mind many are quite elderly and will probably be glad to retire in any case.' Mollie's reasoning cheered her mother, 'We can be generous with the final payment and I suggest we give everyone a bonus to mark their contribution to the war effort.'

'A splendid idea, Mollie, and I'm sure we can afford such a gesture.' Knowing the business had turned over a good profit during the past two years, Philip expressed his support wholeheartedly.

Janine nodded her approval and went on to the burning subject of her grandchildren, 'As soon as Christmas and the New Year are out of the way, we must go up to see Catherina and her little boy, Charlie.'

It was agreed they all go as suggested and after a visit to their local jeweller and silversmith in Exeter, they bought presents for the little one.

On a frosty day at the beginning of January, Janine, Philip and

Mollie arrived at the van Houten house to a wonderful welcome from Jan, Catherina and Bep, not to mention Johan who insisted on carrying all their luggage up to the bedrooms, saying, 'It's my pleasure to help and it'll give you more time with the family.'

Naturally, Janine and Mollie were delighted to see the little boy and both had tears in their eyes as they held him for the first time. Janine declared, 'Catherina you're a lovely mother and you have brought me great joy by making me a grandmother!'

The situation at Framley Park was subdued as Sir Charles and Lady Violet had been informed in late October their son Cuthbert was missing, having dropped with the airborne troops at Arnhem. They and their daughter Helen hoped he'd been captured but as the weeks went by without any notification through the International Red Cross organisation, hopes began to fade and now, early in the New Year, they were resigned to the fact he'd probably been killed.

Christmas and the New Year celebrations at the Manor House, Farndene were quiet as only Clara and her sister Constance were home to join Grandma Fanny and their parents. Unexpectedly, Juliet turned up with Freddie Washbrook to see in 1945 and, with three New Zealand pilots, all went well.

The beginning of 1945 brought an unexpected turn of events on the continent.

The Luftwaffe, perhaps assuming the Allied air force personnel had celebrated the arrival of the New Year and were probably unfit for flying on 1st January, mounted a concerted strike on all the British and American airfields with every possible aircraft they could scrape together, including many from training squadrons. They timed their early morning attack to strike after the Allied dawn patrols had left, but unfortunately for the Germans the weather was not on their side. An exceptionally hard frost had gripped the airfields with the consequence that dawn patrols were delayed until de-icing had been completed. Most were airborne just in time to meet the oncoming enemy aircraft.

Very few of the Germans got through and the remainder suffered horrendous losses of pilots and aircraft. It was referred to jokingly as the Luftwaffe's last fling and there was a great deal of truth in that jest. Hermann Göring's pride and joy had finally been decimated, leaving the skies open for the Allied planes from then on.

Early springtime in Farndene with masses of wild snowdrops, daffodils and aconites in the surrounding woods and forest presented a spectacle many of the Impressionist artists would have been delighted to copy.

In this array of beauty Fanny, walking the dogs with Margot and Francis, spoke of her happiness since moving back to the Manor House: 'I have to thank you two for suggesting my return to Farndene and for putting up with me since.'

Margot was quick to respond, 'Come, come, Mama, we've enjoyed your being with us and particularly being able to see the grandchildren a lot more often than you would have done had you stayed in Bristol. Stay as long as you wish and if you so decide to remain for good, we'll be delighted.'

Francis took his mother's arm as he emphasised his agreement with Margot's comments.

'Mother, you're no burden to us and we have peace of mind if we need to look after you here rather than in Bristol. If, ultimately, you want to return there we'll help you go; meanwhile don't worry anymore about it.

'But changing the subject, I reckon the war is in its last throes and within months or even weeks we shall see the end and our family returning to normality. I hope and pray they all come back safely and this brings me to the reason for my mentioning it. We must prepare for their homecoming, some to stay and others, particularly those now married, to visit before going on their way to new homes.

'I suggest we plan an occasion to welcome them all back and in the future keep the same date for a reunion each year.'

Fanny and Margot both thought the idea splendid and suggested they start planning without delay.

With the wireless announcement the following morning came the news the Allies had mounted a massive attack, crossing the Rhine and already surging into Germany. The speed of the operation was enhanced by glider borne forces with paratroops dropping behind the German lines, linking up with advancing tanks within hours, while the enormous support by Allied air forces blasted away any resistance, uninterrupted by the Luftwaffe, now almost obliterated.

Serving breakfast, Bertie was agog, telling Francis and Margot, 'I wouldn't be surprised if it's over by this time next week. I imagine some of the bookies will have laid out odds and already taken bets.'

Francis and Margot smiled, enjoying his point of view, but Francis urged a note of caution, 'What you say, Bertie, may be true, but we must not underestimate the Germans' resistance, particularly defending their own territory.'

At that moment Fanny joined them; having heard the wireless news, she didn't want to miss the conversation at the breakfast table, 'I just couldn't stay in my room with such exciting things happening, so here I am.'

Margot reiterated what Bertie had said, adding, 'If you want to place a bet I'm sure he'll be able to help you!' That produced plenty of laughter but Fanny agreed with the butler, making the point, 'Bertie has a lot of experience of life and I've always found his observations very profound,' and turning to him, 'Well, Bertie, what's your forecast for the war's end?'

Charmed that Lady Dewar had supported him, Bertie responded, 'Madam, first of all I much appreciate your confidence, but to answer the question I believe hostilities in Europe will cease around the middle of May – a matter of weeks away.'

Francis had the last word, 'Why don't we run a competition, everyone can have one go for half a crown and the winner will be the forecast nearest to the real date; half the money can be the prize and the other half for the British Legion for ex-servicemen and women.'

'Brilliant idea, Francis, and we can include the family and everyone on the staff, with perhaps some of the RAF pilots next door joining in.'

Having dealt with that, Margot turned to the condition of Farndene, stating strongly, 'The whole place looks so dowdy and run down. With the semi-derelict American buildings all round the outskirts, one gets the impression of a shanty town! When will the Yanks take their camps away?'

Fanny joined in, 'I agree. The surrounding area looks a mess and it's an invitation to youngsters to get into mischief; can't something be done about it, Francis?'

'I'll see if I can contact the Americans, but I think their only concern now is to finish the war and go home; we may ultimately have to clear up ourselves and meantime we have to wait.'

With Easter approaching, Francis and Margot invited Helen and her parents for the holiday; the visitors arrived on Monday 27th March at the beginning of Holy Week. Clara was down from Oxford the same day and Constance, Bruce and Dorcas were expected later in the week.

On Good Friday they all went to St Paul's where the rector, Canon Horatio Hulbert, welcomed them. In his address he spoke about the impact of the crucifixion scene on the present-day population.

'The Cross was in fact a Roman gibbet which became the symbol of the Christian faith and to some a talisman radiating goodness to the believer. We have all suffered in one way or another during this terrible war against the satanic force of Nazism but our suffering cannot compare with that of Christ on the Cross. His redeeming sacrifice was for all of us who have faith.

'The war is rapidly coming to its conclusion and very soon as victors we will have to deal with the German nation. For the Nazis we must see justice is done but I firmly believe a majority of ordinary German people are not of that evil system and, as

Christians, we must treat them accordingly. So let the Cross be always in your mind as a symbol of the goodness Jesus Christ died for.

'We made terrible mistakes at the end of the Great War in the way we treated the defeated Germany so we must not make the same errors again. In the words of Mr Churchill, our Prime Minister, in victory let us show magnanimity towards the defeated. We would do well to heed his words.'

Lunchtime back at the Manor House saw a gathering of the family and friends including Robert and Edith Oulton who arrived from Bristol late morning. Unfortunately Fanny's parents were unable to come as her father David, now in his ninety-fifth year, was too weak to travel.

The meal got under way with plenty of views being aired, particularly by Sir Charles who took issue with the rector's sermon, 'It's all very well for a parson to pontificate about the future treatment of our enemy. He means well, I'm sure, but his experience of the conflict is based in his pulpit! I believe we must leave the decision to those men and women who have served at the sharp end throughout the war.'

At that moment Bertie entered the dining room and told Helen there was an urgent telephone call for her in the study.

Less than five minutes later she appeared in the dining room doorway, deathly white, shaking under considerable stress with tears coursing down her face, then staggered and collapsed into the arms of her father with the words, 'It was him.' She sank into a dead faint.

Francis and Violet rushed forward to assist and between them they carried Helen into the drawing room to lay her on a sofa. Bertie arrived with a glass of water and a light blanket which Violet wrapped round her daughter's shoulders as Helen shivered and regained consciousness.

For a moment she gazed at the group surrounding the sofa hardly hearing her mother's voice, 'Helen, darling, tell me whatever is the matter?'

After sipping water she seemed to focus on her mother, almost whispering, 'It was Cuthbert. I heard him say he's coming home.' She stopped suddenly, looking terrified as she gripped Violet's arm imploring her mother's help.

'Oh, Mother, help me please! How could it be Cuthbert? We know he's dead don't we?'

Violet knelt by the sofa putting her arms round her daughter, comforting her with the simple words. 'Darling Helen, nobody has ever told us he's dead, so he may be alive. Now just relax and drink this hot sweet tea Bertie's brought and then we'll talk a bit more.'

She drank slowly and the hot beverage helped as she continued, 'I'm positive it was his voice, that was the eerie part. He said "I've just landed and I'm coming home; give my love to Pa and Ma. I tried ringing them at home but got no answer, so I rang you. I'm at Down Ampney and I'll be with you shortly". Then there was a click and he had gone.'

Francis went straight to his study to telephone and returning shortly, announced with a smile, 'Helen my love, it was your brother who telephoned you. I've just spoken to him and he's being debriefed, after which the RAF promised to fly him here in about an hour's time. It's the most wonderful news.'

The delayed lunch eventually continued with the conversation entirely on the incredible news Cuthbert had survived and was back in England.

Shaking his head, his father declared, 'It's nothing short of a miracle after so long. We've hoped desperately that good news would come but after a time I have to admit my hope gave way to despair and then resignation; as the rector mentioned, I should have had more faith that my prayers could be answered. I freely admit I need to polish up my dedication from now on!'

After the protracted lunch, coffee was taken in the drawing room and well past three o'clock a buzz of conversation and an occasional burst of laughter indicated everyone was enjoying the occasion when suddenly the door opened and the missing paratrooper entered.

A hush gripped the room for seconds until Violet, Helen and Charles moved quickly to greet him, all four standing in a giant huddle, savouring the marvellous moment of reunion!

Soon the whole room joined the family with a standing welcome and to the onlooker the scene resembled a crowd at the first day of a 'sale', with a certain amount of pushing as they all tried to shake Cuthbert's hand or kiss his cheek.

Bertie, always on the ball, handed Francis a referee's whistle and two short blasts brought silence.

'Could we all just calm down and take a seat.' Helped to an armchair, Cuthbert was soon seated as his father asked, 'My dear boy, how on earth did you manage to escape after the Arnhem battle?'

Leaning back with a cup of coffee, Cuthbert surveyed the bevy of smiling faces before putting it plainly to them, 'do you honestly want to hear all that happened to me?' Met immediately by a chorus of, 'Yes please, of course we do,' he smiled as he raised his hand to answer.

'Okay, here goes. I won't bore you with the preliminaries but tell you what happened after nearly three days of desperately bitter fighting.' He paused, focusing his mind on the past weeks before resuming.

'There were many errors, not so much in the planning but in the execution which was hampered by so many unforeseen problems. For example, a lot of our signals equipment didn't work and in some cases was the wrong type of receiver/transmitter – so much so we had to borrow radios from war correspondents to send and receive. Follow-up drops of reinforcements and supplies often landed in areas overrun by the Germans. Inclement weather hampered flying on more than once occasion which was bad for morale. Unbeknown to planners was the presence of a large Panzer unit just north of the Arnhem bridge. On the credit side the help and support we received from the Dutch population was nothing short of magnificent in many ways, particularly in the care of our wounded. They took risks, and the Germans later acknowledged the humanitarian part they played was superb, at times even tending the Wehrmacht badly wounded soldiers.

'Our headquarters, situated in a large residence not a great distance from the bridge, suffered several mortar bomb hits resulting in a number of casualties, including the Brigadier who was badly injured.

'In the afternoon of the third day, we were unable to communicate with our advanced group near the bridge and I was sent forward to ascertain the up to date situation. My route was along a wide, tree-lined street of pleasant detached houses with large gardens and it was here I met some of our men returning to HQ with several wounded. Almost immediately we came under fire and mortar bombs exploded around us, killing many of them. Luckily I was unscathed and I went to the aid of a poor fellow whose lower arm had been severed.

'I applied a tourniquet but more bombs landed nearby and shrapnel finished him off and a piece of the same bomb sliced my left arm open. My face and upper body were covered with his blood, which I didn't realise was going to save me, as at that moment a group of the Wehrmacht appeared, running in my direction. Passing, they glanced at the dead bodies and assuming I was also a goner, went on their way. I lay perfectly still until they'd disappeared and then crawled through the nearby gateway into the front garden which was planted with many shrubs, mostly large lavender bushes, among which I hid.

'Shortly after, I became aware a woman was cutting the stems of lavender flowers and, reaching where I was hidden, spoke to me quietly, "Stay where you are, Tommy, as there are more Germans coming along the street" and went on snipping lavender. I heard the German troops running past and then it was quiet except for the distant gunfire. She called and a man came to help me into the house where they took me to the large kitchen at the rear.

'These wonderful people were Kees and his wife Wilhelmina Westervoorde. By good fortune she was a nurse so, after cleaning me up, she sewed my left arm with twenty-six stitches, the suture used being the boiled "G" string of a violin – I'll probably be able to play a jig on my humerus!'

Cuthbert stopped until the laughter subsided and, looking round the eager faces he said, 'You've no idea how wonderful it is to be back with you all!' He smiled as Violet leaned across to squeeze his hand.

'But I must get on or we'll be here all night. Those two, with the help of others, hid me until I was released when our own troops captured Arnhem en route to Germany.'

'But how did they do that while the Germans still occupied the town?' his father wanted to know more.

'Alright, Pa, but before I go any further I must tell you a bit about Kees Westervoorde.

'For many years he had been the senior industrial chemist at a local factory manufacturing all types of camera film. After the occupation he continued in that position, providing film for the Germans. He made it his business to "cultivate" them and through his job was privy to new methods of aerial photography for Zeiss cameras used by the Luftwaffe; this information he passed on to the Dutch underground movement.

'His lifelong hobby was model trains and in the extensive cellar he had an enormous layout electrically operated by several old car batteries. When the house was bought in the thirties he decided to reduce the cellar size by cutting off a third with stud partitioning. In 1941 he needed access to the other part and neatly made one section swivel on a long vertical steel rod. It was in that section he hid allied airmen as he had become involved in an escape route.

'Having been a founder member of the Arnhem Model Railway Society in 1935, among the membership of which were a number of train drivers and crews, he was able to arrange rail transport for escaping airmen.

'He told me that after the Arnhem battle the Germans searched houses regularly and on reaching the cellar were completely mesmerised by his model railway – so much so they didn't notice the room had been partitioned. Ready for their next search he changed the livery on all the locomotives to the German State style and gave the stations German town names. Two weeks later they searched again and were delighted with the trains, spending half an hour watching the operations, all the while I was hidden behind the partition. In there were camp beds, each with a china "po".' He smiled, 'No, they weren't blue and white Delft!'

The room was quiet as Cuthbert sat for a moment collating his thoughts and then continued his story: 'Wilhelmina worked hard with my arm which, unfortunately, had become infected and gave me a lot of pain; by some means she got hold of some German army field dressings which helped to calm things down.

'My spiritual needs were looked after by the local Dutch Reformed Church dominee [priest] Bernhardt Huisman, who brought communion to the house for the three of us. He was also a link in the escape route for allied airmen as he had more or less free access as a priest and carried messages to the many safe houses where the flyers were hiding.

'Now, I mentioned the interest German soldiers took in Kees' model railway and among those who paid more than one visit was Colonel Dieter Schumacher, the garrison commander. It was late March. Kees said that what he was about to tell me was so astonishing and bizarre I would find it hard to believe. I just waited and he went on. Dieter Schumacher and he were on Christian name terms as he was constantly in touch with the commander through his position at the factory; as a soldier he found him straightforward and fair in all his dealings, being also a devout Catholic from a long established Heidelberg family.

'That day the colonel called and told Kees and Wilhelmina he had a feeling they were involved in helping escaped airmen. He went on to tell them he was convinced the war had only weeks to run its course and that Germany would be defeated. He also told them any deserter or soldier failing to obey Hitler's orders was to be shot immediately. He said he'd had enough of Hitler and wanted to surrender but, as the garrison had been reinforced by Waffen SS troops that week, they would prevent any sign of capitulation. The colonel asked if he could be hidden or helped to escape to the Allied lines.

'Kees told him he'd think the matter over and as soon as he'd gone they called me to ask my opinion.'

'Well, what a dilemma. So, Cuthbert, what happened?' Helen was as curious as everyone listening.

'The principal danger, I told him, was the revelation of the cellar hiding place and if what he said was not genuine they had to beware of falsehood. I suggested the colonel be requested to call at the factory with the secret Enigma code books and his personal commander's file. If he produced them it would be proof he was genuine.

'Sure enough, he complied with the request and the documents were passed to the Dutch Underground Movement for transmission to the Allies.

'The rest was like pure fiction, for once the documents and a letter from Kees were in the Allies' hands they had the presence of mind to make a public declaration to the effect Colonel Schumacher had defected to the west and was being interrogated in a secret place. That took the heat out of the German command in Arnhem where a state of near panic existed.

'Lo and behold, that night what I can only describe as a Gilbertian, topsy-turvy scene took place as I welcomed the German Commander into my humble hiding place.

'You should have seen his face when he met me! My only regret is that our meeting didn't take place on a Cornish beach, in full dress uniform, surrounded by a group of scantily clad Windmill Theatre girls!' When the laughter subsided Cuthbert completed the story.

'Luckily we got on well and, to give him peace of mind and preserve his pride and dignity, he insisted Kees prepare a form of surrender which he signed and I accepted as an Allied officer.

'W.S. Gilbert would have been proud of the whole affair and Arthur Sullivan's music for the Duke of Plaza Toro in "The Gondoliers" would have completed the farce,' and he broke into song, 'In enterprise of martial kind when there was any fighting, he led his regiment from behind he found it less exciting!'

The whole room erupted in laughter and applause, enjoying the fun in Cuthbert's wonderful narrative, but also delighted to find a soldier who had been through hell and had returned to his family, able to look back and see the humour in what had been an extremely dangerous situation at the time.

Francis, standing next to Cuthbert's parents, congratulated them, 'You must be tremendously proud of your son and while England has men like this we never need fear our adversaries!'

Chapter 52

In April 1945 people were saddened when the United States President Franklin D. Roosevelt died after many years of ill health. Mr Churchill was grieved and spoke of the loss of 'our great American friend', at a time when the Allied forces were on the brink of victory in their fight against Nazi Germany.

Daily news coming in from the east and west indicated the collapse of the forces of the Third Reich was gathering pace. The armies of Britain and America, meeting scant resistance, raced for the river Elbe, where they paused as the Russians encircled Berlin in the final battles of the European war. Here on 30th April Hitler committed suicide with Eva Braun his mistress for many years, whom he had married the day before they met their end. As one witty American correspondent said, 'Thank God she didn't survive him or we'd have had to suffer the inevitable autobiography, possibly entitled "Bunk from the Bonker" – obviously a spoonerism – or "Tack in a Hard Back", take your pick!'

At the Manor House, Farndene, Bertie in a buoyant mood welcomed Margot, Francis and Fanny for breakfast.

'Good morning on this very special day and I trust you had a good night.'

'Good morning, Bertie, but what's so special about today?' Margot was inquisitive.

'If you haven't heard the BBC news, I'll tell you, madam. Today, Friday the fourth of May, the representatives of the German forces in north-west Europe sign the surrender document at General Montgomery's headquarters on Luneburg Heath, which means hostilities cease. And the second reason it's special is because I may have won the competition forecasting the date of the end of the war!'

445

'Well now, Bertie, you may or you may not be the winner,' Francis thought for a moment, 'If my memory serves me correctly, the terms of our competition were a forecast of the date for the end of World War II at a cost of half a crown. I think we all intended the European war to be the subject of our competition and here is the problem. On Wednesday 2nd May all hostilities ceased on the Italian Front, and now you tell us a surrender document will be signed today involving the Germans in north-west Europe; but what about the surrender of the Nazi's navy? Surely they will have to capitulate as well.

'I hope you see our difficulty? Perhaps we should wait a little longer before deciding which is the winning day.'

Bertie smiled, nodding his head in agreement, 'I agree we must wait a little longer as you suggest.'

About a week later on 7th May, a fitting act took place at General Eisenhower's headquarters in Reims, where a final surrender document was signed by General Jodl for the Germans, covering all their forces. The ceremony took place in the presence all the Allies: American, British, Russian and French representatives who were witness to the end of Nazism in Europe. The Reims surrender was ratified by General Keitel in Berlin on Tuesday 8th May. This day was also declared VE-day by the Allies.

Once fighting ceased, the Allies put in place armies of occupation and established a military government to enforce law and order and to round up Nazis for interrogation, bringing those guilty of war crimes to justice in due course. The task was enormous and unfortunately some slipped through the net, escaping abroad with false identities.

While the navies cleared minefields in European waters, the air forces ferried thousands of prisoners of war back to Britain and America, as well as dropping food and medical supplies to the starving people of Holland.

As all this took place, large forces were withdrawn from Europe to England, ready to embark for the Far East in preparation for the final assault on Japan.

The final surrender of Germany on 8th May was the signal to the population of Europe to celebrate and the British people let off steam with a vengeance, swarming into the streets in towns and villages, drinking and dancing with perfect strangers, relieved the hostilities were at last finished.

In London the crowds massed to hear Winston Churchill speak about 'the job well done by you all'.

The crowds, in good humour, went on celebrating into the evening and one cockney lady was heard to say, 'I'm gonner tak darn me blackarts an' I don't care if yer sees me gitting inter bed ternite!'

Amid widespread guffaws a cheeky bystander retorted, 'Der yer meen yer kertins or yer bloomers darlin'?'

Great excitement also gripped the Kirkwood household in Exeter when Mollie received a telephone call from Sam, telling her he was coming home on leave in a few days' time. Preparations were made to celebrate and Janine contacted Tom who promised to come down with Hazel for the weekend.

Now that the War Office contract had finished, Philip and Janine were planning to re-open the Madame Baume salon entirely for dressmaking and already they'd received several enquiries from former clients.

And so the great homecoming weekend arrived with scenes of understandable happiness as Sam came into the house to be clasped in Mollie's arms; they stood locked in a tight embrace for some moments, her smiling face wet with tears of joy.

Later that day Tom and Hazel arrived and, unbeknown to them all, Janine had telephoned Rupert who flew down to a local RAF station near Exeter and turned up to join the family for dinner that night.

The happy and relaxed atmosphere made the evening a very special one as the conversation went on nonstop between the brothers and sister, all together again after a very long time. Janine looked on and listened happily and with great pride seeing the success her children had achieved, often against great odds.

It fell to Philip to say something appropriate and smiling, he tapped on the table with a request for a little quiet. Conversation ceased as he went on.

'Many years ago when I married your mother in 1923, you were all "sprogs": Mollie 14, Rupert 12 and Tom 10, all bright-eyed and alert to what went on in your young world. My abiding memory was the wonderful way you accepted me into your family and we became much more than friends from that time. Although later on two of you were away serving apprenticeships and only Mollie was at home, we got on really well whenever the family met, often having great fun. On one such occasion I remember, at Easter 1928, I spoke to you all about your ambitions. Rupert's answer was to be an engineer and you've done more than that by becoming a first-class pilot, Commander,' and with a grin, 'as well as a husband and father.

'Tom, you have achieved all you wanted in aircraft design and, I believe, are responsible for the plans of our successful big bombers. Now the war is over we look forward to your marriage to Hazel in the near future.' Philip paused as he looked at his stepdaughter.

'Mollie, your many ambitions including travelling in Europe; well, you certainly did that and some!

'To get married only if the right man turned up! And what a happy pair you and Sam are.

'I've said all this as I felt it ought to be mentioned because as a family you've done your bit and can now look forward to a normal lifestyle. So, I drink to my darling Janine and to the splendid family she brought along with her when we were married – a family I have been so proud and happy to join.'

After smiles and applause, Rupert responded, 'Your eloquent description of the Tupper kids has been a delight to hear and my only worry may be headaches from a tight halo! I know I speak for us all when I say how much happiness you brought into our family at a pretty desperate time.

'Philip, we all value your friendship and thanks for being so helpful and patient with us over the years.'

They sat talking well into the early hours, as though not wanting to leave each other's company after being apart for so long. Tom announced he and Hazel planed to tie the knot on 31st July, 'We'll get married at her local church as soon as the schools break up. We'll give you all details of how to get there and where you can stay.'

Janine was delighted and gave Hazel and Tom hugs and kisses adding, 'What wonderful news for us all. I think you've been very sensible waiting until the end of the war.' Hazel happily accepted Janine and Mollie's offer to make her wedding dress and measurements were taken before the end of the weekend.

Before departing on Monday morning, Rupert made them promise to come to the van Houten house for a weekend with Catherina and his little son. 'We've plenty of room and my father-in-law Jan and Bep will be delighted to see you again. Once I've fixed my leave I'll telephone and a date can be arranged.' Rupert put his arms round Janine, giving her a big kiss with the final words, 'You have always been a smashing mother and will be an even better grandma!'

Having spent a few days in Exeter with Janine and Philip, Sam and Mollie travelled north to Whitby to see his parents. Once on the train, Sam talked to his wife about the army, 'I couldn't speak to you in front of the family about my prospects as the promotion has not yet been gazetted but I'm sure you'll be delighted when you hear. With the award of the DSO, I'm now a Lieutenant Colonel and – this is the icing on our cake – I'm appointed to the staff of our Military Attaché in Paris from next September. So, my beloved you will be with me in the French capital, which should be fun!'

Mollie could hardly believe her ears and, leaning across the seat, kissed his cheek with a cheeky remark, 'Sam, that's wonderful news but of course I'll need a much larger dress allowance to keep up with the other ladies at the embassy!'

'My darling wife, that will be no problem, but I'll be surprised if your mother doesn't make your clothes and I'm willing to bet you'll have as good a wardrobe as any in Paris.'

They talked at great length, planning for the autumn, and it was then Mollie went quiet and became very serious.

'Darling is something troubling you?' Sam was puzzled by the turn of events.

'Sam, I was thirty-six on 30th June and, if we want a family, time is important from my point of view. Besides that, how would a young child fit in with your job in Paris?'

He put his arm round her shoulder and whispered in her ear, 'Dearest, I'd love some children and appreciate all you've said. From what I hear, there are several families of children of all ages at the embassy, so that wouldn't be a problem.'

After changing at York the train wound its way through the spectacular and beautiful North Yorkshire moors, arriving at Whitby on time.

They entered the Mission House to a fabulous welcome from Madeline, Sam's mother, and Grant his stepfather. Soon seated in the graceful drawing room, Mollie realised how much Sam had been missed from Madeline's conversation.

'Sam, it must be nearly two years since you were here but now you're home we can hear all your news and Mollie's as well,' and turning to her daughter-in-law, Madeline added, 'What you've done is very courageous and we're very proud you are part of our family. Grant and I would love to hear your story, so perhaps later when we have dinner as we expect Marion to arrive by then.'

Madeline had arranged a delicious meal, during which Sam and Mollie related their experiences and later as it was a warm, fine evening they all decided to walk down past the Cook memorial to the harbour to watch the fishing boats leaving for the North Sea.

Gripping Sam's arm, Mollie suddenly felt completely at home, whispering to him, 'Darling, I think Whitby has attracted me so much I could quite easily settle here at some time in the future.'

'Mollie, you might do worse, but before making a final decision it would be as well if you stayed here in the winter to experience a north easterly gale. Whitby faces due north and it can be a bitterly cold spot with driving rain or snow. Personally I think a place in or near Exeter would be preferable.'

During their stay, Madeline told Mollie and Sam they were invited to a big celebration party by Francis and Margot to be held at the Manor House, Farndene, on Sunday 15th July, a gathering of as many family and friends as possible. She also told them, 'Unfortunately your grandparents won't be able to go as Grandpa is too frail to travel. Francis told me Margot and he will to fly up to St Andrews to see them before July.'

Sam explained to his mother, 'Mollie and I intend going on to St Andrews to see them when we leave here and we'll stay for a couple of days if it's convenient. It seems so long since I saw them although I wrote from time to time when I was abroad.'

Two weeks after the family was reunited in Exeter, Philip, Janine, Sam and Mollie attended a similar reunion with the van Houtens in Lincolnshire. They spent a wonderful weekend, made all the more special as Jan's wife Lies had just returned to England after being trapped in Holland throughout the German occupation. The poor woman had aged as a result of the privations suffered under Nazi rule over the occupation years.

Catherina, along with her father and sister, was delighted to have their mother home and promised Lies, 'We'll look after you, Mama, and, with love and good food, your health will be restored.'

Leaving the baby in the adoring care of Bep, Mollie and their two grandmothers, Catherina and Rupert took mounts from the stables and went for a good hour's ride. Being alone together and enjoying the freedom they dismounted in the shade of a small copse, taking in the view across miles of farmland with windmills dotted here and there – in all, a wonderfully relaxing scene.

'Darling Rupert, this is what I've longed for, a beautiful prospect for our future with our children.

'When will you come home to us for good?'

He put his arms round her and his smiling face foretold what his answer would be.

'Dearest, my reply will tell you all you want to know. I have been offered a permanent RAF commission with promotion to Group Captain, but I had already decided I would not accept. My life must be with you and my family and consequently I will leave the air force as soon as possible!'

Catherina was over the moon with joy and hugged and kissed Rupert until he shouted 'Fainites'!

Then, with a cheeky grin, he told his wife, 'I promise I'll buy you a wonderful coming home present,' and after a deliberate pause, 'A brand new tractor!'

'Rupert, you're cheeky, but I love you for your wonderful sense of humour, so don't ever change!'

After a further long embrace they decided it was time to get back to the family.

The weeks slipped by and, as the date of the grand celebration at the Manor House approached, Margot and Francis, assisted by Fanny, planned what was going to be a very large function. To cope with the numbers a very large marquee was erected on the lawns, big enough to accommodate over two hundred guests to be served with a buffet lunch.

The regimental band of the South Hampshire Fusiliers was engaged to entertain the crowd which included all estate staff and their families, the Commanding Officer of RAF Farndene and many of the pilots, the American General Shaun Goodhew, Jack Snapper the retired police superintendent and, of course, all members of the various branches of the family. Having met Wing Commander Rupert Tupper on many occasions, Francis extended an invitation to his parents, Janine and Philip Kirkwood.

On the beautiful July morning of the grand party day, people started to arrive in good time, all thrilled at the spectacle of the whole area as a mass of flags, bunting and streamers. Soon seated in the massive marquee they listened to the band playing selections of popular music and joined in singing the war time songs 'Roll out the Barrel', 'We'll Meet Again', 'We're Going to Hang out the Washing on the Siegfried Line', 'There'll be

Bluebirds over the White Cliffs of Dover', 'Wish me luck as you wave me Goodbye', and some of the Great War songs including, 'Pack up your Troubles in your old Kit Bag', 'There's a Long, Long, Trail a-winding', 'If you were the Only Girl in the World', 'Hello, Hello, Who's your Lady Friend?', 'Mademoiselle from Armentier', 'Let's all go down the Strand (and have a banana)', and 'Keep the Home Fires Burning'. The music continued with music from famous shows while lunch was served.

Towards the end of the meal, Francis took the microphone from the bandmaster and made a short speech after which he called for three cheers for the band. By half past three the visitors made their way home, happily content after celebrating with a splendid meal and entertainment.

As the families left, each child was given an orange, a banana and some 'candy', gifts from the American General Shaun Goodhew and flown over from the United States.

Dinner that evening saw just over twenty friends and family gathered in the beautiful dining room. Those present included most of the Vining family, Margot's sister Madeline with her husband Grant and daughter Marion, Fanny, Alex and Angelina, Algy Vining and Abbot Vincent Logan, Sam and Mollie Shelley and Canon Digby Fletcher. Also invited were Helen's brother Cuthbert and parents Sir Charles and Lady Violet Dauntsey.

Once they were all seated, Francis asked Canon Digby Fletcher to say grace. Digby, now ninety-one, rose slowly and, beaming at the gathering, said, 'Before I proceed I feel I should tell you I have been saying grace at the many Vining functions for the past fifty years and I have never repeated myself. Tonight's grace is no exception!' He paused quietly for a moment and then called for the blessing on the meal.

'Almighty God, please hear our prayer,
Provider of the food we eat,
We thank you for your heavenly care,
and for our daily bread, and meat.
Amen.'

The wonderful sound of enjoyment, chatter and laughing backed by the musical rhythm of cutlery engaging with plates, indicated the occasion was a splendid bonding of family and friends and a gathering none of them would forget.

After dinner in the drawing room they continued talking over coffee and it was well after midnight before welcome tiredness called the tune and goodnights were said.

Once in their bedroom Margot and Francis went over the events of the day, the lunch, and the celebration dinner. Summing up, she said, 'Darling, I'll never forget today as long as I live. It has been the most wonderful experience seeing so many friends and our family together for the very best of reasons.'

'Margot dearest, like you I was deeply touched by our celebration and so thankful our family have all returned safely from the war.'

They put their arms round each other and kissed several times after which Margot suddenly said, 'I don't feel a bit tired, so why don't we get undressed quickly, get into bed and put the light out!'

'That's exactly what I was going to suggest. So what are we waiting for?' Francis was hurriedly discarding his clothes as he spoke.

Moments later they were under the bedclothes with the light out!

The next morning – a beautiful sunny July day – Fanny decided to take a little exercise before breakfast and, walking along the terrace to the rose garden, finally paused to sit in the sun to admire the lovely setting of the old house. She was not alone for long as Algy Vining, walking with the aid of two sticks, approached with Abbot Vincent Logan. Fanny was delighted and as they got nearer she called, 'Do come and enjoy the sunshine and the view.'

They sat talking about the previous day and the spectacular success the whole celebration had been.

'I'm very proud of my son and daughter-in-law for the planning and hard work they put in to make it a day to remember.'

Algy and Vincent agreed at which point the abbot stood up to leave, 'I have my morning intercession to complete before breakfast, so please excuse me.'

Algy and Fanny remained talking about old times and the problems they'd both suffered. He spoke of his admiration for Fanny, 'I look back and throughout the years I've known you I always found you a caring and most generous person, to whom fortune was not always generous.'

Fanny smiled her appreciation, 'Thank you, Algy. That's the nicest thing anyone has said to me for years. I've had a good life and I've got my loving family but as I get older my biggest worry is loneliness, I expect you understand what I mean; the moment one shuts the door of one's house or room there is nobody to talk to.'

Algy listened quietly before speaking, 'Fanny, I know exactly what you are talking about as I suffered the same for many years. Vincent Logan and the monks at Broadbeck Abbey have been the most wonderful people, nursing me back to health and looking after me when I was so terribly injured during the Great War. But after deep reflection, I decided taking Holy Orders was not what I wanted,' he smiled slightly, 'I suppose I'm destined to spend the rest of my days in the seclusion of my cell there.'

Fanny put her hand on his as she spoke with feeling, 'I feel I've let you down as I promised to visit you regularly but I omitted to do so and I'm very sorry, Algy.'

'Please don't feel like that, Fanny. I understand you must have had many family commitments to take your time. However, before we go back to the house I must tell you again, not only do I admire you but I still love you as much as I did all those years ago and would do anything to make you happy. Please forgive a decrepit old man for saying what I've said, but I just had to!'

'Algy, those are the sweetest words any woman would welcome and I think so much more of you for saying them. I remember you telling me you were in love with me way in the past and, if my memory serves me, I told you I didn't love you but I felt great affection for you. Seeing you again after so many years perhaps the affection has ripened into what was really a form of love.

'Whatever we do now, let's not waste more years but make a decision about our future. What do you think, Algy?'

He took both her hands and, looking into her eyes, made the decision he'd wanted to on previous occasions, 'Fanny, you'll never know how much those word mean to me! I hope you will agree to be my wife. Dearest Fanny, will you marry me?'

After accepting with gentle embraces they walked back to the house arm in arm to break the news to Margot, Francis and the family.

Oddly enough a lot of breakfast was uneaten when Algy made his announcement. 'I expect you were all wondering why Fanny and I went for a walk in the rose garden early this morning. Well, I can now tell you. We went there so that I could propose to her and I'm delighted to say Fanny has agreed to be my wife.'

The excitement overflowed as congratulations, with arms round each other and lots of kisses were the order of the day. Francis asked Bertie to bring up the champagne and toasts were drunk.

As she kissed Francis, Fanny remarked with a lovely smile, 'Darling, just think very soon I shall be a Vining again!'

As breakfast resumed shortly after, the happy gathering enjoyed the uplifting news.

Before going their various ways, Canon Digby Fletcher added a few words.

'Old as I am, Fanny and Algy have asked me to marry them and I'm just delighted to be able preside at their wedding. Before you depart may I add a comment about the reason for yesterday's special celebration. It was an accomplishment; a fulfilment of all the dreams and desires of so many families, marking the end of separations and heartaches, and the beginning of what I hope will be bright future years for you all. So go away today, enjoy your lives but take the Vining spirit of generosity and goodwill with you. God bless you all.'

World War II reached the final phase when atom bombs were dropped on Hiroshima and Nagasaki on 6th and 9th August respectively and Japan capitulated shortly after.

The legacy the war left behind is known to all who lost loved ones, who suffered at the hands of the German Nazis or the Japanese, or those who carry the Holocaust scars of body or mind for the rest of their days.